A VISIT FROM THE TEACHER

"Do you have any questions about his prognosis?" the teacher asked.

Dad said, "It's something like autism, they tell us. His difficulty coping with the environment, choosing what to watch and what to ignore. He has these trances—"

"He's very sensitive," said Mom.

"Oh, yes," the teacher agreed. "Autism has its similarities, yes. But an autistic child would be helpless. Ryder is not. With training and hard work, Ryder should be able to carry on normally. He does pay a cost for having such a powerful memory. . . . But we shouldn't grieve for him. When he's like me, old and gray, he'll only have to concentrate for a moment to remember youth." She laughed and said, "Maybe I envy him."

Then no one spoke.

Finally Mom said, "You're very kind," with a certain voice.

Dad said, "Gwinn? Don't be—"

"What?" she asked. "Isn't this rather patronizing? I don't like being patronized, and I'm not sitting through it." She was angry in a quiet fashion. "We wanted a fine healthy boy, Kip and I. We're ordinary people, yes, and I for one take pride in that fact. I don't mind admitting it. I'm part of the last honest generation . . . the good and decent people who were brought up to accept their shortcomings. . . ."

More superior science fiction from Bantam Spectra Books

BLACK MILK

ROBERT REED

BANTAM BOOKS
NEW YORK • TORONTO • LONDON • SYDNEY • AUCKLAND

*This edition contains the complete text
of the original hardcover edition.*
NOT ONE WORD HAS BEEN OMITTED.

BLACK MILK

*A Bantam Spectra Book / published by arrangement with
Donald I. Fine, Inc.*

PRINTING HISTORY

*Donald I. Fine, Inc. edition published 1989
Bantam edition / March 1991*

*Bantam Books are published by Bantam Books, a division of
Bantam Doubleday Dell Publishing Group, Inc. Its trademark,
consisting of the words "Bantam Books" and the portrayal of a
rooster, is Registered in U.S. Patent and Trademark Office and in
other countries. Marca Registrada. Bantam Books, 666 Fifth Ave-
nue, New York, New York 10103.*

To the real spirits of the true woods

ONE

Cody's mothers had heard the rumor, and they had told Cody and Cody had told us, of course, making us promise to keep it secret. Of course. And that's why the five of us were waiting up in the old oak. We were waiting for Dr. Florida.

I remember all of it.

I remember trying to keep calm. It seemed so unlikely, us actually seeing Dr. Florida; but nonetheless I was terribly excited, lying on my back on the long bench with my feet propped up in a window, in the sun, and the dry warm wind slipping between my toes. It was afternoon, and it was spring. I can still smell the old dust and fresh sawdust, and I heard Cody on the roof, walking and then hammering and then walking some more. One of my hands fell to the floor and stroked the smooth, foot-worn faces of the boards, the cool round heads of nails and the empty nail holes fringed with mold and rust. If I had time and the inclination, I would focus my mind and recall where we'd found each of those boards—from old treehouses or trash heaps or blind garages left open. I would retrieve the look and feel of every nail I handled, the angle and scent of every saw cut I made; and I would be able to remember—with utter clarity—every moment of every hour that I spent in that treehouse. Or anywhere else, for that matter. I have a talent, a unique skill. I forget nothing, not ever and not for anyone, no matter how many times I wish it might be otherwise.

The treehouse TV was off. The personal was running,

1

softly humming. Marshall had brought some new game—a hexagon-shaped board with blond and steel-colored pieces—and he had taught the personal how to play it, the two of them facing each other across the little game table. Beth, blessed Beth, was watching the pasture for us, humming a sweet song under her breath. Like always. Jack Wells was sitting on one of the old plastic freezers with his legs crossed and an encyclopedia unrolled on his lap. I watched him changing the pages. He would touch a corner and cause the bright liquid crystals to flow, creating new words and pictures and graphs inside the encyclopedia's thick plastic matrix. The buttery sunshine fell in around Jack, and I watched him. He read and examined and considered, skipping between subjects in a random fashion. Then he quit and looked at me. He smiled at me. Jack had a round face and dirty-blond hair, big freckles beneath his tan and welfare genes beneath everything. I could see his toughness. He was a little kid, several years younger than us, but he had hard old eyes that belonged in an adult's head. Those eyes gave me a smile. "Ryder?" he asked. "How are you doing, Ryder?"

I said, "Fine."

"You excited?" he wondered.

"Oh, yeah," I said. "Sure."

He bent forward. "I've got something." Lying on the floor, in the shade, was a small cloth sack. Jack lifted it to his lap. Its fabric was rough and porous, stains overlapping stains, and the sack's neck was tied with an old leather cord. I saw the sloppy bow knot and his little fingers pulling the bow undone and him reaching inside while something moved, squirming. Jack grinned and told me, "Now watch."

I remember every detail, every feature and face and word.

But I can't tell everything, I realize. There is never enough time for everything. What I need to do now is pick and choose, repeating the essential parts. That's what *he* expected from me—in a different context, true—and so that's what I expect from myself.

I must think clearly and tell it fairly.

And never, never can I pretend to know more than I know.

Jack Wells pulled the snake out by its tail. "Caught it last night," he told me. "It's a ringneck." He held the prize toward me and I saw the smallish body and the dark gray topside, nearly black, and the pale, speckled belly with a slender, fire-colored band encircling its neck. A tiny red tongue was working the air. "I don't catch many," Jack admitted, "but they're sure pretty. Ever catch one yourself?"

I said, "Yes." I had been eight years old and lucky. Ringnecks are sleek and secretive, impossible to anger, and I'd kept mine inside a glass fishbowl filled with dried and musty grass. I'd offered it garden worms and meal bugs and it ate nothing. Not once. Then it died after several months, and I grieved, feeling ashamed for having kept it. I had brought it down here in the end, burying it in the deepest woods, and all of those memories came to me when I saw Jack holding that snake in his hands.

"Where'd you catch it?" I asked him.

"Past the slabs." He motioned toward the west and the woods, smiling and nodding while the snake slipped from hand to hand, weaving through his fingers. Jack Wells loved snake hunting. He loved a snake's looks and life, and he seemed to understand each of them in some mystical way. "Watch," he told me. He held the ringneck behind its tiny head and extended his arm, and I felt something feathery against my bare foot. I saw the tongue working, testing my scent, and Jack grinned and said, "Now he knows you."

"He knows me," I said.

It was Jack's fondest belief that snakes could identify people by their peculiar scents. They were like bloodhounds. Jack measured and marked every snake that he captured, recording the data on liquid crystal paper, and before he released them he made them sniff at him with their tongues. It was a ritual, a routine, and he persisted even when older, smarter people told him he was wrong.

I saw Marshall glance up at us and frown.

Jack took back the ringneck, and Marshall said, "It's way too stupid," with a hard, certain voice.

Jack said nothing. His hard old eyes studied Marshall for a moment, and then his face got a devilish look. He put aside the empty sack and the plastic encyclopedia, jumped off the freezer and approached Marshall with the ringneck wrapped around his right wrist and hand.

"Leave me alone," warned Marshall.

"But he wants a whiff," Jack told him. "He does."

"It's a stupid snake," said Marshall, "and it can't remember shit." He shook his head and set his mouth and said, "How many times do I have to tell you? I'm talking *facts* here. That's a dumb, dumb animal."

"Facts?" asked Jack.

"A tiny, minuscule reptile brain. It's all it can do to crawl." They had had this argument a hundred times in the past. Marshall spoke with conviction—he always spoke with conviction, on any subject—and he had no patience for Jack or Jack's teasing. Motioning with one hand, he said, "I'm busy here. Get away from me."

"Just a whiff," Jack persisted. He held the ringneck close to Marshall's frowning face. "He wants a quick whiff—"

Marshall pushed at Jack's arm and groaned.

Beth quit singing. "Would you quit?" she asked. "Please?"

I heard Cody on the roof. *Bwink! Bwink! Bwink!* The hammering was powerful and steady. *Bwink! Bwink! Bwink!* The noise drove through the roof, making everyone jerk and pause. Then Cody quit hammering and Jack held the ringneck to his own ear, smiling and nodding about something no one could hear. "What was that?" he asked. "What?"

Marshall said, "What?"

Jack told Marshall, "He knows you."

"Oh, Jesus—"

"No, really! He smelled you last week, and saw you." Jack began to laugh, the devilish look growing.

"Leave me alone," said Marshall.

Beth said, "Quit it, please—"

"Want to know what he said?" asked Jack. "Do you?"

Marshall hesitated.

So Jack tilted his head and laughed. "He saw you in the woods last week. Alone."

Marshall shifted his weight, his chair creaking.

"You had some magazine stuffed in a log," Jack said. "A wildlife magazine, I guess. He said it was full of beaver shots—"

Marshall rose and shouted, "Stop!"

"—and you had trouble with your pants. Because you were touching yourself down here—"

"Damn you little shit!" cried Marshall. He came around

the game table, Beth yelling, "Cody!" and Marshall swinging at Jack with one of his clumsy long arms, missing and nearly falling, then shouting, "You little welfare shit bastard!"

Beth was standing now, hands raised high and her face terrified. "Cody!" she called. "Oh, God!"

I heard Cody running on the roof. Marshall bumped the game table, scattering the playing pieces, and Jack screamed, "Ryder!" once and tossed the ringneck at me. I bent and scooped it off the floor. I felt its glossy smoothness and looked up and saw Jack kick at Marshall once and then lift his hard white fists. There was a pause for a moment, both of them hunting for openings; and then Cody came over the edge of the roof, her body hanging in the air and twisting hard with her feet coming first through a window. She yelled. Jack and Marshall started slamming away at each other, and Cody grabbed them and jerked them apart, getting between them and telling them to quit. "Now!" she snapped. But they kept swinging and kicking, wanting one last good blow, and she finally pushed them with one motion, neat and easy. Their butts hit the floor, and I felt the big old oak rocking. Marshall gulped and said, "Welfare shit—!"

Cody struck him. She was tired of their noise, and she popped him in the chest once, and Marshall turned pale and said nothing for a long time.

Beth went to Marshall. "Are you okay?"

Cody looked toward me. She took a breath and wondered, "What happened?" and waited for me to tell everything. Every word and gesture, giving her enough so she could judge—

"Are you all right?" Beth persisted.

Marshall had no color in his face, but he managed to nod slightly.

"What about me?" asked Jack.

"Are you hurt?" Beth's pretty face was long and ever so worried. "Do you need anything?"

Jack didn't answer. He just shook his head and shot hard looks at Marshall now and again, and I picked up the cloth sack and put the ringneck inside it and tied the sack with the old leather cord. Cody was watching me, waiting for my story. So I started to focus, and by chance I looked out the east windows. I saw the early spring grass in the pasture and the far houses and the little gravel road coming down onto the pasture. Vans and limousines were stacked up on the road.

When had they arrived? I wondered. I could see a fresh cloud of settling white dust. I saw little white dishes perched on top of the vans aligning themselves, and several dozen pretty-dressed people stepping into the sunlight. I couldn't see faces, they were too far away. But I knew the insignias on the limousine doors, and one limousine was enormous; and I felt funny in my belly and my legs went numb, a little bit, and the tips of my fingers began to shake.

Cody said, "Ryder?"

Beth said, "Goodness," and pointed.

I was weak and ever so excited. I couldn't have been more excited about anything in the world.

"It's true," said Beth. "Look!"

The rumor was true. Cody's mothers weren't right with all of their rumors, but this was just what they had predicted. Out of all the miles and miles of parkland in the city, Dr. Florida had brought his cars and his people to this pasture on this fine spring day. This was contest time! Dr. Florida had come to launch the contest!

I gulped and moved to the window and saw people walking and cameras flying about their heads, and amid the crowd was a single man, tall and distinguished, wearing his usual wide-brimmed hat and long pale raincoat glistening in the sun. I'd never seen him in person, in the flesh, but I'd seen him on TV ten thousand times. This type of seeing was better, I knew. I felt crazy with nerves, and I leaned forward and squinted. Beth and then Cody grabbed me and pulled me back inside. I'd been leaning out of the window, on my tiptoes, and Beth said, "Oh now Ryder," and hugged me. "Are you okay? Are you?"

Dr. Florida was the richest man in the world. He owned a hundred companies and half of our city, and maybe twenty million people worked for him, on Earth and in space. But he was more than that. He was very likely the best man in the world, I believed. He was kind and wise, a saint in the flesh, and that's what I thought when I watched him from the treehouse. I could very nearly feel the goodness welling out of him.

"You're getting lost," Cody warned me. "Ryder?"

I didn't want to get lost. Not now. No, not with Dr. Florida so close. So I breathed and concentrated, using the tricks I'd learned to gain a measure of normalcy—

"It's really him," Marshall declared, his voice bruised but confident. "Would you look at him?"

"Father-to-the-World," I muttered.

"Father-to-the-World," Beth echoed.

"Let's get closer," said Jack. "Why not?"

Then I didn't hear anything for a long moment. I was staring at Dr. Florida, nobody else, and I felt ice in my blood and a weakness in my legs and finally, from a great distance, I heard Beth and Cody saying, "Ryder? Ryder?" with one voice. "Concentrate Ryder. Focus. Get a hold on yourself," they told me. "Come on."

Our treehouse was high in the massive oak. The oak grew halfway down a short wooded slope. On the slope's high side was the pasture—wild grasses and weed grasses softly rising to a line of fences and trimmed lawns and tiny new houses with solar-cell roofs and candy-colored walls. Plus the old white farmhouse where the Wellses lived. Beneath the oak and the slope were the bottoms—long and narrow and flat to the eye, choked with taller, ranker weeds than the pasture weeds. The bottoms ran straight through the parkland, north to south, and on the west was a long steep slope covered with woods. The woods were dark and cool in the afternoon light, the wind making the highest branches nod. There were maples and more oaks, ashes and elms, plus some huge old cottonwoods with their glittering, singing leaves and the occasional old treehouse perched high and turning pale with the slap of the sun and the rain.

"Let's go!" Jack prompted. "Come on!"

"First," said Cody, "you two shake hands. I mean it."

I looked at her thick arms and muscled legs and her breastless broad chest. Cody was wearing shorts and an army jacket, her hair cut stubbly short and her skin baked brown. Her face was square and adorned with a golden peach fuzz. Her smooth voice wasn't a girl's voice or a boy's. She had four toes on each foot. Her mothers had decided that the fifth toe was vanishing anyway... so why wait? They had also made her powerful and quick, endowed with an incredible sense of balance, of place and poise. Some people made noise about so much tailoring. Old adults liked to say there was too much strangeness in kids and parents were wrong for doing so much. For tinkering with that many genes. The foolish ones called Cody ugly, though usually not to her face. Cody was my very best friend, without a doubt, and everyone who knew her respected her. It was all the colors of her strength, and her independence, and her sense of fair play.

She told Jack and Marshall, "Shake hands," and they did it. They didn't like it, no, but they knew not to quit until she said, "Okay!" Then she winked at us and said, "Let's go watch. Come on."

We broke for the hatch, Cody leading the way.

Our treehouse was a huge creation. It had a flat overhanging roof covered with old-fashioned solar panels and super-loop batteries. The big room below had seats for a dozen kids or more, and all sorts of gear were stored in cabinets and crannies. There was fresh water in a big tank and some old plastic freezers Cody herself had found in a junkyard and brought up with block and tackle. Beneath the big room was our maze—a tapering jumble of wood and plastic braced with old steel, passageways leading everywhere and only one course leading end to end. The maze had been my idea. If kids ever broke through the first hatch, I figured, there were more hatches and false hatches and thumbprint locks coded just to us. Plus wrong turns and dark dead ends. The treehouse and oak were ours by right, no one else's. And no one knew the pasture and bottoms and woods half so well as us—an empire stretching for blocks in all directions; a miniature wilderness full of snakes and obscure corners and marvels only visible to the kids.

We crawled free of the maze, straddling a small branch worn smooth from all the hands and butts. Then it was a hard climb down the trunk to a simple bridge—a flat mess of planks crossing from the oak's waist to the top of the slope. Someday it would be a fancy drawbridge. We had plans in our personal, and Jack knew where an old garage door winch was rusting to nothing. All we had to do was steal the winch and rebuild it, and maybe this summer we'd do the work. We'd have the time, come summer. It was part of our plans, at least.

I felt the old planks under my feet as I ran now, crossing onto the pasture with its grass soft and damp. I saw the crowd spreading out and heard the buzz of people talking. I expected an adult to wave us away, to warn us to keep our distance. But none did. Then I found Cody in the crowd, and we joined her. Beth was behind me. She was breathing hard, touching me and asking, "Ryder? How are you doing?"

"I'm okay."

"You're doing just fine," she assured me. She squeezed my arm and gave the crowd a shy glance, then she sang a couple notes. Her voice made every other voice seem rough and graceless. Her face was pretty in an odd fashion. Her folks were Asian Indians, and her skin was effortlessly dark and her long black hair hung straight and pretty. "Just fine," she repeated. Then she let me go.

Cameras were drifting above their owners—bright new cameras lifted by humming fans, their glass eyes scanning this way and that. I knew faces and names, not even trying to remember them. There were a lot of important newspeople here. Some glanced at us, Cody making them pause and stare. Then Dr. Florida walked past us, his people beside him smiling. I watched two big men carrying a box by its rope handles. A cloth sack was thrown over the box, keeping it hidden, and we moved with the crowd to keep close to them. Kids shouted in the distance. They were coming from the candy-colored houses and from other parts of the parkland. I knew their voices and all of their names, memories welling up inside me; and I worked hard not to think of them, knowing I'd get lost again if I filled my head with too much.

Jack wondered, "What's he got? Anyone know?"

Last year it had been pigs. Dr. Florida had released hairless, greasy pigs. There hadn't been many of them and they were easily caught, and we didn't even see one trace of them. It hadn't been much of a year last year, and I remembered how we'd told one another that we wouldn't even hunt this year unless it was something worth chasing. We'd made a vow to ourselves.

Cody said, "It's supposed to be tough." That was part of her mothers' rumor. "Fast and smart and nothing like it in the world. Whatever it is." The creature was inside the box, and we watched the box and held our breaths.

"Down here, men," said Dr. Florida. I was close enough to hear his quiet voice. "That's it, and thanks." He stood beside the covered box, smiling, and for an instant he seemed to smile just at us. Then he gave the box a gentle kick, and something went *whump whump whump* so hard that the box rocked. *Whump whump whump!*

"Jesus," said Jack. And he laughed.

Cody told us to be quiet.

But Marshall said, "It's something big. Huge. I bet so." And he shivered. "I bet it's enormous—"

Cody touched Marshall's long body, and he stopped talking.

"People?" said Dr. Florida. "People." Everyone turned silent. I blinked and saw Dr. Florida's straight smile and sweet eyes and I told myself he didn't look eighty years old. Except his hands looked old, long and spotted and hanging loose at his sides. "It seems amazing," he told us. "They come faster and faster, these springs. Have you ever noticed?"

People laughed. Dr. Florida's people laughed loudest and quit first, keeping a careful watch on everything.

"Another spring," he said, "and I have to think back fifty years to recall our first Easter egg hunt. Fifty good long wonderful years. Isn't that right?" He waited, always smiling, and I heard the whispering hum of the cameras and the soft wind in the grass. "Then I was so young," he said, "and this lovely town and its wonderful good people had welcomed my first labs and shops into their midst. A brave, brave act on everyone's part. I've said it before, I know, but I'll always say it. Every chance I get. It took courage and vision to do what they did, and I'll never stop thanking them. Not so long as I can draw breath, surely."

There was a stir in the crowd, then nothing. Nobody spoke. Nobody dared interrupt Dr. Florida.

He asked us, "How many communities in that age would have accepted, much less welcomed, a gene-tailor? Do you wonder? Who wanted to be a neighbor to someone who was redesigning plants and animals to serve mankind?" He paused, then he said, "I thank this city. A thousand times every day I say, 'Thank you.'"

He had a silky voice. It had no age and no haste.

"I started the Easter egg hunt for little children," he told us. "I can recall some tailored eggs—brightly colored, low in fat and free of cholesterol. Primitive things by today's standards. Even crude. Yet the contest itself was a success. We gave away little trophies to the children with the sharpest eyes, and after a few years we found ourselves with a ritual. A sign of spring." People nodded to themselves and smiled. He said, "Soon the expectations started to rise. Bigger eggs and fancier trophies, and so on. In a very real sense this annual affair had mirrored the advances in gene-tailoring, in our manipulations of living, replicating DNA. On our tenth anniversary we released live chickens in lieu of eggs—big, ugly birds meant to give a good chase to children of all ages. Our mistake was to neglect intelligence. There was a heavy shower several hours later and most of the birds drowned. The poor things." He halfway laughed. Everyone else shook their heads and smiled, the oldest few remembering the event. I could tell by their dreamy eyes and their knowing happy mouths.

"But we've gotten better," he insisted. "I've watched our skills and cleverness grow by tremendous leaps. Today, at this instant, this world of ours is fed and fat because of our work here. People even live on other worlds because of our commitment to progress." He paused, his eyes full of light. He told us, "Forgive this old husk for his ramblings," and he gestured at the covered box. "We're talking about the contest, aren't we? Of course we are." He sighed and told us, "I swear to you. Even when I'm gone—when my legacy is something you and your children can debate about—this contest will continue. My people and my companies will see to it. In every real sense I am rooted in this fine warm community, and I will make certain that each year some novel and wondrous creature will be set free in the parks. For the children. For always."

People clapped. The five of us clapped with them.

Then Dr. Florida silenced us, lifting a long finger to his lips. "This is the fiftieth anniversary, yes. It's fifty years to the day. So of course we have something special, something extraordinary." He smiled, his gaze coming around to the five of us. We were the only kids standing in the front of the crowd, in plain view. He seemed to speak to us, saying, "I don't think you'll be disappointed."

No one spoke.

He said, "Lillith," and a tall, slender woman produced a trophy from a black carrying case. The trophy's base might have been gold, and there were crystal pillars topped with a brilliant false flame. I watched the flame flicker and curl, and he said, "Thank you." She set the trophy in the grass, and he told us, "Its materials come from my asteroid mines, the ingenuity from my various electronics companies, and the shape is my own design. I hope you like it. The flame is a holo projection, of course, and the super-loop batteries are charged and good for a geologic age. Give or take." He grinned and promised, "If you catch this year's prize, I will personally give you this token and shake your hand. Absolutely."

I blinked and breathed, imagining such a thing.

Dr. Florida nudged the covered box. *Whump whump Whump!* The creature made the box shiver and jump. Beth eased back a step, one hand on Cody and one hand on me, and Cody looked at her face, telling her, "It's okay. It's safe."

"Like every year," Dr. Florida was saying, "we have rules to be obeyed. They'll be published tonight, but suffice to say they're the same reliable rules as every year. You can't be older than fifteen. One trophy per capture. The prey can't be harmed, and we pay for the return of the tailored organism. A modest fee, like always. For the research value it brings." He winked at the five of us, asking, "Do you understand?"

We felt everyone watching us. Nobody spoke.

"So that covers it? We're finished?" He seemed to stare at me, and I felt weak and shaky. "What's left to do? Do you kids know?"

I couldn't talk. Not for anything.

Cody was the one who said, "Open the box," with a soft voice.

"Let it go," Jack added, talking louder. "You've got to—"

"Indeed!" Dr. Florida stabbed the air with a finger. He did it comically, making everyone laugh. Then he said, "But I'm an old man. I don't bend so well, you see," and people sported warm smiles and laughed some more. I felt the newspeople pressing forward, grass breaking under their feet. "I'll tell you what," Dr. Florida announced. "Why don't the four... no, five... the five of you come here and let this marvel go free? All right?"

We couldn't move for an instant.

Even Cody froze.

I glanced to one side, the cameras turning toward us with their glass eyes focusing. I told myself to concentrate. To focus. I was terrified that I might get lost and weird—

"Come on. Don't be bashful," he warned us. "I'm not going to bite. Come here," and he smiled, his voice so smooth and warm that I couldn't help but feel better. I felt at ease.

We went toward him. Cody whispered, "Ryder? Look at us?" and she rolled her head once. I understood. I walked past the box while the others kneeled around it. Then I stared at them and at everything. I saw Jack's worn green jeans and Marshall's long hairless face, Cody stroking her own stubbly hair and Beth small beside Cody, and finally Dr. Florida asked, "Why don't you take off the cover? Go on."

"We're waiting for Ryder," Cody explained.

"Okay. Where's this Ryder person?" He stood on his tiptoes, watching the crowd and adjusting the big brim of his hat.

Beth said, "He's here," and I rejoined them. We stood in a knot, and one of Beth's hard little breasts came up against my arm. Then we weren't touching, and I looked about and saw all the staring faces. I began to shiver, just slightly, and Dr. Florida asked, "What's your name?"

I saw his own hard gaze and his enormous smile. I squeaked, "Ryder," and didn't perish. Here he stood—the great and wise Dr. Florida—and it felt so strange and wondrous to be speaking to him. I wouldn't have guessed that such a thing would happen. Not in my life.

He took a step toward us. "A special skill?" he wondered, his voice barely loud enough to be heard.

"I guess," I admitted, shrugging.

"No one else is like him," Marshall boasted. "No one."

"I thought I noticed . . . something," he responded.

But I felt normal most of the time, in most ways. Didn't I? I felt I'd been doing a good job of acting normal, considering all the things that were happening, all the faces begging to be remembered, and all the voices triggering switches inside my panicking brain . . . wasn't I doing good just the same?

"Ryder? Why don't you and your friends do the service. Please?" He waved at the crowd, bringing them around us but not too close.

I breathed hard and focused on the box. Just on the box.

Cody said, "Here. Get the other edge," and she grabbed the covering sack. Jack helped her lift it, exposing the heavy wooden walls and the double-thick screen door. The door was dented and twisted by something inside. I leaned closer, the sack gone. There was pale yellow straw and nothing else. For an instant I believed the creature had escaped—through a hole somewhere?—and then the straw exploded. I saw white, white fur and tar-black eyes, and everyone else jumped backwards. But not me. I was too well focused, too much a part of things. I saw the creature slam into the screen door with its pointed face, *whump*, and it was part of me. A snake with tiny, tiny legs. And fur. And fury too. Look at it! I thought. Look! There's nothing like it in the world! I thought. Look!

"It's a compilation organism," Dr. Florida explained. "We've named it the snow dragon because of its color and appearance. It's half rattlesnake genes—the venom and fangs removed, of course—and much of the rest is mammalian. With synthetic genes for the extras. Those little feet you see? They can be retracted for speed. The metabolism? It's close to a shrew's. Very fast. Very demanding. The snow dragon is the biological equivalent of a firestorm."

It had thick white fur on its back and sides, golden bits of straw clinging to the fur, and its belly was covered with shiny, ivory-colored scales. I saw its eyes wink, and its broad, triangular head moved left and right and left again, a snake's tongue moving faster than I could follow. The snow dragon was a stout, five-foot bundle of muscle and bone and superquick nerves. Snakes can be fast, sunwarmed and mad, but this thing slipped back and forth too quickly for any snake. Or most anything else alive. Dr. Florida promised, "It will be active year-round. Even in the coldest winters. It eats mice and birds and snakes and . . . well, pretty much anything. My staff tell me it should grow through this year, maybe doubling its size. We're releasing fifty of these marvels throughout the city's parklands . . . this particular specimen being the clone mother to the others . . . and it won't be an easy chase, I warn you. Not this year!"

The snow dragon leaped against the screen door, then hissed.

Marshall stumbled backwards, saying, "Gosh."

People laughed at him. I turned and looked at Dr. Florida, studying his face, seeing little things because I was so close. No, he didn't look eighty. But he was very tired just the same. I saw tiredness in his bright smiling eyes. There was something hard through his face and body—a tension, some spring wound tight, something working against his insides. He was the world's most important person; I thought of all the important work he had to do. People had spoken well of him throughout my life, praising him for his countless good deeds and his ceaseless energy; and I gazed up at him, feeling ever so glad that he'd taken the time to come here today. I could scarcely believe it...

"One last word of advice," he told us. "And tell this to your friends too. We've got no dumb beast here. Not at all. My dragon has a quick brain and great eyes and good ears and a fine tongue." He was smiling with pride. "I wouldn't be surprised if this particular dragon is never caught. How's that for a challenge?" He paused, then he said, "Well? Why don't we stand back and let these kids start the show?"

Cody undid the first latch with a *click*, then grabbed its mate and looked at us. "Ready?"

Jack and Marshall were standing. I stood too. Beth was behind us and off to one side, cautious like always, and Cody undid the other latch and said, "Ready?"

We felt ready.

She lifted the screen in one motion. The dragon launched itself like a torpedo. I blinked and saw a white streak on the grass, and the adults scattered, a touch frightened and giggling because of their fright, and the five of us looked at one another, too startled to move. Then Dr. Florida said: "Get after it! Go!"

So we ran, tearing across the pasture. Cody was in the lead, and Marshall was behind her with his long legs pumping. The dragon moved like rushing water, following the curves and slopes of the ground. I saw its body against the greenness, and Cody sprinted and dove for it, falling short. The dragon had sensed motion and slipped sideways, and now Cody was down and laughing at herself and I was past her. Then Marshall slowed, already winded, and I was ahead for an instant. All I could think was that I wanted to grasp the dragon, wrestle it and bring back its long body, winning the trophy and Dr. Florida's respect. "Look what you've done," he would say to me. "Look what you've managed, Ryder."

The dragon left the pasture. It slipped down onto our bridge, and for an instant I thought it was trapped. I came onto the bridge leaning forward, charging hard, and the dragon turned its head and saw me and turned and slipped past the oak's trunk, leaping into the air—a curling rubbery shape with its fur shining in the afternoon sun.

It seemed to be flying, buoyed up by invisible wings.

I watched it cover an enormous arc, neatly dropping into the brush at the base of the slope, and I was left trapped on the bridge. Everyone else slid down the bare earth of the slope, straight onto the bottoms, Jack hooting and Beth slowing and me turning to look back at the crowd. I saw Dr. Florida watching me, and I felt sick. I had failed and seemed foolish, I was sure, and he was speaking to the tall woman beside him with his eyes fixed on me. Me. I froze and stared back at him for a long moment, then I took a desperate breath and made myself turn and leap.

The snow dragon was streaking down the bottoms.

I paced myself, hoping against hope that I might outlast it. Beth quit and told me to be careful, and Jack stopped and said, "Forget it." He looked small against the tall weeds. "It's long gone," he assured me, and I was past him and closing on Marshall. Marshall found a cramp in his leg, and his face was pale from all the running. Only Cody was ahead, and I focused on her and wouldn't let myself quit. Not for anything. My legs ached and my breath tore at my throat; but she had speed and power, not endurance, and I knew I could catch her if I really wanted.

We approached the end of the bottoms. There was a high roadbed cutting across it, and a stone-lined basin was laid at the roadbed's base. The basin was filled with dark water. We called it the almost-pond. Cody was standing motionless, panting and watching the almost-pond; and I came up beside her and saw the dragon's white body swimming, its head reared high. Birds squawked and lifted from the far shoreline, flapping hard and cursing while the dragon slipped up onto the land again. I couldn't see it now. The watered weeds nodded and nothing showed, and Cody said, "No more," and fell to her knees. She was laughing, sweat soaking her clothes and her face and her gasping voice saying, "Shit," a couple times.

I looked back the way we'd come. Some of the newspeople had followed us into the bottoms, but now they were giving up. Their day was finished. Bunches of kids were hunting the underbrush, kicking up rubbish and joking among themselves. Beth was talking to Marshall, kneeling and touching his cramped leg. I couldn't see Dr. Florida anywhere. Not his hat or his raincoat or anyone tall enough to be him, and I felt a little bit sad.

Muscles aching, I trotted to the far side of the almost-pond.

The dragon was nowhere. It had evaporated. I climbed the steep west slope and reached a flat stretch where there weren't any trees, just tall grass, the outlines of a big old house showing in the side of the hill. Years and years ago the house had burned. All that remained was a partial foundation on three sides, the concrete bricks crumbling to nothing. I pictured the dragon trapped in a corner. Trapped and mine. I moved on my leaden legs, my mouth full of dust, and of course there was nothing but the grass and the bricks and I ended up folding and dropping onto my back.

I lay there for a very long time.

I remember the sky—a clear warm blue, empty of clouds—and there was no reason to fear anything above me, or anywhere. I felt warm and safe in the grass, and I got a little bit lost. For a little while. Then the wind blew and the grass nodded and there was a garter snake that passed within arm's reach, its body dark and the yellow stripes dirty and the lidless eyes hard and patient in a way that people can't be patient. Then it was gone, and I felt rested and breathed easier, my throat pleasantly brassy, and I sat up and smelled the sun on the grass and the shadows in the woods and all the snakes curling in the tangled green growth. Or so it seemed.

Cody and Marshall and Beth were beside the almost-pond. Jack Wells emerged from the woods above me. He was carrying a magazine curled under one arm, and he was giggling. "Marshall!" he shouted. "Rich boy!" He uncurled the magazine and selected a page, the liquid crystals changing into an elegant long body. A naked woman's body. "Look what I found!" he called out. He waved the woman's picture, and he danced—

"Asshole!" Marshall answered. "Goddamn you—!"

Marshall ran after Jack. They vanished into the shadows of the woods, Marshall furious and frantic and embarrassed beyond measure. I laughed and hoped nobody got hurt—but wasn't it funny?—and then I turned and saw Beth and Cody climbing toward me. Beyond them was the motorcade of vans and limousines. They were driving past us, toward the west, and the longest limousine was at the back. I looked at it and looked at it, but I couldn't see anything besides the smoky windows and the shiny body and the reflected, distorted shapes of the ground and sky. It's been years, yes, but I remember every detail. I can focus my mind and see the limousine beside me climbing the hill, and I can freeze that instant and stare hard. Oh yes, I see myself reflected on the limousine's body—a tanned and average-built boy, pretty much handsome but somehow quite strange, particularly in the eyes—and then the limousine is past, gone with the whispering hum of its tires, and I breathe once and blink and turn and start to move again, walking down the grassy slope, walking toward the girls.

TWO

The three of us were at the dinner table. The TV was off and it was late; dinner had been delayed by the news on TV and the phone calls from people who'd seen me with Dr. Florida. Yet still Mom couldn't understand. It didn't seem to fit inside her head. "It was really him? A busy man like him?" She had watched us on several channels, and she had heard me tell it; but all she could do was squint into her steaming corn and hold her mouth closed, skeptical to the end. "Why do you suppose he came *here* this year?" she wondered. "What made him?"

"Had to go somewhere," Dad joked. Then he turned to me, saying, "Ryder? Where's he gone before?"

I named places. I went back several years, recalling different parks scattered about the city.

"See? The luck of the draw," Dad told us. He ate his corn and the dark cultured beef, moving with his usual slow precision. "He had to come here sooner or later."

"I suppose." Mom picked up her fork and stabbed at her food. After a minute, she said, "It's funny what you notice on TV."

"How do you mean?" he asked.

"Oh, things like Marshall getting so tall. Seeing him beside all those people... well, it was obvious. Wasn't it, Kip? And I wouldn't have guessed Cody could run so fast. She just streaked along. Her bulk and everything, and she just flew."

19

I summoned that instant when I'd looked at my friends kneeling beside the dragon's box, my gaze slow and complete. I concentrated on the little details in the milling crowd—the exact curls of the smiles, the angles of the cameras, the shirts not quite tucked into place and the shiny green grass stains on trouser legs. Then Dad was shaking me gently, and he said, "Ryder," as if he'd been repeating my name for a long while. I blinked and realized what had happened. Mom was staring at her plate, the corn not steaming anymore. "Sorry," I said, and Dad said, "For what?" and I ate fast, thinking about nothing else. *Concentrate, concentrate.* I finished and cleaned the table, giving the dishes to the washer. Then we had a sweet and cold dessert, something with strawberries and foam. Mom kept quiet, and Dad, sensing her mood, tried to fill the room with his own voice.

"Yeah, that's something," he said. "A little dragon and that neat trophy," he said. "Quite the trophy, isn't it? Old Florida pulled out the stops this year, coaxing the big networks to send people. A human interest story, all right. Fifty years of the contest, fifty dragons released . . . yours the biggest, right? That's right. Just shows you what they can do when they set their minds to it. Quite the critter—"

I looked at both of them, considering their faces. I knew their expressions and their stances, having seen them pass through every color of mood, and there were moments when I felt close to reading their minds. I asked, "How many people saw us, Dad?"

"On TV? Millions, I suppose. Maybe billions by tomorrow." He wasn't a tall man, yet he looked tall. He was lean and bony, his face full of angles and shadows and wrinkles. Dr. Florida didn't look eighty, no, but Dad seemed older than forty. Easily. His hair was full of tired gray, and if he wasn't smiling I could see the darkness behind his looks. He was forever working to sound happy, keeping his voice bright and cheery; but I knew him. "I guess this'll rank high on your days to savor, won't it?"

"It was fun," I admitted.

Mom asked, "How's Beth doing? We haven't seen her in a while."

"She's fine. Her folks got sick again."

"That's too bad." She nodded and wondered, "Are they better now?"

"They're fine." I shrugged my shoulders.

Mom paused, then she asked, "Does she talk about them much? Her folks?"

"Sometimes," I said. "She talks sometimes."

Dad said, "Gwinn? Aren't you hungry?"

She didn't seem to hear him. "Some people have such sad lives," she told me, and she shivered.

Mom took comfort from other people's troubles. Beth's folks had had terrible things happen to them years ago, in India's civil war, and now they couldn't leave their house for any reason. They were invalids, and Beth served as their nurse on bad days—singing to calm their nerves, tending their old wounds, and whatever else was needed. I didn't know her folks myself; nobody else had ever gotten inside to see them. The most I'd seen were dried, shadowy figures at a window, pale hands pulling aside the curtains and strange eyes staring out at me . . . and I felt ever so cold thinking of them, my mind filling in those gruesome blanks.

Mom brightened all at once. She said, "Marshall's running," and giggled into her uneaten dessert. "He's not exactly coordinated."

"He's got his own style," Dad joked. "He sure does."

I sat and ate.

"So," said Dad, "when are you chasing the dragon?"

"I don't know."

"After school tomorrow? While the trail's hot?"

"Maybe."

"Not too much longer and you'll be on the outside," he warned me, reaching out and touching my closer hand.

I didn't understand.

"You'll be too old for the contest. You're growing up." He said it with a sudden, unexpected seriousness.

"I guess so," I volunteered.

"You think the five of you can catch it?"

"Maybe—"

Mom began to laugh in a gentle, dark way.

"What is it, Gwinn?"

"Just people," she told Dad. "I was thinking about people. Such strange creatures, aren't they?"

"Absolutely," he responded. "Very strange."

"They baffle me. Do they baffle you, Kip?"

"All the time," he laughed. "Pretty much every day."

Mom was nearly my father's height, with short, straw-

colored hair and the roundest face in creation. She had tiny
hands and precise motions like Dad's. People said they were
very much alike and perfect matches for one another. They
shared the office in the basement and the business, selling
real estate, and they cleaned the house together and did the
lawn work on weekends, and our meals came at the same
times every day. A late dinner was strange, even remarkable,
and everything tonight felt askew. The air was tense and
oddly sad, which surprised me, and I tried to see what share
of the sadness I had brought on myself.

With a philosophical tone, Dad said, "Such a day."

Mom said nothing, nodding and studying her dessert.
No, she decided. No, she couldn't touch it. She pushed it
away and sighed.

I was finished. I started to leave, excusing myself and
pacing my steps, knowing the rhythms of the house. I lingered
in the hallway, pretending to climb the stairs but hanging
within earshot of the kitchen. I knew by instinct that precise
moment when they would start to talk honestly—

"I can't stand it," she said. She breathed and said, "I
just . . . I just wish . . . I don't know."

"What is it?" asked Dad.

She didn't say anything. I was on the stairs, taking them
on cat's feet, and she finally admitted, "They saw him."

"Who saw him?"

"Everyone, Kip. Like you said—"

"What do you mean?" he snapped.

"I mean a few billion strangers!"

"If anything," he told her, "they noticed Cody. Not him."
He was impatient and a touch angry. "Ryder looks like a
quiet, inquisitive boy. That's all, and quit it."

"I hope so."

"Jesus, it's a thirty-second news piece," Dad reminded
her. "He was on the screen how many seconds? Ten? You
really believe he's that odd that people are going to care—?"

"Well—"

"Quit it, Gwinn. Just stop."

She was quiet for a moment. Then she said, "I'm too
sensitive. You're right, I admit it."

Dad said something too soft to be heard.

Mom said, "Anyway."

And I finished climbing the stairs, entered my room and
sat on the polished stone floor. I crossed my legs and concen-

trated, escaping into the afternoon again. I began where I was lying on the long bench, holding everything at normal speed, and I ended with Beth and Cody and me walking home through the weedy bottoms. Every sensation was the same. I was existing in a string of wondrous moments, fresh for always, and if I wanted I could have tied the string's ends together and made an endless loop. A million times I could' have seen Dr. Florida smile and Cody leap at the dragon, felt Beth's breast against my arm and the ringneck's red tongue on my bare foot; and there would be Jack and Marshall fighting—and the same surge of fear rising through me, and then the same sudden finish, my adrenalin building and collapsing because certain odd clusters of neurons inside my head knew how to sputter and spark in the same reliable, meaning-rich ways.

People don't think like I think.

Most people barely recall past times, and their memories are forever infected with wishful thinking and impenetrable holes. But I have my way of focusing—concentrating hard on things stored within me. To me a memory can be more real and true than the things of the moment. Memories are reality cured and conditioned into a hard, clear stuff that can be examined with care from every angle and with every sense, new details always lurking, always close.

I have an early memory of the parkland, for example.

We had just moved to the city, and our neighborhood was full of new houses and young families. Mom and Dad walked me down to the old streambed that was soon to become the bottoms. Big bulldozers were gutting out the trash and eroded earth, making room for a modern, efficient sewage treatment scheme. My folks had been reading about it. They spoke of big perforated pipes and special cleansing sands, understanding almost nothing. Mom said, "It's Florida's park," and Dad said, "Florida *is* this town." I wasn't four years old, and a lot of the words were strange to me. They were so much noise. What I noticed most were the huge and magnificent bulldozers with their robot brains and their high, empty seats where people would sit and drive, should the robots fail. I felt their throbbing and clanking, the sensation frightening and fine; and I stood safe between my folks, Dad talking about the dozers now and their invisible riders, and

Mom confessing that the dust was bothering her, so couldn't we go home now? Please?

We walked through the future pasture. I remember more weeds than grasses, and the weeds had a rich stink that lingered on my clothes and skin. We crossed a newly made street and followed a second street up to our house, blue and bright and sandwiched between the other colored houses. I went upstairs to my new room and sat on the stone floor, a big sheet of old-fashioned paper between my legs and a lovely black crayon letting me make lines. I didn't understand tailoring. My idea came to me from a simpler, childish source, and it had nothing to do with genes and splicing.

I remember drawing hard and fighting my clumsy young hands, concentrating on little details. I did the bulldozer as well as I could manage, then I looked in a mirror and made a snarling face and drew it too. Then I went downstairs and found Mom. "Look look look," I said.

"I'm looking." She was sitting on our new couch, my drawing in her lap. She said, "Goodness."

I said it was Dozerman. The dozer was below, the man on top. I was on top. I was the man, I explained. "Dozerman! Dozerman!" I'd drawn it the way I saw it in my head, minus the shakes of my hands and the limits of my crayon. Mom watched me chug-chug around the room. I imagined myself with the funny Dozerman wheels, and I told her I'd grow up the same way. "Dozerman!"—powerful and loud, digging and pushing all day, all night, its big super-loop batteries brimming with juice and no need for food or water, or anything—

"All right, dear. Stop." Mom stared at me, folding the drawing in half and tucking it out of sight. "No more," she said. "What you should do is go upstairs and rest. You must be tired. Aren't you tired?"

Dozerman didn't get tired. I tried telling her so.

"But you're not him, are you? Are you?" She shook her head, saying, "So stop, please. Would you? Ryder? Would you stop now please?"

When I was very young and my folks were talking—at the dinner table, watching TV, or anywhere—I'd catch them forgetting something or telling a story wrong. I would correct them. Of course I meant nothing bad, and I certainly didn't wish to seem proud or to belittle them for their failures. I didn't even understand at first. Couldn't they summon up the past? Did they blink at the wrong moments? I wondered. You put your keys there, Mommy. No, up there. Mr. Evans said the house was on Weavehaven, Daddy. And who cut down that tree? The one by the green house. The green house that was yellow last year, Daddy. Mommy. You remember! We drove past it when it was Christmas and they had all the fake bambis pulling Santa across the yard. We went down this street and turned, and Daddy said, "I feel snow in my bones, Gwinn. Maybe when we're home we can melt it together," and it snowed three inches that night. It did—!

My memory grew as I got older, and I began to have spells.

My capacity to focus was the culprit. Just as I could look inside myself, I could watch the world without and lose myself for times. Once when I was five I climbed a high stool to look at water boiling in a big pot. I'd never gotten lost in such a thing before. The clear water churned and popped, the bubbles skating along the bottom, and growing, and then rising free with such violence that my heart was left pounding and my chest felt tight. Mom was beside me after a while. She took my arms and face, saying, "Oh, what is it? Ryder? Ryder?" Couldn't she see the water boiling? How could she miss such a wonder? I tried to answer her, but I couldn't speak. I was completely lost, oblivious to the scalding steam and my bright burns. And she was terrified, of course. She told Dad so later. Another damned trance, and she didn't care what the doctors said. I was hallucinating! These weren't *discrimination* problems, or whatever they were calling them this week. It was just boiling water, for God's sake! And while I listened I grieved for her and for Dad. I did. That was the moment, precise and undeniable, when I understood that my folks were, in some fashion, blind.

Then I was six years old, and a certain teacher came home with me. The meeting had been arranged and my folks were waiting in the living room, wearing good clothes and smelling of soap. "Go play in your room, Ryder." Mom spoke with her voice slow and tight, her face strange. "Shut your door so we don't bother you. All right?"

I went upstairs. My room was cool and dark with the shades drawn, and my door didn't quite fill its frame. The stone floor served to reflect sounds through the gap at the bottom. I heard talk from the living room. I focused on every sound.

"We're glad to meet you," said Dad. "Can I get you something?"

"A soft drink," said the teacher.

"What can we do for you?" asked Mom. "Is anything wrong?"

"Oh, no. No." The teacher was a fat woman, and old. She was wearing a huge bright dress and paint on her face, and no one liked her. Not at school, at least. The kids called her a witch and worse, and the other teachers said hard things when they thought no one was in earshot. I lay on the floor and thought about the things I'd overhead, the voices like angry bees in my head. "Manipulative," they said. "Two-faced."

"I was studying Ryder's files," she explained, "and I thought this would be a good time to meet his parents. That's all."

"It's good meeting you," said Dad.

"A very special boy. Unique, I think." She wondered, "Where, if I might ask, did you have the refinements done?" Refinement was the same as tailoring. She said the word slowly, as if it was three words.

"In California," Mom told her. "In a Florida clinic."

"An interesting coincidence, your moving here. Dr. Florida's home—"

"A business decision," Dad mentioned. "This is one of the fastest growing states, after all."

"Quite reasonable of you, yes," said the teacher. "Let me thank you for letting me visit, first of all. And I want you to know that we at the school, and myself, want to do our utmost to help your son master his talents and smooth over those points where he might have troubles. I want you to feel assured that all of us wish the best for him, and everything from adapted personals to private tutors will be done on his behalf."

There was nothing. Then Dad said, "Well, thanks . . ."

"Are there any questions about his prognosis?" she wondered.

"More of the same," he said. "It's something like autism, they tell us. His difficulty coping with the environment, choosing what to watch and what to ignore. He has these trances—"

"He's very sensitive," said Mom.

"Oh, yes," the teacher agreed. "Autism has its similarities, yes. But an autistic child would be helpless. Ryder is not. With training and hard work, Ryder should be able to carry on normally. Maybe he'll lack some abilities. He does pay a cost for having such a powerful memory... the brain being finite, after all. But we shouldn't grieve for him. I know I don't grieve. When he's like me, old and gray, he'll only have to concentrate for a moment to remember youth." She laughed and said, "That seems like a precious talent to me." She said, "Maybe I do envy him. A little bit. If I could remember being twenty again, if I could," she laughed loudly for a very brief moment.

Then no one spoke.

Finally Mom said, "You're very kind," with a certain voice.

Dad said, "Gwinn? Don't be—"

"What?" she asked. "Isn't this rather patronizing? I don't like being patronized, and I'm not sitting through it."

"I'm sorry," said the teacher. "I just hoped—"

"Lady," said Mom, "it's difficult to have such a son." She was angry in a quiet fashion. She said, "We wanted a fine healthy boy, Kip and I. We're ordinary people, yes, and I for one take pride in that fact. I don't mind admitting it. I am not gifted. I can't juggle enormous math problems in my head, or paint great paintings, or call myself a beauty. Not even on the old scales. I'm part of the last honest generation... the good and decent people who were brought up to accept their shortcomings..."

"Gwinn?"

"Let me talk, Kip. Please?" She said, "We had the tailoring done, and I guess I am glad for the bulk of it. We made certain that Ryder would be healthy and long-lived and we got what we paid for, yes. But there was this self-serving bastard at the clinic. I'm not blaming Dr. Florida himself, I know better than to do that in this town. But this one man was a demon. Smug. Smart and proud of it. He had his lab coat and his charm, and he seduced us with nonsense about every child being born with enormous talents. Awesome brains and other bankable skills, and we would be unfit parents if we settled for a plain-label boy. That's how he put it. A plain-label boy. And both of us were a little bowled over by him. He told us how a few synthetic genes could be sewn into the fertilized egg—tiny, potent brain enhancers—and we'd make it possible for Ryder to compete in the world—"

"Darling?" said Dad.

"What?"

"What if someone overhears? Don't you think—?"

"What? I'm talking honestly. We spend too much time and breath hiding things as it is," she told him. "When he's old and gray, like she said, he can remember this with everything else. Maybe he'll understand." She sighed and told the teacher, "I'm sorry. I sound bitter, I know, but I've got reasons. I love my son very much, I do, but he can't simply walk home from school. He's always finding distractions. Diversions. An ordinary leaf, and he'll sit on the ground and study it, and then the next leaf, and so on. Then it's after dark, and I'm worried sick and I have to come out and find him. Do you understand? I find him on someone's lawn, and he'd holding leaves up to the streetlights . . ."

"I do understand," said the teacher.

Mom said, "How many times has it happened, Kip? We're talking to some friends of business associates, whoever, and poor Ryder corrects us on this point. On that point. A little boy, and he tells people the most remarkable things, embarrassing things, and everyone knows it's true because they know him—"

"He's not vindictive," said Dad.

"Am I saying he's vindictive?" She paused for a long moment, then she said, "I'm angry because I didn't pay someone for the privilege of having such a child. Special or not. It's not fair, and I realize there are legal rulings that keep us from lawsuits. We signed plenty of papers and clearances and tied our own hands. And yes, maybe I do seem rather simple-minded to you. Shortsighted and all. But I can't help it and I've given up trying to stop myself—I am no saint—and so there. I guess I've said my piece. So thank you."

No one spoke.

Then the teacher said, "Genetics are difficult. At best." Her voice was soft and slow. "Even now they can't predict all the effects from a single novel gene. Particularly the synthetics. A gene meshes with many thousands of genes, and who knows? Who knows?" She paused, then she said, "I don't know." She said, "I see it every day, this new world, and you're right. Not everything is perfect. I see geniuses who aren't smart enough for their parents, and children sculpted according to whims and fancies. We've got synthetic genes and famous genes, and what bothers me most is the parent who can't accept the fact that every child, gifted or not, is a child first. Immature. In need of help."

"These have to be tough times for kids," said Dad. He sounded agreeable and quite sober.

"And yet, you know, the children themselves are such inspirations," the teacher said. "All my life I've worked with the youngest ones, and I've seen the changes. Years ago they would pick on one another for being odd. You know . . . different? I'm sure you remember the horrors. The funny-looking boy was tormented. The ugly or smart girl was friendless. That sort of crime doesn't happen so much anymore—"

"Everyone's smart," said Mom. "And pretty."

"Maybe that's part of the answer," the teacher admitted. "Sure. But there's nothing homogeneous about my kids. There are plenty of chances for viciousness, for in-groups and out-groups. Yet they seem to tolerate the differences. Indeed, if anything, these children nourish a strange, resilient independence . . . based on their own special skills . . ."

"How many children do you have?" asked Mom.

"I see about a hundred every day—"

"I mean you yourself. Have you been a mother?" she wondered. Her voice was wearing an edge.

Dad said, "Another drink?" I heard him moving, his voice turning quiet. Soothing. "It's awfully good of you to come." He was trying to lessen the tension, saying, "We must seem pretty ragged to you, but under the circumstances—"

"Don't mention it. Please," said the teacher.

"Still and all." His voice got louder. "Whatever happens, we do wish the best for Ryder. Always have. We thought we were helping him with the tailoring. The refinements. Because it's tooth-and-nail out there. We wanted him fit to compete for the jobs and the promotions." He paused, then he said, "Think of our position. In a very few years my wife and I will be facing the first of Ryder's generation—their brainpower, their good looks and confidence—and I can confess to feeling nervous." He said, "The tooth-and-nail business of business." He said, "We took our chances and the poor kid suffers for us having done it. And so we make ourselves suffer too. Don't we, dear?"

Mom said, "Kip."

"Sure you don't want another drink?" asked Dad.

"No thank you," said the teacher.

"Where are you going, dear?"

"Downstairs," said Mom. "You mentioned work, and it occurred to me that I might do some. All right?"

No one spoke.

Mom said, "I am sorry. I just want something accomplished today. If you don't mind."

No one spoke while she went downstairs, then Dad said, "Gwinn is a little touchy, that's all. She takes it personally when Ryder does some strange thing or another. When he starts to stare at one of our friends with those big eyes—"

"I should be honest," the teacher announced. "I do have a second agenda today. A request, if you will."

Dad said, "All right."

"A series of studies and papers on Ryder might just help find and treat children like him. And maybe we can learn how to avoid the same mistakes again. For those who wish to consider them mistakes." She paused, then she said, "As I understand it, no one is certain why his ordinary genes and the synthetics merged like they did."

"No one's told us how," said Dad.

"I'm in a unique position, you see. I've access to facilities and I've got the essential training, and so with your permission—"

"I don't believe so."

"Could you tell me why?"

"First," said Dad, "Gwinn wouldn't allow it. And second, neither would I."

"I see."

"It's something we decided long ago. Label us however you wish, but the truth is that we appreciate our quiet lives. We don't want notoriety. A kid like Ryder, with his talents, could become an enormous novelty act on TV. You know what I mean. The public would want to test his memory by every goofy means, and that wouldn't be best. Not for him. Not for us. So I'm sorry, but no."

"Well," she said, "if publicity is the problem—"

"A John Doe? I think not," said Dad. "That doesn't sound appealing. Besides, there's no way you can guarantee our privacy. Is there?"

She said nothing for a good long while. I imagined her sitting on a chair in the living room, filling it, and Dad sitting opposite her and leaning forward with his bony elbows on his bony knees.

She said, "Perhaps I should mention other terms."

"I don't follow you."

She said, "A cash incentive. A gift for the good of the boy—"

"No."

"But you can't—"

"Lady," he said, "let's call it quits." I could hear Dad standing and moving to the front door. The teacher followed. She breathed like fat people breath, quick and shallow. We didn't have fat kids at school, I thought. All of us made our food into heat and motion. "Your intentions are splendid, and thanks," said Dad. "But I ask—I insist—that you leave and forget this conversation." His voice wasn't angry or sad or anything. It was flat and plain.

"I'm sorry if I offended you."

"I'll live." The front door opened, squeaking, and he said, "It was nice of you to take the trouble," with that flat voice.

She said, "You shouldn't be ashamed of him."

"You think we are? You haven't been listening, lady."

She said, "Give him my best," with anger seeping out between the words.

"Sure."

"I can tell," she said. "You *are* interested in the offer."

"A little bit, sure. We could always use the cash flow." Then Dad said, "The thing about being ordinary is that we're weak and we don't have any illusions. And no denials either. I admit it. We're subject to temptations." He made a small, harsh sound, and I imagined him shaking his head. "Maybe there'll come a day when Florida, or someone, learns to tailor out those traits. You suppose? A dose of this, a shot of that, and *poof*! Instant character. Neat and quick."

We were eating that night, sitting at the kitchen table and the teacher gone. No one was talking. No one could think of anything to say, their mouths full and their plates steaming and forks going *click-click* when the peas ran away. I was thinking about my peas. I was studying their wrinkled faces, each face different in tiny vital ways. I was watching the tines of my fork come down on them and stick into their firm green meat, or cause them to jump and run away. *Click-click*. And Mom said, "Ryder? Ryder. Don't you want to know what she said?"

I blinked. "Was it good?" I asked.

They glanced at each other. "Absolutely," said Dad.

"Why? Did you think you were in trouble?" Mom started to watch my peas too. "Have you done something wrong?"

"I don't think so."

"You haven't," said Dad. "Don't worry."

"Is she a nice lady?" asked Mom. "This teacher?"

"I don't know. She's okay."

"What do people say about her?" she asked. "Do they like her?"

"Not really."

"Not really?" She halfway smiled and said, "Go on. Eat."

But I couldn't. All at once a question came into my head, and I thought of how I might ask it. What would be the best way? I pondered and then cleared my throat, looking at Dad and wondering, "Dad? Who's the best person in the world?"

"The best person?"

"Is there one? Anyone?"

"I suppose there must be," he admitted, shrugging his shoulders. "Why do you ask?"

I remembered older kids talking on the playground one day. I saw their faces and heard their self-assured voices, then I blinked and said, "These kids told me it was Dr. Florida. He's the best."

"A good candidate," he decided.

Mom said, "He's not perfect," with that edge to her voice.

"And who is perfect?" asked Dad.

She looked at me and said, "I'm sure he's a decent fellow. Probably better than all of us. Now eat your peas."

I caught three peas and chewed them to slime, then squished the slime between my teeth. I started to daydream, imagining the doorbell ringing and Dad going to the door, finding Dr. Florida standing on our porch. He was so very tall, smiling like he smiled on TV, and he said, "Good evening," and put his hat in his hands. "I hope I'm not intruding."

"Of course not, no," said Dad in my daydream.

Mom smiled and said, "Come in, sir. Please."

We gave him a plate and good shares of everything, and

he took off his raincoat and sat opposite me, looking at me, his smile never wavering. He was friendly all of the time. People said he was a saint, I remembered, and a great genius too, and we couldn't have invented a better person to be so important. I remembered one adult saying, "If someone has to hold the world in his hands, who better than Florida?" Father-to-the-World. He ate his imaginary dinner and spoke with my folks, then he helped clear the table and followed me upstairs. He came into my room and said, "Ryder, you're such a good fellow. I know it." He touched the back of my head, rubbing my hair, and told me, "You're fine as you are, Ryder. Believe me."

I did. It was all imaginary, but it felt so wonderfully real.

"I'm proud to have played a part in you," he told me. "Don't count me with the others. I understand you."

Here was the man who made the tiny, tiny genes that fit inside me, and inside all of us. He was brilliant and richer than kings, and in some sense he was father to my generation— all of those lean and strong and smart kids—and I could practically see him in my room. With me. Me—!

"Ryder?"

"Ryder? Son?"

"Ryder?"

—and I blinked, shaking my head, having to bring myself back to the real and now.

THREE

Because we'd been on TV for several seconds, the five of us became famous for a few days. They talked about us at school and in the parkland, and a couple times strangers recognized Cody and even Marshall, stopping to ask them how it felt to be on TV. It was strange. We talked about it until the thing didn't seem to have any meaning anymore. Then we talked about it without having to think about our words, knowing the story too well, and mostly we were glad when the people around us forgot about it or got bored with the subject and finally quit asking.

Except for Marshall. Marshall loved the attention, and he kept trying to tell people about the shiny hovering cameras and the powerful, swift snow dragon...even when his audiences would roll their eyes and shake their heads, tired of his endless noise.

"They've caught three dragons so far," he told me. "Little ones." We were riding our bikes, pedaling with urgency as the sun set. "Did you see them on TV? Some older kids got one. They were shaking Dr. Florida's hand...just like he promised. Did you see?"

"No," I confessed.

We were riding toward Cody's house. "We'll catch ours tonight," he said. "You wait."

I told him, "I hope so."

"The biggest one. That's ours." I heard something strange

34

in his voice. Something wrong. "Yes, sir," he said, and we picked up speed.

No one was home at Cody's. Her house personal said she and her moms wouldn't come back until late, it was sorry, and did we have a message? We looked up at its single glass eye. Marshall said, "We're going to nab the dragon. Tell her!" Then we climbed back on our bikes, and he glanced across the street at the Wellses' house. "I'm not inviting Jack," he said. "The dirty shit. I'm still pissed."

The Wellses' house was ancient and weathered. Two front windows were broken and covered with plastic plywood, and one of Jack's brothers stood at a good window, smoking some kind of cigarette. All the brothers were older, and they had a reputation for crime and parties. I didn't like going up on that porch, not for anything. I hated the strong, acidic talk and the foul senses of humor. Marshall's grudge was good news. I said nothing for a moment, then asked, "Should we find Beth? She might want to help us."

Marshall nodded and said, "Sure," and led the way. "Come on!"

Beth lived on the opposite side of the parkland, on the high hillside west of the thick woods. Her house personal said, "A minute, please," with its silky Indian accent. We waited and Beth opened the front door with a rush of scrubbed warm air. She was wearing a filter mask, like always. The mask trapped dust and microbes. She said, "Oh, I can't. No." I knew by her face and posture that one of her folks wasn't well tonight. I said, "That's too bad."

She said nothing.

I could smell the air pouring through the opened door. There was a faint stink of medicines and soaps, and I caught a glimpse of the silvery shower build into the hallway. Beth was wearing a bright robe. She'd have to clean herself before returning to them.

"We're going to catch it," Marshall declared. "You wait."

Beth heard something and turned. "Just a minute," she called, the filter mask muffling her voice. "I'll be there in a minute."

Marshall said, "We're going to build a trap." He seemed too eager, I thought. Something was wrong. He said, "See? We've got our bait." A little striped rat sat on its haunches inside a wire cage, the cage strapped to the bike's rack. Marshall was wearing a backpack full of collapsing shovels and ropes, flashlights and an enormous net. The trap was Marshall's. He had designed it on his own personal, running simulations that tested a thousand factors. The speed and strength of the dragon, for instance. The ideal drop height for the net, and so on. "It'll be simple, once we get everything just so."

She glanced backwards again. She had heard someone—

"How are things?" I asked.

She said, "Okay," and for an instant I saw someone in the hallway—her father or mother, I couldn't tell which—and then I blinked and the figure was gone. The medicine smell got thicker. It was sweet and halfway intoxicating, and I could practically taste it in the air.

Beth said, "You poor thing," to the rat. She slipped outside and closed the front door, asking, "Are you the bait?"

The rat stood against one wire wall. Beth placed a finger against its pink nose, and it took a cautious sniff.

"The dragon won't eat it," Marshall promised.

I saw motion in one window, then nothing.

Beth straightened and said, "They've got fevers," meaning her folks. She would never complain about their illnesses or the time she had to spend with them, missing school or time with us. "Little fevers," she added, "but I should stay here. Okay?"

I said, "You'd better stay."

"We'll have the dragon in this cage," Marshall told Beth. "Next time you see us—"

"Take care, you three." She shut the front door, its seals fastening, and I heard the shower running and Marshall coaxing me to hurry up. It was getting dark, he warned. We needed to set up.

I got on my bike and followed him, riding south and then east again. We approached the almost-pond by way of the paved street, dismounting again and pushing the bikes along the widest trail. Evening was drawing up around us. I looked and noticed how the weeds had grown since yesterday. I said so. Marshall said, "Sure. It rained buckets last night," and I touched one of the juicy stalks, remembering it and saying, "An inch, some of them. Nearly an inch of growing."

"Ryder? Would you hurry?" Marshall made an exasperated sound. He had no patience tonight. "Would you come on?"

The almost-pond was black in the long shadows. I looked

across its smooth face and saw feral bambis, spotted and long-limbed, plus a family of little feral pigs—pets gone wild, or wild animals descended from lost pets. And there were all the usual nervous birds too. Marshall saw none of them. He was thinking hard and moving fast, his legs crunching the weeds and tiny brown bugs flying in all directions. Once someone shouted, "Howie!" and I turned, seeing kids up on the pasture. Strange kids. I could just see their faces, and I didn't know their voices. Maybe I'd seen them around town, sure, but that kind of remembering took time and hard concentration. What I knew was that they weren't locals, and weren't we getting a lot of outsiders lately? It was the TV business. Cody said so and Marshall had agreed. These kids had seen the biggest, fastest dragon released here . . . and so they came here to hunt. They wanted our dragon. They knew it was the very best one.

Farther up the bottoms were other springs and smaller stone basins filled with the dark spring water. Our trail passed close to a basin, and we spooked a midget pony as it drank. It was dark and shaggy, maybe twenty inches at the shoulder, and it shot away without any sound, between the trees and gone.

Marshall said, "Here . . . maybe."

We left our bikes standing and studied the basin. It was a modest round thing filled with tar-colored water. The ground around the stones was covered with tracks and little piles of shit. I found a clean spot and kneeled, Marshall circling the basin and me watching him. He was so very tall and clumsy, his face like a little boy's face. Sometimes he boasted that he wouldn't have chest hair or a beard. He wouldn't need to shave, not ever, and he would always keep his scalp hair. His folks had promised him so.

Marshall was going to live to be one hundred and twenty years old.

His folks had promised him that too.

They told him he had winning looks and platinum brains, and they were forever assuring him that people were jealous of his skills. That's what he'd heard since before he could understand words. That's where he got his hothouse pride and the little boy's temperament, and to be Marshall's friend meant giving him a whole lot of maneuvering room.

"There's no place to hang the net," he decided. "Damn."

"Too bad." I felt the stones under my knees and smelled

the dried shit, but the strongest odor was the black spring
water itself. It was seeping through ducts in the earth, rising
from the special cleansing sands. Several yards below us,
night and day, every kind of sewage was torn apart and built
over again. Heavy metals were removed; poisons were dena-
tured; and the leftovers were water and amino acids, sugars
and tailored bacteria—an edible concoction. The water itself
smelled like a cool, thin soup. The feral pigs and bambis and
such drank it for food; otherwise they would starve come
winter. I recalled a day when Cody, on a dare, had filled a
bucket with this very water and pulled it up into the oak and
boiled it hard for a long while. Then she put it into a flask
inside a freezer, and when she poured an icy glass she smiled
and drank half of it, saying it wasn't so bad. Not really. Not if
you tasted around the turds and the dead bugs, she said. And
if you ignored the grit on your teeth.

Marshall had dared her to drink it.

Cody had done it. Then she said, "Your turn," with her
blackened lips, and she chased Marshall around the big
room. She played with him. She cornered him and pulled
him to his knees, jerking back his head and dribbling in just a
few black drops. And he got ill. He moaned and rose and
stuck his head out a window, throwing up on the branches
and weeds below; and Beth said, "Now there," and knew just
what to do. Of course. She put a damp rag to his face and
sang a little song to calm his nerves, mopping up the worst of
the mess. He had had no color, and he was wobbly weak.
Cody said, "You worry me sometimes," but she didn't push
him anymore. She knew when to quit. I remembered her
shaking her head and asking if he was all right. "Are you?
Huh? Are you sure?"

"Let's go, Ryder," Marshall told me. He was shaking me.

I blinked and found myself kneeling beside the stone
basin. I stood and Marshall said, "I know the place. The
perfect place." We pushed our bikes north. "I'm glad you're
along, Ryder. You'll stick with me. I know you will." He
paused, then he said, "You'll see me catch it and be my
witness and tell everyone everything later. Won't you?"

"I'll try."

He pushed his bike with urgency. He was thinking hard
about some important thing, I sensed. Not just the dragon,
no. I stayed close to him, watching the poor rat bouncing in
its cage. I saw the rat's pale eyes and its stripes, and for a

moment I imagined myself in such a cage, frightened, countless strange shapes and stinks rushing past me. I seemed to
know exactly how it would feel—

Marshall was my first best friend.

He lived up the street from me, on the crest of a hill, his
house made from old-fashioned bricks with old-fashioned
rectangular windows. It was a big, fancy house, huge and
sturdy, and Marshall's room alone was larger than any room
in my house. Deep shelves covered two walls, and there
were two enormous closets. He had toys that danced and toys
that flew and toys that spoke like prime ministers. Plus he
had his own fancy personal. One day my folks explained
wealth to me. Marshall's folks had wealth, they said, and I
realized we were poor in some fashion. Never mention
Marshall's good fortune, they warned. Not to anyone ever.
Money was one of those things not given out fairly or often
enough, they told me. "And be sure to be a gentleman too.
Maybe he'll invite you back again. If you're good. Okay?"

We played in Marshall's room, sometimes for hours. I
admired my new friend. We were seven years old, and he
would look straight at me and say, "I'm this smart," and give
me numbers. "Those are my quotient numbers. Aren't they
huge?"

They sounded enormous, yes.

"That's why I'm always beating you at games. Just like I
beat everyone." He knew himself. I didn't know myself half
so well, and I felt sad. I felt particularly sad when we went to
his kitchen for drinks, and back in a special corner were
drawn lines on top of lines. The lines showed how tall
Marshall would be every year. When he was eight, then nine,
and so on. His father had drawn the lines and dated them.
"See? See?" It was like watching Marshall growing before my
eyes, fast and then faster, and I had to climb a stool just to
read the tallest dates. He would be a giant when he was
twenty years old.

"So how tall will *you* become?" he wondered.

I didn't know. I couldn't even guess.

"What are your quotient numbers? Do you know?"

Not one of them. Nobody had mentioned them, and I
was afraid to ask.

"I've got a scientist's brain," Marshall informed me one

day. "And do you know what? I'm going to work for Dr. Florida someday. I'm going to become one of his top researchers."

Nothing could be more wonderful than working for Dr. Florida. I blinked and looked at Marshall, then sighed. He would grow tall like Dr. Florida. Tallness was somehow vital, I decided. But when I asked my folks about my future height, they said, "You'll be a good solid average. Not too much or too little."

"When I work for Dr. Florida," Marshall explained, "I'll invent all sorts of neat things." He grinned and said, "Huge things that'll do what I tell them. You know?" He nodded and then asked me, "What would you build, Ryder? If you could."

I thought of the mythical winged horse—

"You can't," he told me. "A horse is wrong for wings. It's just too big to get off the ground," and he shook his head. "Unless you made it real tiny. Like maybe this big," and he held up his hands, showing me something the size of a rabbit.

"But that's no horse," I protested. "Horses are big. Huge."

"*I* could make a horse any size. If I wanted," he told me. "Even this small." He squeezed two fingers together.

"But that's no real horse."

"It could be."

"It isn't!"

"It is too!"

I breathed and remembered my folks' warning. If I wanted to be invited again I had to be good now. So I said, "Okay. You're right," when Marshall was wrong.

"Good." He was happy with himself. "Let's go play some more. I've got a new game. You want to learn it?"

"Okay."

I envied Marshall. Everything seemed so clear to him. His life was something built, and he would grow to fill that life without having to try. I wished for that kind of purposeful ease. I wanted something solid, some scheme where I might fit even halfway. All my folks would say about the future was that they didn't know, no one understood such things, and I should stick to my studies and do the best I could do. But what was my best? I didn't even know my numbers . . . so how could I tell?

Marshall and I had the same classes in those days. We

did different units, yes, but we always ate lunch together and stayed close to one another in recess. Our playground was huge and square and covered with a giant colored tent. The tent walls were rolled up in warm weather and made transparent in the winter, the sunlight baking the graveled ground. The games of dodgeball and kickball and baseball never seemed to quit, classes coming outside to replace those that were finished playing, the balls always flying and the kids always screaming and the scores huge and muddled by the end of the day.

We weren't good at sports. I had trouble watching what mattered, and Marshall lacked speed and coordination.

"This is different than mind games," he told me. He sounded proud and self-assured. "This stuff is nothing like anything we'll do when we're adults. You'll see."

Cody was in a different class. She had our teachers but at different times, and we wouldn't see her every day. I didn't know her as a friend, but I could recognize her strong looks from across the playground. She sprinted across the gravel with a surprising, effortless grace, on her toes, and she seemed quite ugly to me. Yet she had friends. More friends than either Marshall or me. Even older kids wanted her for their teams—her speed and strength were close to unique—and nobody got on her bad side. Not on purpose. She wouldn't think twice about bruising someone, in warning, and there was even a story about Cody popping a teacher in an accidental, purposeful sort of way. The teacher had said something about her mothers, it seemed, and Cody never let that sort of thing slide past.

One day Marshall got on her bad side.

We were playing kickball. I was concentrating, trying hard to do the simple things well. The strawberry-colored ball sang when it was kicked, a *boing*ing note and then more *boings* as it bounced. I chased the ball, but Marshall was closer and closing when Cody happened past. She grinned and kicked the ball home. It didn't bounce; it flew. Marshall lost his temper and said something harsh and stupid, then he took a stupid swing at her face.

Cody tripped my friend, neat and simple.

Marshall climbed to his feet and charged again, saying, "Dyke," once. She smacked him once, and he was down and crying. I reached him and he rose, wiping at the tears and telling me, "That dyke! We're going to sure teach her a lesson, that dyke! Aren't we? Come on, Ryder! Aren't we?"

This was during winter.

The textbooks and adults always talked about our warm winters, but to me they seemed plenty cold. I knew it was the greenhouse gases that heated the air. People once burned oils and coals and those sort of poisons. Now we had solar cells on all our roofs—efficient and durable—and they sucked up energy without making poisons. There weren't any power lines anymore. Big industries got their energy from orbiting panels, or from inside the earth itself. And everything gathered could be stored forever in the super-loop batteries. That's what we had in our attic, and in both of our cars. Dr. Florida hadn't invented the superloops himself, no, but he had helped make them cheap and tough and simple. He had one big company that did nothing but tinker with the things.

But, like I said, the winters felt cold to me. On that day there was a half foot of snow on the ground, damp and clean, and the two of us waded into it after school. We followed Cody as she walked home, Marshall telling me that we were going to pull off an ambush. "That fat dyke bitch isn't that strong. You'll see," he said. "We get our chance and we pulverize her, okay? We'll smack her hard. We'll *pulverize* her!"

Only there was no place good enough for an ambush.

Marshall delayed and delayed, and then she was inside her house. We were standing on the plowed street, side by side, and Marshall said, "Go ring the bell, Ryder. Ask if she'll come out and play."

I said, "All right."

Cody's house was on the corner of the intersection. It was a soft yellow, nearly gold, with round windows and a tiny round porch. I thought it looked small and neat with its walks cleaned and dried. I rang the bell, and the house personal started talking to me, then quit, and one of Cody's mothers was facing me. I blinked. All the things I'd heard about her mothers, and this one seemed so unremarkable in person. She was just a plain woman, not large and by no means strong. A bright smile emerged, and she asked, "Can I do something for you?"

"Can Cody come play?" I wondered. "For a little bit."

"I don't know," she answered. "I'll ask," and she vanished from view.

I turned and saw Marshall beside the street. He was kneeling, making snowballs. I breathed and turned to my left, my eyes focusing on the old white farmhouse where no one lived. The Wellses were in the future, and the house and its yard had this lonely, empty look about them. Then Cody said, "Yeah?" I turned again. She wasn't wearing a coat or shoes, or even socks. She had four toes on each bare foot, and I had to stare at such a strange thing.

"What do you want?" she asked

I blinked and saw her hard face and curious eyes.

She saw Marshall and said, "Shitstick! What are you doing?"

Marshall came halfway up the walk. He carried two snowballs in each hand, and his coat pockets were bulging. With a little voice he said, "Apologize," and one snowball fell, shattering with a soft, powdery sound. He breathed and blinked, terrified, and with the tiniest whisper said, "Tell me you're sorry."

Cody stepped down to the walk.

Marshall gasped and straightened. His hands were shaking. He said, "Ryder? Help me. Go on and hit her, go on."

But I couldn't find a reason. Instead I watched Cody bend and pull a handful of snow from the lawn, making a perfect snowball in an instant, with bare hands. Where Marshall's efforts were lumpy and crumbling, hers had the solid milky look of pure ice. Panic spread on Marshall's face. His hands refused to throw his snowballs. Cody winked and asked, "Are you watching?"

He nodded once.

"Watch." She turned and threw overhand. A tall elm tree stood in front of the empty farmhouse, two big branches rising from the trunk; and the snowball moved with a bullet's trajectory, hitting the Y. I heard the hard, wet *splat*, and I knew, just knew, that that was the exact point she'd wanted to hit. Then Cody turned to Marshall, saying, "Okay. Let's fight," while she pulled up another gob of snow.

Marshall ran. He dropped everything and made a soft crying sound as he tore up the street toward home, his legs working and his empty arms working and me feeling embarrassed for him. I felt sad.

Then Cody touched me. "You're the kid who remembers, right?"

I nodded.

She said, "I've wondered," and I saw her breath coming out of her smile. It was her mother's smile; I recognized it. "I've got a question," she said. "Suppose you see a snowflake. Could you remember it later? A long time from now?"

"Yes."

"How about a mess of snowflakes? They're all different—"

I blinked and said, "I'd remember them, yes," with a certain tentative pride. "Sure."

"What if I showed you every snowflake in this yard? Or all of them in the city? What would happen?"

"That's too much," I admitted. I couldn't even imagine doing such a thing.

"And all the snowflakes in creation? Try that and I bet this happens to your head." She ground her snowball into icy dust, and the dust fell over the walk and the tops of our feet. I was looking at her feet again. I asked, "Why don't you have five toes?"

"Who's got five toes?" she wondered.

"Everyone," I informed her. "Everyone but you."

"Not the people I know, they don't." She laughed and told me, "I think you're mistaken."

"I'm not."

"You're sure?"

"I am," I promised. "Sure I'm sure." Then I sat on the walk and said, "Look," and yanked off my right shoe and sock. "One, two, three, four, five. See? Five."

Cody was laughing at me.

"I'm teasing you, Ryder." She shook her head and said, "Put those back on. Before you're down to four, okay?"

"All right," said Marshall. "I've got it set."

We were above the slabs, sitting straight across the bottoms from our oak and treehouse. Marshall had staked out his rat and hung his net in the tree overhead—a lump of elastic fabric that would spread as it fell, or so he claimed. Moonlight fell over the rat and its stake and the narrow glimmering wire secured to its foot. I heard incisors chewing on the wire. The trigger string was in my hands, but then Marshall took the string from me. He said, "Thanks," and found a place to sit.

The slabs were pieces of a street that had died. The city, ages ago, had peeled up the tired concrete and dumped it a long way out in the then country. Massive blocks lay at every angle, thick and gray, and tall trees grew on the slope and formed a high, tight canopy overhead. There were snakes and wild rats living in the hollow places. Maybe the snow dragon too, I thought. Maybe it was beneath me now. I shifted my butt on the rough surface and watched the bottoms, spotting someone. Then three someones. They were moving like smoke in the moon's silvery light, and their voices rose toward me—

"Watch the rat," Marshall whispered. "Ryder?"

But who were they? I wondered. I listened to their voices and decided they were strangers, more strangers, toting butterfly nets and cloth sacks as they walked toward the south. They carried themselves like brothers, their bodies the same but for size and with the same smoky motions. "Is that it?" asked the smallest brother. "Look here!" he giggled and said, "Here it goes," and took a swipe at the weeds. They had come from another neighborhood, I realized, and he was teasing his brothers. He was bored. "Look here! Look!" The bored brother attacked a clump of weeds, laughing.

This was the famous ground, all right. I asked Marshall, "Will someone else catch the dragon?"

"What do you mean?" he whispered.

"All these strangers coming through—"

"Forget it, Ryder. No way." He waved his hand, saying, "They don't even belong here. They don't know this place like we know it, so they can't. Okay? So watch the rat now. Okay?"

The rat chewed on its wire. I didn't like the sound of the enamel on metal, and I looked away and asked, "How do you know it can be caught? Dr. Florida said it's too fast and smart—"

"Shush," he said. "Shush."

The bored brother was chucking sticks at our treehouse. Some sticks hit and made a hollow thud, then they fell away. I could see everything in the moonlight. The brother didn't know us—he didn't know what Cody would do to him if she found him chucking sticks—and so he kept doing it while the others moved toward the almost-pond, leaving him.

He finally found himself alone, and he turned and ran out of sight. I heard one of them laughing, then nothing. I stared at our oak and the high dark mass of our treehouse and the nearly full moon just high enough to be seen unobscured. The silvery light angled in beneath the canopy and over the slabs. I wished for binoculars—we had several pairs in the treehouse—and if I was flat on the treehouse's flat roof, I thought, I could watch the moon's moon swinging around the moon. Dr. Florida owned the moon's moon. It looked like a bright dot traveling a snug orbit, skating over the barren land and the new farms and the growing cities. The moon's moon had been a comet, but it had died long ago. Dr. Florida had claimed it and brought it into orbit around the moon. He owned plenty of things in space. There were mines inside asteroids and a science base on Ganymede—I had read about his probes to Jupiter—and there was the moon's moon too. He was taking it apart. Buried at its core were organics and water, and in fifty or a hundred years it would be gone. That's what was planned. He was selling its pieces to the lunar cities and farms. "For a tidy profit," Dad had told me. "A chunk of oily rock, and he's making even more billions. Imagine!"

I stared at the moon with all of my concentration, letting myself get lost. I couldn't hear the rat's chewing for a while. All I sensed was the moon itself, and there wasn't such a thing as time or any other place in creation. I felt nothing. It was soothing to be so lost. I myself didn't exist, it seemed, and a long while passed before Marshall was touching me, shaking me, saying, "Ryder? Hey, I need you. Listen to me a minute, okay?"

He wasn't quite whispering anymore.

My butt was asleep on the concrete. I moved and noticed how the moon had climbed. I said, "Sorry," without feeling sorry. The rat was silent, curled up and shivering, and Marshall was breathing too much. "You want to hear a secret?" he asked. "Promise not to tell? Not anyone?"

"All right."

"My folks made me a promise," he said.

"What about?"

"After they saw me on TV . . . they had this idea."

I waited for a moment. Then I asked, "What idea?"

"If I catch the dragon . . . *this* dragon . . ."

"Yeah—?"

"I'll get a special prize. They'll give me money." He breathed and I saw the excitement on his face. His odd mood made sense all of a sudden. Radiant and wearing a huge grin, he wondered, "Do you want to know how much money?"

"How much?"

"I'm not supposed to tell anyone," he confessed.

I said nothing.

"So you won't tell, will you?"

"It's a secret," I agreed.

"A thousand dollars. Just for me." He barely had the breath to say the words. He shivered and told me, "That much," and my first thought was that so much money would be an enormous burden. I wouldn't know what to do with a thousand dollars, so many things possible and only one choice the best choice. How could someone decide?

"What do you think? Isn't that something?"

"Oh, yeah."

"And you won't tell?"

"I won't," I promised. Then I blinked and imagined Marshall netting the dragon and taking it home. His mother would be thrilled, proud and loud about her pride. A thousand dollars? I watched my friend while he watched the rat, nothing happening, his trap set and nothing slipping out of the shadows to take the bait. This was just the sort of thing his folks would do. Even to Marshall, I thought, that sort of money had to seem huge.

We sat for a little while longer, never talking.

I thought about a tangle of things, and the moon rose higher and began to vanish behind the canopy above us. Then Marshall touched me and asked, "When did we first come here? To the slabs?"

"You and me?"

"Just the two of us. Yeah."

Remembering wasn't hard. I blinked and concentrated, and then I saw us as eight-year-olds. I was sitting on the same slab, only it was tilted at a different angle. A shorter, rounder Marshall was sitting beside me, sharing my perch. It was summer, in the afternoon, and the summer bugs were screaming until the blazing air seemed to rip. We were pretending to be soldiers, dressed in our greenest clothes and sweating under our green plastic helmets. We had plastic guns that spit out authentic noises, and this was India in our minds. This was the last great war, the war we knew from TV and textbooks—real battles and ferocious smart bombs, Moslems and Hindus and U.N. troops fighting in the tropical heat.

"I remember that,'" said Marshall. "Sure."

A couple teenage boys had walked through the bottoms.

I saw them again. They seemed huge and full of danger, their hair raggedly long and their arms thick and powerful. They carried pellet rifles equipped with laser sights and compressed air. They fired and I heard a delicate *woosh*, them swinging their guns this way and that. A couple times the pricks of laser light swept past us, startling us, neither of us moving for fear they might take us for feral pigs.

"They killed something, didn't they?"

I saw a dead garter snake, thick-bodied and shot through the head. We had found it in the weeds after the boys were gone. The pellet had struck the precise center of its skull, between its lidless eyes, and I had marveled at the exactness of the blow and felt sick to see it so dead. I thought those boys were particularly wicked. I tried comforting myself with the thought that their wickedness would someday catch them and destroy them with the same eerie precision. And all summer long, now and again, I returned to the corpse, fascinated, watching it dissolve with rot and the ants. Stringing my memories together, I saw the dark body wiggle and shrivel and then melt away. Gone. Then Marshall touched me and said, "They shot at us, didn't they? I thought they shot at us."

I said, "No."

"But I remember pellets hitting the slabs. Don't you?"

"No." He must have recalled the laser light sweeping past us. I doubted if the boys ever noticed us sitting back in the shade—

"I'm thinking of a different day. With someone else," he told me. "I can *hear* the pellets hitting concrete, Ryder. That's how well I can remember it."

I said nothing.

He said, "Ping, ping," as imaginary pellets sprinkled the ground around us. Then we sat for a few more minutes, nothing said. The rat resumed its chewing, and Marshall got bored with the waiting and handed me the damp trigger string. Nothing happened. We waited and sometimes whispered, and I thought about Marshall getting so much money from his folks. I wasn't exactly jealous, only . . . what? What? Marshall wouldn't catch the dragon, not ever. I couldn't imagine him catching it. I saw the creature in my mind—white fur and those living black eyes, the tiny feet and the working tongue—and its uniqueness endeared it to me. I realized that I didn't want it caught, not by anyone. Then Marshall stood and said, "That's enough. Let's go home."

He climbed the tree in the darkness to get the net, twice nearly falling. Then he turned on a flashlight and undid the rat's wire, saying, "Oh, gosh." The tethered leg was bleeding. Marshall looked at me, embarrassed for having hurt the animal, and he said, "I'll tell you what," and let it go free.

We watched the rat limp into the shadows.

Then we were packing, not talking, and we heard a scream in the distance. It came from the north end of the parkland, and it wasn't any animal I recognized. Marshall turned to me and asked, "What is it?" and I didn't know. I told him so, and he brightened.

He said, "Listen," when it screamed a second time. "I bet I know. I bet I do."

There was a third scream, softer, and I thought of monkeys in a lush jungle. That's how it sounded. I said, "The dragon—?"

He clamped his hand over my mouth, saying, "Shush!" Then he craned his neck and listened to the night sounds, bugs and a soft wind in the treetops, and I smelled the rat on his hand. I shut my eyes and waited, smelling fur and blood; and there were no more screams, not while we listened, and we finally picked up and began to head home.

Like always, we checked the treehouse's hatch and lock when we went past. They were sound. Then we pushed our bikes across the pasture, Marshall talking and talking about the dragon. I wore his pack because his back was sore. The empty wire cage rattled on Marshall's bike rack, and the growing grass caught in our pedals and gears. We came to the short graveled road and passed the Wellses' house. Marshall was wrestling an imaginary dragon, his free arm extended and his throat making guttural sounds. He never noticed one of Jack's brothers standing beside the house. The brother was drunk or drugged, or maybe both things, holding himself upright with one arm and peeing with an odd dignity, the urine sparkling in the moonlight. I felt uneasy. Menaced. I looked away and kept quiet, Marshall busy tying the dragon into knots, and then we were across the street, safe, and looking at Cody's darkened house.

"She's not home yet," I mentioned. "Are you going to leave that message in her personal?"

"What message?" Marshall wondered.

"About catching the dragon tonight?"

"Oh, no. Thanks." He handed me his bike and ran to the front door, talking for a moment and then returning. "I told her we heard it, and that's something." He nodded and smiled, saying, "Come on."

We pedaled up the hill, turning north and arriving at Marshall's house. We put our bikes inside the enormous garage where his father kept old-fashioned cars as a hobby, the air stinking of real gasoline and thick grease. Then we went into the backyard and the bambis and pigs came running toward us. They dipped their heads and demanded to be scratched. I helped scratch them. Then there was a pink dog and a miniature pony, and the dog snarled and shoved the bambis aside. Marshall said, "No," to the dog. He said, "Quit it," in a careless, practiced way.

His mother emerged from the house. "The hunters!" She was a small woman, dark and odd. I felt uneasy whenever she laughed. Laughing now, it sounded as if she was teasing us. Other adults called her a stupid and vain woman, a bitch and worse. As I'd grown older, seeing things with older eyes, I'd come to realize that the hard words were true. She was demanding and tactless and difficult to like. Beneath her flaws was a mess of worries and doubts, and she was Marshall's mother, and he would try almost anything to make her say one halfway positive word—

"How'd the hunt go?" she asked. "Did you get it?"

"We heard it," Marshall answered.

I bent and scratched a bambi behind its ear.

"You heard it? What's that mean?"

Marshall told her, "We just couldn't lure it in—"

"You didn't even see it then?"

"No, ma'am."

"Sometimes," she said, "I do wonder about you, Marshall." Then she breathed and looked at me for the first time. "Ryder?"

I was scratching a pig. "Yes?" I asked.

"Your mother called. She wants you home, as soon as possible."

I said, "Thank you."

Then she turned to Marshall, saying, "You didn't even

get close? You told me you were going to catch it tonight."
She was angry in a teasing way. Maybe she thought she was
being funny. "You left here with promises, young man. So I
told your Aunt Jennie that you'd catch it with that expensive
toy net of yours. Was I wrong? What did you tell me right
before you left?"

He made a low sound in his throat, his head bowing.

I said, "I have to go," and set the pack on the ground.
Marshall glanced at me. His expression was complex and
shifting, pained and embarrassed and angry in a sapless way.
His mother told him, "I thought you were clever," and then
she laughed so nobody would think she was mean.

"Yes, ma'am."

"Aren't you clever?"

"Yes, ma'am."

"Anyway," she said, and she breathed. Her voice was
suddenly weary and disinterested. "Good-bye, Ryder. Good
to see you." She paused, then snapped, "Say good-bye to
your friend, Marshall."

"Good-bye, Ryder."

"Bye."

I rode down the hill in the darkness. I was ever so glad
to be away and alone, feeling the smooth, almost liquid
sensation of rolling. Our street was freshly repaved, and the
ride seemed perfect. Then I pulled up in front of my house,
where only one light was burning in the front window, and
Mom was waiting for me beside that light. She was in the
living room, and she looked as if she had been in her chair for
a very long time. Dad was out showing a house, she told me.
"Sit down, Ryder." She seemed strange, saying, "Please?" I
saw and knew in my heart that it was bad news, awful news,
and I braced myself and tried to seem brave. She told me,
"Something happened while you were out," and she took a
deep breath.

I knew. I had sensed as much.

"You got a call tonight. Just after you left with Marshall."

She said it sadly, but it wasn't sadness on her face. It was
puzzlement and maybe amazement too, and I wondered,
"Who called? Someone called for me?"

"Yes," she said. "Dr. Florida."

FOUR

I was leaving school at lunchtime. I was getting ready in the
hallway, and Beth found me and introduced me to a couple of
girls. The girls had heard this incredible, impossible story,
and they didn't believe it. I was going to Dr. Florida's mansion? Today? The prettier girl said, "You mean one of his
clinics, right? Not the mansion—!"

"But that's where I'm going," I explained. I didn't mean
to sound proud or snotty. I tried speaking matter-of-factly.
"He called me and invited me and my folks—"

"You mean an assistant called," she persisted. "For him."

"You didn't actually talk to *him*," said her friend.

I hadn't talked to anyone, actually. But it had been Dr.
Florida on the phone, and he had talked to my folks for quite
a long while.

"Ryder is having tests done," Beth explained. "With
special equipment at the mansion."

"But you're not meeting *Dr. Florida*," said the pretty
girl. She was like a doll, everything about her face and skin
perfect in a shiny, dead way. "Why should he meet you?
Why?"

"I don't know," I admitted.

"We're talking about Dr. Florida," she reminded me.

I kept quiet. What could I tell her?

"It won't happen." She wagged one of her long fingers at
my face. "You're making this up, I bet."

I shifted my weight from one foot to the other.

Then her friend said, "I know you. You're the kid who remembers things... right? That's you, isn't it?"

Beth frowned. These weren't her friends; I knew her girlfriends. They were classmates, nothing more, and I could tell she regretted having started this thing.

The pretty girl touched me. "You really remember *everything*?"

"I guess—"

She grinned and stuck out her chest. "All right then. Can you remember seeing a girl, any girl, prettier than me?" Her expression was saying, "This is a joke question, but if you want to answer it anyway, go ahead." She smiled so her perfect white teeth showed, then she laughed in a soft, careless way. "Think back," she told me. "Remember all the girls you've ever seen anywhere. Okay?"

"Faces take a long time," I explained. "They're complicated, and I've got to sort through so many of them—"

"I'll wait," she announced. She screwed her face into a clever, proud-of-herself look. "Go on. I want you to."

So I said, "Beth's prettier than you." I wasn't lying, no. But mostly I didn't like the girl's manners, and Beth was the first pretty girl that came to mind.

"What Beth?" she wondered. "This Beth?"

Beth and the other girl began to laugh.

"Well," said the pretty girl, "I don't think you're special. Not at all!" Her clever face vanished. She told me, "You're rude," and then she faced her friend and Beth. "You're rude too!"

"Oh, Corrine," said her friend. "It's a joke."

The pretty girl said nothing. She simply glared at us, her fiery eyes lingering on me the longest, and then she walked away with her back erect and her head tilted high.

"She's full of old actress genes," explained her friend.

Beth was looking at me. "Whose genes?" she asked.

"I don't remember," said the friend. "But her mom's a crazy fan. She's got pictures of the woman all around the house." Then she said, "It's pretty weird." Then she said, "Corrine doesn't even look much like the actress. Not all that much." She shrugged and said, "Weird, huh? Weird!"

The limousine was waiting in front of our house—a smallish limousine, but larger and fancier than any car I had ever ridden in. Its skin was black and warm to the touch and glossy bright. There wasn't any place for a driver. It drove itself. A tall woman was standing beside my father, both of them waiting for me. I knew the woman's face. She was named Lillith. She had been on the pasture with Dr. Florida. "It's a shame your wife feels ill," she was saying. "I'm sure she would have enjoyed herself."

"Gwinn? She would have loved this." Dad winked at me and said, "Ready, son?"

"Sorry I'm late."

He said, "No problem. Lillith? This is Ryder."

"So it is," she said, her voice pleasant. High and soft and graceful. "I just arrived myself, Ryder. Are you ready to go?"

"He was ready last night," Dad told her, and he laughed.

I climbed inside the limousine, the doors shutting after us and the electric motor accelerating and the seats beneath us bending to make us comfortable. There were several rows of seats, and we were in the backmost row. I was thinking how Mom wasn't ill. Not really. Then Lillith touched my knee, saying, "He's quite excited about meeting you too."

She meant Dr. Florida. I didn't know what to say.

"He had me personally research you," said Lillith. Then she turned to Dad, adding, "He has access to various records. For scientific purposes," and she paused for a moment. "We've tried and tried," she said, "but we can't find anyone quite like Ryder. Not anywhere."

"I'm not surprised," said Dad.

She was between us and smiling. "Could I tempt you boys?" Beneath our seat was a cupboard, and she pulled out glasses and asked, "Something sweet and cold?" She was as pretty as an actress, I thought. But she was too old to have been tailored. At least in big ways.

I said I was thirsty. A little bit.

She gave me a lemoned Pepsi. Dad wanted the same, he claimed, and Lillith fixed two more and talked to him. She explained the tests and described what might be found. I listened, absorbing without always understanding; some of her words were substantial and nearly incomprehensible. She spoke of scanning the molecular regions of my brain, even the atomic regions, taking tiny measurements and creating a thorough picture. She said, "We can't make promises," and watched Dad. Then she turned to me, smiling. "Most likely we can offer clues. Clues as to how Ryder can better manage his skills."

"First the tests," said Dad, smiling patiently. "One lurch at a time, I think."

We were passing through bands of parkland and the city's newest neighborhoods. The houses were fresh and the lawns treeless and brilliantly green. The mansion itself was west of the city, buried within a long hill covered with flowering trees and smooth-faced leafy trees, antennas of every shape poking out here and there. I had seen the mansion plenty of times on TV, from all angles. Yet today everything seemed new to me. I pressed my face against the smoked glass of the window and watched while we passed through high gates, then drove along a curling road at the base of the hill itself. I saw quite a few men and women wearing dark uniforms and odd guns. I saw planes rising from the flat country to the west and ordinary cars and trucks coming toward us, our limousine shuddering when the biggest trucks roared past. All at once we turned and slid into a narrow valley. The trees touched shoulders above this smaller road, and everything was in shadow. We were driving into the hillside. I saw a patch of deeper shadow and felt a sudden thudding of tires, and we were inside. I saw blackness through the windows, and we swerved and stopped and the doors came open, and I smelled the cool clean scent of scrubbed concrete and eager warm motors.

Lillith said, "Keep close to me, gentlemen," and stepped outside.

The air was cool and damp. We walked between rows of limousines, and Dad whistled. "Can I take one home? For a while?"

Lillith laughed and said, "I think not," and steered us through sliding glass doors. Guards and cameras examined our faces. I heard water and then smelled it as we walked along a hallway. The hallway walls were beautiful. They were made from metal foams, very fancy, rusted for character and polished until they shone. Then we were in an open space, standing beside a tall shaft cut through the heart of the hill itself. A glass handrail encircled the shaft, and I grabbed the rail and felt the sweat on my palms, looking upwards and seeing more floors and a blue sky and a thin white cloud moving fast in the wind. Lillith asked for our impressions. "Quite the little shelter," Dad muttered. He squeezed my shoulder, sounding rather nervous. I'm sure he felt out of place.

There were more floors below us. Water fell down the far side of the shaft, dribbling across stretches of banded red stone. Vivid emerald mosses clung here and there, plus odd little trees of electric blue and pink, gold and maroon. An empty pool caught the falling water and reflected the sky. "What do you think?" asked Lillith. "Do you like all of this?" She touched my shoulder for a moment lightly. "Ryder?"

"It's nice," I admitted. But *nice* was a silly, small word. I had never seen such wealth, or even imagined money could be so enormous and obvious—the freshness of the air, the neat perfect lines of every surface, the sense that this wasn't merely a home and office, no, but something planned like an artist plans a great painting, the colors and forms strange and yet balanced . . . so well balanced that I couldn't imagine them in any other state.

I gulped. I asked, "Where's Dr. Florida?"

"He's busy just now," she cautioned. "You'll see him soon."

I nodded. He was such a busy man, I thought, and I was taking him from his important work. I knew it. I stood motionless for a moment, feeling so very strange, and then Dad touched me and said, "Our guide's leaving," and he smiled to encourage me. "Come on, son."

We walked down more hallways, seeing dozens of people moving with a formal sort of energy. Many carried personals, and they spoke to their personals and to one another and watched us in a casual yet careful way. They seemed confused to see a boy in their midst. I held my father's hand for the first time in years. We came into a lounge full of food smells, one entire wall built from thick glass and an enormous aquarium on the other side. The aquarium was larger than some ponds, I realized. I had to stop and look at the graceful miniature whales swimming near the surface, each one the size of a man—sleek even with their mouths open, their baleens straining the clean bright water for food. Beneath them were sea turtles with shells made from gemstones, or something resembling gemstones. There were brilliant fish I had never seen in any book, never, and some odd little penguins dashing toward the glass. I stared at the penguins, and one gazed back at me, its orange belly and dark eyes familiar. "They're made from robin stock," said Lillith. I could see the robins inside them. I felt Lillith's touch, and she promised me, "We'll pass this way again. Okay? We have to be going now. All right?"

We passed into another hallway, Dad making jokes. "How many miles are there? Hundreds?"

"In the mansion?" said Lillith. "Counting air vents and service passageways... I suppose a thousand miles, or more."

He laughed and shook his head. "I'm humbled."

"Are you, Kip?"

"Completely."

The laboratory section was deep inside the hill, guarded by thick glass doors sealed tight and strong men with hard, unreadable faces. We were scanned by several means. Even Lillith was scanned. She smiled and told me, "This is where the magic is done," and the last doors parted for us. A *woosh* and a *woosh*, and we were safely inside.

I breathed and concentrated, working to seem utterly normal.

People wore lab coats and glazed stares. Scientists weren't so noisy as the others. The air was cool and dry, and we walked and turned and entered a large room made small by its machinery. A gray-haired man was watching us. "Is this our young friend?" he inquired.

"Ryder?" said Lillith. "Kip? This is Dr. Samuelson. He's one of Dr. Florida's oldest and dearest associates."

"Emphasis on the old," he joked. He had a quiet, firm voice and a friendly laugh. He took my father's hand, then mine, and when we shook I felt all of my hand's bones. He said, "I'm the last of the dinosaurs. You're looking at him."

I remembered Dr. Samuelson from documentaries. He had been with Dr. Florida from the very first days. Had he been on the pasture with us? On the contest day? I tried to find his face—

"Would any of you gentlemen like a refreshment?" asked Lillith. "I'm off to have a late lunch myself."

Dad said, "Some blue tomatoes."

She paused. "Blue what?" Then she understood. Dad was joking, and she laughed pleasantly and said, "Indeed, Kip," and left us. The pleasant laugh quit once she was in the hallway, alone.

I turned and studied the machinery. The room was jammed full of the complicated, interlocking shapes, every-thing smelling new and scrubbed, every surface bright. "Ryder?

Ryder?" I turned to Dr. Samuelson. I wasn't doing very well, I realized. Feeling embarrassed, I said, "Excuse me," and hung my head a little bit.

"Why don't you hop on the table?" he asked me. "Would you?"

Dad was sitting on a little chair, watching everything.

"Should I undress?" I wondered.

"No need," he assured. Then he handed me a glass full of a thick grayish liquid. "Drink every drop, would you?" It tasted sweet, yet wrong somehow. It was heavier than water or any syrup. "There you go. That's the boy." He took the empty glass from my hand and punched buttons on a glowing board. Dad smiled to encourage both of us. "Now, why don't you lie back on the table? All right?" I was down and looking at Dr. Samuelson's wrinkled face. He seemed very tired to me. He must be working hard, I thought, and I was thankful and ashamed, in equal measures, for all of this special attention.

"That's the boy," he said. "You'll sleep in a minute."

The table moved without noise, sliding into the bright new machinery.

"Ryder?" I heard him ask. "Do me a favor? Think of one thing. Only one thing. Concentrate and recall one memory."

I asked, "Which one?"

"Oh, I don't know. Try your oldest memory. Can you?"

I tried. I knew a likely moment—a memory so old that it was close to vague—and I blinked and felt myself turning tiny, ever so tiny, and the happy young faces of Mom and Dad drifted over me. They were waving, their gestures silly and their voices twisted into baby talk. I was full of strange passions, simple and relentless. I thought of food and saw my pink hand in the air, and somehow I stuffed the hand into my mouth and chewed it with my gums, the salty skin delicious. Suddenly there was laughter and strange faces over me, and I felt so scared. All those strange faces, staring and joyful, and me bursting out into tears—

Then I was awake. The machinery was throbbing, then it was silent, and the table moved and stopped and a voice I recognized said, "What do you think, John? Ice cream for our hero?"

Dr. Florida was sitting beside my father. He was looking

straight at me and smiling, and he drummed his long hands on his knees.

Dr. Samuelson was watching him. So was Dad.

"What's your flavor?" asked Dr. Florida. "What would you kill to eat?"

"He loves peppermint," said Dad.

But I said, "French vanilla."

"Not peppermint?" Dad shrugged his shoulders and said, "I thought you loved peppermint."

"Not so much anymore," I confessed.

Dr. Florida rose and said, "Either way, you shouldn't eat now. It's too soon." He grinned and laid his flattened hand on his own belly. Then he gave me a wink. "John? Why not get us a gallon of our best French vanilla? I'm taking our guests into my office. For a chat."

Dr. Samuelson said, "Be glad to." He looked at all of us, his eyes lingering on me. Then he left.

I blinked and took a shallow breath, studying Dr. Florida. There wasn't any raincoat today, and no hat. He was wearing ordinary trousers, dark and simple, and a nearly white shirt. I could see shiny instruments in the shirt pockets, and I heard them rattle when he moved. His hair was streaked with gray and white and combed backwards. His pale skin was freckled. "You want to see my office?" he asked. "I don't give tours to everyone."

I said, "Okay," with a soft voice.

"Well, up! Up!" He laughed and waited for us to rise.

Dad was beside me. He grasped the back of my head as we walked into the hallway, saying, "This is something," with a weak voice. His hand felt damp and nervous; I sensed him trembling. I'd never seen him so nervous about anything. "Quite something," he managed. "Goodness."

"How do you feel?" asked Dr. Florida. "Ryder?"

"Okay." I wasn't nearly so nervous. I had been scared of being scared, but I didn't have any chance now. He'd come while I was asleep, and now he was here and everything felt natural. I felt as if I'd known him for a very long time. "I feel fine."

"That brew you drank? It contains a mild sedative." He stopped at a massive metal door with the name *Doctor Aaron Florida* beside the jamb and a black button under the name. It was a fancy thumbprint lock. He touched the button and the door slid open without sound, and I saw an enormous desk and all kinds of screens built into two walls—TV screens and personal screens of every size—and he let us sit on the swiveling chairs in front of his desk. He sat on his own chair. He seemed so very tall, even sitting. "I was talking to your father while you were down and out," he said. "I was explaining what the data mean and how they're coordinated by my fancy toy. It might be several weeks before we can assemble a complete portrait. At the earliest. But if we can help you, we'll help. I promise you."

I didn't know what to say. I thought about my wonderful luck, me being here with him, and I heard concern in his voice and thought what a wonderful man he was. Surely.

"Say thank you," prompted Dad. "Ryder?"

"Thank you." But the words seemed too small to matter.

"You slept a long time," Dr. Florida told me. "You gave your dad and me a chance to talk about you." He nodded and smiled and said, "I learned about your friends, and everything. Ryder? One of these years you'll look back on these times and see the gold in them. Believe me." He winked and his eyes seemed to twinkle. "Friends and fun and challenges eventually met. That's the gold in growing up."

Dad grinned and nodded, appreciating the words.

"I had time to talk too," said Dr. Florida. "The two of us are similar, you and me. I told your dad so. When I was hope-high to the world, I was labeled as being different. Like you. I had peculiar skills and a rather uncommon perspective. I was labeled a loon, in fact. You know. . .crazy? And in those ancient times it was tough for us loons. It was tough to make friends or to feel as if we belonged in the world."

I tried to imagine that time.

"Maybe that's one way in which things have improved," he told us. "We've gotten clever at finding and using talent. We've become a world of young loons. Rich children and poor. . . all are somehow blessed." He paused, then he said, "We make mistakes, yes, and cause sadness. Yes. But adults can appreciate how much things have improved. They've seen both sides, and they know what I mean."

Dad said, "It's a sweeter world. That's for sure."

"Richer. Happier. Better." Dr. Florida pressed his lips together and stared at me. He didn't blink for the longest time, and I could practically hear the machinery working inside his skull. Then he said, "Anyway," and smiled. "When I was your age, Ryder, I was a solitary loon."

He seemed so friendly and likable. I couldn't believe he had ever lacked friends, and I wondered if he was teasing me.

"I saw that fortress of yours," he told me. "The one in the oak? I saw you and your friends boiling out of it, and do you know what I thought? I thought back to my own boyhood treehouse. I had designed it and built it by myself, from scratch and against my mother's wishes." He chuckled and said, "My poor nervous mother. I was a bookish boy, not a carpenter, and she thought I would kill myself somehow. So do you know what I did, Ryder? I invented a friend to ease her nerves. An imaginary friend who understood nails and boards. That's the only way she'd have let me build my fortress in a cottonwood tree beside the local open sewer."

"A fortress," I echoed.

"Elegant and proud," he declared. "Although no match for yours. Of course. In those days we lacked for the modern conveniences. Just a box of creaky boards, in truth, but I loved it. I get a soft feeling when I think of it now. All of the things I've accomplished in my life—the science and the business, and what-have-you—and my memories of that rude little thing still make me smile."

"She never found out?" I asked. "Your mother—?"

"What mother wouldn't be happier sedated?" He laughed, and Dad laughed too. "No, she didn't find out about my pretend friend. I don't think she ever suspected. I had described him with such clarity that she couldn't have doubted his existence."

He paused, then he said, "Genes are remarkable things, Ryder."

He looked at me and said, "My parents had many fine qualities, but they lacked imagination. A personal possesses more creativity than both of them together, I suspect, and of course they believed my little fib. Of course. It never occurred to them that a bookish boy could invent names and faces . . . whole lives, in effect . . . using nothing more than the electric ramblings of his lonely brain."

I said nothing.

"Genetics." He nodded and said, "One of my first great problems as a geneticist was to decipher my own genetic code and find why two bland people could produce such a loon. And do you know what? I'm still not satisfied with my answers. I'm telling you this in warning, Ryder. Genes are complex. They do enormous dances inside your cells, and there's no way to predict just what will result from those dances. Even today. There are just too many factors."

"What happened to your treehouse?" I wondered.

He laughed hard for a long moment, then he said, "Well, when I was too old to enjoy it any longer... a couple years older than you... I built a bomb from chemicals and fermenting bird droppings. The explosion brought two different fire departments to the scene." He laughed in a mild, amused way. He shook his head and looked at his feet.

Dad was laughing too.

It sounded like a terrible waste, and sad, but I thought it might be one of those jokes best seen from their age. I said nothing. I sat with my hands interlocked and lying on my lap.

Dr. Florida shook his head and smiled. I saw tiredness in his face—the same tiredness I'd seen at the pasture, only it seemed worse now—then it was gone, submerged again, and he told me, "I'm mostly alone in life, Ryder. Even now. Even after all of my supposed successes in science and business. I'm still the loon." He turned to Dad and said, "Kip? I'm trusting you not to make these confessions public. But it's true." He turned back to me. "These multitudes around me? These hallways bursting with energy and ambition? I'll admit something with perfect frankness. The people working for me are adults, and I've never been comfortable with adults. They're a humorless lot. The worst of them, I mean. They collect around me and my money until I can't see anyone or anything else. Which is wrong. Wrong and stupid of me and I'd do almost anything to change these circumstances. Do you see what I mean? Ryder?" He breathed and said, "No. I don't believe you do."

But I thought I did. I leaned forward and said, "I do. I think."

He winked and said, "I hope so." Then he said, "Let me confess one other secret. When I saw you and your friends on that pasture, I took a hard look at myself and felt jealous. Of you. I saw this gulf between us, and when I realized you had a rare talent... well, I decided to offer you my hand. Bridge this gulf between us, in effect... if that doesn't sound too old-folk quaint to you."

I said nothing, thinking hard and nodding.

"In other words," he said, "I'm inviting you back in the near future. Ryder, I've made your father an offer, and he's kindly agreed to take it home and consider it. There are business reasons for doing this thing, but you shouldn't be distracted by them. My great hope is that you, and your four friends, will come here some weekend day, and I'll stuff the five of you with lunch and give you other suitable diversions."

"Dr. Florida wants videos of you," explained Dad.

"For later, Ryder. For TV spots." Dr. Florida smiled and said, "Who knows? Maybe you'll see yourselves on TV all over again."

"Us?" I wondered.

"Absolutely." He sighed and said, "Our justification is that it will make good public relations. Dr. Florida helping tomorrow's people, and so on, and so on." He paused, then he said, "I hope I am helping people. And you."

Dad said, "I've always believed you are. Sir."

I said nothing, feeling . . . what?

Dad cleared his throat and shifted his weight, then he said, "Of course I need to talk to Gwinn first. Before we agree to anything."

Dr. Florida said, "Naturally. Absolutely!"

"It's a question of the presentation." Dad seemed distant while he spoke, the words slow and close to stumbling. "We want Ryder presented in the best light," and he reached to grip my knee. "I'm sure you understand. Sir."

"I wouldn't have it any other way, Kip."

"Sorry to be so sensitive—"

"Say no more. You have my word for now, and legal papers when the times comes. Should it come." He smiled as if he understood everything inside our heads. He saw us better than we saw ourselves, I felt. "Are we set? Are we?" He stood and came around the big desk, saying, "Just one more item, Ryder. I wanted you to hear this from me. Do you know what I've found most impressive about you? Do you? In all of the boasting stories from your dad, do you know what makes the biggest impact?"

I shook my head. I couldn't know.

"Not your memory. It's an impressive talent, yes, but your honesty is the special thing. You've got a sweet, steady honesty."

I managed to say, "Thank you, sir."

"Oh yes," he said. "Someone else with your talent could use your reputation to cause mischief. Do you realize that? You could pick and choose your lies. Juggle the facts. Twist the past until you looked splendid, even perfect, and no one would be the wiser. Do you see what I mean?"

I nodded and said, "But I do lie. Sometimes—"

And he broke into laughter. "Not to help yourself, I'd bet. Do you lie for your own selfish gains, Ryder?"

I kept silent.

"Now I've embarrassed you," he said. "I apologize."

Why do I try hard to be honest? I wondered. What makes me so keen on the truth? I considered the question for a long moment, and I blinked and felt the answer inside me. I was honest, thoroughly and wholeheartedly honest, because no one else could even pretend to be that way. No one else could remember little details, or big ones, and for them the past was a pale stew of crazy wishful thinking.

But not my past. Not Ryder's.

This was my pride, I understood. And pride wasn't a good thing. Dr. Florida didn't see my reasons, no, and so his compliments slipped off me. They were gone. They hadn't mattered a bit.

"I've got projects in the fire," he told us. "I guess we'd better call this meeting finished, men."

"Come on, son." I felt Dad's moist hand once again, and I stood and remembered to say, "Thank you for everything, sir. Thank you," and Dr. Florida said, "No. Thank *you*," and with that I left him.

Dr. Samuelson met us and led us out of the mansion. We took a different course. Dr. Samuelson was carrying a cold gallon of ice cream inside an insulated brown sack, and he watched me and asked, "How do you feel?"

I felt as if I was floating. I couldn't tell if it was from happiness or nerves or the sweet goo I had drunk. So I said, "I'm fine," and nothing more. I walked behind and between the men, Dad offering to carry the sack and Dr. Samuelson refusing the offer.

The garage was partly emptied. The smaller cars were gone, the day finished for their owners. Lillith was sitting in the back of our limousine, a pad of liquid crystal paper unrolled on her lap. She was writing until she saw us approaching, and then she rolled the pad closed and said, "How did it go, Kip? Ryder?"

"You never got my blue tomatoes," said Dad.

She was ready for his jokes. "I'm sorry. Gosh." She laughed in a smooth, bright way, then she said, "What's this?", and peeked inside the sack. "Gifts for the patient?"

I didn't speak. I was thinking.

Dr. Samuelson said good-bye, and the limousine was driving. Dad and Lillith were speaking to each other. Sometimes Dad would watch Lillith. I sat and pulled myself back to the pasture and the snow dragon, concentrating hard, bringing back all of the faces in the crowd. I saw Lillith again. Then I spotted Dr. Samuelson standing beside Dr. Florida's long limousine, listening and then talking to someone on the phone clenched in his hand. Then I was running. I was chasing the fleeing dragon, and I lost it on the bridge again and turned and looked back at Dr. Florida. I saw his raincoat and hat and him talking to pretty Lillith. I scrubbed and polished the memory, the tiniest details becoming apparent. I couldn't hear the words, but I knew how to read lips. I'd had plenty of practice from watching people and thinking about them later. I wanted to see what he had said just then, looking toward me and talking—

"Two things," he had told Lillith.

She had nodded once.

"His name's Ryder. Run checks on him. He might be a maybe—"

"Right—!"

"And two. Tell John to come up with three more teams. Soon."

"Three?"

"I don't care from where. Okay?"

"All right—"

Then I turned and leaped from the bridge. I streaked down the weedy bottoms and missed the rest of it. But what did I miss? And why might I be a maybe? I wondered. A maybe what? Three teams and a maybe, and I sat still and couldn't begin to guess . . .

FIVE

We would play a war game, Marshall and me. We were ten years old and would set up the board on his big dark dining room table. The game had fictional nations and an invented landscape and no particular identity for the troops. Marshall took either color and called himself the U.N. peacekeepers. He wouldn't play any other way. The U.N. was the decent and rightful side in all conflicts, and Marshall always won. "How could you be the U.N.?" he asked me. "You'd get pulverized every time, Ryder."

Marshall grinned when he won. A big smart know-it-all grin.

We played that game a hundred times, and one day I looked at my best friend and saw what he was thinking. I saw the grin and realized how little he thought of me. Why hadn't I seen it before? I wondered. Or maybe I had seen it, only I'd ignored it. Until now.

I took a breath and thought hard.

Then I told him, "Use all your troops this time. Would you?"

He giggled and said, "All right, Ryder. We'll try it." He usually spotted me a portion of his army. "This is going to be a quick one," he said. "Bang and boom and you're done."

I ignored him.

I stared at the board, absorbing it, and I didn't move until I was ready. I took my time and made no mistakes, yet Marshall didn't notice my resolve. He moved and counterattacked and made tiny, lazy mistakes, and sometimes he would manufacture explosion sounds until the spit flew across the table. He enjoyed himself enormously. I was too busy to care. I was remembering all the games we had played to date, recalling every move, and he couldn't distract me. I brought back his own moves and his tactics, and I wouldn't even touch my pieces until I'd picked the best from the past.

Marshall didn't notice my scheme.

Between turns he would read a book, thoroughly unconcerned. Then I got a small lead, and he looked at the board and said, "Well." He said, "I'm going to have to get tough," and he rolled up his book and said, "This is nothing." He counted his casualties and said, "Naw. This is the break I usually give you," and then he leaned forward, putting a finger along his nose.

I said nothing.

He concentrated, playing against himself. I watched the changing alignments and remembered the old battles, and I attacked and attacked, a couple times with luck. Then Marshall looked up at me. He said, "Clever," with a whispering voice. He shifted his butt against the hard dining room chair and breathed and said, "That's clever," with his face changing now. He wasn't smiling. He focused and attacked and broke my lines in two places, his troops streaming through the gaps, and maybe he would have won. I don't know. I was hurt and reeling, and it didn't matter too badly. Not really. I'd done what I'd wanted and wiped the smart smile from his face. That was plenty for me. But then his mother happened into the dining room, pausing for a moment and counting the dead.

"What's this?" she asked. "What is this?"

It was as if she had found an ugly stain on her fancy table. Her voice was harsh, Marshall saying, "I'm winning," and her snapping, "Not by my count, mister." She pricked him with a teasing laugh. Then she shook her head and said, "This isn't like you, is it? Is it?"

Marshall said nothing.

"What do you say?" she persisted.

"No, ma'am."

She glanced at me and smiled in a vague way. "Well, it doesn't really matter, does it? I guess it's just a game."

"Yes, ma'am."

"Don't let *me* bother you," she told us, and then she was gone.

Marshall was left too flustered to play well. He was breathing hard and staring hard at the board, seeing nothing, and when he took his next turn he made blunders. I could have made the attack myself and done better in his shoes, and in three more turns I had his tiny leftover army in a corner, trapped, and his face was red like I'd never seen it before.

We put away the game, saying nothing.

We went into his backyard, the bambis and other pets running circles around us, and I felt bad for winning. I felt I had cheated in some way, and there was a cold hard pain in my belly. So I said, "Marshall," and made him look at me. I said, "You know how I did it?" and I told him my secret. All of it. I thought he'd be relieved to know that he had been playing against himself, not me.

I wasn't smart like Marshall, no. I admitted as much.

But he said, "Asshole." His eyes got strange, his face red and hot, and his hands closed into trembling fists. He said, "Cheater," and spit at me. Then he grabbed a stick and began to swing it. "That's cheating, cheating, cheating," he cried, and he drove the stick into my arm. I felt a white pain in my elbow, and I turned and ran out of his yard. I rushed home and upstairs, never crying and telling no one what had happened; and I made myself a silent vow to never, never have that Marshall shit for a friend again. That cocky shit. Not ever.

We came home from Dr. Florida's, Dad and me. Dinner was waiting. I barely had time enough to call Cody and tell her to tell the others that I was fine and home and I'd talk to everyone tomorrow at school. As soon as I could, I promised. Good-bye.

We ate in the kitchen, like always. Dad described the tests and the machinery, then he explained the delayed results. "A lot of work was done for charity's sake, dear. You can't expect miracles." We finished dinner and had some small bowls of ice cream for dessert. I felt fine. Mom looked calm and passive. She said, "Should you be eating so much, dear?" But I felt all right. I told them so and finished and excused myself to do my homework.

I had to make up my school time. No chatting with friends until it was done. My teachers had fed assignments into the personal in my room, and I sat and looked at it all and thought it was much too much to do. There were long readings and a report to write, plus math problems just beyond my reach. Memory is just one kind of intelligence; I became frustrated in no time. I was numbed. All I wanted was to be with Cody and the others, telling them everything. I didn't want to wait for Mom's permission to return to the mansion. "We're invited," I imagined myself saying. "Dr. Florida invited all of us! Can you believe it? Huh? Can you?!"

One hour at my desk became two, then three, and there was still work begging to be finished. I sat back in my chair and gasped and cocked my head to one side. Mom and Dad were in their bedroom, talking. I could hear them. I sat without moving, and I listened.

Dad was telling her the rest of it, and Mom would ask little questions now and again. I couldn't quite measure her tone. Dad was talking about Dr. Florida and Dr. Samuelson, building toward the climax. In the little limousine, on the way home, he had promised me, "I'll handle your mother. Don't mention Florida's offer, and I'll see what I can do. All right?"

"You think she'll say yes?" I had asked.

"Not the first twenty times, no. But I'll wear her down. Don't you worry."

He was handling her. He said, "Quite the mind, Gwinn. The man is eighty years young, and you should have heard him. Ryder was asleep, and he launched into a string of lectures. He explained the machinery to me. He talked about his first tailoring clinic and lab. Then he told me about the new tailored animals he's producing. Remember that aquarium Ryder mentioned? The little whales and such? Well, they're part of his latest brainstorm. He's starting a new line of household pets from endangered creatures. Tiny whales and flightless eagles, for instance. And miniature tigers, clawless and housecat-sized."

Mom said, "Really," with a flat voice.

"He's going to make them abundant again. A tiny tiger isn't a real tiger, sure, but he explained it to me. What he's doing—isn't this neat, Gwinn?—he's knitting all the normal tiger genes into the pets. They'll be safe, they just won't be expressed." Dad paused, then he said, "When we rebuild the wildernesses and clean up the oceans again...well, these critters will be abundant and ready, and isn't that neat?"

Mom said, "What else?"

"What do you mean?"

"Kip," she said, "I know there's something. I've smelled it all night, and I'd appreciate some honesty. Now."

"You clever wench" he joked. "Okay. Here it is."

He repeated Dr. Florida's offer, saying, "Before you scream and stomp, please do me the favor of listening. Will you?" He spoke for a little while, then added, "We have complete control over what they use. He's given his word, Gwinn. If we take offense at anything, at any time, we have every right to back out of the deal."

"I don't understand," she admitted. "Why Ryder? And his friends?"

"It's the exposure they got on TV. In part." He said, "Three billion people saw them. A third of the world's population. Florida's own public relations people love the idea, using a group of natural kids. Real kids. They say there's an obvious connection between the five of them. It comes across in a moment, and it's something you don't get from professional kids. You see?"

"What's the purpose?" she wondered. "Where would they use—?"

"In a one-minute commercial. If all the parents say okay. It'll be shown in selected markets, at selected times, and it won't be gaudy. He promised. You've seen those commercials before. Those feel-swell things?"

"With Ryder?" she said.

"Portrayed as ordinary. That's assured."

"What about the attention he'd receive? People will be curious—"

"No names are released, Gwinn. The commercials are shown on local stations, not on the big networks. And not near us."

"It takes a day to film?" She sounded stubborn and a little confused. "That's all?"

"Florida plays host for a day, yes." Dad paused, then he remarked, "He's very forthright about his motives, dear. You should have heard him—"

"I would have pressed him—"

"You should have come," he said.

She was silent.

"But no," he said. "You phonied your illness like a schoolgirl, and now you're sorry. Aren't you?" He asked, "What did you expect? If you didn't trust the man, or the circumstances, you should have come and looked after your son's interests. Right?"

"Maybe so."

"Do you want to hear the rest?" I listened hard. I held my breath and there was nothing, then he told Mom, "There's something else and why don't we keep this from Ryder. All right? He doesn't know."

"What?" She sounded meek now. "What is it?"

"Florida's going to pay us and all of the families if, and when, these commercials are aired. Not a fortune, no, but enough—"

"We don't need it," she snapped.

"Am I finished? Did I say I was done?" He paused, then he said, "Gwinn. If we just go along with this game, for now, he's promised to steer some real estate business our way. And soon."

She cleared her throat.

"We could ensure ourselves some rich years, Gwinn. The sort of years we used to dream about having."

She said nothing.

"What are you thinking?"

"He's an angel," she told him. "Everyone says so. Yet doesn't this sound like a bribe? Doesn't it?"

"Dr. Florida," said Dad, "is an enormously successful businessman. Do you think he got that position with luck and sweet intentions? No, dear. No, I'm not fooling myself. He's a tough negotiator and he knows the bottom line. I'm the one who asked for something up front, for something tangible, and he relented when I persisted. This was business. Just business." Dad paused, then he said, "You're mad."

"Am I?"

"Jesus, Gwinn—"

"Just what does he want? I don't understand."

"I told you."

"All this trouble for a commercial? Is that sensible, Kip?" She muttered something, then she said, "We should have refused to allow any of this. From the first. I had a feeling—"

"And what if we help Ryder? You want to risk not doing that?" His voice was a whisper cloaking a full-throated scream. "What *is* your problem, lady? I don't understand."

"I want things to make sense."

"Then let me tell you one other thing. Okay?" Dad said nothing for a long moment, then he admitted, "The great Dr. Florida is alone, dear. And lonely. He's rich beyond measure, but he never married and his family has died. He's surrounded by ambitious people, and he's old enough to see the end. So what I think... are you listening?... what I think is that he wants to spend a little pocket change and have kids underfoot for a day. That's what he wants."

Mom was silent.

"He takes this Father-to-the-World business seriously." Dad waited for a moment, then he said, "You know me. I'm a pretty good judge of people. I'm no genius, but I can read a face as well as anyone."

"You can," she relented.

"So where's the harm?"

And she told him, "Let me sleep on it. Let me think it through."

I couldn't sleep. I tossed in bed and kicked at the clammy sheets, and I got up and opened the window and listened to the night sounds. I was wide awake and remembering the teacher who had come to see my folks years ago. She had offered money for the chance to research me. But she wasn't a good person. Not like Dr. Florida, I thought. My folks couldn't have trusted her like they could trust him, and I imagined Dr. Florida standing over my bed. He touched my head and said, "You're cured of your memory," and I grew scared. How would such a thing feel? How could I stand losing chunks of my past? Or having my surviving memories grow fuzzy and dull? And never, never being able to pick which moments I would save? I couldn't stand the thought. I curled tight beneath the clammy sheets, feeling an ache in my belly and shivering.

I got sick just after one o'clock. I didn't reach the bathroom in time, and Mom found me puking a second time, my head dangling over the perfumed white bowl. She said nothing. She got a sponge and ammonia and loaded our upstairs maid, and while the maid ran she took a towel to my face—a dry white towel frayed at the edge—and she mopped away the sweat.

I puked a third time and felt better.

The sickness was past, and I was simply dry and weak. It must have been the sweet goo I'd drunk at the mansion, and the ice cream, and Mom helped me to bed and felt my head, her hands stinking of the ammonia. She asked if I'd slept. I hadn't, no. "Then stay home tomorrow," she told me. "Sleep late and rest."

"But I'm okay." I wanted to see my friends; I needed to tell them everything that had happened. "If I go straight to sleep—?"

She wasn't listening. She was thinking to herself, her eyes focused on a point a thousand miles past me.

I said, "I'm not sick."

"What?"

"I'm fine," I promised.

"You're lying warm under covers at home." She said it carefully. "You're weak and tired and you don't even know it," she told me, sounding wise and a little bit angry. Then she bent and kissed my forehead and left. The lights turned off as she walked from the room, and I heard her leading the maid back into its closet. Then everything was dark and calm in the house. For a long while I hovered on the brink of deep sleep, and all at once I heard a scream. Or I thought I did. I blinked and sat up and heard nothing through the open window. Was it the dragon? Or a dream? I lay down again and found myself in a tree, climbing slippery branches, and my toes let go, and my hands, and I was tumbling . . .

. . . and I jerked awake, feeling empty and tired and powerfully happy. To sleep again, I conjured up one of Beth's songs and played it in my head, once and then again, and the song lingered, threading its way through all of my dreams that night, bringing me safely to morning.

I was ten years old and friendless, and on a cold Saturday morning I went down to the bottoms to wander. It was early winter, after the first hard freeze, and I still hated Marshall for all of his cocky shit. The air was so still that my breath hung around me, and every tiny sound seemed important. The tall weeds were shriveling and browning. The dark spring water in the little stone basins was steaming, heat bleeding from the earth, and I watched the birds drinking wing to wing, jockeying for position.

The almost-pond was prepped for winter. City crews and

city robots had done the work yesterday. The intakes were closed and the water was inoculated with certain tailored bugs—special microbes that consumed and transformed the sugars and amino acids into a plastic, the dark almost-pond turning clear and now capped with a false ice. The freeze had helped the process, I knew. That plastic was slick and tougher than real ice. It would shoulder aside the warm days and sunshine once it was cured, and kids would skate and play hockey and race one another. Then come spring the crews and robots would return, carting off the plastic and opening the intakes, the water turning dark and sweet again for the birds and bambis and such.

The false ice wasn't quite cured that morning.

I sat on my butt on the stony shoreline, staring through the clear new inch of flexible plastic. Bits of dead and sodden leaves drifted in sluggish currents. I tried the pressure of one gloved hand, the false ice bowing a little bit. I knew it wasn't cured; I remembered past winters. So I just sat and watched the morning light spreading through the orange and red trees. Leaves had fallen and the woods themselves looked less substantial, less mysterious, autumn turning them transparent. I saw the high stone walls bordering the west woods and the neat homes perched above the walls. I didn't know Beth. I hated Marshall but missed his predictable nonsense. I thought about him for a while, then blinked and noticed two shadows on the false ice. My shadow and a second shadow. I blinked and turned, finding Cody.

She was wearing hockey pads and an orange Russian hockey helmet, her skates velcroed together and thrown over a shoulder. She had a puck and stick in one hand. She was smiling through her helmet's cage. "Why aren't you out there?" she asked. She sounded tough and friendly in the same breath. "What's the holdup here?"

I said it was too soon.

"You think?"

"It's dangerous," I warned her, and I backed away from the shoreline. I meant to impress her with the danger.

Cody laughed, removing her pads and helmet. She was wearing white jeans and a heavy shirt and running shoes worn smooth from use. "It's Ryder, right?" She said, "Watch *this*, Ryder," and she ran past me. She slid out onto the weak false ice, never pausing, never doubting herself.

I cried out, startled and frightened.

The almost-pond had its deep spots, like wells, and I remembered stories of kids pulled dead from such holes. I felt a horror, knowing Cody would break through and become trapped, dying while I watched, and how could I help her get free? I couldn't. I was half her size and a tenth her strength, and I hated Cody for being out there while I was watching. For giving me no choice.

Cody pretended to skate. She took long smooth strokes and the uncured plastic bowed and cracked behind her. It was like a cartoon—a visible white line jerking and jolting its way across the surface, the sound deep and menacing. I jumped and clasped my hands on my head, shouting for her to hurry. "Faster!" I cried. "Faster, Cody! Go!"

She was laughing. She laughed all the way across, dry and happy, and then she was standing on the far shore and I saw the almost-pond moving beneath the false ice. There was a rubbery rise and fall to the cold water, waves rolling from shore to shore. It was strange to see, and unexpected, and I stared until I heard my name. "Ryder!" shouted Cody. "Come across. Come on. Quick and smooth and it's easy!"

I didn't want to seem frightened.

Cody was fearless, and it seemed important not to act scared now. I moved. I didn't give myself time to think. I just took an enormous breath and moved.

The plastic gave beneath me. It wasn't so slick as real ice, and the telltale cracking sound chased me. I let go of my breath and rushed forward. I told myself that I wasn't so heavy as Cody, not nearly, and the ice surely would appreciate my scrawniness. And then I was terrified. I pumped my arms and managed mammoth strides, crossing the middle of the almost-pond, and I was past the middle and came sliding up onto the earth, safe and grateful and belatedly full of courage. I nearly tripped, and Cody caught me and patted my back, pointing to the slender white fissure that had chased me from shore to shore. "You're one of the club," she informed me.

"Am I?" I wondered. "What club?"

"It's an expression," she explained, laughing hard.

I looked at Cody's square face. I saw her early chin fuzz and the heavy square teeth and the boy-short hair sprinkled with perspiration, bright in the sunshine, and she didn't seem ugly anymore. She was transformed, and now she was just

Cody. I thought: "This is Cody." I thought: "This is how Cody looks."

"Want to go again?" she wondered.

I said, "Sure," and we took turns again. It was a delightful thrill to slip over the danger, real or not, and I could have done it all day. We crisscrossed the false ice until it was laced with cracks, and I was sweating hard and laughing too hard to stand when we were finished. I was down on my knees on the cold dirt; and Cody took a long look at me, then she said, "I've got two big rules. If you want to be with me, there are two things you can never, never do."

"What things?" I asked.

"First of all, you can't be rude about my mothers. Not for any reason." Her voice was calm and certain, saying, "I don't want you to ever say anything against them. I won't take it."

I nodded. "Okay."

"And second," she said, "if someone else says something about them, or even about me—anything stupid or ugly—you don't come tell me. Understand? You're not my spy. You're not my eyes. So you keep it to yourself, okay?"

"All right."

"You've got it?"

I said, "I understand."

Cody smiled. I stared at her face until she turned away, and she bent and picked up her gear and then turned back to me, saying, "Look," and pointing at the almost-pond with her hockey stick. "You know what that looks like?" I saw the water still moving beneath the false ice, its waves crossing the almost-pond once and then again. I felt a little bit sad for having scarred the false ice—it would stay that way throughout the winter—then Cody said, "It looks like we're still out there. You know? Can't you almost see us skating out there still?"

Dad worked on Mom while I slept through the morning, and then into the afternoon. It was nearly three o'clock when he came from the basement to tell me, "She's relented. Ask your buddies if they want to visit the mansion, and I'll call Florida and get the big ball rolling." He breathed and said, "She's got rules and restrictions—you know Mom!—but at least she's come around." He shook his head and grinned, glad for the way things had turned out.

"Can I leave now?" I wondered. "I feel better."

"Isn't it early?"

School would let out soon, and I had plans—

"Go on," he relented. "Just take it easy. Okay?"

I walked straight to Cody's house and left a message. "Come down to the oak as soon soon soon as possible! And make sure you bring everyone else! Everyone!" Then I slid past the Wellses' house and across the green pasture, no one else in sight. It was the rarest of days—a whiff of solitude over the parkland—but I felt ever so excited with my news, and I was hungry to tell it. I wished my friends were with me now. I would have traded the solitude for their noise and nonsense in an instant.

I crossed the bridge and muscled my way up the oak's trunk, finding crescent-shaped depressions around the thumb-print lock. Someone had been beating the hatch with a hammer. Probably yesterday, I thought. The lock had held tight. Cody built for keeps, I told myself; and it opened to my thumb and I crawled inside, up into the big room. I opened a cabinet and dug out our best binoculars—huge and black with electronic workings and palm-sized eyes—and I sat on the long bench and looked out the east windows, waiting, the binoculars on my lap.

I'd invite everyone at once. All four of them, I planned, and I wouldn't play favorites. I promised myself not to play favorites.

I smelled the warm wind and sat motionless, imagining them smiling when I told them. The oak gave a lazy groan. I lifted the binoculars to my eyes, the dusty white rocks of the road now close enough to touch. I adjusted the dials and kept my hands steady, and the electronic workings adjusted for my little trembles. I saw bits of broken glass and a small black beetle crossing the whiteness. Then I felt an urge, a tempta-tion, and swinging right and lifting, I found myself looking inside the kitchen window at the back of the Wellses' house. I saw an ancient sink—stainless steel dented and the faucet dripping and sprouting rust at every seam—and there were dirty dishes and dirty glasses on the countertop, and big metallic green flies clung to the filth. A puffy woman—Jack's mother—passed into view, a sweating beer bottle in one puffy hand, her face colorless and somehow dead. Suddenly I felt wicked for spying—a little bit. I pulled back and breathed and then lifted the binoculars, thinking that I shouldn't wimp out now. I wasn't doing anything wrong. I would never spy on other people, no, but it didn't count so much with the Wellses. I sat still and told myself that the taboos didn't apply to them, so it was okay.

Jack's room was straight above the kitchen.

I hadn't been inside his house, no, but everyone knew which was his room. I could see a cheap chest of drawers, each drawer painted some different loud color, every knob a different shape. There were old-fashioned books stacked on top of the chest, with tattered bindings and yellowed pages working free. They were given-away books, or cheap, and when I saw them I imagined Jack Wells sitting up late and reading. Is that what he did? I wondered. Were those books about snakes? Or what? It made me realize that I didn't know Jack very well. Cody might be the one to know what he read, and when. She certainly knew plenty of stories about his brothers and folks—their drinking and drugging and the night-long parties and the run of small-time stealing that had started in the neighborhood the day the Wellses arrived. Jack was the only tailored brother. The other four brothers were quite a bit older, and each had seen prison time. At least Cody said so. I asked myself how Jack could live in such a house . . . how anyone could manage that kind of life. I hadn't any clue. They were like a different species, those Wellses. They were like wrong-colored ants in a nest.

I put down the binoculars and started to daydream.

I imagined the five of us at the mansion. Dr. Florida met Jack Wells, and later, on the sly, I told the Father-to-the-World: "He's got such a hard life, sir. But he's not bad himself. Cody will tell you, sir. All of us will, except maybe Marshall." I said, "Jack's a good, smart kid. He is."

"I know it," said the imaginary Dr. Florida. "I can tell."

"He's smart and tough, sir."

"Oh, he's got talents. They show." Then he smiled and rubbed my hair and said, "I'll tell you what. I'll help your friend. Jack deserves a good boost, don't you think?"

What could Dr. Florida do? I wondered. Buy liquid crystal books for Jack? Or give him his own personal? Or maybe, just maybe, he could get Jack out of the house entirely. I took a deep breath and vowed to bring the subject to Dr. Florida's attention. I trusted him to know how to help. If anyone could know such a thing.

Time passed.

I got a little bit lost, staring out at nothing. Then a boy was shouting, his voice strange, and I blinked and heard another boy shouting, "Go! Go!" Someone was running on our bridge!

"It's open," called the first voice.

I blinked and gazed downwards. Boys were starting to climb the oak. They were older than me, and larger, and I didn't know them. "Climb!" One was carrying a long crowbar, another had a battered old electric saw, and the lead boy was awfully close to our hatch. I'd left the hatch open. Open? I gasped and moved, and someone shouted, "I saw a little shit! Get the fuck up there! Go!"

I climbed into the maze, scooting face-first through the dark, turning passageways. The voices outside became muffled, almost peaceful, and my own breathing sounded huge. I was stupid for leaving the hatch open. I came around a corner and saw a hand reaching inside, fighting for a grip, and I panicked and slammed the hatch shut. *Whomp!* The hand vanished. I heard a wailing scream while I secured the lock, then I retreated to the first corner, breathing hard and trying to collect my senses, my poise.

The air turned stale after a minute.

I heard more voices and motion, and there came the sudden piercing whine of the saw. Its spinning blade bit into the hatch, sawdust and beams of sunlight playing over me. I retreated. The voices beyond sounded furious. Vengeful. The saw stopped and then started again, cutting again, and I locked the next hatches and worked upwards and thought there wasn't any hope to stop them. Not by myself. I was scared and so sorry for the boy's hand, and I thought that maybe an apology would help. If I was to say I was sorry? So when I reached the big room I secured the floor's hatch and went to the window to speak, and someone saw me and chucked a ragged lump of concrete at my head.

It missed me by nothing.

"You fucking broke my hand, asshole! You hear me?"

Maybe I deserved to be hit, in payment, but all of them were throwing concrete. They had brought chunks of it in their pockets. I ducked and slipped under the game table, clinging to the binoculars and shivering with a bad case of nerves.

Five voices, plus the boy with the saw. I heard the

cursing and the saw working and felt vibrations through the floorboards.

The concrete stopped flying. I heard grunts and old nails being jerked from wood, and I realized what they were doing. They were angry enough to dismantle our bridge. *Bang* and *skeeek* and the boards came up, faster and faster, and the saw was getting closer to me. It was cutting through layers of the maze, ignoring all of our intricate turns and twists.

No one was throwing at me. I rose and saw five boys dragging boards down onto the bottoms, making a heap in the green weeds. They were laughing. They were dancing. They saw me and said, "You fucking shit, we're going to kill you! Hear? We're going to murder you, you shit!"

Cody was standing on the bottoms.

She was with Beth and Marshall, the three of them near the slabs. For a terrible long moment I thought they didn't see me. How couldn't they see me? I was trapped and doomed, and Beth said, "There it goes! I see it!" with her voice close to singing. It was an opera voice, her words carrying over the whining saw and shouts. She was pointing at something. Or nothing. "Do you see it?" she sang. "Look, look!"

The strangers paused.

"Is it the dragon?" called Cody.

"I saw it!" sang Beth.

"The dragon!" Marshall screamed. "I see it too!"

My three friends ran toward the slabs. Cody sprinted and jumped and missed grabbing the fleeing dragon. The strangers watched her without speaking, curious now. Then one of them asked, "What is it?"

"The snow dragon?" said another.

"You think?" asked a third boy. He rubbed his sore hand. "What the hell? The shit's not going anywhere. Let's take a look!"

The floorboards trembled when the saw started to cut again. But the other boys were leaving. I watched my friends chase nothing up past the slabs, all of them pointing and shouting, and then the boys were in the woods too and no on else was in sight.

I waited, standing motionless, my breath galloping and my guts aching.

Beth and Marshall came from the north, Cody from the

south, and Cody was first to reach the oak. I shouted to her about the boy in the maze. She told the others to hide, hide and wait, and she took an enormous leap and scampered up through the ruined hatch. The saw kept cutting. Then it quit and there was shouting, then shoving, and I heard the boy saying, "Fuck you! You're not goddamn taking my saw! It's my dad's—!"

The shoving continued. The boy and Cody emerged from the maze, the boy dangling on the oak's lowest branch. His face was sweaty and scared. Cody said, "Jump or climb," and he tried to climb. Only there weren't enough handholds with the bridge gone. He ended up leaping and tucking when he hit the bare slope, dust rising and his sweaty clothes turning muddy in an instant. Then he was up and running, his friends gone and him rushing onto the bottoms with his hands cupped around his mouth, his scared voice calling for John and Larry and Pete. "Jesus? Where are you?"

Beth and Marshall were hiding. I couldn't see them.

Cody came into the big room. "What a mess, would you look?" She winked at me and dropped the saw on the game table. "A good thing you were here to slow them, Ryder," and she opened a freezer and got ready. She picked a dozen hard white snowballs and told me to be alert. "We're going to teach them," she declared. And she winked again.

The boys came out of the woods after a while.

They stopped for a moment, watching Cody and me, and then they came toward us and I picked up a snowball. It was smooth and wonderfully round, Cody-made and pure ice. It felt heavy and bitterly cold in my hand. I stood beside Cody. She yelled at them, taunting them. "You jerks! There's no dragon! You toad-gened dickless jerks!"

They began to charge us.

Cody threw the first snowball with a sidearm motion, putting so much force into it that she grunted—a hard, from-the-gut grunt—and the snowball spun downwards and struck the lead boy with a *slap* in the chest. He stumbled and picked himself up again and kept running. Cody let them come close. She waited for them to congregate beneath us, presenting easy targets, and she flung the snowballs down at their heads. They didn't have much to throw at us; the concrete was too slow to hit Cody. I watched the joy in her face and how she turned to me, practically calm, and asked,

"Can you get me more, Ryder?" and I handed her fresh snowballs from the freezer. "That's the boy. Thanks."

One boy climbed the oak's trunk. His fingers jabbed into the bark itself, and Cody struck his face with a half-strength blow, striking him just above the right eye, and his hands went limp and he fell backwards to the bare slope, all of him limp. He looked like something boneless. Dust rose and the skin over his eyes was split open and bleeding. He was lying motionless, and I saw the vivid crimson color. One of his friends bent over him and said, "He's dead," and for an instant I didn't just believe him, I was glad. For a tiny wicked sliver of a moment I was so glad that he had died, thinking of the fear he had caused me. I could have been the one dead on the ground, not him. And then the wounded boy stirred, moaning and lost under all the blood, and I saw how the heart had gone out of his friends. The other five gathered their tools, minus the saw, and they helped their fallen comrade to his feet. A couple of them remembered to shout at Cody. They called her, "Fella," because they didn't know better. "We'll get you, fella!" But they were broken. It showed in their faces and in the stooping curl of their big bodies.

Beth and Marshall returned when it was safe.

Cody hammered extra handholds into the oak's trunk, everyone coming into the big room. "I hope he's all right," said Beth. "That one—"

"He asked for it," Marshall declared. "He deserved worse."

Beth shook her head sadly.

"I wished I could have popped him too," said Marshall. He pounded his fist into his hand, saying, "They make me mad."

No one thought about me or Dr. Florida. They wanted to hear about the strangers trying to break into the treehouse. I was telling it when Jack arrived, and he sat with us and listened. Then I was finished and ready to tell about Dr. Florida. Only Cody stood and said, "I've got to start fixing this mess. Can you tell me later?"

Not really. I had something special to say—

"I wish I could have plugged those assholes," said Marshall. He shook his hands and moved his feet and turned toward Jack. "It was great! You should have seen Cody pounding them—"

"Where were you? Hiding?" asked Jack.

"Cody told me to stay below," he explained. "In case."

Cody rolled her eyes. "Listen. I'm tired of you two—"

"In case you shit your pants," said Jack.

"So where were you?" asked Marshall. "We could have used you for bait, you little shit—"

"*All right!*" Cody got between them and said, "Now shut up!" and glared at both of them. She hadn't been half as furious with the attacking boys. "Listen. Ryder wants to tell us about Dr. Florida, and we're going to sit on our tongues and listen. You understand? Do you?"

And so I started to tell it. I was a little angry with the way events had pushed my news aside, spoiling my timing. I told them how it felt to meet Dr. Florida in his home, to see his office and labs while he talked about his childhood and treehouse and the crazy ordinary things he did when he was like us, a kid. Then I told them what a good man he was, truly; and that's when I got a stabbing feeling that maybe, just maybe, I didn't deserve the honor of a return visit. I had believed that the boy was dead, and his death had made me happy. For a moment, I felt quite ashamed of myself. I wished I could take back that vindictive instant. What would happen if I made no mention of Dr. Florida's invitation? Could I avoid it? And then I stopped talking, losing myself inside my tangled thoughts, and Beth touched me and said my name until I blinked and looked at their calm faces.

I ignored my doubts.

Everything was starting, after all. Dad was making the call and the big relentless ball was rolling.

I swallowed and blinked, saying, "And guess what?"

"What?" they wondered. "What is it?"

I told my news. We would go to the mansion together, all of us; and my friends straightened and turned wide-eyed, the notion too large to be swallowed neatly. I watched them shake their heads in disbelief, and then they gave quick shy smiles. Their faces were vacant. Their hands were open and limp. It occurred to me that they were now the ones who were lost, and this is how I must sometimes look to them; and I sat and waited patiently, feeling the breeze and smelling the green woods and the sun.

SIX

Lillith came to my house and my folks walked me to the limousine. Mom never spoke. She stood with her arms crossed, and Dad spun jokes for Lillith and told me to enjoy myself. "I mean it!" Then we were leaving and they were waving at me, both of them, and Lillith told the limousine where to stop next. It was a cloudy day, rain coming. Marshall was waiting for us. He was wearing a suit and tie, and his mom beat him to the open door. "So good to meet you!" she announced. "Lillith? Is it Lillith?" Marshall's dad was a quiet, empty-faced man who hung in the background. "Now take care, dear!" Marshall's mom couldn't have sounded nicer. "Remember your manners, and good-bye! Good-bye, Ryder! Good-bye!" She was waving and then his dad waved too. As soon as Marshall was sitting, and safe, he pulled off the tie and breathed like someone who'd been choked.

Jack and Cody came from Cody's house. They were dressed in clean shirts and new jeans. Cody's mother May walked from the backyard with a wad of weeds in one gloved hand. She was a pretty woman, and large, and it was strange how she resembled her daughter. May said something to Cody, her free hand hanging in the air between them. Tina must be gone, I thought. Tina was the small plain one who had answered the door years ago. Cody had inherited Tina's plainness and May's build, and I sat watching them. I was sitting beside Lillith and feeling ever so fine.

Jack climbed inside.

"You must be Jack," said Lillith.

He was looking out the opposite windows. "Fuck," he said.

I turned and saw two of Jack's brothers standing on their porch. They were wearing nothing but shorts, and they were reaching inside the shorts and scratching themselves. I saw them digging and grinning without any shame or hesitation.

Color rose in Lillith's face.

Cody arrived and we were moving, Jack saying, "Fucking jerks," with a soft, fierce voice. We turned right and passed the almost-pond, and Lillith quit blushing, saying, "One more stop." We turned right again and pulled up in front of Beth's house. She was wearing a bright cream-colored dress and black shoes that shone despite the clouds. A window shade lifted while she walked toward us, then it dropped, and then we were moving again. The sky began to spit rain, and the rain became strong as we drove west. "It's no morning to be outside," said Lillith. Her eyes were red and tired. She asked if everyone was comfortable and would we like drinks, and then she repeated herself. "I wouldn't want to be outside today. No thank you."

Jack touched his shirt pocket.

I blinked and saw motion. There was a tiny snake in the pocket, squirming, and Jack noticed my stare and halfway smiled, as if to say, "Our secret, okay? Don't tell."

Lillith was silent, her eyes faraway and intense. She seemed lost in some rainy-day mood. For a little while I watched the rain too. The ground and trees and even the people took on a sodden, chilled appearance. I found myself shivering. Marshall started to talk about the dragon, saying, "It's not weather for hunting it, no," and then he asked Lillith, "What are we going to be doing, ma'am? I'm curious."

Lillith blinked. "Do?" She blinked again. "Well, you'll get a tour. Of course. Then I think you'll end up in the surf room." She shook her head and said, "I hope everyone can swim."

Marshall said, "I don't have a swimsuit."

"We'll find one." Lillith didn't seem herself. She bit her lower lip, then asked, "So. Have you been chasing the dragon?" She must not have heard Marshall talking to himself. "Any of you?"

"I'm too busy," said Cody. "Our treehouse got torn to hell the other day, and I'm fixing it." She pretended there was a hammer in her hand and a nail in the air. "Marshall's our dragon man."

"Are you?"

"And I'll catch it too," he declared. "I've got this system with live bait and nets. Everything's figured."

"Well," said Lillith, "good luck to you."

"Ryder helps me," he persisted. "Don't you, Ryder?"

A few times. But I didn't like waiting in the dark with nothing fooled by the bait. I said nothing, nodding and giving a shrug, and I thought how a part of me didn't want to catch the thing. It would be a lot happier in the woods hunting wild rats and birds, and whatever. That's what I told myself.

"Do you know anything about the dragon, ma'am?" Marshall was hoping for clues. For advice.

"It's not my department." Lillith offered a thin, weak smile. I kept watching her red eyes and the way she chewed on her lip, and she sighed and said, "I'm in a different division."

Jack said, "You aren't going to catch it. Not ever."

"I bet I do."

"I bet it dies of old age first."

"You two don't get along?" asked Lillith.

"They feud," Beth admitted. "That's all, really."

"Not today," said Cody. "They have a truce. They shook on it."

Lillith stopped listening. I could tell by looking at her eyes.

"Ma'am?" said Beth. "What do you do? If I might ask, ma'am."

"What do I do?" She blinked and said, "Public relations. Coordinating departments. Those sorts of chores."

Marshall asked, "Are you important?"

"I'd like to think so."

"Myself," Marshall announced, "I'm going to be a scientist. Maybe a tailor, I'm not sure."

"Oh?" Lillith asked. "What about the rest of you?"

"Beth sings," said Cody.

"A little." Beth dropped her eyes, her mouth clamped shut.

Cody said, "Sports for me," and grinned, imagining a baseball and throwing it out the window. "The men's leagues."

One of Lillith's pretty hands curled into a fist, knuckles showing through the stretched skin. She gave a little sigh and said, "You sing?" to Beth. It was as if the words had finally percolated into her mind. "Maybe you could sing now. A little something?"

Beth said, "Now?"

"You can't pay attention," Cody explained, "or she clams up."

So we stared out the windows, and Beth gradually broke into a song. It was slow and cold and matched the falling rain, and it was pretty in a fragile way. "That's precious, dear," said Lillith, and she smiled with sad eyes. "I've always liked that one." She rubbed an eye with a finger, then she crossed her arms on her chest.

Beth said, "Thank you, ma'am."

Lillith kept quiet. She was watching us.

Jack said, "I'm going to be a thief when I'm grown up."

I looked at Jack, waiting.

"Pardon me?" said Lillith.

"Or a street-corner pharmacy," Jack added. He smiled and touched his shirt pocket once lightly, teasing Lillith. "Everyone says I'm going to end up in jail, you know."

"I see . . ."

"But you're not," Beth whined. "You don't mean that."

"Maybe yes," said Jack, "and maybe no."

Marshall said, "Let him do what he wants."

Cody said, "Marshall."

"What?"

"Leave him alone."

"What did I do?" Marshall wondered. "Huh?"

Then Lillith nearly spoke. She leaned forward and opened her mouth, and I watched her and waited until she sat back again, her hands knotted together in her lap, her lips pressed into a seam, and her dark eyes damp enough to shine. She was watching us. She stared at each of us. I kept asking myself: "What is she thinking? What's in her head?" Then her gaze came around to me, and we stared at one another for a moment. And she blinked and said, "Anyway," and put her head back, shutting her eyes and not speaking again. Not until we were inside the mansion itself.

The surf room was a long beach against a long high wall, everything else saltwater and the illusion of sky. The waves rolled and collapsed onto the hard-packed sand, time after

time, and somehow the lighting was brighter than outdoors,
brighter even than a sunny summer day.

"We mimic the tropical sun," Dr. Florida explained to
me. "And the tropical heat, I'm afraid." He was sitting beside
me. He had a folding chair woven from liquid-filled tubes,
and the liquid was chilled and keeping him from suffering too
much. He wore light clothes and his usual hat. It wasn't the
same exact hat he had worn on the pasture, no. It had the
same fabric and colors—smooth almost to shiny; tan with
curling black lines—but there were differences in the wear
and exact weave. I told him some of the differences, and he
chuckled. "You've got exceptional eyes," he told me. "Don't
you?" I felt glad to hear his praise, and he looked at me and
said, "The truth is that I've got closets full of these things."
He ran his long spotted hands along the big brim. "They're a
symbol for me. Aren't they?"

I nodded.

"People think in symbols, Ryder." He shook his head and
sighed, then he said, "Now consider yourself warned," and
grinned.

I said nothing. I saw Jack and Beth standing up to their
knees in the water, waiting for the next wave. Jack's swimsuit
was too large, tied too high around his waist. He looked
tough and silly, both things at once, and I could have laughed.
Dr. Florida's guards had found his garter snake in the shirt
pocket, using their scanners, and Dr. Florida had promised
that he would get it back when it was time to leave. Absolutely.
The snake would be kept safe and sound.

"I like your friends, Ryder. You're fortunate to have
them."

"I know I am, sir. Thank you."

Beth turned her back to the next wave, her eyes squashed
shut and the clear bluish water crashing over her head. She
and Jack were pushed off their feet. She got up, laughing,
and Jack looked mad. Beyond them, in the deepest water, I
saw two heads bobbing and then diving, then coming up
again. Marshall and Cody had donned goggles and snorkels
and fins. I saw streams of salty vapor blown from the snorkels. A little camera moved over them, its fans blowing at the
air. At least a dozen cameras were flitting about the surf
room, scanning and listening and mostly keeping out of plain
view. I couldn't find any close to us now. I turned and turned
and didn't see one.

Dr. Florida touched me. "Ryder?"

I looked at his eyes and nothing else.

"How do you like this place?" he wondered.

"Just fine." It was so bright and warm on a rainy day. The air couldn't have tasted fresher. I sat and thought, then I told him, "It's like the one on the moon, isn't it?"

"There are several—"

"Tranquility City. The fake rocks, and everything . . . it's the same." The image had come to me. Dad had been turning through the channels and I had been sitting on the floor, my legs crossed and a coloring pad uncurled on my lap. Dad had lingered on one of those channels that showed views of exotic places. I'd seen the shoreline and the enormous slow waves, and people were thick on the beach and in the water, giggling and moving with the strange skipping motions of people on the moon. I watched them running on the sand, kicking up little lingering clouds, and Mom had said, "Kip? Kip? Could we find something a little more dull? Please?"

"The similarity," said Dr. Florida, "is simply explained. My own engineering firm designed and manufactured both surf rooms." He touched my shoulder and squeezed. I was lying on an ordinary blanket, the heat of the sand seeping into my bones. "It's an indulgence for that parched land, but a wise indulgence." He said, "It's too bad I'm too old and frail to travel in space. The moon has grown so much since my last visit. So have all our farflung adventures. Isn't that so?"

Just in my lifetime much had changed. I said, "Yes, sir. Quite."

"The people who visit Tranquility City tell me that the surf room is easily, easily the most popular attraction. They have to employ a lottery system just to regulate who gets to feel the clean spray and the false sun."

Dozens of glimpse-quick memories came to me. I saw glass domes and the vivid green farms beneath the domes, the brightly lit caverns and the long, razor-straight magnetic launchers. There were robots working the huge and bleak strip mines, plus people who seemed too tall and thin to be healthy. The earth hung full in the sky—a vast round blueness bordered with an honest surf of its own—and the moon's moon passed overhead, moving fast, black like velvet and studded with tiny bright lights.

"Ryder? Ryder?"

I blinked and turned toward him again.

"You were a little lost, I think." He patted my shoulder. "It's fine. Don't worry. I just wanted to ask a question."

"Yes, sir?"

"Are you interested in space?" he wondered. "I was when I was your age. The wild worlds. The great unknowns. The adventure of the thing... does that sound familiar?"

"I read about space," I admitted. "And watch TV—"

"I know you do." He breathed once, then again, and said, "I had a dream when I was a boy. Do you want to hear it? I dreamed of becoming a great explorer and going on long, long voyages around the solar system, finding wonders." He said, "Living wonders," and stared at me. "I imagined fishes swimming in underground Martian seas. And bat-winged monsters soaring in the Venusian clouds. And forests of methane-sapped trees standing beside some Titan lake. Do you see what I'm saying? A solar system stuffed full of living creatures. Do you see?"

I had done the same things myself, in a fashion—

"None of those wonders are possible. Of course," he said. "We know that now. No doubts about it. But when I was a boy I took them as fact. It wasn't a game. It was possible. The image of alien creatures... well, it captivated me. It was addictive. And so beautiful."

A flood of random facts jumbled in my head.

"Tell me," said Dr. Florida, "are there any native life forms on any nearby worlds?" He leaned toward me and waited.

I said, "No, sir."

"Exactly." He nodded and sat back into his folding chair.

I grabbed a handful of sand, dry and coarse and warmer than blood.

"Venus had oceans when it was young," he told me. "Did you know? It was the earth's mirror twin for several hundred million years, which is quite a long time. Long enough to let life forms evolve into proficient, if somewhat simple, microbes." He nodded and squinted at nothing, saying, "We've sent robots into that hell—my own robots included—and we've found the sketchy traces of life chemically bound with the rocks. Imagine an early Venus full of life—a durable, adaptable bacterial life—and the sun huge and scalding in the sky. The seas slowly evaporate. The water vapor lifts. Because of the strength of the sunlight and the extra heat, the clouds form at much higher elevations than on the earth. Light radiation from the sun shatters water molecules, bleeding off the precious hydrogen gas, and do you know the result? The seas shrivel and die. They are doomed from the start, and that's the truth. That's what happened, Ryder."

The sand fell through my curling fingers, leaving my palm warm.

He said, "It's a different story on Mars. Life was much more blessed on Mars. It reached a multicellular stage. There were jellyfish blobs, delicate and almost certainly lovely in life. There were worms in the muck and creatures on stalks, and so on. They left wonderful fossils. There are countless fossils on Mars, more than you could find on the earth. and they are truly ancient, Ryder." He paused, then said, "Nearly a billion years old. Do you know why my survey teams have uncovered so many fossils? It's because there hasn't been much volcanic activity on Mars. On the earth, in the last billion years, volcanoes and the drifting continents have crushed and melted and otherwise destroyed old rocks. But little Mars is too small and cold for that kind of drama. Which, in turn, is the reason it's empty of life today." He breathed and his expression became rigid, something sorry in his eyes. He told me, "The young Mars had volcanoes and the first rumblings of continents. There was plenty of carbon dioxide in the atmosphere then. And that was good—"

"The greenhouse gases," I blurted.

"Exactly." He nodded and said, "On Mars, so far from the sun, that carbon dioxide was a saving grace. So long as it was liberated from old rocks, life evolved. Life could find new forms, more intricate and beautiful and precious forms, and it was very much like the youthful Earth. Only it didn't last, Ryder. Mars went to sleep. The air thinned and its citizens retreated and froze and died of thirst. The changes didn't come in one year, or in a million, and it wasn't a steady slide either. There were sudden late summers. Teasing summers. But there was no doubting the end." He shrugged his shoulders and said, "The last tough microbes died inside the permafrost. They're locked there today, and researchers can find them and use them as reliable markers. An entire biosphere—an entire world—became extinct hundreds of millions of years ago, Ryder, and I think that is just so sad."

"It is sad," I agreed. My remark seemed small, even useless, when set beside such an enormous sadness. I stirred the sand beside my towel, using one finger. Why was Dr.

Florida so serious today? I recalled him asking my friends, Cody and the rest, to leave us now, for a little while, because we had to talk. Just the two of us. I looked out at Cody and longed to be swimming. This wasn't the same Dr. Florida I'd seen on the pasture, or the one who had given me ice cream. Like his hat, I thought. He looked very much the same. But he wasn't.

He told me, "My entire life has been spent with life, Ryder."

I blinked and watched him.

"I have this curious passion for things living. I do. There's something fundamentally special about even the simplest organism. Life is the universe's attempt to save itself from entropy. Do you know what I mean? Entropy? Heat death?" He paused, then he winked at me. "You don't need to understand every word. Suffice to say that life is more precious than even I could have guessed when I was your age. Infinitely so."

I nodded.

He nodded with me and watched the tumbling waves. "Think of the very largest planets. The gas giants." He breathed and said, "Ryder," and turned back to me. "They aren't like Venus and Mars. Did you know? Each gas giant has zones where there's plenty of water and energy in several flavors and temperatures that wouldn't feel much different than this beach does now. I mean Jupiter, and the rest too. Isn't that something to consider? When I was a boy, maybe a touch older than you, I imagined a Jupiter stuffed full of exotic, wondrous creatures. Before I made a living tinkering with earthly life, I spent hours and hours devising planktons and plankton-eating beasts that would live in the Jovian clouds. A game of childish pretend, yes. And futile too. Do you know what happens on Jupiter, and on every other gas giant? Do you know why they're as sterile as the glassware in my cleanest lab?"

I shook my head. I had read things, but I couldn't focus—

"Take Jupiter," he said. "It has regions where sunlight and lightning bolts—enormous lightning bolts—work together on simple chemicals and airborne dusts. The dusts themselves come from meteorites, and they serve as catalysts. Chemicals cling to them and form RNA and DNA. Each year, without pause, Jupiter fabricates several billion tons of pure genetic material. Plus proteins too, and complex fats. And so on. The basics of life, yes. But the wind always blows. The atmosphere is torn by storms and unstable thermals. Those precious compounds—listen to me!—are eventually carried into the deepest regions of Jupiter's atmosphere. The pressures and heat destroy them. They're shattered into atoms again—wasted—and so life never has its chance to evolve on Jupiter. Or anywhere like Jupiter. Gas giants are doomed to remain sterile for all time."

I watched him suck on his teeth, nodding. I watched him press his hands together. I felt tired and sorry for his sadness, and I was sad for the empty worlds. "It's too bad," I offered with my inadequate voice. "It would be nice... otherwise."

He didn't seem to hear me. He said, "Neptune and Uranus are cooler, true. And smaller. But the results are the same. Saturn too. This self-murdering goes on and on forever. Without pause."

I said nothing.

"Only one world cradles life, Ryder."

Earth. I had known that fact all of my life, but *knowing* is many things. Now I understood the fact. I saw it in the clearest of terms. Around us was a remarkable wealth, and we were blessed. Even the poorest weed rooted in the driest, poorest soil—

"Life is so precious," he told me.

I understood. I said, "I know, yes," and felt like crying.

"For a century," he said, "we've listened to the skies, and watched the skies, and nothing resembling life has been heard. Not once. No one has any answers as to why it's quiet, but if pressed I could make a few reasoned guesses." He paused, then he asked, "Would you like to hear?"

I said, "Okay."

"All sorts of nonsense can happen to a planet, Ryder." He squeezed my shoulder. "Asteroids can slam into one. A swarm of comets can pepper it, leaving craters and devastated land. Or a passing star might explode and spread its poisons willy-nilly across the sky." He was looking at me. "I don't mean to sound black," he told me, "and I don't wish you to take this the wrong way. What I'm saying—what I want you to see—is that we, our world and all its sugary passengers, could have been swept away by any of a dozen cosmic events. That is the simple truth."

I believed him. I dipped my head and said, "Okay."

"The dinosaurs went extinct because of a rain of comets. We know it to be fact. But comets come in many sizes, and the largest comets exceed a hundred miles in diameter. A thousand times larger than the dinosaur killers. One giant comet impacting on our world, anywhere, would boil the oceans and sterilize the land. I've seen the simulations. Little would survive. Just some tiny bacteria accustomed to scalding heat, perhaps. And the forests and reefs and so on . . . well, I'm afraid nothing and no one would remain."

I said nothing.

"Such a nasty truth, isn't it?" He laughed without humor and shook his head. "As it turns out, Ryder, our chances of being hit by a giant comet are not small. We've probably had several near misses, in fact, and we remain a tempting target. Don't think otherwise. Don't."

I looked at my sandy hands, wondering why he was telling me this stuff. I felt uncomfortable. I wished he would at least look elsewhere when he talked to me. Why me?

"Indeed," he announced. "If I add up every potential world-killing mishap—heat death and cold death, comets and asteroids, plus exotic horrors like supernovae and quasars at our galaxy's core—the chances of us sitting here now, like this, have fallen to almost nothing. Which is why the sky is so quiet, and so empty, and why we have no one to listen to but ourselves."

I concentrated hard, trying to understand.

"Ryder?" he said. "Do your friends ever tell you things? Things they want to have remembered?"

I looked straight at his eyes and nodded.

"I hope you consider me a friend." He waited, then he said, "I can't tell you why this is important. Not yet, at least. And maybe not ever. All right?"

"Okay."

"It's something between the two of us. No one else."

I nodded again.

"It's a dismal load to carry, I know. But there are reasons, and you'll have to trust me. Can you trust me?"

He was Dr. Florida, and everything involving Dr. Florida was an honor. "I trust you, sir." What were my choices? Painful words or not, he had thought enough of me to give them to me. A gloomy sense of despair. . . I felt it with every breath, a part of me wishing I could cry hard and long.

"Mention this to no one," he muttered. "For now."

"Yes, sir."

"Life is precious," he reminded me.

"Life is precious," I echoed.

"Indeed."

Then I breathed and had to ask him, "Who would forget such a thing, sir? Who?"

And he shook his head sadly.

After a moment, almost without sound, he told me, "You can never be too sure, Ryder. You can never be too sure."

We ate lunch on the beach, the six of us. My friends loved talking to Dr. Florida, Marshall making half the noise, asking him endless questions about the snow dragon. Dr. Florida was like the buoyant man I remembered from the pasture. He smiled and joked, once telling Marshall, "I can't diagram *everything* about the dragon, can I? Would that be fair?"

Marshall shrugged his shoulders and stared at the bright white sand. I could see him blushing, embarrassed now. Then I looked past him and saw Lillith emerging from the false rocks of the wall.

She came with several other adults from the room's well-hidden entrance. They were wearing office clothes and looked very much out of place. Dr. Florida saw them and rose from his cool chair, and I watched his face and how he walked to them, slowly but not slowly. Jack touched his chair and said, "We ought to get one, Cody. For the oak."

The adults were speaking with Dr. Florida. I couldn't hear them over the crashing waves. Lillith was looking at the five of us. At one point she started to say something; and Dr. Florida, without fanfare, touched her chin and dipped her face out of sight.

He returned in a little while.

"I have to leave," he told us. He looked at me and halfway winked. "Enjoy yourselves and I'll be back soon. All right?"

We nodded. We watched Dr. Florida vanish through the door, and Beth touched me and asked, "Ryder? Why are you so quiet, Ryder?"

"What did you guys talk about?" asked Marshall. "Before."

"Oh," I said, "nothing really."

Cameras hovered around us. A moment ago they had been far out over the water.

"Come swim," Marshall told me. "There are all kinds of neat fish in the water. And turtles. And these tiny whales—"

"Are you tired?" asked Cody.

"Some," I said.

"A swim would make you feel better," she told me.

"But we have to wait," cautioned Beth. "Because we just ate." We had had sandwiches and lemoned Pepsi for lunch. Now we belched into our hands. There was strange fruit waiting in a cool tub and more food than twenty of us could have eaten. Cody started picking the meat from several sandwiches, wrapping it in plastic, and she stood and tried biting a rust-colored ball of fruit. "Sour," she snarled, and she spit out the dry pinkish guts.

Beth said, "Cody?"

Cody walked toward the surf, her plastic-wrapped meat in one hand.

"Where are you going?" asked Beth.

"I'm going to feed the fish," she announced. Sand clung to her butt and the dark backs of her legs. Her swimsuit was straining against her muscles, the cords showing in her arms and hamstrings and across her broad, flat shoulders. Beth said something about cramps, she might get cramps, and Cody looked at us and smiled, saying, "Me?" and then winking.

Beth shrank down a little bit.

We watched Cody position her goggles and dive into a rising wave. We waited for her head or her back, counting seconds, and then she emerged in the deepest water. Her hands tore the meat to pieces. The water itself was halfway still, and I saw the fish breaking the surface—colored fins and eager mouths, flashes of red gills and Cody surrounded, seemingly fish food herself.

I thought hard about the fragile, precious business of life.

I wanted to weep for all the dead and lost creatures on other worlds. But I didn't. Dr. Florida had told me to keep our conversation secret, and I knew if I cried I would tell everything. So I bit my lower lip and tucked my knees to my mouth and never, never made a sound.

Marshall talked about the dragon. On and on. "Dr.

Florida knows I can figure it out for myself. How to catch it. That's why he did what he did. I bet so."

Jack said, "You're an idiot."

Beth said, "Guys."

"Platinum brains, my ass," said Jack.

"I'm not listening to you," said Marshall.

I thought about Jack Wells. I hadn't yet mentioned him to Dr. Florida, believing we had the entire day. But where was Dr. Florida? Had something gone wrong? I remembered a cool hardness coming into his face when Lillith appeared, and I tried to guess what was happening. I made a hundred good guesses, all of them wrong.

"We can swim now, Ryder?" Beth touched me and told me that our lunches were settled. We grabbed more sandwich meat and waded into the surf, and Jack was beside me, not strong in the water but kicking hard and refusing to quit. A long rainbow-colored eel stole the meat from my hand, fleeing into the rocks far below. I dove and my chest burned, and I quit and rose again and laughed a halfway laugh. Then Cody shot past me with Marshall and Beth clinging to her back, and she dove and they rode her down. Then she shook them off and kicked to the surface, treading water, her working legs making it look as if she was standing in shallow water.

"Want a ride?" she wondered.

I was too tired. I told her, "Later," and swam toward shore, letting the waves do the hardest work. I came in fast and the beach itself seemed to be pitching beneath me. I blinked and saw Dr. Florida waiting for me. He was wearing office clothes. He didn't have his hat anymore. I saw his sweat in the false sunlight, and he told me, "I'm sorry. An emergency has arrived," and he took a long ragged breath.

I blinked and waited.

He said, "There were other things I wished to tell you, to try to explain . . . but maybe later." He said it hopefully. He said, "You and your friends keep on playing. Don't worry about anything. We've got people watching you, of course, and if you want to leave just go through the door. All right?"

"Dr. Florida—?"

"Yes, Ryder?"

"I was wondering." I could see Jack's arms and head, his strokes slow and disjointed. I explained my concern for him, trying to make Dr. Florida appreciate his circumstances and needs. "Maybe, I was thinking . . . maybe there's something you could do for him? He's not like the rest of his family. Not at all. Ask Cody, sir. She'll tell you. Jack tries to keep away from his brothers, and if he could just get some help—"

Dr. Florida said, "Ryder. Ryder, Ryder," and shook his head.

"If you could, sir—"

He stared at Jack and the others for a long moment, then he took a breath and looked at me. I felt his eyes. Something made me nervous. Then he began to laugh in a strange way. I thought he was close to crying, and he sniffed and said, "Nothing. Forget it."

"What, sir?"

He kept silent.

"I like Jack," I said, "and I was hoping—"

"Ryder? Let me tell you something." He bit his lower lip, then he said, "A lot of people have bad luck. I know you mean well, but trust me . . . I'm doing the best I can for everyone, for you *and* for him, and there simply are things more important than giving a disadvantaged kid a bunch of books. All right?"

I watched him.

"I know. You can't understand." He turned and began to walk across the beach, climbing to the high powdery sand. "But maybe soon you will, the way it looks. Good day to you, Ryder."

"And to you, sir."

He seemed oblivious of me. He had an old man's face and an old man's stooped back, and perspiration dripped from his forehead and hands, glittering and then vanishing into the dry white sand.

SEVEN

"Emergencies happen," cautioned Mom. "You can't expect someone like him, with his schedule, to spend an *entire* day with you."

Dad said, "Gwinn?"

"Gwinn, what?" she responded. "You pumped up his expectations, and now look at him. He's worn out and depressed because of the way things went." She paused, giving Dad a fierce look. Then she sighed. "Anyway, it's over." She nodded and the fierceness dissolved. "Now, can we get back to a normal life, at least?"

I hadn't mentioned my long talk with Dr. Florida, of course. My folks just knew about us eating with him and swimming after he had left us. Jack had gotten tired in the deep water, a warning horn blaring and Cody nabbing him in time. In plenty of time, really. Then Marshall said something to Jack, teasing him when everyone was back on the beach, and Cody had had another fight to dismantle. That's when we decided to go home. Lillith met us in the hallway, saying, "Dr. Florida sent me to say good-bye. He's in a meeting... and he wishes all of you the best and hopes to see you again. Soon."

Dad cleared his throat. "Sounds like some emergency," he said. "The suits-and-ties showing up on that beach like that? Getting him?"

"What about it?" asked Mom. She showed no interest.

"Oh, I'm just thinking." He looked at me, needing an

audience. "I showed a house last week. To a pregnant woman." He shaped a swollen belly with his hands. "Her husband works for some accounting department in one of the local Florida divisions. I don't remember where, but anyway . . . he couldn't see the house too. He was out of town for some emergency, and she didn't know when he'd return. So naturally I asked if he was being transferred. Was it wise buying a bigger home now—?"

"It's her decision," cautioned Mom. "Not yours."

"I forgot to tell you this story, Gwinn." Dad turned to Mom and said, "The woman didn't know his whereabouts. And that was the funny thing. She said no, he'd be home soon. It was just some big secret assignment; she didn't know where or why, but he was supposed to be back in a few days. Or weeks. She said she wasn't worried."

"That's good," said Mom. "So what?"

"I never asked if she was worried. She volunteered the information, as if maybe she was worried. As if she wanted to reassure herself—"

"She didn't know where to find her husband?"

"Not a clue, I guess."

"So he ran off with another woman and she was too proud to say it—"

"Gwinn," said Dad. "I just thought it was funny."

"It's silly." That was Mom's verdict. "Kip," she said, "I never understand the points of your stories."

"So what kinds of secret assignments involve accountants?" Dad shook his head and laughed. "I ask you."

"And I, for one, do not care."

"Oh, Gwinn," he muttered.

"Oh, Gwinn," she echoed.

Dad kept smiling. He touched my closer hand and said, "Anyway, we're glad you had a good time and nobody drowned. I'm sorry if things didn't quite meet expectations—"

"It's all right," I promised.

"You're sure?"

"I'm just tired."

He seemed heartened by that news. "Well, a good night's sleep will fix what ails you."

I nodded, agreeing with him.

Then Mom repeated her fondest hope. "Now life can get back to normal, just maybe," and she sighed. I looked at her blonde hair and her wishful eyes, and I wished the same thing. As hard as I could, I did.

I fought with Marshall over the game, and then that next winter I became best friends with Cody. I did make up with Marshall in the end. I'd go to his house because he'd plead, though we never played war games again. And I insisted that Cody meant more to me now. I wouldn't let him think otherwise.

In spring I went snake hunting with Cody, and she taught me how to find snakes in the growing grass and underbrush and beneath junk and old boards. She showed me how to pin them with my foot or hand and how to bring my hands at them from behind, avoiding their slashing jaws. In the summer we began building our first treehouse. It was in a big ash up above the slabs, overhanging the main trail cutting through the woods. I told Marshall, "You ought to come see it." He was afraid of Cody, and jealous, and the three of us rarely played together. "If Cody lets you," I told him, "you can climb up and help us work."

"I don't know," he muttered.

"She's got all sorts of plans." I was proud of my best friend. "She knows where we can get solar cells, good ones, and super-loops. And maybe a freezer too—"

"Why a freezer?" he asked.

"We'll make snowballs year-round," I said. "For protection."

His eyes went round. "Protection? Who from?"

"Everyone," I assured him. "Maybe you can join us. You can ask!"

Marshall joined. In a fashion. At first he'd pick fights with Cody and then run home crying. It was as if he was testing her patience and anger, calling her names and refusing to help. Cody reacted by popping him or dropping a hammer inches from his feet... anything to make him behave. One day they had a wicked shouting match, and afterwards Cody told me, "You've got an immature friend, Ryder," with her most adult voice. "I'm getting tired of him. Tell him so." I did. Then Marshall returned and they didn't fight as much. He seemed to realize he had reached some brink, and he didn't want to be left alone. Anything but that.

Marshall helped with the work—nailing and sawing, the

treehouse growing—and Cody fixed his blunders without fuss. He made plenty of blunders, but he also had excuses. Of course. Marshall did nothing wrong without good reasons. One day his coordination would fail because of his allergy medicines—the allergies sprang from his special genetics—and another day, in different circumstances, he was distracted because of some hairy math problem he was working in his head. Marshall was always working on problems. He talked about mathematics because Cody had no interest in such things. We tried to ignore him. Or sometimes, when nothing else worked, Cody looked straight at him and said, "It's a good thing you're smart. Otherwise you'd be nothing at all."

Marshall spent an entire day carving equations into a long board, telling us, "These are the bones of the universe. This is how matter and light, and everything, is put together for us."

I felt sorry for Marshall, and so did Cody. Cody told me, "I let him pull shit because it's not all his fault. That bitch mother of his is part of it." She shook her head and said, "My moms tell me stories. Maybe that mother acts sweet around you, Ryder. But she's a terror. Believe me."

We finished the treehouse at the end of the summer—an enormous rambling structure with few windows, little circulation, and nothing fancy—and Cody looked at it and admitted the truth. "We did it wrong," she told us. "The wrong tree and the wrong design, and we've got to start again."

"But school's starting," said Marshall. "We don't have time—"

"Next year," Cody announced. "The three of us will do it right next year," and she turned and glanced at Marshall for a moment, and he smiled and felt ever so glad to be included. He did.

They didn't fight during the fall.

We were playing cards one day, sitting inside our ugly airborne box, and I heard someone coming. I heard a pretty voice singing nothing in particular, and when I glanced outside I saw a dark girl, smallish and alone, passing beneath us. She was walking north on the trail. Marshall asked, "Who's that?" and Cody looked downwards. "Hey," she said. "Little girl. Wait a minute, would you? Hey!"

The strange girl bolted.

We climbed down and chased her. Our card game was

boring, Marshall always figuring odds and strategy; but running the trails on a bright, brisk day felt splendid. The girl used a tiny trail and climbed a set of stairs leading up a stone wall. Cody reached the stairs first, pointing and saying, "She had too much of a lead." The stone wall was massive, every block square and the mortar white as sugar. The stairs themselves had been built from smaller stones, rough and clumsily shaped. A metal handrail was stuck on the outer edge. I climbed the first few steps, curious, and when I touched the rail it moved in a sluggish way. "Don't trust me," it seemed to say. "Don't trust me, and you'll be fine."

I didn't go any farther. I thought there might be trouble.

Marshall was of the same mind, and Cody knew it. "Scout her out," Cody told him. "I bet she lives up there. Go on. Are you chicken? Go on." We watched while Marshall crept up the stairs, then watched him sit at the top, in a suspenseful crouch. Then he wheeled and ran back down to us, almost stumbling. "I saw her," he said. "In a window. Maybe she saw me too. I think so, maybe."

"I bet she's calling the cops," Cody told him.

"You think?!"

Cody giggled, and I did too. I knew she was joking. Then she asked, "So? What did you learn?"

"Well, I think I know her. Sort of. She's in my literature class, and she's new. Her name is Beth . . . Beth Something. Her folks are foreign. Asian. And she's real quiet."

I focused, trying to summon the girl's face from hundreds—

"She's younger than us," said Marshall. "Good at literature and real good at music. But she misses a lot of time from class. A whole lot."

"Why?" asked Cody.

"I don't know," Marshall admitted. "I don't *know her*!"

"Do you remember her, Ryder?"

I found a suitable face, and Marshall said, "Yeah. That's her," when I described the shy pretty face. Afterwards I found myself fascinated. Intrigued. Maybe it was because Beth was pretty in odd ways. Maybe it was her singing. She seemed very much alone to me, and lonely, and I would remember her singing in the woods . . . something tired and sad in the notes. I began to watch her at school, on the sly, and I imagined all sorts of sadnesses in her heart. Compassion would well up inside me, often without warning. I felt she had to have great secrets that made her sad, and endless pains. Sometimes I would sit and recall tiny details about Beth—the angle of her gaze, the pursing of her lips, the dampness of her eyes—and I convinced myself that I knew her in some special, intimate way.

One day, on a blue November afternoon, Cody said, "You know that girl? Beth, was it?"

Marshall said, "What about her?"

"I got the poop from my moms. I know the story." Cody looked at both of us, then she said, "It's pretty crazy. You want to hear—?"

"Yes," we said.

"Well," she said, "okay. Listen."

Beth's folks were *Indians*, it seemed. *The Indians*. They'd come to the States after the civil war, and this was their second house. Or their third. Of course we knew about the war itself, Marshall fancying himself an expert on the subject— naming the enormous battles, the famous generals, and telling us with a matter-of-fact voice that more than one hundred million people died from all sorts of causes. Cody watched him for a minute, then she said, "Shut up." She said, "I'm talking about the big prison camps. What do you know about them?"

Not much, Marshall conceded.

"So shut up!"

There were special camps for special prisoners. The prisoners were fed and clothed and treated with medicines, pampered in most senses, the enemy doctors wanting them healthy. Hospitals were built beside the camps, and when enemy soldiers were injured and in need of spare parts— tissues and organs, glands and living bone—matches were found and plucked from the prisoners. As required.

Those prison camps were quick and easy sources of living matter.

And if the doctors were smart, not taking too much too fast, those poor prisoners could be coaxed into regrowing what was stolen from them. With new medicines. With cloned tissues and such.

Cody explained the grisly business with a steady dry voice, something odd in her eyes. Then she stopped and breathed deeply and said, "That's where her folks come from. Those camps."

Marshall said, "No," stretching out the word. "NNNooooo."

"It's true," she maintained. "That's why they never,

never come outside. They're scarred and sick, and I guess
maybe crazy too. A little bit. Because of all the shitty things
that happened."

"What kinds of scars?" asked Marshall.

She blinked. "They got skinned alive. At least once.
Maybe twice." She paused, then she said, "The doctors made
them grow new skin, only it's not the same. I guess they're
all smooth and shiny and pale—"

Marshall said, "No!"

"It's true."

I remembered stories about these things. But they had
happened a long way away, a long time ago, and nobody liked
talking about them.

"You're telling me what?" Marshall persisted. "Someone
plucked out their guts too. Their kidneys and lungs—?"

"I don't know what else," Cody admitted. She narrowed
her eyes and breathed. "I guess their bug-fighting systems are
shot. The prison doctors had this way of harvesting antibod-
ies. White cells. Those sorts of things."

"That's crazy," declared Marshall. "Why would anyone
do that stuff?"

"I don't know."

"If they wanted skin and stuff, I don't know...they
could have just frozen them whole instead. It would have
been simpler."

"Freezing people whole?"

"Yeah!" said Marshall, forever practical.

"You don't get it!" Cody told him. "Beth's folks were
from the *other side*! They were *hated*! So why kill them neat
and clean? Huh?" She snorted and said, "You don't understand, do you?"

Marshall shrugged.

"I give up," she decided.

Then he said, "No, I understand," with a stiff, lying
voice.

Cody didn't seem to hear him. We were sitting on a
downed tree, Cody at the highest point, her thick legs
dangling and her square face slack and calm.

"You know what we ought to do?" asked Marshall. "Do
you?"

I was thinking about poor Beth. Now I knew her terrible
secret, and it was worse than I could have imagined—a
thousand times worse. I tried imagining my own folks being

so sick and strange, and I couldn't believe anyone might live under such a burden. Not for one day, I thought. Not me, surely. The girl must be an angel. Surely—

"We ought to scout trees for our new treehouse," said Marshall. His face was bright and cheery. "Cody? Ryder? What do you say?"

Cody was thinking about Beth's folks. She said, "No," and lifted her hand into a beam of sunlight. Her meat turned pink on its fringes, and then she put her hand on her lap and said, "Let's just sit awhile. Okay? For a little while."

We had gone to the mansion and the surf room on a Saturday. Sunday morning saw more rain, steady and cold; but then the skies cleared after church and I changed clothes and ate and went down to the oak. Everyone was supposed to meet there. Cody was already working, hammering sheets of tough metal over the surface of the maze. Nobody with a saw was going to break their way inside. Not again. She was hanging in the air, ropes tied to her waist and to the beams of the roof, and she looked as brown as a nut against the shiny metal surfaces, her hair bleached and her hammer pounding with smooth, easy strokes. *Bang-bang-Boom! Bang-bang-Boom!*

I climbed into the big room and looked down at Cody. She said, "Ryder! How was God today?"

"God was fine."

"Great!" *Bang-bang-boom-Boom!* "Do me a favor? Ryder? Check the super-loops. Make sure their juices are up, okay?"

"All right."

There was a tiny hatch in the center of the roof. I popped it open and climbed into the brilliant sunshine. There were no handrails or any substantial branches to hold, and I stood with my knees and back bent, feeling the gentle swaying of the far-below trunk. It was a frightening sensation, and fun.

The roof was built from weathered boards and rain-proofed with clear plastic sheets, and maybe half of it was covered with old-fashioned solar cells, their slick black faces soaking up the light and feeding the old super-loop batteries. Cody had pulled the super-loops from old cars. They were heavy and scattered so their weight didn't buckle a beam. Newer batteries were built from organics, nothing else. Nowadays they were grown in vats, just like people grew steaks and human hearts. They could hold enormous amounts of energy too, almost forever, and they weren't touchy to abuse. Not like our super-loops were touchy. Not at all.

Rain and lightning could make ours fail. I kneeled over each of them, peering at gauges, every needle well into the green zone. The wind gusted one time and pulled my shirt up my sweating back. I pulled it down and sat while my heart pounded, waiting for the wind to cease. I was very close to the edge of the roof, and I happened to notice a certain old board. Marshall had carved his mathematical figures in that board when it was part of the old treehouse. Here they are, I thought. The bones to the universe.

I fingered them for a moment.

Without trying, I recalled what each figure meant and some of what each equation said. Definitions are easy. But for my life I couldn't have appreciated the significance of the equations. Did Marshall really see their deepest meanings? I wondered. I felt the hard old boards under my butt and wondered about Dr. Florida and his talk about the empty skies. If they were truly empty, like he claimed, then only people knew the essence of everything. All the stars and all the galaxies, and it wasn't even people who understood these bones. It was people like Marshall. A few of us. A very few.

I climbed downstairs and found Beth and Jack in the big room. Beth was reading. Jack was making notes on a big sheet of liquid crystal paper. A sack of snakes was between his feet, and when he wasn't writing he was fixing tags to each of their tails. They were last night's catch. "Look." He handed me a thick-bodied bull snake. I held it by the neck, watching its strange, hard eyes, and then he took it back and put it away, tying the sack closed and saying, "You want to see where it bit me?"

"It bit you?"

He stood and said, "Yeah! You want to see?"

I rose and he pulled a trick on me. He made me look at his bare shoulder, freckles but no bites, and when I wasn't ready he popped me with his fingers. I hadn't seen his hand. Then Jack was laughing, saying, "Gotcha!" and I had to sit down.

"You're blushing," said Beth. "Why, Ryder?"

"I don't know."

She looked at Jack and then me. She smiled and went back to her book.

I picked up Jack's snake notes. Touching the paper's corners, I sifted through the pages, the liquid crystals flowing and flowing, remembering hundreds of snakes—

"Eleven hundred and nineteen," said Jack. "Not counting recaptures, of course." He was smiling and proud. "It's taken a year and a half to get that many. And there aren't many that I haven't caught. I bet not."

I said, "Gosh," and let myself get a little lost in Jack's work. I read about garter snakes and bull snakes, ringnecks and milk snakes and king snakes, and so on. Then Marshall was yelling. I blinked and heard him on the ground. "Let me have a rope, would you? I need a rope."

"Marshall needs a rope," cried Cody. She was still hanging in the air, still hammering from time to time. "Someone help him!"

"People? I've got to have help!"

Marshall had brought add-on equipment for the personal. I looked down at him and Beth said, "Here," and dropped one end of a rope. Marshall had the equipment in cardboard boxes, stacked on his old red hover-style wagon, the wagon running, humming and blowing at the pasture's grass. I watched him tie the rope to one box, saying, "There. Now lift it *carefully*," and Jack, standing behind me, said, "Don't warn him, Ryder. But I'm going to show him where the snake bit me. Okay?"

I said, "I won't tell," and smiled inside myself.

The three of us lifted the boxes through the window. Then Marshall came up and started to assemble everything. There were speakers and cable and special electronic gear. He plugged the gear into our personal—an old model, slow and quirky—saying, "I've got this great idea. You know what we'll do, you and me? Ryder?"

"What?"

"We're going to call the dragon. That's what."

I thought for a moment, then I guessed what he meant. "Like someone calls ducks? Is that it?"

"Right." He was grinning. "Remember the screams we heard that first night. All right? We're going to build our own scream with the personal, and we'll pump it through these speakers. Pretty clever, huh?"

He seemed very clever.

"Because the dragon's territorial, I bet. I bet." He punched on the personal and plugged in a couple pairs of headphones. "I'll hang the net right off the oak itself." He started to laugh, saying, "We'll lure it in with its own screams. They'll be the perfect bait—"

"Can I watch?" asked Beth. She smiled, her eyes big and interested. "Ryder? Marshall? Could I come watch?"

Marshall told her, "You can't make *any* noise."

"I won't."

Jack said, "I saw the dragon last night." I thought he was joking. I thought he would say, "It bit me on the shoulder. You want to see the bite, Marshall?"

Only he didn't say that.

Instead he told us, "It was hunting near the almost-pond. I saw it catch a little pig in its mouth and eat it whole. Near midnight."

"Oh yeah?" said Marshall.

"I didn't get close to it. I didn't want to spook it."

"I bet not." Marshall giggled, not believing a word of the story.

"What? You think I'm lying?" Jack laughed and snarled at the same time. "I've watched it plenty of times. Night and day."

Cody grunted. One of her calloused hands gripped a windowsill, and she jerked hard and brought herself up through the window. Her hammer went *bang* on the floor, and she untied her ropes and asked us, "What's going on? Ryder? Jack?" She was watching Jack.

Beth said, "I believe you, Jack. I do."

Marshall ignored everyone. He was wearing the headphones, concentrating on sounds while he punched buttons. His eyes were fixed on some far point, and his head was cocked to one side. "Ryder?" he said. "Listen to this. Does this sound close?"

Jack said, "It won't work," with his voice soft.

"What did you say?" asked Marshall.

"What did you say?" asked Cody. "Jack?"

"That it'll work," he answered. "I've got a feeling."

Marshall nodded. "Yeah, I got the idea last night." I couldn't think of a time when he was half this happy. "Out of the blue. I just got it."

"Can I watch too?" asked Jack. "Please, Marshall?"

"All right. Sure." He had no enemies today. No pains,

and no suspicions. "Sit here, Ryder. Wear this and listen." He told me to recall the screams we had heard, and he showed me how to use the dials to coax the right sound from the machinery. "You got it? You understand?" I could scarcely hear him speaking, the headphones snug around my ears and humming like air squeezed from a tiny leak.

The scream became truer every time.

I began to feel as if the dragon was calling to me, saying something meant for me. Then I removed the headphones and warned Marshall, "We can't just play it over and over again."

"Why not?"

"Dogs don't bark the same way twice," I explained. "You don't say, 'Ryder!' with the same exact voice. There have to be little—"

"Fluctuations!" he said. "From the norm, sure!"

"I guess so."

He seized the idea, changing the program. Then the scream was ready, nearly perfect, and everyone wanted to hear it for themselves.

"Cute," said Cody.

Jack said, "That's it, all right."

"When have you heard it?" asked Marshall.

"Some nights when I'm hunting," he confessed. "Plenty of times."

Beth tilted her head and pressed an ear against the headphones. She listened to the scream and then began to sing, bending the dragon's call into something bubbling and sweet.

"Everyone can come," Marshall told us. "Tonight. But I'm going to hold the trigger string, and you people are just helping me. All right? You've got to promise to keep quiet and out of my way—"

"You're such a jerk," said Cody.

Beth kept singing the scream.

Marshall crossed his arms, saying nothing. He was too happy to be insulted by anyone now.

"Just don't be such a jerk," said Cody. "Please?"

Marshall glanced at me, and I knew what he was thinking. He was imagining the thousand dollars his folks would give him, and he was hopelessly proud of his cleverness, and he could almost feel the snow dragon in his two hands—

"I had a good time yesterday," said Jack. "Ryder?"

"Yeah," said Cody, "thanks for inviting us, Ryder."

Dr. Florida had invited them, I started to correct them—

"It was great meeting him," Beth admitted. "I think that was the best part of it. Don't you guys think so?"

Everyone nodded. Yes, it was the best part.

Then Jack said, "A fish bit me when I was swimming—"

"When you were drowning?" snapped Marshall. He smiled at his wit and put the headphones snug over his ears.

"Don't you want to see?" asked Jack. He rose and stared at Marshall, one hand pulling up his short shirtsleeve. "It's an ugly bite—"

"Show me," said Cody. She jumped to her feet and stood beside him. "Go on."

Jack gulped. His hand was dangling between Cody's legs, and I knew he wouldn't do anything. Then I knew she knew what he might have done. "I don't see anything," said Cody. "You must have healed."

"I guess so."

"You must be eating right, huh?" She glared at him, her eyes cold and hard and never blinking. I decided something was going on besides the words. What else was I seeing? I blinked and looked at Beth, but she was looking at me, not them. And Marshall wasn't aware of any of it, leaning forward in his chair and playing that scream again and again, his daydreams practically visible in the way his eyes danced and his head rocked and his soft hands played baby games with one another.

The moon was half full, a little past straight overhead, and the scream was going to begin in a minute. Beth was sitting beside me. We were in the underbrush close to the oak. The big binoculars were cradled in my hands, and every so often I would lift them and peer between the branches, catching quick partial glimpses of the moon itself.

I couldn't find the moon's moon.

I did see the faint green smudges of the big farms, however. They showed on the night side of the moon, lit by their own stored sunshine and obvious against the inky darkness. Those farms lay in a belt about the moon's waist, built from the dead comet's precious guts. I recalled Dr. Florida's tales of impacting comets and worlds destroyed, and I was so very thankful he had corralled this particular comet.

For a moment I tried picturing a future age, wondrous and safe, when every comet was corralled and the moon and Mars and Venus were fat with water and with happy, safe people, and I set the binoculars on the ground, smiling to myself, feeling certain that that age was surely coming.

Every so often Beth would squeak a note, or a half note, catching herself before she actually sang. Cody and Jack were somewhere on the opposite side of the oak, sitting apart and hiding. Marshall was squatting behind the oak's trunk, on its side, the trigger string in both hands. We had piled brush and old boards on the slope below, burying the speakers and their wires, and the net was overhead, suspended and ready, and any time now we would hear the first false screams beckoning to the dragon.

There was an excitement to the scene. A delicious suspense. I was aware of little motions and the swelling buzz of insects, and I worked to keep alert and ready. I wouldn't get lost, I told myself. I was eager and part of things and I wouldn't—

—the scream!

It was too loud. I trembled and hugged myself, thinking all the wild parkland must have heard the sound. The insects stopped their buzzing for a long moment, in respect. Then they started again and I could scarcely hear anything else. I felt Beth's hand take mine and the warm moist skin of her palm and fingers squeezed hard. She said, "You're shaking, Ryder," with her mouth close to my ear. "Don't shake." I couldn't help myself, however. All at once I was remembering something . . . this place and Beth tripping some switch in my head.

We had had a rare blizzard, and afterwards the wind was still ripping from the north and Cody called me and asked if I wanted to meet her at the almost-pond and help shovel it clean. I had said, "Okay," and dressed and crossed the pasture, following Cody's prints in the new snow. I had passed beneath the then-empty oak—this very ground—and I saw again the bright white bottoms and the woods beyond. I left Cody's trail so I could walk beside the woods. I paused at one of the stone basins, smelling the warm sweet water, and suddenly I looked up and saw Beth standing beside a massive cottonwood tree, out of the wind. She said, "Hi," and I gave a little jump, startled. She blinked and smiled, saying, "Hi," once again.

I said, "Hello," with the wind pulling away my white breath.

"I've seen you," she confessed. "You're down here a lot, aren't you?"

"I guess."

She told me her name. She seemed small and very pretty, but she wasn't so shy anymore. And not nearly as mysterious. I felt warm when I looked at her face. I told her my name, and she repeated, "Ryder," aloud. Then we spoke for several minutes, the conversation small and bland. All the countless hours spent thinking about Beth and her amazing circumstances—me envisioning her as being one sort of person, sad and profound—and yet now she seemed like anyone else. I asked why she had run away from me, from us, that day last fall. "Was that you? All I heard was someone shouting at me!" She had an ordinary voice, not at all foreign, and she told me she had always been in the States. She made no mention of her poor folks. Instead she told me some ordinary jokes and talked about school with the same giggling voice any girl would use. She admitted to being shy, yes. "But I'm getting better," she told me. "I'm just not comfortable around people right away, see?" She seemed pleasant and contented, and I was disappointed. All those terrible tragedies—her folks living sad, painful lives and her trapped in that house with them. I felt cheated, and I felt a little angry. I had put so much time and compassion into her plight, and here she stood giggling. She was telling some story about a funny teacher and how a classroom personal had been reprogrammed to curse every so often...and I did something stupid. I couldn't help myself. I looked at Beth and wondered aloud, "Why don't your folks go outside? Huh?"

She blinked, startled. "They can't," she told me. "They're sick a lot, you see. They can't."

"Why are they sick?"

Beth watched me. "Reasons," she said, and she shrugged.

"They were in prison, weren't they?"

She didn't speak.

"And you take care of them. Don't you?"

"Sometimes."

I asked, "Why aren't you taking care of them now? Huh?"

"Because they're fine—"

"You're sure?" She wasn't special. I had envisioned Beth

as being such a good person. Tireless. Saintly. But she could
be any kid, it seemed to me. She didn't want to talk about
her sick folks, and that wasn't right. I said, "Maybe they need
you now. Maybe."

"They don't."

"How do you know?"

She opened her mouth, but she made no sound.

I told her, "I'm glad you don't take care of me."

"Why?" she squeaked.

"Because you're not doing much of a job, I think." I was
angry, barely able to think.

"Why are you so cruel? You're just wicked—"

"Are you ashamed of them?" I felt wonderfully cruel and
angry.

"Who?" she wondered. "Who do you mean?"

"Your folks. I bet you're ashamed—"

"Will you stop?" she sobbed. "Please?!"

And then I felt awful. My anger evaporated, and I
realized just how terrible I must have sounded. All at once. It
wasn't me who had been talking. Not the real me. I had been
carrying this perfect image of Beth inside myself, and this
Beth had seemed so...I don't know...run-of-the-mill. Ordinary. Unworthy of my admiration...

Beth turned and fled, crunching through the snow.

She must have been crying, and I stood watching her
retreat, feeling wicked and tainted and foolish. It was my
fault, all mine, and I was so stupid. So thoughtless. Then
some distant part of me said, "You're lost, Ryder. Ryder?
Blink hard and come back, Ryder. Come on." Which I did. I
blinked and focused and found myself sitting in the underbrush again, in the spring, and nothing was changed, but a
coat of guilt lay over me like new paint...and I blinked
again, trying to shake free the guilt. Trying to peel it off me.

—the scream!

It seemed louder this time, and closer, and I felt it
through my bones and my teeth and the sockets of my eyes. I
held my breath for a long, cold moment, trying to concentrate, wondering how long I had been lost. Not too long, I
decided. This was the second scream, wasn't it? I felt Beth
next to me and nearly asked. Then I heard something moving, and I tensed and realized it was the wind in the trees.

Relax, I told myself. Relax. I glanced at the oak and saw Marshall pressed against the trunk, waiting—

—then the scream!

Only it came early. I was certain it was early—that was my first thought—and I blinked and knew that the sound had come from across the weed-choked bottoms, from the woods, and it wasn't so loud this time. There was something alive in that voice, challenging everything and everyone to make way. Beware! This wasn't amplified synthesized sound, no. It was from a flesh-and-bone throat, from muscles and lungs. I could very nearly understand its intent; and I sat motionless, never blinking, knowing the dragon was shouting at me. *Back off! Blow off! Don't screw with me!*

Our own scream repeated itself.

I could find differences, subtle but distinctive. The speakers distorted the sound just slightly, and maybe the dragon would mark the differences and hold its voice—

—no! It answered at once, no hesitations. I shuddered and turned to my right, the scream coming from somewhere north of the bottoms. I blinked and wondered if it was circling us, listening and measuring and maybe approaching us. Maybe not. Beth stirred beside me, grasping my hand once again. She understood. And Marshall did too. I saw his face moving, his expression tense in the broken moonlight; and our scream came again, clumsy and false and shattering the night sounds.

Beth squeezed my hand.

The unseen dragon answered us after a short moment. It was closer now! No doubts! I heard its voice carry off the pasture, from straight behind us, and I imagined it slipping through the high grass with its big triangular head lifting to survey the scene. The tension was bracing. I quit thinking about Beth and my guilt, wondering what if the dragon was crawling toward us now? The wind made branches nod again, and I nearly jumped. Then I breathed and bit my lip and waited, the fear diminishing to fun again. And again our personal screamed.

The quarry answered. I thought I heard a certain fury— that was my first thought—and then I realized the dragon was toward the south now, very close. Beth pushed her arm against me and held her breath and straightened her back, starting to tremble. I watched the bottoms. The weeds were fat with sunlight and rainwater, and something low-built and sleek was passing through those weeds. I heard a gentle rustling and saw seedy heads nodding, ever so slightly nodding, and I held my breath and focused and saw the big white rattlesnake head emerge at the base of the slope. In the dull moonlight its fur had a lustrous quality, almost a glow, and I thought of milk and new snow and bright white cotton, watching it pull itself into the open now. I could see all of the dragon.

It had grown through these last weeks—a foot was added to its length, and bulk to its muscled sides. I didn't breath. I waited. It wasn't quite beneath the net, not yet, and Marshall moved the trigger string ever so slightly. Our scream rose from the pile of brush and rubbish. The dragon answered the challenge at once, lifting its great head and opening its mouth and roaring. It moved forward when it roared, probably by reflex, and I can still see Marshall jerking the trigger string and the dragon catching that motion—or maybe smelling a human scent on the breeze—and it dove backwards into the high weeds. The net was tumbling, spreading until huge and catching nothing. The dragon was gone, and Marshall was up and charging hard down the slope. "There!" he shouted. "Don't let it . . . there!" Cody and Jack boiled out of their hiding places, Jack saying, "I told you. I said so. He couldn't catch it." He was talking to Cody, and Cody said, "Shut up." Beth and I rose and went down to the empty net, and she bumped me so I could feel her hard breast against my elbow, for a long moment, and when the breast was gone she said, "Let's go look for it? Okay? Ryder? Okay?"

I had a flashlight snapped to my belt. I took it and pulled the beam in every direction, searching for motion and confident we wouldn't see the dragon again. We were walking toward the northwest, roughly toward Beth's house, and Beth stopped and said, "Hear them? Can you?" The others were a long way off, their voices muffled by the trees. I listened to Marshall cursing his luck, I saw a weak flash of light and then a bug bit me on the back of my hand.

I swatted it.

Beth was close to me. I smelled her breath and felt the heat from her body for a moment, and then the guilt began tugging at me again. I couldn't help but remember how shabbily I had treated her, and it didn't seem like something in the past. I felt sick inside. I felt weak and sorry, but I couldn't speak—

"Anyway," said Beth.

I shifted my weight and waited.

Then she said, "The time," and passed her glowing watch in front of my face. "I should go home, I think."

I looked at Beth.

"Walk me?"

I said, "Okay," and we cut through the woods to her staircase. We climbed the uneven steps in a cautious, practiced way, the ground falling away and the tree branches close enough to touch. Beth said, "Ryder?"

I stopped and asked, "What?"

"Nothing," she said.

We climbed to within a step of her back fence and gate and yard, and she tugged at my belt with one hand, saying, "Let's rest," and then she said, "Look at everything. Isn't it pretty?"

We were level with the treetops. The moon seemed brighter now, and I wished I hadn't left my binoculars under the oak. I would have liked a long look at the moon. Again I felt Beth's hand on my wrist, and suddenly I remembered the day a couple years ago when Marshall brought his newest friend to meet us. "This is Beth, everyone." They had become friends in their literature class. Cody and I were working on the new treehouse, Cody carrying the first long boards into the oak; and Beth looked at me and said, "I know Ryder," with a hard, quiet voice.

"Do you?" asked Marshall, irritated to find his introduction spoiled. "From where?"

"Somewhere," she said.

I made no sound.

She told Marshall, "He's a cruel boy. I know him well."

"Cruel?" Marshall shook his head. "Oh, no! You're wrong, Beth!" I was amazed by his conviction, and I felt so unworthy. "Ryder's a whole lot better than any of us! He is!"

"He's cruel!"

"No no no!"

"Ryder?" said Beth.

I blinked, returning to the present.

"Are you cold?" she asked. "You're shaking now."

I felt so terribly cold. I was leaning against the smooth stone wall, and Beth got on the step above me and hugged me and rubbed my closer arm, saying, "There, there," with satisfaction. "You're okay."

I found myself crying.

"Tell me," she said. "What is it?"

"I'm sorry. I'm just so sorry—"

"For what, Ryder?" She didn't understand. She had forgiven me long ago, in a series of gradual easy steps, and I knew there was no point in telling her what I was remembering. It wasn't real anymore. Not for her. It was something forgotten, and gone...

It was just the past...

EIGHT

Dad was watching the news and Mom was beside him, her eyes shut and her head resting on a fluffy lemon-colored pillow. I was on the floor, a book unrolled on my lap, but my eyes were fixed on the TV the moment someone mentioned shuttles to the moon's moon. The reporter was a stocky woman with make-up and a rough voice. She stood at the entrance to Dr. Florida's private launch facility in Hawaii. Uniformed guards were staring while she told us that over twelve hundred passengers—an enormous number—had embarked for the moon's moon during the last weeks. All of them were employees of Dr. Florida's, and recent unconfirmed reports stated that there were significant irregularities in the records kept. Dad said, "Gwinn," once, softly. Mom lifted her head and started to speak, and he told her, "Quiet. Listen," and nodded at the big flat screen.

The reporter mentioned U.N. regulations and how *all* space traffic was suppose to be monitored. She couldn't name sources or culprits, but she told us that several Florida companies had falsified a certain number of cargo manifests—

"What is this?" asked Mom.

"I don't know," Dad confessed. "Shush!"

"An investigation is under way," said the reporter, "and while not admitting to any wrongdoing on anyone's part, U.N. officials are quick to call the violations minor and assure the press that there is no danger to public health or public concerns. The irregularities likely mean nothing, one official told me. And a Florida spokeswoman is certain the issue will be resolved in a few weeks. At the most."

"That's a lot of people," said Dad. "Twelve hundred? What do you suppose our dear friend is doing with them?"

He meant Dr. Florida, I realized.

Mom asked, "Why make a point of saying there's no danger?"

"I don't know, love. To avoid needless worry, perhaps?"

Mom was sitting upright. "Remember your story about the wife and the absent husband? Kip?"

"I sure do."

"Well," she said, "do you suppose he's one of the twelve hundred?"

"Could be."

"Has he come home yet?"

"I don't know. Honestly." Dad paused, stroking his mouth with a fingertip. "I know she was getting messages from him. He was fine and happy, and so on. Full of reassurances."

I sat motionless, thinking to myself.

"It's nothing," Dad cautioned. "What do you bet?"

"Oh, I know," Mom nodded, but her eyes were concerned nonetheless. After a moment she made herself smile, then giggle. "Do you suppose it's going to fall? Maybe?"

"What's falling, dear?"

"The moon's moon. Maybe those people are trying to keep it from tumbling down—"

Dad saw the joke and laughed. Then he said, "Ryder? Ryder? Can you explain to your mother about orbits and gravity? Please?"

I felt so very strange. "Can I go to bed now please?" I asked.

They looked at me for a moment, then Mom said, "Of course, dear."

"Good night," I told them, and I rose and left.

They told me, "Good night," with one voice. I climbed the stairs, sports scores and commercials rising after me; and I undressed and slid under the sheets, thinking hard, trying to focus and remember clues from everywhere. Dr. Florida's tiredness and moods seemed important. I thought of Lillith's empty stares. Then I brought back that moment on the pasture, Dr. Florida telling Lillith to tell John—Dr. Samuelson? —to find three more teams. Teams of what? What could it mean? I wondered. My clues were like crooked branches in a tree. After a lot of good hard thinking, I was full of possible clues; but all I could see was a shadowy tangle without the faintest sense. None.

Marshall wasn't sad for long about the dragon's escape. He had lured it in with his cleverness, after all, and that was something to tell people. The same as he told people about us going to Dr. Florida's and sharing lunch with the man. Two things worth bragging about for weeks. At least. And maybe— no, positively—he could lure in the dragon again and nab it this time. Net it and put it in a box and bring it up to school to show the kids and everyone.

The two of us were sitting in the big room, and Marshall was patching the net. It was stretched out on the floor, with a ragged hole near one edge. I bent forward and touched the frayed ends of the fabric, and he admitted, "I did it. With the clawed end of a hammer."

"Why?"

"Because I told *her* that I got it into the net." He meant his mother. I knew because he stiffened a little bit and halfway smiled. "I told her it ripped loose." He paused, then he said, "I pretty much lied, huh?"

"Why?"

"Because she bought the net for me," he said and shrugged. "I don't know why I did it. I don't know."

Just the two of us went hunting the next time. Marshall didn't want any excess noise, he claimed. But despite our silence and Marshall's new confidence, we only managed to make the dragon scream at us from across the bottoms. We couldn't coax it closer . . . not after an hour of trying . . . Marshall fiddling with the scream and the volume and me thinking: "It knows better now. It's gotten wise to us."

"I've got a better plan anyway," said Marshall. "For the next time."

The next time we crossed the bottoms and hung the net where he had hung it the first night. Marshall had rigged a model car with a speaker, plus a tape of the scream, and he had rigged a phony dragon around the car body. It was long and white, made of tough paper and plastic, and it was silly. Nothing was going to be fooled, and I had to tell him so. "We'll see," he said with a brittle confidence. "We'll just wait and give it a chance. All right, Ryder? All right."

Nothing answered. Not once. It was a warm night full of sucking bugs and biting bugs, and I swatted myself a hundred times. For all I knew the dragon was watching us from the shadows, laughing to itself. After a while the silly car tipped and smashed itself on the slabs. Marshall cursed and stomped for a moment, then he lifted a chunk of gray concrete over his head and crushed the car and everything. "Okay," he said. "All right. I'll just figure something else."

"It's too bad," I admitted. "Maybe next time."

He sucked air through his teeth. "No problem," he said.

I shrugged my shoulders.

"Anyway, I'm glad you're sticking with me, Ryder." Marshall nodded and gave me a long look. He wasn't going to let himself be unhappy. He said, "That's the important thing. I can trust you."

I was hunting for Cody after school, but her house personal said, "No one's home, Ryder. I'm sorry."

"Tell her I'm at the oak for a while?"

"I promise, and good day to you." It was a summer-hot day, brilliant and dry. The dry white dust rose while I walked down the graveled road, taking my time, then out of the corner of my eye I saw one of Jack's brothers. He was standing on the back porch, fingers cocked inside his belt loops. He was watching me, I realized, and I began to pick up my pace.

"Hey!" he shouted. "Don't fucking run on me!" He waved and said, "Get over here, kid. Hey, I'm not going to kill you." He laughed and said, "I just want to fucking talk a minute, okay?"

I turned and blinked, holding my ground.

"Yeah, you!" He was a tall, lean young man dressed like a shabby boy. He had Jack's face and a weak beard and the Wellses' wiriness too. Something about him made me feel cold. He smiled and waved and said, "What the fuck are you scared of, kid? Come here. Right now. I got a question to ask."

I walked to the old fence encircling their yard—a thing built from wooden posts and hog wire and partly flattened by the vines and brush growing through it. He shuffled toward me. What could he do to me? I wondered. It was daylight and I was ready to run, on my toes and halfway leaning to one side. I almost wished he would make a grab for me, just so his intentions would become clear.

I was scared.

I was ever so alert.

"What question?" I asked, my mouth dry as the road itself.

He said, "I've got a friend," and he coughed into his balled-up fist. His eyes were red and sleepless, but he spoke as if he was sober and straight. "The friend's got a buddy who works maintenance out at the big house. You know. The mansion? Florida's?"

I nodded.

"So I thought maybe you'd know, one way or another." Jack's brother blinked and said, "What with you and His Majesty being so tight."

I waited.

"This maintenance guy? He's been telling stories. Crazy things. He says people at the mansion are talking about something going on inside the moon's moon. Some sort of wildfire burning." He paused and looked straight at me, his tongue pressed against one cheek. He said, "I don't know. Maybe Florida hasn't said anything. But I figure you're a clever kid. Aren't you? Like my shit-for-brains brother thinks he's clever? So tell me. How can a fucking fire burn in outer fucking space?"

I said, "It can't."

"You don't sound too sure to me." He breathed, his breath hot and sour. We were several feet apart, and I blinked when the smell hit me. He said, "What I was thinking... I was thinking maybe this moon's moon is full of weird chemicals. It's a comet, right? Comets are full of oils and that sort of shit. And Florida's got all that machinery up there doing the mining for him, and maybe... well, who knows what?"

"I don't think it can burn," I admitted. "The comet."

"Maybe not. I don't know." He didn't want to debate the point. "I just think it's fucking crazy to push things around in the sky. You know? Someone could do something stupid, and then what?" He jabbed his own temple with a long finger, telling me, "Florida's got those genius genes, sure. But don't think he can't screw up. No matter what he's got for brains, let me tell you... all of us are pretty damned stupid. You just think about that, okay?"

I started to nod.

"You think I'm right, squirt?"

"I guess so," I said.

"I fucking guess so." He laughed and grinned, saying, "You're not so bad a shit. Not a snob like most kids." He reached for his back pocket. "Tell you what. Let me slip you a little sip of something. Just the thing to put hair on your cock—!"

I eased away from the fence.

"Hey, kid!" He laughed and turned and slapped his butt. "Nothing in the pockets, I guess. Sorry." Then he farted with force, laughing louder and shouting, "Run, kid! Run! It's a goddamn chemical spill!"

I turned and fled, racing through the pasture, and the ugly laughter faded into the wind sounds on the grass. Nobody was chasing me. I was alone, running because it was fun to slip through the grass, watching the bugs and moths and grasshoppers leaping out of my way. I caught one of the grasshoppers, then another, and I stopped long enough to press their faces together, their strong front legs starting to wrestle. Then I tossed them into the air. They were springtime hoppers, small and green, and they flew without weight or strength, the gusting wind catching them and carrying them over into the trees.

I turned and looked back at the Wellses' house.

Nobody was outside. I remembered how empty it had seemed for years and years, spooky in a harmless way, and then the Wellses had arrived in their old cars, their possessions stacked high and tied down with knotted straw-colored ropes. That's when I saw Jack for the first time—ill-dressed and tiny next to the others. The house had seemed neater when it was empty, I realized. In a matter of hours, after much cursing and two fights between brothers, the Wellses had settled and a strange volatile quality hung in the air. The four of us were building our treehouse; it was summer. We sat on the treehouse's new bones, wondering aloud what might be happening inside the white walls. There were odd parties at unusual hours. Feral young women arrived, and we heard the harsh music mixed with shouts, and sometimes a beer bottle would sail out a window, shattering on the graveled road. I remembered Cody's mothers telling about radios being stolen and tools lost and wallets misplaced and then found empty in street gutters. It was the Wellses who were to blame, of course.

Everyone knew it, and we were part of everyone. They were the sworn enemies of the neighborhood, and we would watch them to keep track of them . . . and because they were so different and fascinating, at least to us.

One night we were in Cody's bedroom. Marshall was playing a game against Cody and me. Beth was reading. Cody's mother May knocked and came inside. "Do me a favor? Stay away from the windows, okay?" Her pretty face was excited about something. Not scared, but concerned. We asked what was happening, and she told us there was trouble across the street. "At the Wellses' place," she said, and she left us.

Of course Cody turned off the lights and lifted a window shade. We were curious. Police cars lined the street, red lights spinning, and Cody said, "Quiet," and nudged open the window. "Shush."

The humid summer air poured inside. Jack's father was standing on the porch—a loud, harsh man who was lean but for the considerable gut over his belt. His beard was gray and ragged, his hair gray and ragged, and he was staggering whenever he moved, I thought he must be ill. He raised his arms over his head, then he dropped them and said, "He takes he gives he rises and falls to the bumpy places," with every word slurred.

"What's the matter with him?" asked Beth.

"Drugs in his blood," said Cody. "Quiet."

The police approached Mr. Wells. One of them said, "We have a warrant to search your home, sir—"

"The sun the sun the sun!" he shouted. "Look!"

"Crazy talk," mumbled Marshall.

A policeman said, "Let us pass, sir. Please."

Mr. Wells wobbled, stumbled and then righted himself with a sudden strange poise. His back was straight and I saw his face in the porch light. Later, knowing more about the world, I would remember that face and realize that he wasn't drunk or drugged. He was pretending.

"Mice!" he snapped. "Mice mice mice!"

"Sir—?"

"God's sweet cheese!" He staggered forward and stomped at the porch steps, trying to crush phantom mice. He seemed to be rushing the line of policemen, and they shot him several times. I heard the rush of air and saw one of the darts smack home on his chest. He straightened for a moment, then he moaned and tumbled. He was lying on his back, on the sidewalk, and the policemen handcuffed him and brought out the rest of the family. Jack was among them. One brother was missing. I watched Jack standing apart from the rest, his fists trying to stuff themselves into his pants pockets, and later, wiser, I would remember his hard eyes and the defiant expression on his face. He was already staking out his independence.

The house was searched several times, nothing was found, and Mr. Wells vanished into jail for the night. For disorderly conduct.

Then came the rumors. Cody's mothers heard every rumor, of course, and they repeated the one that smelled truest. It seemed the missing brother had been seen slipping out the back of the house two seconds before the police cars arrived. He had grabbed a shovel and carried a box under one arm, running into the parkland, and when the police were gone again he emerged from the woods with just the shovel. No box. And no one knew where the box might be buried. Or what might be inside it.

"We could dig it up," said Cody. "Just think! We could do it now."

"You'll get into trouble," cautioned Beth. She shook her head and told us to think first. So we sat and thought and three of us thought it was a fine idea. Marshall and Cody slipped little garden shovels into their shirts, and we left Beth at Cody's house. We walked past the Wellses' house and felt terribly clever and bold. My job was to hunt for ground that had been disturbed. Was there some place recently worked by a shovel? I warned them, "I can't walk everywhere. He could have gone anywhere."

"It'll be in the woods," said Cody. She smiled and told us, "There might be a reward or something. Just think!"

We crossed the bottoms and climbed the tilted slabs, and I found a small patch of freshly turned ground. Marshall took two bites with his shovel, then stopped and stepped backwards. "Maybe we shouldn't."

"Why not?" asked Cody.

"They might . . . see us." He meant the Wellses. "They might—"

"So?" asked Cody. "What'll they do? Kill us?"

Marshall shook his head. He was sweating like a runner.

"I'm not staying, guys." He put down the shovel with both hands, and he said, "Are you coming with me? Ryder?"

"No." I felt safe with Cody, and I said so.

Cody said, "Enough talk. Let's dig," and she smiled at me. Marshall melted into the trees, and the two of us got on our knees and began flinging the soft soil to either side. I was wondering what the brother had buried in the hole. Something stolen? Drugs, maybe? Or what? I took a deep breath and stabbed with the blade, and something went *thunk* with a forbidding hollow sound.

Cody said, "Great!" and swept away the loose earth. "A box, all right. Look at it!"

She lifted the box from the hole and looked everywhere. She even glanced up into the trees. It was an ordinary box of pressed wood and plastic seams, and its lid was fastened with a single bent nail.

I asked, "What about booby traps? Bombs?"

"Then we're dead," she said simply. She gripped the nail and jerked once, straightening it, and then she bent low and hunted for wires or other triggers, smiling and saying, "Now watch."

The lid creaked as it opened.

I looked inside. Wrapped inside thick plastic, snugly secured, was a small dead dog halfway rotted to nothing.

The stink of the rot welled up into our faces, and we coughed. Cody said, "Shit," and slammed the lid down and laughed. Then she rebent the nail and eased the box back into its hole, always laughing. Then we kicked the dirt back over everything and tamped it flat, and we pulled twigs and dead leaves over the grave, thinking that was right, working hard to make certain that it resembled nothing but the surrounding forest floor.

I was at school a couple days after talking to Jack's brother. It was my morning algebra class, and I was wrestling with problems. The answers evaded me, but I wouldn't let myself cheat—remembering a solution from somewhere else, say, or finding a similar problem stored in my head. Those would be cheating tricks... so I poked and picked at one problem, then at another, accomplishing nothing until the school principal's voice came over the intercom.

Every teacher was to meet in the auditorium, she said. At once, no delays.

There was an odd nervousness to the voice, I thought. A shakiness that I didn't recognize. Our own teacher was gone for twenty minutes, and I sat and pretended to work, fooling the personals while I thought about a tangle of things. Our teacher came back into the room—a small, homely woman with white hair and a sudden nervousness of her own—and I watched her standing at the head of the class, mustering courage, then clearing her throat and saying, "People? People? Please look up at me, people."

No one made a sound.

"You'll hear this soon enough on the news," she told us, "and I want you to understand. Are you listening to me? There's been an accident in space, out at the moon's moon." She paused, weighing words. Then she said, "It's a sad disaster, actually. Very sad. People have been injured, and some killed—"

I turned cold and dead inside myself.

"A lot isn't known," she admitted. "But every network is broadcasting news, and maybe we'll learn something soon. We can pray it's not too terribly bad."

"How many people killed?" asked one boy.

"I don't know," she said, her voice level and careful. Then she took a deep breath. "We'll have to wait and see. I'm sorry."

A girl beside me asked, "Is Dr. Florida all right?"

"Pardon me?" asked our teacher.

A boy wondered, "Was he up at the moon's moon, ma'am?"

She said, "No." She shook her head and told us, "I'm sure they would have said something . . . if he was . . ."

But I knew he wasn't. Dr. Florida didn't travel in space anymore; he had told me that fact. I nearly said something to my neighbors, and then I stopped myself. I caught my tongue and for some reason kept myself from reminding people that I knew Dr. Florida, personally knew him, and that he was my friend and I was his confidant—

"Ryder?" whispered a boy beside me. "Ryder? Why are people so weird? It's a long ways away." He waved his hand toward space. "Ryder? Who cares what happens on the moon's moon? Huh?"

They were little kids in this class. I was the oldest,

slowest student, and some days I felt huge and ancient and wise among them. I explained to him that the moon's moon belonged to Dr. Florida, and it was important for many, many people. I thought of the man with the pregnant wife, then I told him that maybe, just maybe, local people were among the dead. It was possible. And then... then I clamped down on my tongue again. I had this awful swelling sense that something enormous was beginning to show itself. And maybe our teacher had the same sense. I watched her standing at the window for the rest of the hour, her eyes fixed on the outdoors, and she didn't once notice the kids talking among themselves, algebra forgotten, or even blink when the bell trilled and it was time for us to rise and leave.

We heard the truth in bits and pieces through the long day.

There was always one kid in every class who knew something authentic, from peeking at a TV or from a tiny hideaway radio plugged into an ear. He or she would always tell this knowledge with a sober, breathless voice. It was astounding and forever surprising news, and even the tiniest kids in my classes would listen intently. No embellishments were required. And no theatrics, either. Our teachers would stop their work too, perhaps adding what they knew for themselves. Then they would take away any radios, out of tradition, and when they thought nobody was looking they would tuck the little things into their own ears, out of sight...

Debris was raining down from the moon's moon, puncturing some of the big farming domes on the moon itself. One kid reported how the moon's moon looked different. It was missing a couple chunks of its lumpy black surface, and the insides were visible to telescopic cameras. What were its insides? we asked. What could they see? "Crystal things sprouting hairs," we heard. "That's what they looked like to me." He breathed and thought, then he tried describing it in detail. "You know? Like a bunch of dark, dark diamonds with all these real long silvery hairs—"

"Just some inner structure," our teacher assured us. "The explosions must have exposed the mine itself."

One girl told of the moon's government declaring an emergency, all shuttle flights canceled until whenever. She wasn't sure for how long. And the militia was being activated in all the lunar cities for the first time in history, and food and water were already being rationed. Why was the militia being used? we wondered. Who needed soldiers now? Our history teacher—a smallish man with fiery eyes and a squeaky voice—explained how crowds needed to be controlled, hoarders found and punished, and the social order maintained. He reminded us of the delicate hold people had on the moon. It wasn't the earth with free air and easy water. Maybe more farming domes would be punctured by falling debris . . . and then what? "Anarchy!" he cried, lifting a finger to the ceiling. "They have to take a hard stand against such a thing. Against panic!" His fiery eyes began to water, and his upthrusted finger started to shake.

Later in the day, in science class, a boy reported some craziness he had overheard. "There's something loose inside the moon's moon." He paused, swallowed and said, "That's what started it, they think."

"Who thinks?" we asked.

"The government. The people on TV. Everyone. They say it's some sort of infestation—"

The teacher laughed in a gentle, disarming way. "An infestation? Are you sure you didn't hear some other word?" She herself hadn't been following events, busy to tears with her students; but she felt confident enough to tell us not to be concerned. "This is all very bad, yes," she said. "It's easily the worst disaster in space history, and I know we'll always remember today. But an infestation? I don't think so, no. No."

The boy told us, "That's what I heard. I'm sure—"

"All right." The teacher gave a challenging smile. "An infestation of fruit flies? Cheese mold? What?" There were scattered laughs, then she said, "Of what? Tell us."

The boy rocked in his chair, admitting, "I don't know, ma'am."

"The moon's moon is a mining camp, nothing more. The only thing *I* can guess is that some strange alien life form has been living inside the moon's moon. But does that stand to reason? No. No, because why hasn't the life form been seen before now? They've been tunneling for years, and nothing. Nothing. And now this explosion? No, it's a simple bad accident of some kind or another. It's not a biological infestation, thank God."

The boy said, "Yes, ma'am."

"All right," she told us. "Does everyone understand?"

I wanted to believe her explanation. I did. But I kept thinking of the dark diamond interior with its strange hairs, thinking that it didn't sound like a mine's guts. Did it? Through lunch and most of the afternoon I kept to myself, concentrating on all the clues plucked from around me—from Dr. Florida and Lillith, and from today's rumors—weighing each of them and trying to fit them together. Then it was the last class of the day, art class, and a girl in the back said the word "Spark-hounds" to the kids around her.

The teacher's head lifted, turning while his mouth turned grim. "What did you say, young lady? Where did you hear that word?"

"In the hallway. During break—"

"Class!" he cried. "Eyes forward!"

We jerked in our seats, everyone startled.

"Miss Blackmere? Tell the class what you know please. Now."

"Pardon, sir?"

"Did you hear anything more? In the hallway?"

The girl said, "Some older kids were talking. About things called spark-hounds. I guess they're monsters of some kind. They got loose inside the moon's moon, and they're doing all the damage. They just got out of social studies—"

"The spark-hounds?"

Kids giggled, then stopped themselves. No one made a sound.

And the girl said, "No, sir. The kids I heard talking. Their teacher had let them watch the news on TV—"

"I see. Thank you, Miss Blackmere." Our teacher was a youngish man with chiseled features and long blond hair. He dated the girls' physical education teacher, and the current rumor was that they did it on the smelly wrestling mats after school. In the gym. Then they burned the mats to hide the evidence . . . a story I found unlikely and intoxicating in equal measures. I couldn't help but see them naked and making love on the sweaty slick plastic. But I didn't believe it, no. Why would they do it there? I couldn't see any reason.

The art teacher watched us for a moment, then he said, "Spark-hounds."

I had never seen him so intense, so emotional, his chiseled face becoming angry. But not angry at us, no. He cleared his throat and said, "I hoped you'd go home and learn about this from your parents." Then he sighed and thought hard for a long moment, finally saying, "Listen."

No one spoke.

"Apparently Dr. Florida has been operating an experimental lab inside the moon's moon. In secret. Spark-hounds are some kind of tailored organism, and I guess they're terribly dangerous. That's why he did his work so far from here. And somehow those hounds have escaped and done awful things, and I don't know much more myself. I wish I did."

Someone asked what they looked like. The hounds.

He said, "They have wings, and they spit electricity some way or another." He shook his head, saying, "It's a tragedy. But we shouldn't worry too much," and he sighed. "This business is happening a long ways from here. I don't think these hounds can live long in space, and of course we're fighting them. We'll kill them." His handsome face and his poise meant a lot to us. I know he made me feel brave, a little bit, and he told us, "Get back to work now. Go on," and I didn't think too much about the moon's moon or those spark-hounds. I focused on the drawing on my desk. I was making a sky full of clouds, fighting my clumsy fingers to make it look real . . . and somewhere in the midst of one cloud I started to draw Dr. Florida. I made his face full of pain and tears on his wrinkled cheeks, and I stopped and looked up and shivered, tears in my eyes and my fingers starting to mash the tears as they crept out onto my cheeks.

Beth was crying after school. "All those poor dead people," she said, and I said it was too bad. It was very sad. I wished it wasn't so.

Cody and Marshall came out together and found us. Cody said, "Let's go to the oak and watch. At least for a while." She touched my shoulder and said, "Isn't it crazy, Ryder? Huh?"

I said, "It is."

"I hear those damned hound things have been running free for weeks." She snorted and told me, "While we were swimming at his place? And eating his food? Florida knew about them. All along."

"I guess so," I admitted. "He must have."

We hurried to the parkland, crossing the pasture and

pulling ourselves into the treehouse. Jack was lying stretched out on the long bench with his feet in a window, his toes pink in the sunlight. "Hi!" he said, winking and rising. "All of you at once?" Then he saw Beth's damp red eyes. "Hey! What's happening?"

"Didn't you go to school?" asked Marshall.

"Hunted half the night, so I skipped." Jack missed as much school as he could manage. To the day. He shrugged, saying, "I read the encyclopedia all afternoon, which is better than listening to teachers anyway—"

"So you don't know?" Marshall persisted.

"Know what?"

"He doesn't!" Marshall gave a strange little giggle and danced for a moment, banging his head into one of the wooden beams.

Jack laughed and then quit, watching us.

Cody said, "Shut up, Marshall," and brought out the TV. She didn't want to explain anything now. She set the TV on the game table and then sat in a west window, helping to cut the sun's glare. Beth told the boiled-down brunt of the story to Jack. Then Marshall hit him with some alarming details, trying to bother him. Cody said, "Shush!" and glared at everyone. She filled that window and her face was full of tension, and she told us, "Watch. Would you watch this?" and pointed at the colored screen.

A reporter was talking to a man—a sour, exhausted man halfway drunk and sitting in a bar in Hadley City—and the reporter said, "You used to work for Dr. Florida. Am I right?"

"Absolutely." He nodded and swirled the red liquor in the massive knobby glass. "A good twenty years, lady."

"And you're here now. On the moon," she said.

"Meaning I'm not where I'm supposed to be?" He pointed toward the unseen sky. How many times had I seen people make that gesture today? The man said, "Lady," and shook his head. "My team is dead. Every last one of them, and I'm a coward. I'll admit it. Go on, shoot me. Who gives a good goddamn? You know? Who cares? I ran from there and escaped, lucky me, and now you want to hear all the sweet details, right?"

"Tell me whatever you want," she said.

"'Tell me whatever you want,'" he repeated, mocking her voice. He had wild eyes and a fleshy face, exhausted to the bone, and I thought to myself that he was a very unsavory person. I didn't want *him* telling stories. I almost asked Cody to find a different channel and a better-looking witness, since I didn't like this one—

"I was once a soldier," he said. "In the U.N. Then I went to work for Florida, as one of his security people, and I did okay for myself. I did my work and went home afterwards and had my own life." He sipped his drink and cleared his wet throat with a cough, then he said, "So about eight weeks ago . . . it seems like eight years ago . . . my supervisor came and said, 'You can get a big boost in pay, Pete. If you want. You'll get to do some traveling—I can't tell you where because they haven't told me—but they say it's exotic and it's got something to do with your military time. They want your skills.'

"So I said, 'More pay? Sure, I'll go,' and one day later I'm shipped to Hawaii. I wasn't supposed to tell a soul about any of it; the operation was that secret. And you know what? They put me *in charge* of my own team. A bunch of overweight ex-soldiers from other Florida companies. A whole lot of gray was in that team, and no one had done military time in years. At least most of them hadn't. But the gal in charge of the whole show said, 'Don't worry. You won't need muscles where you're going.'

"I asked, 'Where am I going, lady?'

"And she said, 'I don't know. But it must be fun. No one's come back yet.'"

"From the moon's moon?" asked the reporter.

"Yeah." He finished his drink and said, "First I had one day's practice in zero-gee combat, then a day's ride on an express shuttle. The best guns money can buy, and no one was to know anything. Ever. We were sworn to secrecy, and they made us sign a thousand forms and threatened us with brigades of lawyers if we ever so much as oozed a word of this thing. As if we'd have audiences to tell up there, you know? They went as far as making family men record messages for the wives and kids, for later, making everything seem swell and so on." He stopped, his eyes fixed on a point several inches in front of his face. Then he said, "Up there we were. Inside that chunk of grease and rubble, and nothing with us but those spark-hounds and their goddamn nests—"

"Spark-hounds?" she asked.

"It's funny," he said, and he laughed for a moment. Then he rolled his shoulders and produced another drink from somewhere. "We thought they were aliens from the stars, or something. We couldn't think of them as being *tailored*. Me? I've seen plenty of odd critters in my years with Florida and his big-money freak show. But I've never, never seen armor-plated skin and bloodless meat and super-loop batteries instead of guts, plus mouths to put a damned shark to shame."

"The spark-hounds?"

"Nothing like anything else," he said. "We're not talking bambis or cultured beef here. Spark-hounds. A week after it started for me—the fighting, I mean—they thought to tell us the truth. Florida built them for Neptune, or someplace. He had this crazy idea about seeding those places with the hounds. He'd designed them to live in the clouds, chewing up organics and each other and building their floating nests, the nests busy soaking up sunlight and fat-free bolts of lightning—"

"Lightning?" she said skeptically.

"A damn good energy source in some places." He nodded and said, "What you see now? That crystal stuff inside the moon's moon? It's all nest material. It's a lot like the solar cells on anyone's house, only a thousand times tougher and wired to take big blasts of juice all at once." I thought of those dark diamonds studded with silvery hairs, and the man said, "Spark-hounds build them like bugs build their nests. Together. They're social critters in a big way."

"If you can, please, explain the spark-hounds to us." The reporter kept her voice slow and calm. "As best you can."

He took a drink and said, "Hounds are organic factories with brains and wings," and he shrugged. "Too simple? Well, think of it this way. You and me? We eat and burn what we eat with oxygen. But the hounds . . . the hounds live off stored electrical juices. Like robots do. They're living batteries—thinking, breeding, mad-as-hell batteries. That's them."

"How do they look?" she asked.

He sipped and said, "Sort of like a bulldog in the face. They've got these simple hands and sharp crystal brains and long, long stinging tails that hang out their asses. They eat electricity with those tails too. Hit you with their juice and they'll cook you to ash and smoke—"

"They're like electric eels?"

"They're like power plants, lady. Power plants." He said, "A hound is stronger than twelve men, and the biggest one is my size. They don't need oxygen, and so they don't need atmospheres. And they don't drink water either. Punch a hole in their armor plates, and you've made them mad. Punch a hole in their super-loop guts, and maybe you'll kill them. Or maybe they'll get you first. They're full of redundant systems—with plenty of room for excess juice—and suppose they fry you and eat the ashes. Okay? Then they can heal themselves fast. And I mean fast, lady! I mean a few days and they're a hundred percent again!"

"What kinds of organics . . . do they like?"

"Any kind." He grinned and shook his head. "I suppose they're made to eat Jupiter's red spot, but they sure do love comet stuff. And people. Everything gets built in their body cavities—super-loops and new flesh and nest materials and eggs too. They're always making eggs." He paused and stared hard at his hands, then he breathed and lifted his eyes toward the reporter. "You know how long it takes them to cook a man? Maybe two seconds. A big flash and it's done."

"I see . . ."

"What else can I tell you?" He thought for a moment, then said, "You know what happens when two hounds from two nests meet? Huh? They fight. They're really touchy bastards, and they'll try to fry each other and it's something incredible to see up close. Sparks everywhere. The heat enough to boil blood—"

"And they were meant to live on Neptune? Or was it Jupiter?"

"I really don't know." He lifted the big glass and said, "My guess was that Florida made them to kill me. At first. It was crazy to think that someone would invent hounds just to stock an empty planet. But now I can see it. I can. They'd do all right on a gas world, I think. Those nests of theirs would float in the wind—they're strong but light, full of huge rooms—and maybe I can see Florida's thinking. A little bit. Nests all over Jupiter, and trillions of pissed-off hounds busy scooping up raw organics and each other."

Beth interrupted, saying, "I'm tired of watching this—"

"Shush!" said Cody.

The reporter wanted to hear about the nests. How were they built? How did they look up close, and what were those silver spines—?

"Yeah, the nests," the man said. "Catch a hound with lasers and bullets and you can kill it. It's tough but not *that* tough." He breathed and told us, "The hound gets inside its nest, however, and God help all miserable sinners. Nests have tunnels and turns and dead-end rooms everywhere. The walls are tough plastics...like I said, made inside the hounds themselves. I don't know how exactly. I wasn't on a nature hike when I was in close, believe me. There's veins of conducting plastics that bring the juices in from the outer walls. You know. Light energy? And lightning? Then there's an enormous mass of super-loops near the center of the nest. The core. That's where the hounds feed. Like bees sucking up honey in their hive, except they use their tails. Not their mouths." He paused, then he said, "A big nest can hold more power than a big city could use in a year. Believe me. I've seen the figures—"

"Really." The reporter sighed.

"The big spines?" Those silvery hairs?" he said. "They bend when they sense a stranger. Either spark-hounds with unfamiliar electrical fields, or people. Any people. If you get close and clumsy, lady, you can find all flavors of misery. I've seen it plenty of times."

The reporter said, "I see," with her voice flat and impressed.

"Florida has managed a real trick. He's taken things we see every day that no one even thinks twice about. Like tailoring. And organic super-loops. And hardened energy sinks. And that's how be built his spark-hounds. A bunch of ordinary things mixed together and made to work somehow.

"And you fought the hounds," she said.

"Yeah, I did." He nodded and said, "We fought them. We thought our best hope was shaped explosives and getting inside the nests through blind spots. That's what we were doing in the end. Careful blasts to break the nests apart...only someone screwed up and we had a big *kaboom*. That's when the chunks of the moon's moon got scattered, and the last of my team was killed. And I was left alive somehow. The lucky one."

He had a bitter expression. He said, "I just gave up then. Snuck my way on board a supply shuttle, came down to the moon and walked straight to the nearest bar. Here."

The reporter made a small sound. Not a word, just a sound.

He said, "I got pretty close to those guys. The ones on my team?" He set down his glass and looked at the reporter, saying, "Fuck it," and then he pulled one of his hands across his mouth.

She made no sound for a long moment.

Then she asked, "Couldn't you have used something else? Against the nest, I mean."

"Pardon?"

"A strong laser, for instance. It seems to me—"

"Were you listening?" He blinked and restrained some sudden fury, then he said, "The nests were built to be struck by big Jovian lightning bolts. All right? Do you know what kind of power that means?"

"Well, I—"

"Sure," he said, "a laser might melt some of the nest. But the rest would suck up the power. It would store it. Then the whole nest would grow stronger, fatter, more juice in its super-loops and more for its hounds, more for the stinging tails and for frying people, and so on."

She waited, then asked, "What about nuclear charges?"

"What about them?"

"It seems that bombs of sufficient sizes—"

"Who has bombs today?" he asked.

"Dr. Florida has facilities," she told him. Her voice turned tough, her reporter instincts coming into play again. "He's certainly proven himself able to keep secrets."

"So okay. Suppose he nukes the moon's moon. All right. The blasts would have to vaporize every piece of every nest, and the moon's moon is miles across and full of water and dust and the sort of garbage that's perfect for blunting fireballs. Okay? So let's say we miss killing every last hound. Hard radiation doesn't mean the same thing to a hound that it means to us. Say some little nest in a deep mining tunnel survives. It's blasted free to God knows where. Maybe down here. Wouldn't that be a joy? Or maybe, just maybe, it gets kicked clean out of lunar orbit. A few days of drifting in the darkness, and down it comes into the earth's own sweet air. Plop!"

"You're saying... what? The earth is in danger too?"

"Lady," he said, "I don't think you see the picture. That chunk of dead comet is sick with spark-hounds. Let anyone anywhere do anything wrong, today or whenever, and some hounds might just reach the dear old Mother Earth. Believe me."

"But the impact—"

"Twenty gees isn't going to do much more than piss a hound off. A big chunk of nest would survive reentry and spill its hounds, and what those hounds would do is fly and eat organics where they found them, build new nests however they could, and if they didn't have a nest, they'd steal the electrical juices they needed. From wherever." He said, "Remember. The earth is full of super-loop batteries, all charged and waiting to be robbed. Hounds are built to milk super-loops whenever they find them. Why not in an apartment building or a grocery store . . . you see?"

"I see," said the reporter.

Then the drunken man said, "Now we're going to call it quits. I've got to pee." He suddenly rose from his seat and vanished. The five of us were staring at the gloomy air of the bar, and then the camera swung back to the reporter. She said, "That's the story from Hadley City, from the first firsthand witness to this ongoing disaster," and she gave her name and shuddered. She looked pale and weak, and the screen went blank after a long moment.

Beth made a sound.

I looked sideways and saw her crying again.

Marshall saw her too. He said, "It won't happen," with confidence. He stood and turned down the volume, telling us, "We'll stop them first. There are plenty of things we can do."

Cody echoed him, saying, "That guy was a coward anyway, running like he did. And he was drunk besides."

Beth shook her head and tried a smile.

Jack said, "I still don't get it. What's going on?"

No one spoke.

"*Is this real?*" wondered Jack.

Cody said, "You bet."

I looked outside and saw no one. There weren't any kids hunting the dragon or any adults working in their yards.

"No, I get it!" Jack announced. "This is a joke, isn't it? Cody?"

"What?"

"This is something from a movie, right? A tape?" Jack brightened and sat up straight and tried to laugh.

"What are you saying?" asked Marshall.

"This stuff on TV . . ." Jack pointed and looked at us, his face beginning to doubt his words. Just a little. "What was it?

You rigged a tape, didn't you? You were trying to scare me—?"

Cody said, "We didn't."

"—because you wanted to play a joke. Right?"

Cody said, "I wish it was. I do."

Marshall said, "Jack," with his voice stretching the word into something long and fragile.

"Ryder?" said Jack. "Ryder? Tell me it's pretend. Tell me!"

I couldn't talk. I glanced out a west window, feeling empty and cold. There was no one on the bottoms, just a pair of bambis with their heads dropped while they drank from the stone basin nearest us. The weeds near the basin were beaten flat, and I could see the bambis with their pretty white spots and their dark eyes moving, always moving, and I thought of all the times I had seen bambis and watched them and how I'd never really appreciated how scared they looked. All the time, whatever they were doing, they looked scared.

NINE

I came home in time for dinner. Mom told me Dad was showing a house, he would return soon, but until then we'd eat without him. The TV was off. Mom said, "I've heard enough news today, thank you." Then she stayed quiet, her face grave and her eyes distant.

Dad was working, like always, and nothing was truly changed from yesterday. People in the world were still purchasing houses, and so of course nothing was about to collapse. How could it collapse? I let myself be bolstered by confident words and stances—my art teacher's, my friends', anyone's. I reminded myself that the man in that Hadley bar was a drunk and a coward too. Just like Cody had said. What did he know? He had fled his post. Abandoned his fight. What possible value could his fear hold for me?

After dinner, still without Dad, we went to the living room, and Mom decided to watch the latest nonsense. That's what she called it. A spokesman from the U.N. was on every channel—a little black man with one of those lovely African-English voices, almost musical at times—and he spoke about top-notch troops being gathered and trained, and the best shuttles being readied to take these troops to the moon. Not to the moon's moon, no. He told his audience, and the world, that to attack and win meant patience. Insufficient forces would do little good. Better one killing blow than a hundred wasteful assaults. Wasn't that the sensible course? Of course.

"I want to know why," Mom muttered.

I said, "Pardon?"

"Why did Florida do such a thing?" She sucked air through her teeth, her eyes fixed on the TV screen. "Do you know?"

I started to collect my thoughts. Not to tell Mom, no, because I was sworn to secrecy. But I wanted to know in my own heart why he had done such a thing. Had he explained it to me? That day on the false beach? I concentrated, trying to decide.

"*They* say he wanted to stock Jupiter and Saturn. With *hounds*." Mom said *hounds* as if she wasn't comfortable with the word, as if it was in a foreign language and she was speaking it for the first time. "They keep saying nonsense about him bringing *life* to those worlds," she said, and I glanced at her disgusted expression. "But that's not why. I know why he did it."

I waited.

She said, "Ego."

I said nothing, and then the front door opened, squeaking in a slow comfortable way. Dad peered into the living room, asking, "How are things going?" with his long face gray and tired and smiling.

"Kip?" asked Mom. "Is it ego? Tell me the truth."

"What's ego?" He blinked and started to shrug.

"Dr. Florida and his hell-hounds."

"Spark-hounds," I corrected.

"Underneath the charm, is he an egotist?" Mom asked. "Is he so self-possessed that he needs to play God for empty worlds? Is that why?"

Dad was quite tired. He had been working long days lately—I suppose because of the business Dr. Florida had given him, though I wasn't sure—and I watched him breathe and say, "I honestly don't know, Gwinn," and he paused. Then he said, "All right?"

"You're a friend of his," she said. "I just thought—"

"Listen. It's been a shitty day for everyone." He lifted his hands, seemingly pushing her away. His face had lost all trace of his smile, and he told Mom, "Just let me chew on something and unwind, okay? Then we'll sit around and bad-mouth people. All you want."

"You don't have to be so coarse—"

"Shut up," he said with a careful voice. "Now? Please?"

Mom sat without moving, without breathing, and then Dad was in the kitchen and she told me, "Playing God is always wrong. I hope you realize it, Ryder. I do."

I halfway nodded, then I said, "We watched a man who thinks the hounds might come here," and I swallowed.

She said, "Plenty of others say they can't. There's a lot of space between us and them." She asked, "Are you scared?" and pulled her little hand through my hair. "Don't be, honey. We're not on the moon. Those are the people being hurt, the ones out there." She watched me and tried a smile, then said, "The only one here who's going to be hurt, I think, is Dr. Florida himself. At least his precious reputation."

The U.N. man was telling us that within a month, without doubts, all the world's energies could be focused on that dead comet. The threat would be finished by then. "In six weeks," he reassured us, "this will be over and done and we'll have learned a valuable lesson," and the people in the audience began to applaud him, a few of them cheering.

Mom said, "See?"

Dad emerged from the kitchen, a plate of food in both hands. "What's the latest?" he asked, smiling again.

"It'll be finished in six weeks," said Mom. She made no mention of his harsh words and voice. "They just said so."

"Good." Dad took a hearty forkful of meat and chewed, then he said, "You should have seen it."

"What, dear?"

"Like a parade." He swallowed and said, "There was a line of cars stuffed with reporters and whomever . . . all heading west. They were going out of town, and guess where?"

"He was playing God, wasn't he, Kip?"

"I suppose so," Dad admitted.

She touched my head, and for a little while no one spoke. Then Mom said, "Maybe if he'd spent more time fighting them and less time entertaining children—"

"Gwinn?" Dad interrupted.

"I'm sorry," she said. "I was just thinking aloud."

There were moments, now and again, when life seemed so very strange and fun, and knowing the terrible truths only made it more fun. A kind of pattern emerged, and it held for weeks. There was news on TV—the same kind of news repeated without pause and virtually without change—and at school there was constant talking and teaching about the spark-hounds. Summer was approaching, and the adults wanted us to understand things and not be afraid.

We saw pictures of the brave soldiers sitting in neat rows, like us, and then the mammoth shuttles lifted from the concrete pads, climbing toward the moon and the forward bases. We saw endless pictures of the lunar cities and the lunar people who were building barricades and weapons. There were railguns and cannons, and sometimes there were patrols combing the dusty countryside, groups of armed militia hunting for hounds. Maybe some had fallen with the chunks of the moon's moon. Maybe the hounds had launched themselves downward in some fashion. Nobody seemed to know for certain. "The news is being sanitized," said Dad. Which was a good thing. Never again did we see one of Dr. Florida's soldiers drunk in a bar. Not for a minute. His surviving soldiers had been pulled off the moon's moon, and now they were teaching the U.N. troops how to fight the hounds. Everyone was preparing for the final assault; there were no doomsayers, no cowards; and no one doubted who would win.

The hounds were smart, sure. But not human-smart.

I learned everything about them one day. Our science teacher showed us a true-to-life model of a hound. Its authenticity was guaranteed. One of Dr. Florida's own companies had built it, distributing it free to many thousands of schools and public groups. They wanted to help people know the enemy.

There was a bulldog face, all right. It had grappling arms and legs and retractable wings. The hands had two fingers and a thumb. The tail was long and built like a rudder, and the stinging came from the tail's tip, longer still and needlelike. Everyone knew what that stinging tail meant. Electricity in potent bursts. Our teacher said, "What about these wings?" as she unfolded them from the body. They were long and narrow, like gull wings, and she gave a weak smile and tossed the model into the air. We gasped and some giggled, the model gliding an amazing distance. Then it dropped and she said, "It's shaped to glide forever in the strong Jupiter winds."

The model skidded on its belly. I bent and picked it up and saw the odd round eyes covered with clear crystal, the entire body encased inside a sharp-edged insulating armor.

Then the teacher said, "Ryder?" and I flipped my wrist and the hound rose and fell hard, everyone laughing when it crashed.

Our teacher found a seam in the side of the body.

She opened the belly and showed us the strange internal organs—robotlike, I thought; shiny and angular—and she pointed to the five super-loops and the big empty chamber where raw organics were made into hound meat and nest walls and fresh eggs. Then she touched a hidden button and the hound's mouth came open, its plastic turning flexible and our teacher reaching inside with care, tugging on the lip and making the mouth huge. There were gill-like gaps in the flesh. I remembered the tiny whales in Dr. Florida's aquarium, their baleens straining out the plankton. She said, "The tongue," and showed us something resembling a file. It was round and covered with hard, sharp surfaces, and she read from an instruction booklet. "The tongue is intended to tear apart foreign nests. The large mouth can collect organic matter from Jovian clouds." She nodded and brightened, lifting her head. "Remember, class! Nests fight one another. Just like ant nests fight among themselves," and she set down the model with a flourish. Full of hope, she said, "Maybe all we need do is wait and watch, and the hounds will kill one another. Maybe so."

There were moments, dreamy odd moments, when I saw hounds in the sky. I imagined myself on the treehouse roof, in the open, and they were dropping toward me on those big gull-like wings. A dozen hounds, maybe more. Their stinging tails were going to suck the electrical juices from our old super-loops, but I was shooting them with some secret ultimate gun that killed in a suitably gruesome way. I imagined sparks and flames and then exploding corpses, and the images made me smile for a little while. But then the satisfaction faded. I grew bored and drifted away from my game, leaving a few imaginary hounds soaring in the sky.

One Saturday evening, early in the war, four of us were up in the oak tree. Only Beth was missing. Her mother had cut herself by accident, and Beth had to stay home and wait for infections. But she would watch TV too, she had promised. There was going to be a big news conference with Dr. Florida himself. A lot of questions were going to be answered at last. At least that's what everyone was saying.

Cody was filling a west window again, blocking the sun's

glare. Nobody spoke. The news conference started late, Dr. Florida absent. I blinked and saw Lillith and Dr. Samuelson at the podium. Dr. Samuelson's gray hair was bright in the lights of the auditorium, and I watched him smile and beckon for Lillith to speak first.

She explained that Dr. Florida couldn't appear tonight. Grief and stress had pushed him into bed and a doctor's care. But he was taking all blame on himself, and naturally he would do everything in his power to fix all damages and care for survivors. Maybe next week, God willing, he would appear in public again. It was all a matter of his strength. She thanked the audience for their indulgence and invited questions.

The questions came in waves, and Lillith took turns with Dr. Samuelson. They would point and cock their heads, listening and then giving their best answers.

Yes, oh yes! They wanted the hounds dead and thoroughly extinct. And of course no expense was being spared in the quest to find new ways to kill the monsters. Dr. Samuelson himself outlined plans to form diseases that could infect hounds, and for poisons that might be introduced into their nests and for hunting weaknesses in their super-loop guts. Those were the best hopes, he told us.

Was Florida helping the U.N. in every way? someone asked.

"Of course," said Lillith. "Absolutely."

How did the beasts escape in the first place? someone wondered. Was it human negligence? Sabotage? What?

Dr. Samuelson said, "Apparently simple errors were involved," and he looked at the cameras with his voice absolutely calm. "Several fertile hounds escaped from a test chamber, and due to clerical malfunctions there was no discovery until they had bred and started two separate nests in the deep interior—"

But why was the problem hidden from the world? If more help had arrived at an earlier time, perhaps—

"Another mistake," he conceded. "But we were convinced, absolutely convinced, that the hounds were being destroyed. We wanted to avoid a panic, you see. And we had no way of realizing their numbers and power." He paused, then he said, "They had stolen considerable energy from our own super-loops, and due to the hard fighting there was no way to take the needed measurements."

But what could be gained by keeping such a thing secret? Who was to be helped with such a lie?

Lillith said, "You're right. We erred. No one's cause was aided. Panic and overreaction haven't been an issue. Not like we imagined." She paused before saying, "Dr. Florida did wish to make a full disclosure at a much earlier date, but associates convinced him to wait. To bide his time. And naturally we hope that once this business is finished, soon, we can sit down and discuss these issues in depth—"

What about rumors? asked someone. Rumors about a deal cut between the U.N. and Florida? Was there any amnesty granted in exchange for technical cooperation?

A hush fell over the auditorium.

Lillith told them, "Certain people have been cleared of criminal wrongdoing, but no," and she seemed very cool and collected, gazing out at the faces, at us. "No," she said, "Dr. Florida himself will face full criminal charges at the end of this incident. Naturally."

What about the hounds themselves?

"What about them?" asked Dr. Samuelson. He seemed relieved to have the subject changed.

Some authorities were projecting that the entire comet would become a single nest inside eight weeks—

"There are thirty to forty nests today," said Dr. Samuelson. "I don't know *your* familiarity with hound social systems, but all valid experts are on my staff. And we don't see any single-nest scenario. The hounds will increase their numbers, yes, and weaker nests will succumb—"

Will they kill one another off? asked a lone voice.

"Unlikely," he admitted. "Our best simulations show several months of slowing growth and increasing competition for the comet's organics, and for sunlight. The only new energy source is sunlight, and the U.N. is sensibly pursuing several schemes to put the entire comet into shadow. Which would be an enormous help." He breathed and said, "If they are given ample time, ladies and gentlemen, those nests will become large enough and strong enough to generate vast amounts of energy. The hounds are aggressive by any definition. They were intended for aggressive environments. If we wait too long before attacking . . . well, there's a remote chance that our worst fears will be realized. The heat and blast effects of hounds and nest fights could perhaps demolish the comet, scattering its pieces through the sky." He paused, scanning the room and then adding, "Of course, by then our soldiers will have attacked and the war will be won. So this is an academic problem, and I'm digressing. My apologies."

No one spoke for a long instant.

I saw sober expressions as a camera panned the auditorium. Then out from the back of the stage came an aged figure. I didn't know him for an instant. Dr. Florida had aged thirty years in these last days. At least. Lillith and Dr. Samuelson went to him and spoke to him with quiet voices, telling him to please return to bed, please, and rest. Just rest. But he waved them aside and shuffled to the podium, gripping its sides and shivering for a moment.

His face was torn with anguish. His colorless skin was waxen, virtually dead. He put his mouth to a microphone and moaned, "I'm . . . I'm so terribly sorry," and then he slumped forward and collapsed.

People grasped him under the arms, lifting, and more people held his legs and helped carry him from the auditorium. The news conference ended in chaos. I kept seeing him collapsing, in my mind and on TV, and then we turned off the TV and sat in the gathering darkness, talking and then not talking. Then we turned on the TV once again.

Dr. Florida was resting comfortably, we learned. The weather for the next week would be wet and warmer than normal. Cody plucked a snowball from a freezer, offering it to me, and then she found three more of them and we ate them with the TV's sound down and none of us watching it.

Jack finally announced, "I've got to pee."

We turned our backs. He did it out the window. It was a moonless night, dark despite the stars, and the warm wind broke up the stream of urine before it hit the ground. I know because I listened. There were the sounds of bugs and sleepless birds, and we sat still and listened for the urine to hit. Only it didn't hit. Not anything. We sat and sat, and it was like Jack was peeing off into nothing.

Mostly people were mad, sure. Even furious. But it didn't last.

They would say, "Florida shouldn't have done it and we'll see him poor before he's dead, sure, but what the hell? The guy's done a helluva lot of good in his life, and you can't fault him for everything. We're still miles better for having him around, and we've got to figure that into any final equation."

My dad went farther. "What if it had worked?" he asked.

"What if what had worked?" answered Mom.

"Stocking Jupiter with those hounds." He laughed and told us, "That would have been some legacy, wouldn't it? He populates the biggest planet with his own critters, making it his own biosphere . . . isn't that the word, Ryder? Biosphere?"

"I guess."

"Legacy?" said Mom. "Legacy? For a man who thought himself immune to human laws?" She was angrier than most people, and I think she took pride in her anger. "That's the situation, isn't it? He got caught and now he should be charged with murder. Fifteen hundred counts of murder. And probably more on the way."

"Gwinn," said Dad. He shook his head and wondered, "How many people has he saved in his life? Guess." He looked at both of us, pushing aside his plate. "Medicines. Tailoring. Help me count them, Ryder. Would you? He's got one division that makes the best artificial hearts in the business. Doesn't he? And what else—?"

"Stop," said Mom. "I know what you're doing. You're defending him because he's done us some favors. Aren't you?"

"No," he said. "I'd defend him in any case. I would."

Mom shrugged and said, "I just want the nightmare finished."

"They're working on it, Gwinn."

She rose and carried her half-filled plate to the sink, giving its contents to the drain. To the sewers. To the bottoms, I thought.

"We're going to win," said Dad. "There's no doubt."

"I know." She seemed to believe him. I could tell by the way she stood straight, nodding her head and gripping the sides of the sink. "I just wish it was done now. Now. Not tomorrow. Not next month, or whenever they're promising—"

"I know what you mean," he told her.

"I don't appreciate the tension. I hate it."

"Sure."

"Ryder? Love?" Mom asked, "Can you clear now please?"

Then there was a different night. I had eaten a light meal, and I was dressed for Marshall's birthday party. I was clearing the table and Dad said, "I caught a minute of the news on the way home. Another couple hundred soldiers arrived at Tranquility City—"

"So?" asked Mom.

"Usual enough, I admit. But then they said something about bringing back half a thousand kids too. Coming here—"

"Earth?"

"All those damaged farms," explained Dad, "and a chance for serious fighting . . . I guess they're coming here for their own safety. And so they don't have so many mouths to feed up there."

I remembered hearing about the moon kids. They tended toward tall and ridiculously lean, Marshall muscle-bound by comparison, and it wasn't altogether good for them to be plopped down on the earth without preparation. They lacked strength and durable bones—particularly those born up there— and I couldn't help but wonder how alien things must seem to them. No domes. No shortages of water and air. Clouds and rain and trees all tending themselves—

"Ryder?" asked Dad. "What's on the agenda tonight?"

"Marshall's birthday." I felt a pang of excitement.

"That's right. I wasn't thinking." He grinned and asked, "What'd you get him this year?"

"A puzzle."

"Appropriate," Dad decided. "Have a grand time!"

I climbed the hill with the present under one arm. I paused just short of Marshall's house, for a moment, and glanced down at the dark rooftops and the treetops and thought about the moon's kids. Then I turned and went on.

Marshall's mom met me at the door. "Just put that over there. With the rest," she told me, gesturing toward a tottering stack of brightly wrapped gifts. "All right, dear?"

"Yes, ma'am."

"Everyone's out in the back. You just go right on."

I did. I saw Beth among the faces. Then Marshall. And Cody with Jack. There were other friends—Marshall's neighbors and so-so pals—plus a few cousins thrown into the mix. Everyone stood about the backyard holding cans of cold pop, most of them watching Marshall tinkering with the day's biggest present. It was a huge white tube set on a tripod, the tripod itself set on the concrete lid where his father stored gasoline underground. The tube was a large telescope with electronic enhancements and a big flexible mirror aligned and adjusted by on-board personals. It was very expensive, I knew. Such things were nearly impossible to find in stores, what with everyone eager to look at the sky. Marshall was plugging the telescope into a portable TV. Sometimes a bambi or pig would come close and sniff, and he cried, "Get! Get out of here, get!" He would flip his hands and chase them off, and they would race between the kids and come back again. They thought this was some wondrous new game.

Marshall's mom brought cake and more drinks outside, his dad helping. Marshall's dad was small like his wife, quiet and somehow distant. Beth helped him carry, and he thanked her. Then he didn't speak for hours. We formed two groups and ate the cake. There were five of us on the concrete lid, including Marshall, and the others stood scattered on the yard itself.

At one point Cody nudged Jack and motioned, and Jack cleared his throat and thanked Marshall for inviting him.

"You're welcome," said Marshall, and he shrugged.

Cody came tonight because Jack was invited. That was the deal.

"What's this thing?" asked Jack. He took the heel of his shoe and struck a metal plug at the center of the big lid. "Huh?"

"It's the valve. To the gasoline—"

"What's gasoline?"

Marshall said, "They used to burn it for fuel," and he rolled his eyes in amusement. "My father's got a bunch of old, old cars in the garage. Big gas burners. He's got to pay all sorts of taxes just to own them, and he buys his gas special. There's a big tank way underground."

"Yeah?" said Jack. "What do you know?"

Marshall's folks returned with the gifts. It was nearly night, and the kids came together and watched Marshall tearing away the colored paper. The bambis loved the paper, stealing pieces and running wild in the yard while they chewed it. Marshall liked my puzzle gift. Cody had brought him a game, and he said, "Thanks!" Beth got him a puzzle too, and he said, "Neat!" and set it with the rest. That left him with a paper sack, brown and plain, taped shut and marked with the simple declaration: "From Jack W."

Marshall held the sack with both hands.

Jack said, "Go on."

So Marshall tore away the tape and opened the sack, reaching inside and removing... something.

"What's this?" he wondered.

"A puzzle too." Jack was smiling. I couldn't tell what the smile meant. "Try guessing," he told Marshall. "What do you think?"

Marshall was holding a lumpy piece of something. A rock? Only it wasn't a rock. It was solid and heavy, but not rock-heavy. He shook his head and said, "I don't know. What is it?"

"Look at it," Jack prodded. "Close."

"Where'd you find it?"

Jack said nothing.

Beth asked, "Where did you get it, Jack?"

"Near our place." His smile grew. "Down in the woods."

"So what's it made of?" asked Marshall. His curiosity was pricked now. He pulled a hand lens from the tool kit beneath the tripod, opening it and squinting at the strange puzzle by the soft bluish light of the porch. "It looks like hair, this stuff," he admitted. "What's this? Squirrel hair?"

Jack kept quiet.

"And these are what? Bone? Bits of bone?"

Jack started to nod.

"And this!" Marshall looked at Jack's smile, his confusion balanced with a desire to know. "This thing here . . . it's a snake tag, right? One of yours, right? It's mashed in with everything else."

Cody glanced at Jack. She understood what was happening, and I almost understood. Almost. Marshall peered through the hand lens for another long moment, then he stared at Jack's smiling eyes and said, "What? Has this got something to do with the dragon?"

"I guess so," said Jack.

"What do you mean?"

"I think the dragon must have coughed it up."

"What? A hair ball?" Marshall shrieked and dropped the puzzle, and it hit the ground with a substantial thud. Everyone stared at it. One tiny bambi came forward and gave it a tentative lick. "You gave me what? An old ugly hairball?" cried Marshall.

"Hey!" Jack protested. "I thought you'd be interested."

"What the hell kind of gift is this?" Marshall knelt and wiped his hands on the grass. "God . . . that's just so gross! Just gross!"

"You still hunt it, don't you? The dragon?"

Marshall's mom stood behind Jack. She was watching us and listening.

Marshall said, "I sure do."

"So this is a clue," Jack told him.

"For what?"

"Don't you want to know what it eats?" Jack was honestly amazed. He had expected thanks—I could see as much as on his face—and now he was turning angry, a little bit, hands on his hips and his lower jaw thrust forward.

"You're an ugly little shit," Marshall decided.

"And you're not so smart, you asshole."

I glanced at Marshall's mom. She was angriest of anyone. Marshall said, "Get out of my yard!"

Jack said, "Fuck you!"

Marshall's mom pressed forward. "That language," she said with a disgusted voice. "I forbid such language in my house! I'm going to ask you to leave, young man. I mean now!"

"Fuck both of you," Jack said with passion, no hesitations or qualifications or room for apologies later. "You asshole shits with your fucking money—!"

Cody grabbed him, saying, "Enough. Okay?" and she practically carried him from the yard. Everyone stood silent, embarrassed or furious or maybe amused. I heard Cody talking to Jack, telling him, "It's his fault, okay? Don't worry. You came and tried, all right?"

Jack said, "He *could* use that thing, if he wanted—!"

"I know."

"He could study it!"

"I know."

"I'd even show him where I found it, the shithole!"

"Maybe tomorrow," she told him.

Then I turned and saw Marshall. He was listening to Jack too, his face empty. I couldn't tell what he was thinking. Marshall's mom came with a rag and picked up the hair ball and carried it to the garbage without speaking. I watched her set it and the rag into the chute, then she wiped her hands on a clean second rag. "Got rid of two uglies," she muttered. The night sounds weren't loud, but she didn't notice me listening. "Two uglies." She didn't care if anyone else could hear.

*   *   *

It became a clear, fine night, the moon a thin crescent over the western horizon. It looked pretty and insubstantial, and Marshall said, "There," when the focus was right. We were standing around the big TV screen. He said, "I checked the schedules and we'll see it soon." We could see the darkened limb of the moon and some vivid green patches inside small craters, and there was a sprinkling of lights and an eerie sense of depth that didn't come with binoculars. Marshall pointed to the little cities, naming them. Then he checked the time and said, "Now," and something rose from behind the moon.

It had changed since the first explosions.

Marshall tinkered with the magnification, bringing out minuscule details. I saw the blackish facets of the nests bursting from the blacker surface of the moon's moon, and I could make out the longish hairs protruding from the largest nests. I felt cold and strange to be looking at the scene. It was as if we were hanging in space, exposed and vulnerable, and I had to shake my head and look away for a moment. For reassurance.

Beth was beside me.

She took my hand and said, "Maybe we shouldn't."

"What?" I asked.

"Bother them." She said it and breathed and squeezed my hand. "If we left the spark-hounds alone—"

"They'd come after us," said Cody. "If we let them."

"Maybe we could push it all into space." She gave me a look, fearful and confused. "Why not? Just let them live somewhere else?"

Marshall said, "It's not so simple."

"Why?"

"You can't just push big things like that," Marshall told her. "I mean, wouldn't Dr. Florida have thought about that? If it were possible?"

It seemed an easy answer to me, but then I didn't know enough about such things. Marshall must be right, I thought. It couldn't be done.

One of his cousins said, "Look!" and I saw lightning on the moon's moon. Everyone became quiet, watching the screen. There came another bright flash, and Marshall said, "They're fighting," with his matter-of-fact voice.

"We'll finish them soon," Cody told Beth. She grinned and told us about the army's commanding officer—a handsome, tallish man from Old Israel. "No reason to worry. Six thousand soldiers and they're almost ready. Any time."

People began to drift away in the darkness.

We watched the moon's moon, but there were no more bursts of lightning. So Marshall turned the telescope to Jupiter. He focused it and we saw the colored bands and three big moons and listened to Marshall's sudden lecture on Jovian weather and the harsh environment and the tough old Red Spot. Then his mom came to us, his dad shadowing her. "One last event for the evening," she said, and she clapped her hands. "Kids? Kids? Would you please come with us? Marshall? Come on, son."

"Oh, gosh." He rolled his eyes.

"It's a tradition!" she said brightly. "This minute. Right now!"

We filed inside the kitchen. The air was humid and warm and filled with the heavy odors of drying cakes. I walked to the corner in the back, knowing what to expect, and Marshall lingered at the door, his eyes dipped.

"Oh he's pretending to be ashamed," said his mother. She put on an enormous smile. "Marshall waits for this like we all do. Don't you, dear? Of course you do."

Her husband stood beside her, saying nothing.

"Come here, birthday boy. Please?"

We looked at Marshall's eyes as they lifted, his mouth frowning even as he walked forward. The kitchen was crowded. People had to press against the walls and appliances to let him pass. I studied the neat horizontal lines in the corner. Marshall's dad was making ready, finding the appropriate line with a pencil. Then he backed away and let Marshall turn and ease himself against the wall. "Your shoes. Remember?" his mom said. Marshall removed his shoes, his face placid and indifferent. His head tilted slightly to one side, and his dad straightened his head and then pressed the pencil flush to the top of his head. With confidence and a quick smile, he put a dash on the white wall.

Marshall stepped away as soon as possible.

His mom said, "There!" and approached. Her expression turned from a toothy smile to puzzlement, then to something darker. "What's this?" she wondered. "What? I don't believe *this*!"

There were two lines on the wall. They were close but

not quite the same, the new pencil mark maybe a quarter of an inch too low.

She turned to her husband. "Let me try." She made Marshall press back against the wall. "You have to keep the pencil level, *dear*." Then she finished and found the new lines overlapping one another. Marshall was shorter than predicted, no doubt about it, and her response was to snort and ask, "How did this happen? Can someone tell me how?"

No one made a sound.

Then Marshall's dad said, "At least I did it right," and sighed, genuinely relieved.

"But explain this!" She wheeled and looked at her son, her face close to angry. "What is it? Are you eating enough? Dear?" Then she seemed to hear herself, and she tried defusing the tension with a careless pretended smile. "Not that it's absolutely important, of course. But I just wonder. Is everything fine?"

Marshall watched her, saying nothing.

"What's wrong, dear?"

He said, "Leave me alone," with a quiet voice.

"What? What was that?"

He dipped his head and bit his lower lip so hard that I saw the clear pink imprints of his straight sharp teeth afterwards. He said, "Nothing."

She didn't know what to say or think.

"What we ought to do," said her husband, "is try again come morning. That might do it."

No one spoke.

"Your spine grows while you sleep," he persisted. "It's the lack of weight, right? Someone back me up on this. Am I right?"

Marshall drummed on the wall with one fist, then the other, and he shook his head as if he was in mortal pain.

"You sleep, you expand," his dad declared. "We'll wait for morning, dear. All right? Okay? We can do that." He stared at his wife, desperate for some agreement; then he looked out at us, asking us, "Wouldn't that be fair? What do you think? Yes?"

TEN

We built our treehouse high in the oak, Cody doing the bulk of the real work. She lifted and she pounded, and she had the better sense for where things belonged. Marshall would talk. One day he said, "Do you know why kids like trees and treehouses? It's because of old monkey genes and ape genes and stuff. They tell us to climb and be safe above the ground."

"Is that true?" asked Beth.

"Absolutely," he declared. "The genes are expressed when we're kids, and then they're tucked away and forgotten."

We built our floor and the bones of our walls, then the roof, no maze below and no bridge even on our plans; and one sunny summer day we took a break to lie in the blazing sunlight, stretched out on the roof on colored beach towels. We were talking, drifting into a strangely honest conversation, telling each other how and why we had gotten to be like we were, gene-wise. I told about my folks wanting a healthy boy with a few synthetic genes, just a few, and Cody said, "They got a surprise, huh?" and laughed in a peaceful, understanding way. Marshall spoke in technical terms, outlining the effects and interactions of several dozen potent genes—a real stew of biochemical extras—and then no one spoke for a long while.

"What about you, Beth?" said Cody. There wasn't much to tell, Beth claimed. Her folks, her dear sweet folks, had had simpler kinds of tailoring done. The clinic doctors had mapped and sorted their own genes, picking and choosing for fruitful combinations; and no, she wasn't blessed with synthetics or famous people's genes, or anything like that. She was the best her folks had to offer. That's what she told us. "I'm the best they could give me," and she smiled and hugged herself, saying nothing more.

Then it was Cody's turn to tell.

She held a hammer in one hand, and every so often she tossed it up against the cobalt blue sky. It would roll and rise, roll and fall, and she caught it every time by its massive metal head. She never slipped. She didn't seem to think about her motions, and her words ran along at a steady pace.

"My mothers," she said, "were pissed when they were young. You know what I mean? Tina's folks hated her because she lived with a woman, and May's folks pretended they were just roommates. Only they knew better. And my mothers were part of some radical groups that were big back then. The old lesbian groups. They were charter members."

"They've told you this?" asked Beth, doubtful.

"They've told me everything, sure." I watched the hammer against the sky, then there was just sky. "Anyway," said Cody, "they decided to have a kid. A girl. It would have been hypocritical to have a boy, what with the lesbians talking about societies free of men. All men. That's why my moms went into debt and did a lot a crazy tailoring. They were getting ready. They were pissed at the world and wanted a daughter who could do anything a boy could manage. And more."

No one spoke.

"That was long ago," Cody told us. "Those lesbians got crazier and crazier, talking about going to war against men. Shit like that. So my moms dropped out and May had me, and May's folks didn't have any other grandkids to spoil. So things got good with them. In a gradual way." She paused, then she said, "I don't know. Things have always felt pretty ordinary to me. Life, I mean, I don't feel all that strange."

"Are they sorry?" asked Beth. "For doing so much with you?"

"Sometimes. Sort of." She shrugged and threw her hammer, then she said, "I'm not." She snatched the hammer and rose. "I get a real charge out of doing stuff. You know? Stuff no one else can do." She stood on the edge of the roof, walking toe-to-heel with her arms outstretched and the hammer balanced on top of her head. "We've got a great relationship, my moms and me. They talk to me and I talk to them." She went up on one leg, saying, "Every kid thinks his or her folks are the best, I guess. But I know mine are." She started to laugh, and the hammer slipped and hit the roof with a *thud*. "Oops," said Cody. "Oops."

We finished the walls to the big room, and Cody told us, "It's not enough. I know where we can get super-loops and solar panels . . . but we've got to have cash. Some green. We can't do it for free."

Everyone glanced at Marshall, waiting.

"I'm not giving. Not more than my share," he said, licking his lips. "I don't want to. I shouldn't have to. And forget it."

"Not even if we name the treehouse after you?" asked Cody. "Not even if we put up a big sign with your name?"

Marshall licked his lips again, considering the offer.

But Cody said, "No, wait! I've got a better idea!"

"What is it?" asked Marshall. He broke into a frown.

"A contest," she told us. "We'll hold a big contest and get the little kids to pay to enter. The winner gets the money, of course. And I'll be the big winner. Me."

"You?" said Marshall.

"What kind of contest?" said Beth.

"Snake hunting." Cody smiled, her square teeth showing. "What do you think? We'll judge the snakes on length, and weight too. Every kid pays a dollar to enter, and I'll just catch more than anyone else. Okay?"

She was a good hunter, all right. She knew the rich spots and she was quick enough to snatch them without fuss. Fuss was what took time with the little kids. We hadn't hunted snakes much that year, true—the treehouse filled our time— but I could imagine her plan working. Absolutely.

We held the contest on a Saturday morning.

We had posted signs on trees and streetlamps. Forty-two kids came from the neighborhood, and most of them were small kids. The ones as old as Cody, or older, could be beaten. She felt sure. She had a huge cloth sack, ready for anything. Beth was in charge of money. I was going to help

Marshall patrol the parkland, making certain nobody even tried to cheat.

"Are pennies okay?" asked Beth. "Cody?"

"Yeah?"

"It's that little Wells kid," she explained. "He's got pockets full of pennies—"

"If there's a hundred, sure."

"Okay."

We started the hunt in the pasture, close to the oak, and maybe half the kids didn't last an hour. They got bored or they saw other kids doing better and became discouraged. It took patience to walk and listen for the right sounds. A very good hunter could smell a garter snake—a faint sour odor that became strong when it was in your hand, flipping and shitting its musk gland dry—and the very best hunter, like Cody, could even hear a tiny snake slipping through the grass and brush, even on a windy day. The contest was to last until noon, no later, and by eleven the parkland was nearly empty of kids. Cody had ten or twelve competitors. I caught two of them pooling their snakes into one bag, and I told them even those weren't enough to win and they were disqualified. By noon there were eight kids according to my count, plus Cody, and I walked back to the oak and found Cody sitting in the shade, smiling. Her big sack was heavy with all kinds of snakes, and she whistled and said, "Would you look?" It was obvious who had won. The other kids dumped out their sacks and left without trying to compare. Cody nodded and looked into the oak, saying, "It's over. It's done."

But it was a minute short of noon.

Marshall came from the opposite direction, one kid on his trail. I saw Jack Wells struggling with his sacks. His old clothes were torn and his freckled face was streaked with new dirt and fresh thorn cuts, and the two sacks in his hands were at least equal to Cody's one. Cody saw him too. She rose and blinked, saying, "Okay," and she turned to Marshall when he arrived. "Did he cheat?" she asked. "How'd he get so many?"

"I don't know how." Marshall shrugged his narrow shoulders, then he told us, "You should have seen him. Plucking them out of everywhere, the little welfare shit—"

"Hey," said Cody.

"What?"

Jack Wells had heard Marshall talking. The hard adult eyes showed a slow anger, staring at Marshall, and he put down both sacks and said, "Now what?" He didn't talk like a little kid. He acted ready to kick shit where he found it. "What do I do now? Huh?"

We weighed the sacks, and Jack's two weighed a bit more than Cody's.

"So I win?" asked Jack. "Is that it?"

"Weight *and* length," reminded Marshall. "Just wait."

The feud had started. I can point to the precise moment. Marshall spoke to Jack with a certain voice, and Jack stared at him. Something inside Jack wouldn't bend an inch or forget a single ugly word. And then Marshall made it worse by refusing to explain how he was judging the snakes. "You couldn't understand it. It's a big formula, kid."

So many inches equalled so many ounces.

Marshall invented the system as he went along. I helped Beth put the squirming snakes against the tape measure, and Marshall kept track of everything on a big sheet of liquid crystal paper. He would say, "Cody's ahead." Then he would say, "It's Jack Wells. For now."

Cody herself said, "Play fair, okay?"

"Who said I wasn't? You think I'm cheating?"

Cody couldn't tell what he was doing. And besides, she wanted the money for us. So she didn't look at the numbers too hard.

Finally Marshall straightened, smiled and said, "It's done. Cody won."

Jack Wells said, "What? How come?"

"Look for yourself," Marshall told him. "See here? See? You know how to add, don't you?"

Jack said, "Asshole."

Cody stepped between them. For the first time.

"It's as simple as simple can be," Marshall explained. "Cody won by three inches. So many inches equals an ounce, see? And you've got more weight, but Cody's got more inches. Enough more that it's not even close. Can you see?"

"Three inches?" said Jack. "You asshole!"

"It's the rules," Marshall told him. "We've got to obey the rules."

Jack glared at Marshall.

Cody pressed her tongue against a cheek, her eyes narrowed. She was watching Jack Wells.

Jack opened one of his sacks. After a minute, he said, "Wait. Wait! I had another one."

"Another what?" asked Marshall.

"A little garter snake. In this sack, right here."

"Maybe it got away."

"No way, asshole!"

"Quit saying that," Marshall protested. Then he laughed and shook his head, pleased with his cleverness.

Jack got on his knees and picked out a big king snake, speckled and pretty, and he wrapped it around his hand and tossed it into the air. Then he chased it through the long grass. I watched him catch it with a graceful stab of the hand, and he shook it and then stroked its belly and spun it in a wide circle, making us dizzy. Then he said, "Okay. Watch."

The snake vomited its morning meal. We saw the fresh bright carcass of a tiny garter snake, and Jack said, "More than three inches. Look!"

"You can't!" cried Marshall.

Cody told Marshall to quit it. "It's done."

"This is stupid," he insisted. "This is so stupid!"

"You're stupid," said Jack.

"Welfare shit!" said Marshall. "Cheap ugly welfare genes—!"

Jack launched himself at Marshall, and they fought their first fight on the grass. It lasted five seconds, nobody was bloodied, and then Cody was between them and shoving them to the ground. She told Jack, "You win. The money's yours, okay?" Then she looked at Beth, saying, "Can you count it out now? Please?"

Beth was beside Marshall. "Are you all right?" she wondered.

"I'm just fine," he blubbered. His face was red, his anger slow to leave. "Just go. I don't need a goddamn nurse," and he fled her grasp. He started walking home, and Beth was crestfallen. They had been the best of friends, never fighting. Now Beth sat in the grass, her face pushed shut and both hands wringing the fat green stalks.

Jack counted his own money, then he dumped the sacks and watched the rushing snakes spreading across the pasture. I emptied Cody's sack for her, and when I turned I saw her talking to Jack. I thought she was trying to calm him down. I went to Beth and sat. She looked lonely. I didn't know her well enough to know what to say, but I sat because that seemed the right thing to do. When I looked again, Jack was handing his money to Cody. Minus the pennies. Then he turned and started walking toward our oak, walking straight through the grass.

"What happened?" I asked. "What's he doing?"

Cody picked up her empty sack. I could smell its snakes on my hands, the musk and shit. "Oh," she said, "we made a deal."

"Yeah?"

"I don't think he's all that lousy. I really don't."

I waited.

Cody told me, "He's just a kid, I mean. And tailored. And his big brothers would rather piss on him than give him the time of day."

"Why'd he give up the money?"

"He wanted to," she said. "He's joined us. The money's so we can finish the treehouse."

I saw Jack Wells climbing the oak's trunk, his arms reaching and his feet on the lowest step. "Marshall's going to be mad," I said.

"He can't always win," she told me.

Jack couldn't reach the next step, and while I watched he slipped and fell with a hard thud and a cloud of dust. Then I blinked and he was up again, climbing again, sore and hurting; but he didn't quit until he was sitting in the big room itself.

Summer came, school closed; the spark-hounds stayed in the sky.

There was still homework during the hot months, assignments fed into the home personals, but there was plenty of time to wander and talk and do nothing at all. The U.N. was getting closer to the great assault, and the TV was full of the news. But the strangeness of it all was turning ordinary. Sometimes it felt as if the war's finish would be nothing. An anticlimax. When it came—"Soon," said the generals, "soon!" —the spark-hounds would be pulverized with every terrible weapon—beams of neutrons and X-ray lasers coupled with freshly minted hydrogen bombs. And the very worst result for people would be a dusting of fallout on the moon's surface. Surely nothing more, we were told. Because every factor was being weighed, and every dark possibility was being considered.

Come summer, with no warning, Jack moved out of his house and into the oak.

His folks and brothers didn't care, and Cody said it would be a good thing to have a guard in the treehouse. There were still plenty of kids hunting for the snow dragon, or just walking the trails late at night. Maybe some of them would try something. "If they do," said Cody, "pop them. Okay? If the snowballs don't stop them, I've got slingshots and marbles in that cabinet. Way in the back."

Jack said, "Great," and nodded. He pretended to throw a snowball out the window. "I'll cream them."

"Scare them," Cody corrected him. "All right?"

"But how's he going to pee and stuff?" asked Marshall. He glanced at Jack and wondered, "Where will you wash? You want to stink?"

"I'll go home and shower, you dick. What do you think?"

Beth asked, "Won't they miss you at home?" She squinted, not understanding what she heard.

"They don't care," Jack assured her. "Just go ask if you don't believe me."

"What'll you eat?" Marshall persisted.

"Canned stuff. Wild stuff. Whatever."

"We ought to vote," Marshall decided. "Can Jack actually *live* in our treehouse? That's the question."

Cody thought it was a good idea; so did I. I knew Marshall was just jealous that Jack was getting his own way. Sure. And Beth couldn't see why he wanted such a thing. "You're too young to be alone up here," she told him. I saw her breathing, then she said, "You're leaving your *family*. Your *home*," and she made a soft whining sound.

Jack glanced out an east window, shrugging once.

"Jack stays," said Cody. "His vote makes three, and he wins."

Beth said, "Ryder? Do you always do what Cody wants?" She was angry. I knew it when her bright eyes focused on me.

I said, "I thought it was a good idea."

"Why?" she asked.

"Because it's what he wants," I began.

"Is it?"

"He's happier here, sure."

She shook her head and wondered, "What if everyone did the happy thing? Would that be right?"

I blinked, trying to think—

"Ryder? What about obligations?"

"But it's different—"

"And duty?" she whined.

Jack was staring at Beth now.

"Sometimes," she said, "you disappoint me, Ryder."

Now I was angry. "Cody's mostly right," I countered. "She almost always knows what to do."

"You're sure?"

"Mostly."

"You think Jack's old enough to live here?"

I looked at Jack, and he seemed so very much like a little boy—

"Beth?" said Jack. "Butt out of it."

Beth sighed and shook her head, then she sang one soft, sad note. I was watching her now. Her eyes were fixed on some point far beneath the floor, her head still shaking, and I felt sorry for being angry and tried to say something nice. Only she didn't hear me. She couldn't hear me. She was sitting on the long bench, tangled up in her thoughts.

Jack brought a foam pad and an old water-cooled sleeping bag into the treehouse, plus extra clothes, canned food and frozen food and his assorted snake equipment—liquid crystal records, maps and numbers and such, with cloth sacks for carrying the snakes and lucky sticks for whipping the ground or pinning the big ones in one place. He slept on the long bench and used a portable burner to cook his meals, and he stored his gear in one of the maze's dead ends. Cody made him clean the room every day. It was part of the deal. And Jack seemed happier than I could remember him being, with something fresh in his eyes and quick in his honest smile.

I had to wonder what had happened in the Wellses' house. Really.

And what would happen when cold weather came again? Jack couldn't stay up in the oak with the snow and ice. No way.

"You should have seen the storm," he told me one day.

"Did you hear it? Last night? Wind and lightning and me just holding on!"

I had slept through the night, unaware.

"A lot of noise," said Jack, "and maybe ten drops of rain."

"Yeah?"

"And I heard it scream afterwards," he told me.

"The dragon?"

"It was close." He pointed at two spots on the pasture. "It screamed twice, and you know how fast it was moving? About as fast as Cody runs in the open, on good ground."

"It's sure quick," I agreed.

He was watching me and thinking something. "Nobody's catching them anymore. Did you notice? They've gotten too smart." He said, "I'm glad I never tried nabbing them. Really!" Beans and beef were heating over the burner. "And this big one? I really like having it around. Just knowing it's close. You know?"

"I do," I said.

He dipped a finger into the bubbling sauce. "Want some?"

I was hungry, yes. But dinner was going to be served at home in a little while, so I said, "Thanks, no," and left Jack to eat by himself. I arrived to find Dad cooking and the TV full of news. "It's the big attack, Ryder," Dad said. "They've finally squared away the D-day."

I sat at the kitchen table and watched shuttles standing in rows on the blasted dead ground of the moon. "Ten days," said the newscaster, "and our future will be determined by several thousand brave soldiers. The most powerful army ever created, and it will be launched with considerable fanfare, its purpose as noble as any ever imagined—"

"Yams?" said Mom. She brought a plate of yams from the oven.

I said, "Thank you, yes."

"This animated sequence," said the newscaster, "shows the assault as it is supposed to happen." I saw tiny shuttles maneuvering around the moon's moon, nests sparking and teams of soldiers being dispatched to fight their way into the deepest regions. They would plant nuclear explosives. And more explosives—enormous hundred-megaton charges—would be placed in the nearby space, all lunar-based artillery aimed and waiting. At a preplanned moment, at a preplanned position, the full-scale attack would blow the moon's moon to ashes and gas and hot light quickly fading. "Neat and quick and thorough," said the man's steady, knowing voice. The TV simulation ended with a brilliant flash, then blackness. "Simulations and endless practice," he claimed, "have made the army ready, and according to all accounts, our soldiers are eager to do their jobs."

"Eat," prompted Mom. "It's getting cold."

"Ten days," said Dad, and he winked at me. "It should be quite the show, Ryder. Don't you think?"

Mom began to eat, her fork clicking against her plate.

"History in the making," said Dad.

"I don't like history," Mom responded.

Dad waited, then he said, "You did in school. I recall—"

"I meant being stuck in it, Kip." She sighed and looked into her steaming food, never blinking.

Then it was nine days to go.

Then eight days.

It was afternoon of a blazing hot June day. Marshall was with me in the big room, Beth and Cody were on the roof and Jack was scouring the pasture for any snakes foolish enough to come out in this heat. "We've got somebody on the west," Cody yelled. "Someone coming."

I lifted my head. I had been reading.

"You know him, Ryder?"

He was a neighbor kid, sure. I remembered his face and name and age—seven years old, and small for seven—and he crossed the bottoms and climbed the short slope with his gaze fixed upwards at us. I remembered where he lived, way past Beth's house. I saw the jade-colored house and his folks standing in the front yard, each with a bambi on a leash. Then I breathed and blinked and came back to the present. The kid wanted to talk to us. I watched him summoning the courage, then he asked, "You got any shovels?" with a brittle little voice.

Cody poked her head over the edge of the roof. "What do you want?"

"You got anything to dig with?" the kid wondered.

Cody asked, "Why?"

He didn't want to say why. He rocked from one foot to the other, then back again. He said, "I'm not supposed to use my dad's tools."

"So what are you digging for?" Cody persisted.

"Nothing."

"Nothing?"

"We want to dig a hole," he whined.

What was Cody thinking? I didn't understand. We didn't loan tools to anyone, not ever. I looked down at the kid's eager face, and she asked him, "Where are you putting this hole?"

Beth's face came over the edge, her black hair streaming downwards.

"Where are you digging?" Cody asked again.

"Oh," he said, "over there," and he pointed in some random wrong direction. I looked at his face and stance and knew he was lying.

Jack came up behind the kid, saying nothing.

"So what are you chasing?" asked Cody.

The kid wheeled and saw Jack. Beth said, "Don't do anything to him, Jack," and scared the kid without meaning to do it. Fear came up into his face, into his eyes, and he bolted. He was down the slope and running with a frantic, clumsy motion, and Cody shouted, "Keep on him!" She gripped the edge of the roof and swung out into the air, holding tight and coming feet-first through a window. In an instant she was beside me, and I watched the kid and Jack racing across the green bottoms. Cody was telling Marshall to hurry and help with the shovels. Now! She had a feeling—

"What?" He looked up from a puzzle, interrupted and angry. "What's going on?"

"Ryder?" Cody shook my shoulder. "Come on."

Beth crawled down through the hatch. We threw shovels to the ground, then it was quick through the maze and across the bottoms, Cody prompting us all the way. I still didn't understand. Neither did Marshall. "What's the point? I don't get it!" We climbed the slabs and heard voices—Jack's voice and then a couple of kids talking to him—and we pressed up into a stand of second-growth trees where the light was dim and cool and damp. Jack was standing beside a lone beam of sunlight that showed dust in the beam, and three kids clumped past him. Jack was asking, "What'd you see?" Then he turned and told us, "Something went down this hole. *They* saw something."

Cody threw her shovel into the earth, the sharp blade

knifing deep and the handle standing in the air. Then she breathed a couple times and looked at the kids, smiling.

There were two boys and a girl. They rocked in place and hunted for escape routes. Cody said, "Boo!" and lifted her arms, spooking them. Then she jumped and grabbed the boy who had come to us, and the other two shrieked and fled. I heard them running in the shadows, then there was nothing. Cody was smiling. She showed her square teeth and told her captive, "You know what I'm going to do to you? Do you?"

He went limp in her arms. "What—?"

"Kiss you. On the lips."

Horror came into the boy's tiny face—

"I'll use my tongue," she threatened.

"Don't!" he squealed.

"What went down that hole?" she asked him. "Tell me!"

"It's ours," he said. "We saw it."

"What'd you see?"

"Nothing."

Cody pursed her lips and bent toward him—

"That dragon thing!" he cried. "It was lying right here," and one hand lifted, pointing at the packed earth and the sunbeam.

Marshall came forward, his face intense. "What hole?" he asked.

"Let me go," said the boy.

"This hole?" said Marshall. "Tell me!"

"I saw it. It's mine!"

"It's got to be here," said Marshall. "It's the only one big enough." He lifted his shovel and drove the blade into the earth, cutting roots and the heavy moist soil. The hole had been dug long ago by some animal, its sides smoothed by use. I started helping Marshall with the digging, and Beth told Cody, "Let him go. You'll hurt him."

"You didn't see a dragon." Cody shook the kid. "Did you?"

"I did!" He was angry to be doubted. He said, "It was white and furry and this big," and he stretched his arms to show that it was longer than he could stretch. "It went down there, and it belongs to me. It's *mine!*"

"So catch it." She released him, pulling her shovel from the ground and telling him, "Help us dig, and maybe you'll be the one—"

"That's not fair!"

"Yeah," Cody agreed. "It's not."

"I'm getting my dad. He'll whip your ass."

Cody looked at me. "His dad worth shit?" she wondered.

I remembered the man with the bambi on a leash. He was fat and pink and not much taller than her. I said so.

She told the kid, "Go on then. Get him," and she laughed.

The kid turned and ran, vanishing, and I started to dig again. I smelled the exposed earth and the root saps, and soon Cody was telling me to help pull the loose soil away from the growing hole. She'd bring up the big clods herself. With Marshall. "Some stroke of luck, huh?" she asked Marshall. "You know what tipped me off? When I saw that kid coming toward us. He was wrestling something. In his mind. And he was sort of playacting while he walked, using his hands—"

"I've got dibs," said Marshall. He grunted and jabbed with the shovel, his hands already blistering. "I call dibs!"

Cody stared at him for a moment, saying nothing.

"Don't quit," he said. "Dig! It might get away!"

Jack wasn't helping. I saw him sitting on a slab of concrete, rocking it and watching us with his face showing nothing.

"There you go," said Beth. "There." She was picking worms and the moist fragments of worms out of the shovel-chewed clods, then she put them on quiet ground and coaxed them into digging. She seemed possessed with the work, singing a string of la-la-la's, and I found myself moving to the rhythm of her song.

Cody was sweating. Her arms were pumped full of blood, and her face too, and when she moved the drops of sweat would fly in all directions. Once she drove the shovel like a spear, striking something solid. We heard the *clang*, and I paused to look into the growing pit. A crescent-shaped wound showed on the surface of some concrete block. A few more shovel strokes showed one edge of the block. The animal hole curled beneath it, vanishing into who-knew-what.

Marshall dug with his blistered hands, and Cody helped him.

They got beneath the block, bringing up bricks and pieces of bricks—red and dirty on the outside, red and bright at their core—and Cody paused and studied the bricks. She said, "You know what it is? I bet?"

Marshall grunted and brought up another clod. "What?" he muttered.

"Just a minute." She dropped to the ground, crawling into the pit and forcing her hands and then her face under the concrete block. When she came up again, she said, "A well. It's some old well capped with this thing," and she swatted the block one time: *Whap!*

"The dragon's in there?" asked Marshall.

"Trapped, I'm guessing."

Marshall said, "Trapped," without sound. Then he grunted and worked until an entire side of the old well was exposed. Our pit was deep and wide, bricks missing from one spot at the well's lip. A badger or something might have slipped through that hole at one time. Now the dragon had made it its home, I realized. Cody told Marshall to quit digging, and again she climbed down as far as possible, putting an ear close to the dark spot. She didn't move for a long while. Then Marshall asked, "Do you hear it?"

"Something," she said. She climbed back out again.

"What'd you hear?"

"Your damned heart beating." She stared at Marshall. "Settle down. We'll get it for you somehow. Don't worry."

The pit grew even larger, clods and a few more bricks scattered on the ground all around us. The concrete block was entirely exposed, and the neck of the well too. "What do you think?" Cody asked Marshall. "We sure can't squeeze through that gap there."

"We've got to move the cap. This thing," said Marshall. He jumped onto the block and dulled his shovel with some wasted stabs. His hands were a sorry mess, I saw. But he didn't seem to notice, concentrating on the problem. "If we had a real big lever," he said. "Maybe we could—"

"Maybe," said Cody.

"I don't think so," said Beth.

Marshall looked at Jack. "Please?" he asked. "Go and get us some axes, okay? And my net too?"

Jack glanced at Cody.

"Go on," she said. Then she turned to Marshall. "What are you using for a lever?"

"A tree."

"Which one?"

"That one. It's good and straight."

Cody stared at Marshall for a long moment, then she

went to the tree and swung her shovel with both arms. The curved blade struck the trunk with a dull *thud*. I saw a slice of bark cut free and the sappy meat beneath it. She swung again and again, and Marshall did his best to help. But there wasn't any coordination between them, and his poor hands were so raw that it was agony just to hold the handle, much less aim and swing and strike with any force.

He quit. He had to quit. We stood watching Cody chopping at the tree, and Marshall whispered to me, "We've got it finally."

I said nothing.

"What'll she say?" he asked. "When I show her?"

"Your mom?"

"She'll just shit," he said with enormous, crazy satisfaction. He shook his head and smiled and took a long, ragged breath. "I'll bet she'll just shit."

Jack returned with axes and the net. I helped Cody chop, and my hands were sore inside a minute. The tree's wood was springy and damp and I couldn't do much more than bust away the slivers. It was Cody who drove her blade deeper every time. She made the whole tree shake. Beth was sharing Jack's concrete seat, their knees near their mouths. Marshall himself couldn't stand in one place, and he was pacing and planning and making us nervous.

Cody finally paused, wiping sweat from her face and saying, "You ought to hang the net now. Get it where you want it."

"Yeah!" said Marshall. "I will."

The tree wasn't large, no, but it took a lot of pounding before it tilted and dropped. Cody had to shove it. Branches in the canopy snapped, and the sunshine fell onto us while the last of the trunk bent and broke; and then the tree was lying at our feet with the faintest traces of a wind making the leaves move. I looked up at the patch of clear blue sky. Cody said, "Okay, boss. Now what?"

Marshall said, "Drag it over. Shove it right in here!"

It took everyone. Cody prodded Jack into helping, and we found good handholds in the branches and shoved together in a string of jerks, and Cody herself kicked the trunk into alignment. We got the axe-clawed end of it into the gap beneath the massive concrete block. If nothing else, I thought, the dragon was really trapped now. I stopped and gasped, my sore hands stinging with my sweat; and Cody rolled Jack's perch over to us. She said, "The fulcrum," and positioned it between the pit's edge and our newly made lever.

We were ready.

Marshall had the net hanging overhead. "We tip the slab," he said, "and I drop the net, and we've got it. Neat and quick."

Cody looked at him and shook her head. I couldn't guess what she was thinking. Then she grabbed the tree where it jutted into the air, and she asked, "Are we doing it? Marshall?"

He stood motionless for a moment. "Yeah," he said. "Yeah."

I used all of my muscles, my back and legs and arms, grunting hard and thinking that nothing would move that block, that a hundred of us couldn't have made it slip an inch. Then came the first tentative sounds—the concrete rubbing against the bricks, grinding them to dust—and Cody screamed behind me and the tree itself bowed a little bit. I gasped and jerked harder. I imagined that gray-white block rising up on its side and tumbling backwards with a thunderous crash, and again the block slipped several inches, Cody roaring, my hands burning against the tree's bark and each of my fingers ready to pull loose and nothing happening, nothing moving for the awfullest age, and then Cody let the tree spring from her grasp. I felt myself lifted, briefly airborne, and the tree shook and Cody staggered out onto open ground, in the liquid sunlight, squatting on her hands and knees while she gasped and dripped sweat and shook with exhaustion.

"You quit," said Marshall. "Why'd you quit?"

She said nothing. Her head lifted, her eyes narrowed against the glare, and she didn't say a word.

Marshall was too close. He couldn't think of quitting now, his own clothes drenched and his hands a mess and him unable to understand what people wanted. "Rest," he told us, sounding as if he was granting us a favor. "Rest and we'll give it another try. In a minute."

Jack said, "Forget me."

Marshall wheeled and glared at Jack.

"We're finished," Cody whispered. She rocked backwards and rose to her feet, shaking she was so tired, her arms and shoulders trembling with the exertion. "We just don't have the meat—"

"We'll get help," Marshall countered. "We'll find help."

She said, "It's getting late."

"So we work tonight—"

"It'll keep, Marshall. If it's there, it's trapped. Okay?"

Marshall turned and asked, "Who's staying with me? Anyone?"

The ground around us was covered with clods and the crushed underbrush and the freshly killed tree, and I felt a sudden sadness for having helped tear everything apart. It was as if I'd had a fever and spoken crazy talk for a while; and now I was healthy again and remembering what the feverish Ryder had said. All of us had acted crazy. We had made an awful mess—

"Ryder?" said Marshall. "You'll stay and help. Right?"

I looked at him. I was hungry and ever so tired, and I couldn't seem to speak.

He said, "I can pay you," with his voice rolling out of control. His eyes were wild; he moaned and glanced at each of us. "I'll pay everyone. Anything. How much do you want—?"

"Marshall—" Cody began.

"Twenty dollars. Fifty!" The voice rolled faster. "A hundred real dollars! I can do it! If we catch it, believe me, I can pay you at least that much. Or more!"

"Stop it," said Cody.

Marshall said, "Ryder? Ryder? You'll stay, won't you?"

"Quit!" Cody rushed toward Marshall and pushed him off his feet. "Will you just fucking quit, goddamn it! For a second!"

"I'll pay—"

She slapped his face, then made an ugly sound and turned away. She took a couple steps and shook her head, saying, "Stop." She turned to face him again, telling him, "I know all about it, Marshall."

Marshall stayed quiet, watching her.

"What is it? If you catch it, what do you get?" she wondered. "My moms heard it was a ton. A big fucking ton of money." She breathed through her nose, her mouth clamped tight. Then she asked, "How much are you getting? If you make your mom proud?"

"It's my business," Marshall claimed.

Cody watched him, and she shook her head again.

"So how'd they find out? Your moms."

"I don't know. One of your aunts blabbed to some woman who works with Tina. Something like that," she said, and she blinked before telling him, "She's such a fucking jerk—"

"Who?"

"Your mother."

Marshall rose to his feet. There wasn't any color in his face. His long arms were hanging at his sides, apparently boneless, and he was breathing so fast that I expected him to faint at any moment.

"Don't," he warned. "Just don't—"

"A royal blue bitch," said Cody. "Don't you know it?"

Marshall said, "Shut up. Would you—?"

"Watching her at your party," she said, "know what I thought? I thought I was so goddamn lucky. I told myself, 'A good thing I didn't pop out of her tight little cunt—'"

Marshall grabbed the handle of a shovel and drove hard, the blade *woosh*ing in the air. I heard the *woosh* and nobody else moved, everyone watching, and maybe Cody wasn't ready. Or maybe she thought Marshall would pull up short. Or maybe she wanted to get hit, pivoting at the last instant and the dirty backside of the blade striking her side, her ribs, just missing an arm. Then Cody dropped. She was down. Her face was red and her mouth was clamped shut and nothing else showed on her face but a fine layer of sudden shiny perspiration.

Marshall dropped the shovel, startled but still angry.

"Jesus!" cried Jack.

"Oh, no!" said Beth. She knelt beside Cody and laid her hands close to the wound. I saw blood on the shirt, and Cody lifted the shirt to show the ugly bruises blossoming over her ribs. She said, "I'm okay," without any breath in her lungs. "I'm fine."

Beth touched her bruises. The blood came from an ugly shallow gash on the wound's upper edge. Cody gasped and said, "Don't."

Beth said, "You need help," with slow certainty.

"You could have killed her," Jack told Marshall. "Murdered her! Jesus!" He picked up another shovel and held it like a ball bat.

"Cut that," Cody managed. She pulled down her shirt and stood and breathed in a regular, labored way. "Help me get home," she told us. "Jack? Help me walk."

I looked at Marshall. His anger was dissolving out of

him, leaving him too weak to stand. He took a few wobbly steps and sat on the tree trunk, close to the pit and the capping block. He didn't seem to see me. He sat motionless. The others were leaving, and Beth said, "Ryder?" until I turned and joined them. We walked a gentle course through the woods and across the bottoms. Cody was carrying herself. We kept close to her, watching her feet and legs and the drooping tilt of her head. Jack said, "You should have smashed him! The turd!"

Cody said, "No," and breathed slowly.

"He could have split your brains!" Jack was the angriest one of us. "He could have *killed you!*"

She said, "Help me up the slope. Okay?"

It was strange to see Cody weak. The world seemed wrong when she couldn't bound up the bare slope with ease. We held her hands and reached the pasture, and she said, "We'll rest a minute," and she sat down in the warm tall grass.

"You let him hit you," Jack decided. "Why didn't you dance out of the way, Cody?"

I knew why. It was because Cody had said those things about his mom, true or not, and she said those things knowing that she had to stand up to whatever happened. That's how Cody saw things. She didn't take shit about her mothers, and turnaround was fair. I was sitting beside Cody, watching the wind running in the grass, and Jack touched me. "Did you know about it? What Marshall was doing?"

I nodded. "Yeah."

"He tell you himself?"

I nodded again.

Jack broke into a hard angry smile. "I knew too. Cody told me—"

Cody said, "Jack?"

"—and we made a deal," he said.

"Who made a deal?" I asked.

"Cody and me." The smile was harder and angrier every moment. He told me, "She'd let me live in the treehouse come summer. If I promised not to hunt the snow dragon."

I glanced at Cody, and she gave a half nod.

Beth said, "Your bleeding's stopped. I think."

I asked Cody, "Why?"

Cody breathed and sat back in the grass, staring at the

hard empty blue of the sky. "Don't tell Marshall," she warned. "None of you tell him. I mean it."

"Why'd she do it?" I asked Jack . . . and then I didn't need to ask him. I saw it for myself. Jack would catch the dragon first, and then Marshall would never quit being angry. Their feud would become a war and someone would have to leave the group, sure—I could see everything—and then what we were, this little family that we were, just wouldn't ever be the same.

ELEVEN

Dad woke me at four in the morning, running a hand through my hair. "You want to watch it, Ryder? Ryder? It's starting now. Ryder? The big hound hunt...it's going on."

"Not now," I managed. I sat up in bed and ran my own hands through my hair, then across my face. "It's days early. Isn't it?"

"Must be a change in plans," he said.

"It's on TV?"

"Come downstairs. I'm going to make a doughnut run myself."

Mom was sitting on the sofa, her face puffy and her red eyes slow to move. Dad left us with a cheery wave. I sat on the floor, feeling spent, and the two of us watched rows of shuttles lifting off the moon's surface. They were near Tranquility City—their hot exhausts chewing the rock to dust, the dust spreading to all sides—and the cool voice of a woman saying, "Robots brought the warning, as we understand it. One government spokesman has stated that the military anticipated such an emergency—"

"What sort—?" I started to ask.

"Shush," said Mom.

"—although one wonders about the consequences of this sudden rush. A few more days of preparation now seem like a luxury." The images of lifting shuttles dissolved into a sober handsome face. I recognized the woman reporter and Tranquility City's main mall stretching out behind her. She said,

"Recapping events: There is growing evidence of structural weaknesses within the notorious Florida comet. It's feared that fighting between spark-hounds could—I repeat, *could*—cause explosions and a scattering effect." She paused, grave in a professional way. "The moon itself is at risk... although sources indicate that the dangers are still quite slight."

Mom muttered something.

I turned and looked at her, saying nothing.

The TV shifted to shuttles at Hadley, and then at other cities. The moon's moon was somewhere behind the moon, out of view, and the reporter spoke of the complex maneuvers required to catch it in the proper fashion. From somewhere came images of tiny robots—the armored spies used to probe hound nests and old mining tunnels. They were insect-sized and blackened, weaponless but equipped with hardened senses and fearlessness. The military had been sending thousands of these spies into the moon's moon, seeking information. The reporter read from the prepared text, describing the robots' mission and their benefits; then the images dissolved into an animated view of the dark organic heart of the moon's moon, pressures building and massive bolts of lightning flaring and the narrator's voice feeling the pressure, telling us, "This *is* very much a race against time. The hounds number near a hundred thousand, and the nests themselves have been gathering solar energy despite the obstruction schemes—"

"What's the word?" Dad burst through the front door, a box of fresh doughnuts under his arm.

Mom said, "The best laid plans, Kip. The best laid plans." Her voice was strange. There was an edge to every word.

"It's sure the odd morning." Dad sat and opened the box and pushed it across the floor to me. "Know what I saw? More than a couple fancy campers on the street, heading straight out of town, and it sure isn't hunting season. Is it?"

No one spoke.

"As if the mountains are going to be safe ground," he said.

I took a doughnut and bit once, chewing and realizing that I wasn't hungry. I put down the doughnut, the cherry filling bulging outwards.

"Where do you suppose *he* is hiding?" asked Mom.

Dad rolled his eyes. "Now, pray tell, *who* do you mean, Gwinn?"

"Wherever he is," she said, "he'll be safe." She sounded angry. She told us, "I bet he's built himself a fine pillbox somewhere. A fortress."

"But nothing's going to happen," said Dad.

"You think not, Kip?"

He said nothing. I watched him sitting with his back straight, eating nothing, something working behind his face.

Another woman reporter was talking. She was in a noisy room inside U.N. headquarters; official announcements had been made moments ago. She told the details in brief—how the earth's defensive systems, orbital and ground-based, were being activated as a precaution, and people everywhere were being asked to keep in touch with events throughout the next two days. These were the critical times, she promised. Then, almost as an afterthought, she added that everyone remained confident despite the changed schedule. "Buoyant," she said and smiled, assuring us that everything was under complete control. No problems were expected. And there was no truth to rumors of confusion in the ranks or shortcomings in the training or the simulated attacks—

"Ryder?" said Mom. "You've seen the mansion twice. Is it a fortress?"

"Gwinn," said Dad. "Just quit."

"What?"

"Nothing's getting this far. Okay?" Dad was angry, blood in his face and his knuckles white, his fists pressing into the sofa's soft fabric. He said, "Trust me. It's as good as done. Okay?"

She rolled her eyes and said nothing.

I blinked and focused on the TV. Shuttles and bombs were destroying the moon's moon in simulation, in slow motion, and I wondered about Dr. Florida while I watched. I couldn't seem to blame him for these troubles. At least not like Mom blamed him. Besides, I thought, he felt so very awful about what was happening. I knew it. I knew he would give his life a hundred times if he thought that that would save us—

"Ryder? Hand me the box. Ryder?"

I pushed the doughnuts to Dad, reclaiming mine first, and he set the box on his lap. He touched several with his fingertips, taking none, and the TV showed dots of fire crossing the moon's black sky.

"Look at them," said Dad. "It's an armada, all right!"

I had to go to the bathroom. I felt better when I was out of the living room, alone. I returned without hurrying, pausing at the front door and looking outside, noticing the first red splashes of light on our street, everything absolutely ordinary in that quiet, scrubbed early morning way.

It was more of the same throughout the morning—shuttles maneuvering while the reporters talked in delicate, graceful loops, plus pictures of the moon's moon and scenes from the lunar cities and everyone everywhere bursting with confidence—and finally Mom said, "I've had enough. I've got work to do, Kip, and this is driving me crazy. Crazy! I'm not going to sit here all day!"

"So go." Dad shrugged and said, "It's not much of a show, you're right," and he winked at me. Dad wasn't worried about anything. "Would you keep tabs on things, Ryder? For us?"

"I'll try."

"I think I'd better take a look at some properties," he told Mom. He halfway grinned, asking, "Would you like to come, love?"

She shrugged. "Can you make your own lunch, dear?"

I said, "Sure," and they left together. I waited for a time before building sandwiches and pouring myself a huge glass of lemoned Pepsi, and I sat on the floor again and skipped through the channels. Then our house personal said, "Ryder? Someone wishes to speak with you—"

"Who?" I asked.

"I don't know the voice."

I lifted the receiver. "Hello?"

Lillith said, "Hello," and I felt a moment of confusion. I hadn't expected her voice, but then I blinked and some voice deep inside me said, "Are you really surprised? No, you're not."

She asked, "Are you busy, Ryder?"

"No."

"Come outside. He wants to see you. For a bit."

"Now?" I asked.

"Just come outside, Ryder. It's important."

A delivery truck was waiting. It was across the street, large and brown with its engine purring, its driver watching me and me knowing his face. I had seen that face at the mansion, on one of the uniformed guards, and he waved to me. He beckoned me, and I felt calm beneath the strangeness. The truck's back door opened, and Lillith stepped into the sunshine. She squinted and said, "Hello, Ryder. How are you?"

"Okay."

"Quite the day," she offered. Her eyes were red and tired, and she looked as if she hadn't slept in an age. "I'm glad we found you. Come on. Step up and in, if you please."

Dr. Florida was sitting inside on a reclining chair.

I said, "Hello, sir."

He said nothing. For a long moment I believed he was asleep with his eyes half-opened, his long face pale and cool and his mouth hanging relaxed. Then he said, "The door, please," and Lillith shut the door. The truck's interior was brightly lit, screens in the walls showing all sorts of images. I glanced at the largest screen and saw inside one of the U.N. shuttles—a view not given to the networks, I realized—and the troops were drifting in freefall, their harsh voices giving orders or making suggestions or simply telling jokes, crude and simple jokes, that most times would have made me want to blush.

I waited a long while, and Dr. Florida merely stared at me. I could hear him taking slow breaths. He moved in his chair like someone terribly weak. He wasn't the man who had stood on the pasture. He wasn't even the despairing man sitting beside me with the surf pounding at the beach, his voice raging about the preciousness of life, and so on. This particular Dr. Florida glanced at Lillith, and he said, "Why don't we drive? Someone might notice us sitting."

Lillith touched an intercom, telling the guard to drive through the area—in a natural fashion.

Then Dr. Florida asked, "Are you surprised to see me, Ryder?"

"Not really."

"You're a bright fellow," he said.

I said nothing.

He touched a control panel, changing the image on the large screen. For a long while he did nothing but stare at the moon's moon as it rose over a crater wall—a darkish lump now flaring with blue-white electrical light—and then he said, "You're not afraid of me, are you?"

"No, sir."

"Do you blame me? For these terrible things?"

I said, "No," and paused. "They were accidents..."

Lillith touched my shoulder. I was sitting on a small chair, and I could feel her long fingernails through my shirt. I could smell her old perspiration. The truck was moving, turning every so often and going nowhere; and I had to ask myself what was so important that Dr. Florida had gone to this much trouble on this particular day—

"Accidents," he said. "Accidents?" He seemed to weigh the word on his tongue, then he shook his head. "I really meant nothing but the best, Ryder. You believe me. Don't you?"

I kept quiet. I wanted to believe—

"I wanted lifeless places to bloom. I told you that much when we talked last time...and it's the absolute truth. Anything else you hear is wrong. Simply and totally wrong."

Lillith said, "Aaron," as if to bolster him somehow.

"You were helping life," I said. I wished Mom could be here to hear his explanations. I wondered what she would say if she witnessed his deep sincerity for herself.

"But it is my fault, Ryder. If I hadn't started this insanity, none of this would have happened." He breathed and looked at me, and his eyes came wide open for the first time. He seemed alert and clear-headed for the first time. "People are dead, Ryder."

"Tragedies happen," Lillith told him. "You can't carry the weight yourself, Aaron," and she pulled her hand from my shoulder.

"How many dead?" he wondered. "So far?"

"And how many richer and happier because of you?" she asked.

"Lillith," he explained, "is my most loyal fan." He smiled without joy or humor. "The fact of the matter is that whatever happens, good or awful, people will say certain things about me. And for a long, long while they'll talk. Damning me for an eternity, I should think—"

"Aaron?" said Lillith. "You don't know that."

He blinked and told me, "I kept everything secret. Particularly once the hounds were loose...for as long as physically possible, I kept it hidden." He breathed and said,

"Ryder? Do you know why I worked so hard—why all of my people worked so hard—keeping the truth invisible?"

I remembered what they had said on TV, about cowardice—

"There was a rationale behind the deceit, son."

"A good rationale," snapped Lillith.

I waited.

Dr. Florida smiled and sighed. He told me, "For fifty years, without pause, I've been enlarging the public's consciousness. As bright as you might be, Ryder, I think you're too young and naive to appreciate how fast people have come to accept tailoring. I did it with plants, then animals, and then people themselves. The larger part of the struggle hasn't been scientific. Oh, no. We've always been able to do much, much more than the public believes possible. No, everything's hinged on public moods and perceptions." He shook his head. "I've labored long to build a society that could use and appreciate such special children as you." He breathed deeply and lifted one hand to his face, examining it in an idle fashion. "Not that there aren't wastes or injustices, no. And of course there are cruelties. Some of the tailored children are being scarred right now. I admit it. Troubles with their parents or their peers, and the scars will linger throughout their lives. Yes. Yes, it's sad." He breathed and said, "But growing up has never been easy, Ryder. Not in my time. Not in any. There are always days when it seems impossibly hard—"

"Aaron?" said Lillith. "Aaron."

"Pardon me," he offered. Then he grinned. "I'm rambling like an old fool, I fear."

I kept silent.

"Imagine, dear boy. What would have happened had the world learned about the spark-hounds too soon? Do you sense my point? There are limits, strict and unbridgeable limits, as to what the average person accepts. Synthesize a unique organism, a virtual alien, and you've crossed those limits. I knew that when I started the project, and that's why I maintained secrecy from the outset. And when the hounds were running free in some old tunnels, deep inside 'Florida's hell,' I couldn't very well make public announcements. The reasons for secrecy were just too enormous. You see?"

"You had no choice," said Lillith. Her expression was passionate and utterly convinced. "None."

He said, "The hounds were a mistake," and he nodded.

"I was old and mortal and rather obsessed with life and its sanctity. That's why I made them in the first place. I didn't believe anyone would ever occupy my position again—the money, the prestige, and so on—and so of course I had to be the pioneer. What government or corporation would have had the imagination to attempt such a feat—injecting life, robust and elegant, into a wild, empty world? It was *my* duty and *my* risk. Let this world debate my worth when I was dead, I decided. Damn me or make me sit on God's right hand. Either way—"

"But people adore you," Lillith told him. "Even now."

"She means there have been no major backlashes, Ryder. Yes. People are generally holding their breath and expecting the best."

I said, "Shouldn't they?" We? Me?

He said nothing. I felt very cold when I saw him looking at me, his mouth closed and his hands wringing one another. Then Lillith said, "He's devastated, Ryder. You must believe—"

"In the best of all possible worlds," he told me, "there will be an ugly backlash. There's no escaping it. The dust will settle and a large number of adults will think for two minutes, maybe three, and then claim it's wrong to tinker with life, for any reason and at any time." He shook his head and said, "I can imagine the sorts of political and religious movements that will try to undo the good . . . and that's in the best of all possible worlds, Ryder."

"Such a tragedy," said Lillith.

I looked at her, then at him, then I stared at the floor and listened to the purring of the truck's engine.

"My secrecy," he admitted, "was a hopeless bid to protect you and your friends. And the billion-plus other children around the world."

"To protect us?" I whispered.

"I was so afraid . . . afraid that if the world learned of the hounds, particularly if they weren't beaten . . . well, I was sure hysteria and the fanatics would do worse things than shout and march. Much worse."

"We've been fortunate," said Lillith. "No children have suffered. That we know of—"

I'd never have guessed such a thing were possible. I said so.

He said, "It is," and shook his head. "There have been three maniacs, in three separate cities, who were making plans to assault schools and other places where 'contaminated' children could be found." He sighed. "As sad as it seems."

Lillith touched me again. "We aren't saying these things to scare you, Ryder. We want you to be informed."

I saw tears welling up in Dr. Florida's eyes, and he leaned forward and grabbed my hands. His own hands felt cool to the touch, like always, and they shook without strength. "In the best world possible, I promise you, I will care for everyone injured because of me and this business. I make that pledge to you just as I do to everyone I meet. Believe me."

I swallowed and asked, "What's going to happen today?"

No one spoke.

"Are we going to win?"

Lillith breathed, and Dr. Florida pulled away from me.

"The soldiers are going to kill the hounds, aren't they?" I asked. "Everyone says so!"

And Dr. Florida explained, "Sometimes, Ryder... sad as it seems... public moods and public perceptions have no absolute worth. What happens, happens. I am sorry."

Once again he touched the controls and changed the image on the big screen. I saw the moon's surface dissolve into salmon-colored clouds and the piercing wail of wind, and now the sun fell into view over the far horizon, tiny and bright in the soft bluish sky, and moving fast. I said, "Jupiter," and he said, "Good," and the camera tilted upwards, showing me the bulging clear plastic balloon—"Heated by laser light and the weak sunshine, Ryder"—plus the lightweight gondola encasing the camera itself. The wind shrieked and then paused, then it struck again, the gondola jerking and twisting with the impact. Then we looked down into those salmon-colored clouds, and somewhere in the back of my mind textbooks and science shows explained what I was seeing—the distances, the wind velocities, the mammoth proportions of the electrical blasts and the seething heat beneath everything. Jupiter seemed so very vast and beautiful, and Dr. Florida apparently read my mind. He said, "A shame it's all empty, all this loveliness and no admirers," and I started to cry.

"Now don't," he warned. "Please?"

I blinked at my tears. I felt so sick and sad, wishing

everything were different. Clearing my throat, I said, "I'm scared. Sir."

He was crying too. He used the backs of his long hands to dry his cheeks, and he told me, "I'm terrified, Ryder. I wouldn't want to lie to you or pretend otherwise."

Lillith seemed impatient. She touched my wrist and said, "Tell him."

I swallowed and waited.

"About what's happening today," he said. "You should know one thing."

I said, "We won't win," with a flat, defeated voice.

"I don't know," he admitted. "But I don't think so, no."

"The eggs," said Lillith. "Explain the eggs."

"What eggs?"

A strange slender grin broke out on his face. He told me, "When I knew the secret would leak out—before that first explosion by several days, Ryder—I brought the high U.N. officials into the picture. I told them the story, and do you know what happened? They took the secret for their own. Yes, they did. They began to apply the governmental tricks used to control people's attitudes. And they put shrouds over certain ugly facts." He paused, then he asked, "Have you heard or seen anyone on TV, on any of the networks, discussing spark-hound eggs? In these last weeks?"

I remembered nothing.

"And do you know why? Because that's part of the plan. They've obscured the eggs from the start." He glanced at Lillith, then he told me, "Remember my lecture on Jupiter, if you will. All right? All that heat below, and the enormous pressures?"

I said, "All right," and glanced at the bright screen.

"And you're seeing it now. Here." He tapped the screen with one knuckle lightly and said, "Enormous sheer winds and downbursts and vast turbulences that would rip apart the strongest hound nests. In time. It's an abusive environment, Ryder. Even for the hounds. There are no close comparisons on the earth, but a pounding surf has similarities. Think of a beach. Water shifts and the winds blow, no good cover anywhere. And the native animals are prolific out of need. They need tough bodies and tough abundant eggs, all of the elements wanting them dead—"

"For us," said Lillith, "the eggs are the greater danger."

Her eyes were exhausted and sincere. "World governments are aware of the danger, and each is preparing its defenses—"

"If we can't sterilize the moon's moon in one stroke," said Dr. Florida, "then there's a likelihood of infection. For us."

"We can't count all the eggs," said Lillith.

"Not that we're helpless, of course. And maybe with good shooting... well, we'll see."

I started to cry again. I had to blow my nose, and I hunted for something to use but nobody paid attention to me. The two of them sat upright and motionless, and I found an old napkin stinking of mustard, blew hard and looked at Jupiter again. I listened to its raging winds and felt a chill, and I blew my nose again and folded the napkin over the wet warmness and tucked it into my pocket, out of sight. I said, "They'll kill all of us, won't they? Right?"

"The hounds?" he responded. "If they arrive now, I don't know how we could fight them." He seemed to think for a moment, then he declared, "My labs are working nonstop trying to find a synthetic virus, any form of contagion, to cause epidemics. The problem is that the hounds are the most rigorously designed organisms of all time. From the first DNA strand we have kept them devoid of weaknesses. Believe me."

Lillith told me, "The eggs can tolerate enormous heat and pressure, you see. More than the adults, by several factors."

Dr. Florida nodded. "The eggs are buoyant and full of energy. They've got big super-loop yolks that can power a youngster until it and its fellows have a nest built." He said, "Our simulations of hounds on the earth are sobering. Small nests lifted by warm air would drift on the wind, and the larger ones would settle and form hill-sized mounds, the mounds dotting a broiled, organic-impoverished landscape."

"Eggs don't die easily," said Lillith.

"Nuclear fire will do the trick," Dr. Florida told me.

She said, "We can't know how many eggs are in the moon's moon. A hundred thousand? A million? We just don't have the information." Then she paused, adding, "Of course lasers and neutron beams will help—"

"Absolutely!" He said. "Don't count us out yet, Ryder!"

But then their sudden courage was gone. They fell silent, and I felt the truck rolling and thought hard for a long while. Lillith called the driver on the intercom. She asked about people tagging along behind us, or anything else suspicious.

The driver's hard voice said, "Nothing. We're clear."

I felt hollow now. Drained.

Dr. Florida fixed his eyes on me. Then he put his hands on the arms of his chair, squeezing hard and asking me, "Do you ever ask yourself why I'm telling you secrets, Ryder? Have you ever wondered what I want?"

"I do," I admitted.

"All of the time, I bet."

"Yes, sir."

"Well," he said, "quite a long time ago, even before I saw you for the first time, I realized just how badly things might turn out. In the end. So I started drawing up a worst-case plan. And when I did happen to meet you and your friends—by the purest chance—I realized something at once. Without hesitation."

I waited.

"This is a grave secret," he said. "Let's both hope you can keep it to yourself for years and years, maybe for the rest of your long life. Okay? Maybe everything will work out, every last hound and egg killed, and just maybe I can die with a shred of my dignity intact—"

"We have an outlet," said Lillith. "An escape."

"Exactly." He sighed and said, "I won't explain the details, but we've come today to tell you that we're thinking of you and that you and your friends need not be terrified for your own lives."

"Everything's ready," said Lillith.

"I wish there hadn't been this need for a sudden assault," he confided to me. "The soldiers aren't ready. And we're struggling to make ready. What I was planning to do . . . if the attack happened in a week or so . . . was come to you and your folks. No need for this drama, this camouflage," and he lifted his hands, gesturing at our surroundings. "What with the chaos of the moment, I felt I owed you some explanations. And some warning—"

"We'll still come talk to your parents," said Lillith. "If there's any need."

I swallowed and managed to say, "I don't understand."

"These friends of yours?" he said. "They're your very best friends in the world, aren't they? You rely on them for countless things, and the five of you are a unit. A team. Isn't that so?"

Lillith said, "You're all quite talented. We've seen your records, and we're certain that you merit the honor."

"Honor?" I asked. I started to move in my chair.

Dr. Florida said, "We're making ready for the worst possible end, Ryder. That's all I can tell you now."

"Don't mention this to anyone," said Lillith.

"Not even to your parents," Dr. Florida warned.

"Or anyone," Lillith added. She pressed at me with one hand, not wanting me to move.

I tried standing anyway. I said, "Don't. Please."

"We don't wish to seem cruel," said Dr. Florida, "but the chances are good that we'll see you again. You must try to prepare yourself mentally, Ryder? You're the perfect candidate, Ryder."

I was weeping again, pushing at Lillith's arm.

"This isn't going well," she admitted.

"Try concentrating, Ryder. Be brave, for God's sake."

"You'll be safe," Lillith assured me. "Whatever happens—"

"And your friends too," Dr. Florida said. "Plus other children."

"Many others, Ryder."

"I want out," I muttered. "Please? Now?"

Dr. Florida glanced at Lillith, his eyes saying that this wasn't as he'd imagined it. But he said, "Fine. We'll take you straight home."

"Now!" I cried. "Let me go now!"

"But you're not a prisoner," he promised.

I suddenly felt like a prisoner. I was trapped and desperate to be outside again, and safe—

Lillith told the driver to stop.

The truck quit moving, though the engine was still humming.

"I'd hoped for more from you," Dr. Florida told me, shaking his head.

"I'm sorry," I said.

"You're not cowardly, are you, Ryder?"

I stood, and nobody tried to touch me. "What happens to my folks?" I asked. "If?"

No one spoke.

I shivered, and Lillith said, "Good-bye, Ryder. And thank you."

"Remember," said Dr. Florida. "Everything is hard for everyone now. You're no exception, and I just wish this could all be neater—"

"You'll do fine," Lillith promised, and she smiled. "Just fine."

I saw her strong smile.

The back door of the truck opened, sunlight flooding inwards; and Dr. Florida said, "You'll understand it better. Someday."

I said nothing.

Lillith kept smiling.

"Regardless what happens," he promised, "I know you'll appreciate our efforts and our good intentions. Ryder?"

I climbed out of the truck, down onto the pavement.

"Good-bye, Ryder," said Dr. Florida.

I kept silent.

The door began to close; and for a moment, between the door and its reinforced frame, I saw him take Lillith's hand and holding it flush to his face, to his cheek, saying, "Love," with a crumbling voice. "Oh dear love."

We were on the west side of the parkland. The truck pulled away, and I crossed the street and followed another street until it ended with a row of bright houses and the woods beyond. The day was hot and brutally dry, every lawn watering itself and the trees shaking in the furnacelike winds. I cried for a little while, then I stopped myself. I cut between houses and a man yelled, "Use the street, you little shit!" and I climbed his back fence and eased myself down a series of vine-choked terraces, down into the cool dark woods. The faint but unmistakable odor of a dead fire hung in the quieter air. I froze, my confused mind wondering if a hound had come to the parkland. Already? I thought. Was it somewhere close? Somewhere broiling trees into ashes, into food . . . my skin grew cold and my hands trembled, something stirred in the brush and I turned and bolted across the bottoms and up toward Cody's house.

Of course it was too soon for any hounds. I realized that much when I was running, feeling foolish, feeling like a hopeless coward on top of everything else.

I rang the bell and knocked. Tina answered the door. She saw I had been crying, and she nodded as if she understood. "Hasn't been much of a day, has it?" She and May had been lying on the sofa together, watching TV. "Cody's in her room, Ryder. Healing. She took quite a fall."

May was watching me. "Did you see her fall, Ryder?"

"No, ma'am."

"It must have been quite a drop," said May. "As bad as that bruise looks."

"I guess so."

Tina asked, "Do you want a drink? A snack? Help yourself."

I was desperately thirsty. I slipped into the kitchen and filled a hefty glass with ice water. Fixed to one wall was a liquid crystal bulletin board, and while I drank I watched the words "THIS IS A HAPPY HOUSE" form in bright pink letters. My head ached from the cold water. I set down the glass, and the words changed. They were tall and vividly blue: "CONGRATULATIONS TO CODY—ANOTHER FINE SCHOOL YEAR!" I passed through the living room on the way to Cody's room. Tina was snuggling against May on the sofa, and May was purring into Tina's ear. Tina giggled. May giggled. They looked up at me.

"Nothing to eat?" asked Tina. "You're sure?"

"Thanks, no." I slipped into Cody's room. She was dressed and sitting upright in bed, on top of her sheets, and the hot wind was passing through an open window. She seemed to relish the heat. She said, "Hey!" and smiled. "You been watching TV?"

The TV was hung on the wall. The news hadn't changed since morning, except more shuttles were in position and more teams were ready to be dispatched. I saw men and some women inside their armored lifesuits. They were carrying powerful recoilless guns and strange bulky packs—"For bleeding away stray lightning bolts," Cody told me—and each of them looked brave and self-assured. They knew nothing about the dangers, I thought to myself. They believed, wrongly, that they could win.

Cody was watching me. "You're in some state," she said.

"I'm just worried," I told her.

"Not me."

I sat on the edge of her bed, on a corner.

"I didn't break any ribs yesterday. When I fell," she told me. "I feel a whole lot better today anyway. I'm healing fast."

I hadn't thought about Marshall or the shovel for a long

while. It didn't seem to have the slightest importance anymore. Not to me.

"Anyway," she said, "you want to hear the latest?"

"The latest?"

"About the great dragon hunter." She poked me with a bare toe, smiling with all of her face. "After we left him yesterday? After my spill? Jack saw him later. Late at night. Jack was in the oak and Marshall was coming and going from the woods. All night long he carried stuff through the pasture and straight under the oak, and Jack told me everything this morning. You know what Marshall was carrying?"

I shook my head.

"Cans. Buckets. Big bottles. Bunches of little bottles. I'm talking about the middle of the night, Ryder." She shook her head, her smile huge. "His folks were out somewhere or asleep. Because they didn't hear him out in the backyard pumping gas—"

"Gas?"

"Pure old fashioned gasoline!" She paused, halfway laughing. "Jack went to sleep late. After midnight, I guess. And maybe at two o'clock there was this *wham* and the oak jumped and he fell off the long bench, flat on his butt, and he saw an enormous flash of light—"

I could smell the ashes again. I said, "What happened?"

"Marshall poured gas into the old well, I guess. I don't know how many gallons. And then he set a fire—"

"Is he all right?"

"Oh, sure," she told me. "Jack went to watch the fire. He saw Marshall sitting there, baking in the heat," and she blinked and watched me. I felt strange. A little voice inside me told me that Marshall had tried to kill the snow dragon, that such an event was somehow important . . . but I couldn't find any excitement inside myself. Not the weakest drop of interest.

"You don't look so good," said Cody. "You don't."

I admitted, "I've got a story too."

"Yeah?"

"A giant secret," I warned. "No one can know it."

Cody was staring at me. Her eyes were round and so was her mouth, and her round mouth said, "All right," with a whisper.

And I cried. The soldiers on TV were dropping toward the moon's moon, singing old military songs, and I was dissolving to pieces. Cody grabbed me. She squeezed me until I ached and told me, "It's okay. Your speed. Your voice. Explain it however you want, Ryder," and that's what I did.

I told everything.

And Cody shook her head, crying too. "Assholes, assholes," she said. "Everywhere you look it's assholes."

TWELVE

Mom and Dad were drinking coffee from their largest cups, trying to stay awake. It was after midnight, and the attack was still grinding along. I was sitting upright on the floor and feeling no need for sleep. "Are you all right?" Mom asked me. "I don't like your color."

"I'm okay."

"You're sure?"

"Yes, ma'am."

She didn't stop watching me, however. "Maybe you should climb into bed," she said after a little while. "You can see what's happened when you get up tomorrow."

"This isn't some football game, Gwinn!" Dad's voice glanced angry and then settled on tense. He was tense. He looked at her and forced a laugh, then asked, "More coffee? Love?"

"Thank you, no."

"Well," he said, "don't let them kick a field goal till I'm back. Okay, Ryder?"

I made myself say, "All right."

We were watching the moon's moon from a higher orbit, watching it passing against the gray bulk of the moon itself. I saw scattered farms and occasional lights, plus bright discharges between nests in the foreground, and I thought of the soldiers fighting to plant their nuclear charges in special places, just so. There was talk of casualties, maybe a lot of them, and the hounds were proving hard to kill. No network gave us a close-up view. The U.N. was keeping its secrets, I realized. And the newscasters kept telling us that soon, maybe in minutes, the last of the killing bombs would be in place and the final countdown would begin.

"What did you do today?" asked Mom. "You never told us."

I said I went to Cody's and watched TV. And I walked too. I just walked.

She scratched the top of my head for a moment, then quit, saying, "I changed my mind," to Dad. He had come back into the room, and she handed him her empty cup. "Half full. Please?"

"Yes, love."

I blinked. Dad had turned and taken a long stride, and I blinked and saw a flash, brilliant and short-lived, and the unseen newscaster sputtered, "Goodness! Something... goodness, something's happened!"

"What?" said Dad.

"Kip!" said Mom.

"A premature detonation?" said the newscaster, her poise shaky but reemerging. "One of the shallow nuclear charges... has somehow detonated, and we're awaiting an official explanation. Perhaps this means nothing. Perhaps..."

The shuttles around the moon's moon were beginning to fire their engines, pushing themselves clear of the blast area; and for an instant I thought of the teams inside the tunnels and nests, fighting and working to place their charges. And then the next blasts came fast, even brighter now, and when they quit there wasn't any sound but for the soft breathless gasps of the newscaster herself.

The moon's moon was shattered.

Debris was scattering from clouds of hot plasma, turning red-hot and still much too large. There wasn't supposed to be any visible debris. The moon's moon hadn't been in position, none of the big lunar guns had been able to do their magic; and the newscaster tried to explain, saying, "A back-up plan was triggered by the premature blast. The Florida comet's orbit had been changed, you see... it might have shattered and scattered hundreds of... of large pieces pell-mell. So the assault commander ordered the detonation of all nuclear devices... and it's hoped, we can all hope, that what little debris you see can be tracked and destroyed. As soon as possible, yes..."

Mom said, "Kip?"

"Shush!" he answered.

I was thinking about the eggs. How many eggs had survived?

The newscaster spoke of the earthly defense systems: enormous radar installations, ground-based and in orbit, which had the capacity to track tiny objects; newly installed lasers able to cook hounds in a millisecond; plus the very best artificial intelligences calculating orbits and ranking the dangers even now, even as she spoke.

"What are we going to do, Kip?"

Dad settled on a chair, leaning forward. He said, "Search me," with his face sad and weary.

"If those . . . those monsters . . ."

"I don't know, Gwinn. I just don't."

I said, "I'm going upstairs to watch," and no one spoke to me. I climbed the stairs and sat in the dark, and from time to time I heard Mom speaking with a voice turning tighter and more frightened by the minute.

"There must be something we can do," she said.

"What do you want me to do?"

"Is there someplace we can go?"

"None I know."

"But there must be a way to hide from them."

"They're not at our door, Gwinn. Not yet."

"If they come—?"

"I don't know. Just . . . we'll wait and see."

"Sit and do nothing? And what will *they* do to us?" She said, "I can't believe this. You'll be twiddling your thumbs until they break through our walls, won't you?"

"Gwinn—?"

"That son-of-a-bitch," said Mom. "Him and his ego and his damned slimy charm—!"

"Gwinn?"

"You're defending him!"

"I'm not. Believe me," Dad told her. "If he walked in here this minute, I would shoot him. I mean it."

She said, "It's what he deserves."

Dad said nothing.

"This isn't real," Mom decided. "It just can't be happening."

And Dad told her, "I know what you mean. It feels like a dream." Then he added, "It's a blessing, that feeling. It's the only thing keeping me sane."

*   *   *

I slept and woke, and it was still dark. My head hurt and the quiet was a little frightening while I climbed out of bed and dressed. I told the house personal to keep the lights off. I went downstairs, finding no one, and told the personal that I was going to the parkland, just for a walk, and not to let anyone worry. Please.

I didn't want to be home when Dr. Florida arrived. He would come this morning, I thought—or someone would come in his stead—and Dad would shoot him. I could almost see him doing it. *Pow* and then *pow* again.

I walked past Cody's house, where no lights were burning.

The Wellses' house was nearly as dark, every good window opened to the cool night air, and I could hear two songs playing and someone laughing and someone else shouting, "Fuck!" one time. Then there were just the two songs banging their heads together. Brown shattered glass littered the graveled road. I slipped past and onto the pasture. The air was humid. The grass itself felt warm against my bare legs. A soft wind blew one way, then another, and then died away entirely. Someone threw another bottle, and I heard it burst on the road.

A light showed in the oak. It was the flickering, campfirelike light of the TV, and I heard TV voices. I said, "Jack?"

"Ryder?"

"I'm coming up," I told him.

Jack was sitting on the floor of the big room, working by the TV's colored glow. He had been crying. He said, "They're coming. Did you know?" and he breathed once and shuddered. "Shit's falling on the moon, all over, and hounds too. And there's more shit coming our way. They're saying so now."

"I know it."

He looked at me. After a minute, he said, "Glad you're here."

"What are you doing?"

"Working." He brought out a sack, untying its neck and pulling a big garter snake out by its neck. I saw the tag fixed to its tail. Jack read the tag and marked down the number and location of capture, then its length and girth and its weight according to a little scale. He said, "A female," with a distant voice. "Know how I know?"

I remembered a field guide, imagining it in my hands—

"Her build. See how thick she's built, and big? Female garter snakes are always larger."

I remembered. I said, "Sure."

He watched the snake moving in his hands. He said, "You hear about Marshall?" and he lifted his eyes to find mine. "Did you?"

I said, "Cody told me."

"Left a real mess over there. You see the mess yet? No?" He shook his head. "Jerk," he said without heart. "The jerk left our tools over there, and his damned net. I brought them back here for him. Yesterday," and there wasn't any anger in his voice. "He blew the shit out of the place, Ryder."

"Did he kill it?" I wondered.

"The dragon? I don't know." He shrugged. "I haven't heard it, but then it doesn't always scream. You know? Maybe it got out first. Maybe there was another way out of that thing."

I kept quiet.

"Anyway." Jack stood and looked toward the east. "It's getting light," he said, and I looked up and saw a touch of red on everything. He asked, "Do you want anything to eat? Drink? What?"

"What do you have?"

"Canned shit. Fresh mulberries. And some of this." He pulled a plastic flask out of a freezer. It was covered with frost and full of heavy liquid, and when he took off the lid, in an instant I could smell the contents.

"From the springs," I said.

"And not too bad." Jack took a long swallow and smiled, and he told me, "Go on. I filtered it and boiled it and it's not bad at all."

I tilted the icy flask and sipped, the stuff tasting like cold, thin soup. It tasted okay. I thanked him and he put the flask back in the freezer, then he turned and asked, "Are we all going to die, Ryder?"

I said, "No," and realized that I was being truthful.

Jack said, "I'm going back to sleep. Okay?" He didn't mention my answer, nor did he give his own opinion. He turned off the TV and made his bed on the long bench, then he put his snakes and his snake records beneath the bench and lay down. I pulled a pair of binoculars from their cabinet and sat alongside the east windows, watching Jack's house and as much of Cody's as I could see. The sun was close to showing. My stomach began to growl, so I opened a can of spaghetti and meatballs and ate it cold, using a grimy fork and my fingers. After a while an ordinary car pulled up beside the Wellses' house. I heard it on the gravel, glass breaking under its tires, and I focused the binoculars and saw Dr. Samuelson stepping out. He seemed cautious and wary, looking in all directions and then crossing the street. He was going to talk to Cody's moms first.

I waited.

Jack was asleep and dreaming. I saw his eyes flipping about beneath his eyelids, and I breathed and waited and wished I could sleep too. I so much wanted to lie down and dream, dreaming something happy. Only I couldn't relax. Not now. Not with the heat of the day starting and the sun breaking over the trees on the horizon.

Dr. Samuelson left Cody's house. May was beside him, and she was crying while he spoke. She stopped and shook his hand and went inside, and he turned and turned, looking everywhere, then he crossed the paved street and vanished into the Wellses' front porch.

I heard him knocking in the morning's stillness. Once, then again.

No one answered. He came to the back of the house, and I saw the way he walked, so straight and yet tired, and he mounted the porch and knocked and knocked, then he turned and shot a look down at me. I felt his eyes. I didn't think he could see me—he was watching the treehouse—but with my binoculars I could see his weathered face and his red unblinking eyes, his mouth set and hard gray whiskers starting to cover his chin.

Lillith arrived in a second car. She got out and joined him, and I watched them talking and gesturing. Jack said, "What's going on?"

"Just peoplewatching."

He was sitting up now. "I had this dream. What to hear?"

"Sure."

Jack stood and pulled the flask from the freezer. He took a long drink and farted once and said, "I was a snake. You know?"

Lillith and Dr. Samuelson were walking to the front of the Wellses' house, to the front porch, and I heard them knocking hard on the door, without pauses.

"Are you listening, Ryder?"

"You were a snake?"

"In the dream, yeah." He sat on the bench and rubbed his face. He farted again. "I've had the same dream . . . I don't know how many times. I'm always a snake out hunting. I'm always smelling things with my tongue. This time I was in the grass, slipping along, and you know what I saw? I saw you."

"Me?"

"Just lying on your back in the grass, Ryder. I saw your face in the bright sunshine, just so plain, and when I came past you, you turned and looked at me, right at me, and said, 'I know you.'"

I couldn't hear anyone knocking on any doors now. They must have gotten someone up out of bed at last, and now they were inside. I could see Marshall coming down the hill on his bike. He rode up to Cody's house and vanished, and then Lillith and Dr. Samuelson appeared again. They were talking. I pressed the binoculars to my eyes, trying to read their lips. Lillith glanced at the Wellses' house, just once, and then they climbed into their plain little cars and drove out of sight.

"What else happened?" I asked. "In the dream."

"Nothing." He looked at me and asked, "Who are you watching now?"

Marshall had reappeared, Cody beside him. They were coming toward us. Marshall was tense and pale. I couldn't tell much about Cody. Her face looked wooden, I thought. She seemed so very short beside Marshall, and Marshall was even clumsier than usual. I loved him for being clumsy, I realized, and I felt so very glad that they were walking our way. For a slippery strange moment I was actually thrilled, knowing all of us would survive . . . that Dr. Florida had some wonderful plan and we'd be saved in some wonderful fashion.

"It's them," said Jack.

I put down the binoculars and looked at Jack. I studied his face and the way he slouched forward. He was just a kid, I thought. A little kid, and scared. Sure. "What do you want to do today?" he asked. As if he could pick and choose.

"I don't know."

"Let's hunt snakes, okay?" He brightened and said, "The four of us. And Beth too. How about that?"

I said, "Maybe."

"Maybe?"

I didn't say anything.

Marshall shouted, "Ryder!"

Cody shouted, "Ryder!"

Jack looked at his hands and said, "We don't have to decide yet, I guess."

"Your mom said you were down here," Marshall explained. "She sounded nervous as hell on the phone. So I told her we'd come get you and explain things, only then she said you knew it already. That lady, Lillith, had come by yesterday and told you to be ready."

Cody was sitting beside Jack. She was holding him like she had held me yesterday, to comfort him. The morning's chill was finished, the air blowing hot through the windows, and I was so very tired that I felt sick and cold and numb.

Marshall was on the floor. "You didn't tell *me*," he said.

I shrugged.

"You told Cody. Not me." He wanted to be angry, only everything was too crazy. He sat with his knees up near his mouth, and he said, "I guess it doesn't matter, huh?" and he shrugged too.

Marshall had been crying. I could tell.

"How did Lillith explain things?" I asked.

"She told my folks about the eggs coming for us. Maybe the orbiting defenses would get them, but in case not we ought to be ready for the very worst. Soon."

"Did she say where we'd go?" I wondered.

"Not really." He shook his head, his lips pressed together. "I guess somewhere in space and they don't want us telling anyone. Not anyone. It's all some huge secret."

Cody said, "There's Beth," and I lifted my eyes. Beth was crossing the bottoms, and I expected her to be crying worse than any of us. Only she wasn't. When she was below us her face was almost calm. She had a strange look to her eyes and around her quiet mouth. She climbed up to us and sat at the game table, sighing, and Marshall asked, "You've heard?" with a careful voice.

She seemed deaf.

Marshall said, "Beth?"

She blinked and told us, "I'm not leaving them," and bit her lower lip. Then she nodded, satisfied.

"What?" said Cody.

"What did you say?" asked Marshall.

I said, "Beth? What happened?" I went to her and touched her face, my own hands shaking, and she felt so warm to the touch. She started to cry, but only slightly. "Who came to your house?" I wondered.

"A man."

"Dr. Samuelson?"

She nodded and gently pressed my hands away from her. "He stood on our porch and talked to them . . . telling them there wasn't much time and if they wanted me to live, if they loved me, I needed to be packed and ready in a few hours." She sobbed. "I heard everything." She picked at her tears and said, "Quit," to herself, and she stopped crying.

"What did your folks say?" asked Cody.

"They need me." She wasn't answering the question. She was speaking without thinking, without doubts, saying, "He scared them," as if that was somehow wrong. "They didn't have time to think . . . but I can't just go! I can't leave them here, can I? I'm not going to do it."

"You've got to go," Marshall told her. "All of us are going."

"They'll come get you," I said. I was too tired to be scared, the numbness insulating me. I told her and everyone, "They won't let you decide. Not if your folks say yes—"

"I'll hide," said Beth.

"Hide where?" asked Marshall, skeptical.

"In the woods. Anywhere." She had given it careful thought, I realized. She said, "There are plenty of places."

"And then what?" he persisted.

"They'll stop looking for me and I can go home again. When it's too late for them to make me leave."

Cody made a sound. It might have been a word choked off inside her throat, or it might have been nothing. Just a sound. She seemed angry now. She told us, "I don't want to leave my moms, either. I've been up all night thinking about it, and I don't."

I blinked and turned to face her.

Marshall said, "You're nuts!"

"We don't *know* the hounds are going to make it here," she said. "And do you know where we're going? Huh, Marshall?"

"Florida's trying to save us," he said. "Like Ryder said. You can't just say no."

"Why not?"

Marshall didn't know why not. His face filled with color, his mouth pressed into a tight pink line.

"I'll hide you," Cody promised Beth. "Don't worry." She was using her smoothest, surest voice. She didn't want to leave her family, not now, and when she spoke with that voice I myself saw a glimmer of choice. I hadn't even imagined that I could do what I wanted. Not until then.

"They'll be here in a couple days," said Beth. "The hounds. I heard it on the news." She hummed a soft note, fuzzy and dark. "If we can just stay down here that long, maybe—"

"I'm going," Marshall declared.

"So go," said Cody.

"I will." He licked his lips and looked concerned. He wished one of us would argue with him, or that he could change Beth's mind, or Cody's. "I am going to leave," he repeated.

"So leave," said Cody.

"Soon."

"Ryder?" said Cody. "Ryder? Do you want to know what I think?" She touched me. "The rest of us are invited because of you. It's you that Florida wants to save."

Jack said, "Why?" and stared at me.

"Because I can remember certain things," I admitted. I felt absolutely certain. "Later," I said, "when it's over, I'm suppose to tell people what happened. The true story. That's what he wants me to do."

"That's what I figure," said Cody.

I started to breathe harder, the blood in my face and my heart pounding, and they were looking at me. All four of them were watching me. Marshall said, "When everything's destroyed, you'll be the one people go to. So they don't forget. Sure," and he blew air between his knees with his eyes fixed on me.

Beth asked, "Are you going to leave now? Ryder?"

I looked at Beth.

"Stay if you want," said Cody. "Or find Florida and go."

And I heard myself saying, "No." I said, "No, I'm staying."

*   *   *

Dr. Samuelson drove a van onto the graveled road. It was nearly noon. I saw his suit and his bright gray hair and a dark little briefcase in one hand, and for a long moment he stood gazing down at the pasture. Then he turned and went to the Wellses' front door. We couldn't hear him knocking, since the wind was too loud. Maybe he didn't have to knock this time. Maybe someone was waiting for him.

"I bet he's looking for you, Jack," said Marshall. "Then all of us."

Cody said, "Anyone else? Anyone see anyone else?"

Everyone was holding binoculars. There was nobody until Dr. Samuelson reappeared, coming out of the back door. He didn't have the briefcase anymore. He paused and stared down at the oak, and us, and I felt his eyes playing across us. Cody said, "Down. Now," and we hunkered on the floor, waiting.

I saw the pasture through a tiny crack in the wall.

Dr. Samuelson didn't like the long walk. He seemed old and heavy, sweating hard enough to soak his good clothes. He said, "Kids?" to us. "Can you hear me? Kids?" I saw a strange bright redness to his face. Then he was below us, and I couldn't see him anymore.

Nothing happened for a long moment.

He was waiting, I knew. Standing and waiting for us to jump.

Then I heard him sliding down the slope, kicking loose clods of earth and the soft dust, and Jack pressed his face against the opposite wall, peering through another crack. Jack motioned when he saw Dr. Samuelson. Very softly, almost without breath, he said, "He's looking up." Then he said, "Now he's just looking around."

We waited.

Finally Dr. Samuelson climbed back up the slope and crossed the pasture, whirling before he got too far away from us. He had hoped to catch sight of us, I suppose. But we were down and hiding. He was frustrated, maybe angry, but he didn't say anything. He went to the van and drove it himself, leaving in the direction of my house.

I wondered what had been inside that briefcase. The briefcase he had left inside the Wellses' house.

I sat up and looked at nothing in particular, thinking hard.

Cody said, "We need weapons," and waited. Then she

said, "If we're going to make a stand, then we'll need more than we've got."

Nobody spoke.

"In case they do find us," she told us.

Beth said, "Can't we just run somewhere else?" Her eyes were big and round and sorry for things.

Marshall muttered something about leaving us. Now.

"Ryder? Jack?" said Cody. "We're going to do this fast."

The three of us climbed out of the oak and crossed the bottoms, each carrying a bucket. We gathered chunks of concrete from the slabs—chunks that would fill a hand—and then we climbed past the slabs, needing more ammunition. We found the old brick well and the concrete cap and the dead tree beside them. The cap had been blasted to one side—I tried to imagine such an explosion—and I smelled the dead fire and crept up to the edge of the well. Shards of bricks were everywhere. I could see sunlight falling into the shaft, but when I bent forward my shadow blotted out the light. Was the dragon dead? I couldn't tell. I was looking at how the intact bricks were stacked, with plenty of slots where little feet could cling. Then Cody said, "Ryder?" and shook me. "Come on! We've got to go."

She carried my bucket for me.

The van appeared when we were climbing the oak. It came straight down onto the pasture this time, its engine racing, and I crawled up into the big room, panting. Cody was pulling up the last bucket, pulling the rope hand over hand, and the van jerked to a stop and my folks climbed out. Dr. Samuelson was behind them. Marshall was watching the van with binoculars, saying, "Ryder? I think your suitcases are in the back, aren't they?"

I saw them. My folks had packed for me; I was ready to leave.

Cody said, "Help me, Jack," and she spilled concrete and bricks onto the floor, one bucket and then the other two. She said, "The slingshots, Jack. They're there," and she pointed at a cabinet. "Marbles too."

Mom called, "Ryder?" when she was close.

"Come down, son," said Dad. "Right now, would you?"

They looked limp and tired, but they also seemed remarkably brave to me. I imagined them sitting with Lillith, listening while she explained what would happen to the earth and them, but not to me. I couldn't imagine either of them saying, "Take us too, please. Save us!" I tried to picture such a thing, and I just couldn't.

Mom said, "You've got to go, honey."

Jack poured marbles into a big stew can.

"Climb on down! All of you kids!" said Dad.

Dr. Samuelson told us, "A flight is being readied. At the mansion. You'll be leaving for Hawaii just as soon as possible—"

"No!" cried Cody. "We won't!" She stood at a window and held a piece of raw concrete in one hand, in view. "We've voted and decided to stay up here." Jack was behind her, setting slingshots on the game table; and I watched how neatly he put them in a row, just so, Cody shouting, "Now you people just stay away. Please."

I looked at my folks. "Dr. Samuelson?" I said. "We want them to come too. Our parents."

Beth made a sound.

"Honey!" cried Mom. "There's no room for us."

I couldn't picture them asking for themselves, no, and so I had to ask for them. Wasn't that right? I watched Dr. Samuelson. "Tell Dr. Florida what we want. Please, sir?"

Dr. Samuelson straightened. He shook his head and said, "No."

I felt unsure of my next step.

Marshall said, "Let me leave," with his voice barely more than a faint whisper. "Right now."

"Go on," said Cody. "We won't stop you."

Marshall didn't move.

Dad said, "Son? This is no time to be noble. Why don't you climb down and bring your friends? Please?" He made a slow, sad sound. Then he turned away. He put his hands in the small of his back, not showing us his face.

Mom shouted, "Ryder! Come down here now!"

Cody stood beside me.

Mom said, "Cody, dear? Would you please, please make him come down? Do what you want, but don't pull him under too—"

"Gwinn," said Dad. He tried to hold her, and she pushed at Dad. She told me, "I want you standing *here* in one minute! Do you understand me?"

"Dr. Florida's waiting," said Dr. Samuelson. "He's counting on your cooperation, and he wants a last word with you—"

"He's not going with us?" I asked.

"No." Dr. Samuelson shook his head. "His duty is here, son."

"So where are we going?" asked Cody. "Why not tell us?"

"Not now. Not here."

And Cody turned to me. "Look. He's scared." She halfway smiled and turned back to Dr. Samuelson, saying, "Bring Florida. We want to talk to him here!"

Dr. Samuelson turned as if someone might be listening to us. He was very much afraid.

"We aren't budging until then!" said Cody.

Dr. Samuelson couldn't stand it anymore. He straightened once again, declaring, "You're not in any position to make demands, young lady—"

And Cody threw the piece of concrete overhand. Not hard, not for Cody, but the gray thing streaked through the air and struck the van's windshield, the glass bursting inward and collapsing. Dr. Samuelson was startled, ducking too late and then tensing for the next blow. He expected to be the target. It was my father who told him, "Easy, easy. She's just trying to rattle us," and he offered him his hand.

Dr. Samuelson accepted it, rising now.

Dad told me, "We'll be back, son."

And behind me, speaking with some certainty, Marshall said, "All right. Okay. I'll stick it out with you guys. For now."

THIRTEEN

We ate snowballs to slake our thirst and Jack's canned food for lunch, and we watched TV for a little while. They were fighting spark-hounds on the moon now. We saw a live hunt, the militia patrolling inside an armored wagon that came over a low rise and almost collided with an injured hound. I saw the angry alien face and its wings extended for no reason, one wing and part of its body misshapened, apparently melted, and the deadly tail gone. The nuclear blasts had left it crippled.

Cody guessed they were showing us an easy fight. She said they might have spotted this hound beforehand, and the victory was supposed to make people feel better everywhere. Bolstering courage and that sort of shit, she said.

The hound shouted in the vacuum, making no sound. The wagon halted and the militia began to fire. I saw the hound's enormous mouth extending and the rasping tongue dangling outward, explosive bullets bursting in its face and chest and the enormous wings. Its glaring eyes were inhuman, I thought. I heard people talking on radios, telling one another to keep firing and don't let up and drive the bastard down. Now! The hound tried to leap, only its legs were too weak. It could barely stand against the moon's weak pull. Then the bullets pierced its armor and its salmon-colored meat shattered, and I saw sparks from its opened bloodless belly and its three-fingered hands trying to close the wounds. None of us could believe the thing was alive, not after so much, and then it was down and thankfully dead and the people inside the wagon cheered. I halfway smiled myself, for a minute. Then there came a sudden motion and flash, the wagon rolled over on its side, the TV image spun and people screamed and there came a second flash, brighter now, and a section of a wall melted as a bolt of brilliant white bored its way through—

The network switched away from the scene, or the camera died.

Another hound, I understood. A healthy hound. I breathed and shuddered, and Beth asked, "What will they do next?" She wasn't paying attention to the TV, but was staring out the window instead.

"They aren't going to wait long, whatever they do," said Cody. She stood and put her hands on her hips, watching the pasture and thinking.

"We'll be ready," said Jack.

Marshall coughed into his hand.

"If Florida comes," said Cody. "Then we can talk to him. That's our big hope."

We nodded.

Cody looked at Jack, and she said, "I was wondering. What would you want him to do for you?"

"Do?"

She paused. "Who do you want brought along, Jack?"

His hard eyes stared at the floor for a long moment, then he said, "Nobody." Then he said, "I don't know," and he blinked several times. He sat up and told us, "I'll think about it."

I turned back to the TV. There were reports of fighting inside the main Hadley domes, and several of the largest farms were infested with hounds hunting organics. The entire lunar population was armed, all that world a battlefield, and the saving grace—if there was such a thing—was the absence of good organics. Given time, said the newscaster, the hounds would run out of raw materials. The key was to keep them from the farms in the meantime.

We ourselves had nothing to do but wait.

Marshall napped on the floor, Beth on the long bench, and finally I had to lie down beside Marshall and shut my eyes, just for a moment, and when I opened them again the angle of the light had changed. It was later in the afternoon, and I sat up and found only Beth with me. I breathed and turned and saw no one else.

"Ryder?' said Beth. "Cody's on the roof."

"Where are—?"

"Below," she said, "They needed toilets."

I heard Cody on the roof. She was standing near the east edge, boards creaking. A long minute passed, then she whistled hard, slicing at the air, and she shouted, "Get up here now! Now! Now!"

Two new vans were pulling off the main street. I saw the sun on their windshields.

"Climb!" she cried. "Fast! Now!"

The lead van was filled with uniformed guards. They drove hard over the pasture, the grass whispering beneath them. I counted eight guards, and they were nearly to the oak with Jack in the maze but Marshall still below. He was in the open and pulling at his pants, and one guard shouted, "That one!" and Cody threw a chunk of concrete. I saw it dropping and the windshield shattered, and she threw a larger chunk that struck the roof and left an ugly dent.

"Get in! Get in!" shouted Cody.

Marshall's long body was clinging to the trunk, then it folded and vanished into the maze. One guard stepped down, brandishing a dart gun. Another said, "Don't." He said, "They aren't squirrels, you shit. We're not dropping 'em from trees!"

Cody used a slingshot now. I saw the streaking colors of the marbles, guards ducking, some hugging the van and others digging helmets from the back end—plastic riot helmets with long face shields. There weren't enough helmets for everyone, and Cody could still punish their bodies. A blue streak, a green streak, and a guard would flinch and moan. Then one of them yelled, "It's kids, Jesus! Go on! Get up there!"

The second van—a fresh one with an intact windshield— had crept up behind them.

Dr. Samuelson and Lillith emerged. Behind them were my folks and Marshall's folks and Cody's moms. All of them looked like rags wrung dry. They were talking among themselves and watching us, and Marshall's mom cupped her hands around her mouth. "Son?" she shouted. "Son?"

Marshall and Jack were beside me, panting.

Jack picked a target and heaved a chunk of concrete. It struck the grassy ground, and he said, "Shit."

"They're climbing," said Cody. "I don't have the angle here!"

I saw two guards managing the trunk, clinging to our little steps. They had cutting tools and helmets and dart guns in their black holsters. I was scared and helpless. I couldn't make myself fight them, but I kept holding my place; and then Jack was beside me with a huge rough piece of concrete in both hands, his body leaning into the open air and bending at the waist and him throwing hard, grunting hard. The higher guard took the blow between his shoulder blades. He turned rubbery but somehow held tight. Blood soaked his shirt, and I saw sweat on his face and the pain making him tremble. He was looking straight at me. Then Jack said, "Back, Ryder. Out of the way," and he threw a second piece of concrete, hitting the man square on the faceplate.

The guard tumbled, his feet catching the man beneath him and both men ending up on the dirt slope. They cursed and rolled in agony. Cody kept the others from approaching, marbles flying. Another guard said, "We need more gear. They said kids in a tree, Jesus." And still another said, "We haven't time. We do it now."

Dr. Samuelson came forward.

He spoke to one guard, and the guard said, "Kids in a tree! You never told us they were fucking criminals!" All the guards were retreating, the one man stripping away his bloody shirt and glaring at us, hating us. Dr. Samuelson said, "Talk to them. Convince them there's no time for nonsense." He was talking to our folks.

"We're not leaving!" Cody cried from the roof.

Tina said, "Cody? We know where you're going. You're going to be absolutely safe, believe us!"

May said, "There's no place for us, dear. Understand."

Marshall's folks pressed to the front, panic in their faces. I could see them trembling, his mom the worst in the bunch . . . a sickly kind of panic on her face. "Marshall?" she shouted. "Dear? Listen to me."

He stepped to the window, obedient and silent.

"You're going to be with other children. And some astronauts too. In a kind of ark, I guess. You've been chosen out of millions of children—"

"Not me!" he answered. "Florida doesn't give a shit about me."

She blinked, not certain what to say.

He said, "Ryder's the one he wants. Not me."

Cody asked, "Where's the ark?"

Tina answered, "Inside some asteroid, dear."

Marshall's dad grasped his wife's hand, squeezing hard. He told us, "Enough of this. Now listen. We want you to come down now, and no excuses. Do you hear?" His voice sounded unnatural, him trying to be harsh and frightening and not knowing how.

Marshall's mom said, "Please now?"

The hatch on the roof opened, and Cody dropped into the big room. "What do you think?" she wondered.

"They're not so tough," said Jack.

Beth sniffled and said, "I'm not leaving," with a desperate certainty. "I just won't."

"Look at my mom," said Marshall. "See? She's all pissed because it's Ryder they want. Not me," and he laughed. He shook his head and laughed and all I could see was his mom crying to herself.

"We just need to talk to Dr. Florida," I said.

"Only he's not coming," Cody decided.

Dr. Samuelson stepped forward. He said, "Jack? Jack Wells?" I saw the guards talking among themselves. Lillith climbed into the second van, started the engine and turned toward the street. "Jack?" Dr. Samuelson persisted. "I was talking to your parents this morning, and can I tell you something? My honest impressions?"

Jack said nothing.

"This is a big opportunity for you, son. Both of us know how much you need to get out of here." He paused, then he said, "Think of the amazing things you'll see in space. And do. Aren't you curious? Don't you want to ride a rocket to the stars—?"

"Fuck off!" said Jack.

Dr. Samuelson didn't seem to hear him. He said, "There's a large nickel-iron asteroid—one of Dr. Florida's mining asteroids—and it's honeycombed with chambers and bright lights, plus water and fresh new soil. A zero-gee park, in essence. We're stocking it with plants and animals, and it's going to be junglelike and green, and I will bet you anything, son, that you'd love to be there. I will." Dr. Samuelson stopped, then he said, "Awful things might happen here soon, or maybe not. Either way, you get a free ride to this place. All right? Jack?" He kept his face turned up toward us, waiting for someone to answer him.

Dr. Samuelson had taken a briefcase into the Wellses' house and left it, and I had to wonder what was inside the briefcase. Money? Drugs? Some sort of payment, I realized. He had come to the Wellses and asked permission to take their youngest son, and they had said, "Okay. If you pay us," and that's what he had done. All at once I could see it very clearly.

Cody said, "If there's so much room, there's room for our folks too."

Beth sang a few rising notes.

Dr. Samuelson shook his head. "Just children can go. And mission specialists." He looked straight at us, saying, "That's the deal!"

"Then there's no deal!" Cody screamed.

And Dr. Samuelson cursed under his breath and gestured at the guards. "Go and get them," he said, "and now, and don't make fools of yourselves this time."

My dad said, "Listen. Isn't there some other way—?"

"Sir?" said Dr. Samuelson. "Kip, wasn't it? Kip, I'm going to ask you and all of these people to stand aside. For a minute."

Jack was beside me, crying hard without any sound. And Cody touched me and touched Jack, saying, "All right. Okay. Here's what we're going to do."

This time the guards returned Cody's fire, throwing gravel and sticks to keep our heads down. Cody was back on the roof, punishing them, and the two smallest guards rushed and climbed the trunk, trying for speed, and none of us throwing at them. Jack went into the maze, and I followed. We were carrying clawed hammers and Marshall's net, and when we were in position we busted facing holes in the maze walls. The guards were using a potent, industrial-grade drill to destroy our thumbprint lock. We heard the whine of the drill, and I was lying on my belly in the blackness, reaching through the small hole and touching Jack's hand. I felt its moisture and heat, and he gave me one end of the net. I heard him say, "Ready," just as the lock died.

The hatch flew open.

The lead guard grunted and cursed and scooted up inside, blocking the sudden light. The net was tucked low and tough to see, and I kept quiet while he pulled himself closer in the blackness, feeling his way. I could smell his sour breath and his sweat, and I felt his body heat. I wanted him in the perfect position, just like Cody had described, and then his waist was beside me and he didn't seem quite there and Jack yelled, "Now!" and the guard snorted, saying, "The fuck—?"

We tugged on the net, and it unfolded itself with an explosive ease. The guard's hands and head were in the tangles. He couldn't reach us or move. Shards of sunlight let me see his waist and belt, and Jack was screaming, "Ryder? Ryder? It's on your side. Can you reach?"

I forced my hand to move, to grope, and suddenly I felt the hard angry shape of the gun, a small dart gun. I pulled it free of its holster. I had it in both hands and took an enormous breath, then yelled, "Got it!" with my lungs tearing.

Cody yelled, "Bring it!" from far overhead.

I hurried.

The big room seemed unnaturally bright and cool, sweat soaking my clothes. Cody took the plastic gun from me and studied it for a long, long moment. Then she said, "I think it's like this," and she aimed and fired, the *woosh* soft. A guard on the pasture gave a little cry. I peered out a window and saw him collapse, his face relaxed and his whole body helpless under his bulk.

She shot again, then a third time, dropping another guard.

No one climbed for us. Dr. Samuelson was shouting, his words smeared into nonsense and his face red and furious; but there wasn't anything he could do. We had won, I felt certain; everything was going as we'd wanted. There wasn't much time, no, but I imagined Dr. Florida coming anyway. I pictured him standing below—I saw him in his raincoat and hat—and he listened to me and nodded, saying, "I understand, Ryder. And I agree, yes, we sure will make room for your folks. At once."

I blinked. The daydream wobbled and vanished.

Dad and May were walking together across the pasture, and I watched them and wondered what they were saying to each other. The guard we'd netted came sliding out of the maze, having pulled free; and he practically fell to the ground, then got to his feet and ran hard as Cody watched him, making little *wooshing* sounds with her pursed lips.

"Let me hold the gun," said Marshall.

Cody didn't answer him.

Jack was sitting on the long bench, his face happy and sad at the same time, in equal measures. He said, "We showed them," without any light or life. "We sure did."

Cody asked, "Is there anything to eat?"

Jack made himself stand. He opened a freezer and removed the flask of cold dark water. "There's this."

"Give it," she said. I saw her take a long swallow, a faint black moustache on her own moustache, then she said "Anyone else?"

It didn't taste too bad this time. I remembered the flavor of lemoned Pepsi, and it was like Pepsi mixed with the spring water. Beth had a tiny sip. Jack took three long sips. Then we stared at Marshall. The four of us had decided that everyone would have to sample it; and eventually Marshall wetted his lips, saying nothing. All of us had the same moustache, and we sat for a few minutes and looked at one another. I had never felt so empty of words or ever so close to anyone, not ever in my life. Then Jack looked outside and said, "They're coming," and I rose and looked.

May and Dad were carrying a long ladder across the pasture. The other parents joined them, walking alongside them. I heard them talking. Dr. Samuelson was standing behind the van, and he said, "Why not wait? I've put in a call—"

"Enough of you," said May. "Good-bye!"

We watched them plant the ladder and adjust its settings, the highest section extending and then dipping toward us. My dad and Marshall's dad and both of Cody's moms were making sure everything was secure, and then they looked at one another. It was my dad who said, "Let them dart me if they want," and he started to climb.

The ladder nearly reached the east windows.

Dad shouted, "You don't have darts for everyone," and he laughed as if something were truly funny. He was almost to us, and he said, "Well, it's time I took a look at this place, anyway."

We backed away from the windows.

Tina followed Dad, and Marshall's dad came last. The three

of them stood in the big room with us, studying their surroundings. Tina was crying without noise. Marshall's dad looked winded. My dad cleared his throat and told us, "I think we're in agreement about one thing, kids. We've never been so proud of you in our lives. Not ever," and he didn't cry. I could see him not crying. He wasn't crying with his eyes or his mouth, and he blinked and said, "The thing is, however, that you're leaving. All of you. You've got absolutely no choice."

I made myself get lost. I didn't want to listen, so I shut my eyes and let myself drift on memories and found myself as ten years old, on a day like today, walking the bottoms. There was a knot of kids and they waved at me. They were standing beneath a scrubby elm. They had found something in the weeds. Could I help them? Could I?

I trotted up to them and saw a baby bird—a featherless, flightless robin—lying on the ground inside a thick green stand of stinging nettles. One girl said, "We'll take care of it if you can get it for us, please. We can't quite," and I got on my knees and tried. No hesitations. I put my hands into the nettles, and then all of my bare arm, and the stinging began at once and got worse every moment. The nettles pumped their poisons into my flesh, and I cried out and breathed and bit my tongue and tried harder. The kids crowded around me, and I swallowed and tried to shake off the agony. The robin was desiccated, feeble, its head rising and dipping and rising again, its future set and me old enough to know its future and still I was breathing and bending, my shoulder starting to burn now, and now the side of my poor face—

—and Cody touched me.

I blinked and found myself back in the present. I couldn't feel the nettles anymore, but I moved my hands just to be sure. Tina was telling us, "We just don't have skills. We can't go with you and eat food, waste air, and be in everyone's way." She smiled weakly and said, "Cody? Honey? You understand, don't you?"

"So you learn things," said her daughter. "You just learn."

"If it were that simple," said Tina. She shook her head and sighed.

Marshall's dad said, "There'll be adults. Some are at the asteroid now, making ready, and I'm sure they're trained and thoroughly professional and..." His voice collapsed. He took a deep breath and said, "Not so talented as you, son. Of course. But I'm sure you'll be patient with them."

"Ryder?" said my dad.

I blinked and looked at him.

He said, "Why don't we go down? All of us?"

"I just wanted to talk... to Dr. Florida," I persisted.

"Only he can't come here, son."

"But—?"

"Ryder. He has his own problems now. All right?"

I felt terribly selfish all at once. I hugged myself and thought for a long moment, then decided, "If the others go, I'll go."

Tina said, "Honey?"

Cody stood and put down the dart gun and took a long breath, then she closed her fists.

Tina said, "We want you safe. Please?"

Cody drove her right fist into the ceiling, one long board screeching and jumping loose; and she shook her hand afterwards, grimacing.

"Please?" Tina repeated.

Beth said, "I'm staying," with a soft voice.

"No," said Cody. "You're coming too."

"I'm going to go," Marshall announced. Then he rose and started to cry. I didn't think any of us could cry anymore. I felt embarrassed and wished he would stop himself.

Jack said, "You big baby," and tried to kick him. Jack's face was dark and crumbling. "You big shit baby—"

Cody pushed between them, saying, "Quit."

"Can we climb down?" asked Dad. "In peace?"

"Sounds find to me," said Marshall's dad.

I glanced outside. Dr. Samuelson and the guards who were still awake were standing in a ragged line in front of their battered van, watching us, and beside them were Mom and Marshall's mom and May. I saw the blowing grass and the houses beyond, a couple of Jack's brothers sitting on the back porch, smoking and watching us—

Dad said, "Ryder?"

I turned.

He smiled at me and said, "Never mind."

Beth told us, "I'm not leaving." She looked tiny sitting in the corner, on the floor, and Cody knelt beside her and said something into her ear. Then she said, "Come here, Marshall. Help me."

The two of them picked Beth up by her arms.

She said, "They need me. I'll just talk to them," without strength, speaking about her folks.

Cody said, "Easy," and Beth was standing. Cody said, "Go first," and Beth climbed into the maze. Cody followed, making certain she wouldn't try to hide. Then Marshall left, and me. Dad was swinging a leg out the window, straining to catch the topmost rung of the ladder, both of his hands clinging to the window frame and his knuckles white and sweat beading on his forehead.

"I'll lock up," Jack promised.

"But you're coming?" I asked.

"In a minute."

I slid through the gloom, smelling people and feeling so very tired, yet no longer able to imagine sleep. I would never sleep again, I told myself. I was stupid with fatigue. Turn and turn and turn, down and up and down again, then out of the maze for the last time. For the last time I was straddling the branch worn smooth by all of our butts, and Beth and then Cody were on the ground, then Marshall, and I came down and jumped the last few feet and stumbled. I was down and tasting the dust in the air, very dry and rough against my teeth, and Mom asked if I was all right. I said, "Yes," and rose, dusting myself with both hands.

Dad was off the ladder.

Marshall's dad was as clumsy as Marshall, almost falling before he was clear of the window. Then Tina came out without hitches, Cody's grace showing through. She didn't look where she was setting her feet, and I watched her and then Jack. Jack was sliding out onto the polished branch, a snake sack dangling from one hand.

"What's that?" asked Marshall's mom. "What's he got?"

Cody said, "He caught them yesterday."

"Snakes?" she squealed.

Dad was looking for Lillith. He asked Dr. Samuelson, "Where did she go?"

"The girl's house," he explained. "Beth's."

Dad said, "All the luggage is in the van."

"We'll walk," May suggested. "Why don't we walk them over?"

Everyone nodded in a sluggish way. We organized ourselves, kids with their folks and Jack jumping down among us. He untied the sack and pulled out bull snakes and a pair of tiny ringnecks, throwing them into the brush. He didn't bother putting their tongues to his face. He left his garter snakes in the sack.

"Call Lillith," said Dad. "Have her wait."

"You're walking straight over there?" Dr. Samuelson seemed worried that we might cause more trouble. "Is that the plan?"

"Straight over," said Dad.

We walked down the slope and across the bottoms. Suddenly Jack shot past us, running, and for a moment I thought he was escaping. Then I saw the sack in one hand and him flipping boards and concrete with his free hand, moving quickly ... with enormous intensity ... as if there was no work more vital in the world ...

"What's he doing?" asked Marshall's dad.

"What are you doing?" asked Cody. "Jack?"

But he had no time for answers. He shook his head and found something, chasing it through the highest weeds and kicking up brown bugs and coming into view again, his arms bleeding and black bugs sucking at his flesh. A broad female garter snake, pregnant and placid, dangled from his free hand while he opened the sack, putting her inside now. Safe now. Saved, I told myself. I realized what he was doing.

We crossed into the woods.

"Where are we?" asked Mom. She admitted, "I am lost."

I was walking between my folks. Cody and Cody's moms were ahead; Marshall and Marshall's folks were behind, Beth in front of them. Mom told me, "I guess we should tell you to be careful ... out there ... and behave—"

Dad made a sound. It wasn't a word, it was a sound.

I glanced behind us. Jack had come up alongside Beth. "I'm getting as many as possible," he explained. "They're tough and adaptable, so I'm going to take them."

Mom sobbed.

"I meant what I said," Dad told me. "About being proud, son." He paused, then he said, "We're both so proud. And would you please promise us something? Remember we were proud? Every so often, please?"

"I will."

Mom stopped and hugged me, crying.

I hugged her back and then Dad too, and we were

walking again, climbing through the shadowy woods. I saw a pair of bambis hiding in the brush, their bodies rigid and their eyes like glass. I saw Cody hugging her moms and Beth now coming closer to us, and I felt like a brown leaf in the sun. I had no weight besides my skeleton. I wished I was an old, old man and all of this was some ancient memory and with a blink of my eyes—I blinked—I could be past it, beyond it, free of the ache.

Then I heard a voice, soft and colorless.

It came from up in the trees, I thought. I heard someone calling for Beth, and I was so very tired that I started looking for someone on a high branch. Did I know that voice? It was a woman's voice, and I knew which woman. I said, "Beth?" as she bolted past me, racing up the path, Mom now asking, "Who is it? What's happening?"

Beth was past everyone now. Cody said, "Look," and pointed and then ran too. I followed her.

Three figures were standing on the stone staircase.

I came out from under the trees and saw Lillith's face, then blinked and saw two people dressed in flowing long clothes with enormous hats on their little heads, and gloves, and veils, and the weak soft urgent voices were saying, "Beth? Beth?" through filter masks.

She ran up the stairs to them. "Get inside!" she cried. "Are you crazy? You get inside, now now now!"

Her father said, "You have to leave."

"No arguments," said her mother.

"I told you! I'm not!" Beth was with them now. Cody and I were climbing after her, nearly there, and Lillith was behind them and leaning against the stone wall, so terribly spent that she was taking this chance to breathe.

"You're going with your friends!" said Beth's father. His voice was dry and strange. "We told you—!"

"You can't make me!" Beth screeched.

Her parents seemed to glance at each other, and then something was decided. They moved with deliberation. Her mother said, "If we have to," and reached, slapping Beth with one gloved hand.

"You're going!" her father said. He slapped her too.

Beth was shocked. She crumbled on a step and wept, and her parents wept too. Then her mother kicked at her body. Not to bruise or break bones, no, but hard enough.

Lillith was moaning, "Please! Please, no!" and Cody was beside me, stunned like me. Motionless.

They pleaded for Beth to leave, and now, and they swatted her. Beth held up her hands and tried to fend off their blows. But at last she couldn't take any more, and she promised, "I'll go! Stop! I'll go with them, just stop!" and Cody grabbed Beth's father. She told me to get Beth's mother now. Fast.

The woman felt tiny and cool beneath her clothes. She had no strength. I could have split her arms without trying, yet she managed to kick at Beth a few more times. "You have to go! You have to!" I had them apart, and the wind gusted. I had her turned toward me, and the wind parted her long veils, for a moment, and I saw the pale false skin etched with enormous scars and one glass eye and no trace of hair on her chalk-colored scalp. I was startled. I gasped and stumbled and hit the old handrail with the small of my back, the tired metal flexing, and I wheeled by instinct with my eyes gazing out at the shaggy trees and the bright open air, half a dozen hands grasping me and pulling me back to safety...

FOURTEEN

Dr. Samuelson drove fast along the mostly empty streets. It was late in the day, and too much time had been wasted. Lillith was in the seat beside Dr. Samuelson, clinging to her door and gnawing on one of her fists, and the rest of us were bunched close and waiting. I felt Beth on my left, her knees pulled up to her face and her face dipped so her eyes were covered and her mouth, and her glossy black hair hung long and loose over everything. She wouldn't move or make a sound. I was between her and Cody, and sometimes Cody would glance at Beth and shake her head sadly. Once she reached past me to squeeze Beth's shoulder, trying to give reassurance.

For a moment I smelled Cody and felt her gentle heat.

Jack and Marshall were behind us. I heard them stirring among the big suitcases. "We're leaving the world," I told myself. "The five of us are going to Hawaii, then into the sky, with hundreds and hundreds of kids..."

How did I feel?

I didn't know. There were moments—brief and terrifyingly strange—when it seemed as though I'd forgotten what was happening to us. Almost. I would blink and look out the van's windows, wondering where we were going and where were my folks and why was my heart beating so fast and hard inside my aching chest. Stress and exhaustion were doing it, I was sure. And the sheer enormity of events. Then I would blink and remember everything in a flash, and I would shudder. And maybe Cody sensed my mood, because she touched me like she touched Beth, squeezing her hand strong like a vise and steady like a vise, and warm.

We slowed as we approached the mansion's gates. Dr. Samuelson said, "Who brought *them*?" and I saw several dozen soldiers wearing the green U.N. uniforms. Large guns were slung over their shoulders, and they were working to build a low wall of sandbags just beyond the gate. "What happened to the guards?" snapped Dr. Samuelson.

"Will they let us through?" asked Lillith.

One soldier lifted a hand, and Dr. Samuelson braked. Then a different soldier came close and stared at him, nothing showing on his face. At last he said, "They pass," and we were waved through the gates and the sandbag wall, most of the soldiers pausing long enough to watch us. I could see their eyes and their hard, worldly expressions. Did they know where we were going? I wondered. How could they know? Dr. Samuelson had told us it was an enormous secret—the shuttles and the asteroid and everything. I was watching the soldiers over my shoulder, and Jack said, "It's okay. I've got you here with me." His snake sack was in his lap, one hand around the well-lashed neck. "We're doing okay," he promised. "We're doing fine."

Marshall said, "Let me see one."

I watched the two of them.

"Please?" asked Marshall. "For a minute?"

Jack said, "I suppose," and unlashed the sack. Then he reached inside with his free hand, his eyes narrowing, and he nabbed a male garter snake with vivid yellow stripes and red blotches on its green sides. Jack was bleeding from one finger. Minuscule red drops formed a U-shaped wound, and when he handed the snake to Marshall he wiped away the blood, closing the tiny punctures in an instant.

Marshall held the snake close to his face, watching it slide between his long fingers. The forked tongue appeared and blurred and then vanished again. Marshall put the snake's face flush to one ear.

"What are you doing?" asked Jack.

"Listening." He seemed to be smiling with the corners of his eyes, finding something funny. "It's talking to me."

"Yeah?"

"Yeah."

We were driving alongside the mansion, approaching the turn-off for the underground garage. Dr. Samuelson asked if there were any more soldiers lurking nearby, and Lillith said, "No. I don't see any. Does anyone?"

Nobody answered.

"What's he telling you?" asked Jack.

"About the fire. The one in the woods." said Marshall. He breathed and put down the snake and scratched his ear. "A couple nights ago."

"The one you set?" asked Jack.

"Maybe."

"Did he see the fire?"

"Maybe."

"I saw it too," Jack told him. "Are you done holding him?"

We reached the turn-off. Dr. Samuelson cranked the wheels, steering us up the tree-lined road. There wasn't any other traffic; we hadn't seen a single vehicle since the gates. The shadows were long and black, the day close to finished. The emptiness and darkness sent out conspiratorial vibrations, and I felt suddenly chilled.

Jack took the snake from Marshall, returning him to his mates and then securing the sack.

"What did you see?" asked Marshall. "Everything?"

"You didn't notice me?"

"No."

"I was there." Jack described the blast and the fire and how he ran across the bottoms while the flames were still visible. "Some big hell of a blast," he told Marshall.

"Did you see the concrete block go flying?"

Jack said, "No. I couldn't."

Marshall seemed ready to speak, then he stopped himself. His hands lay empty on his lap, side by side, and he held himself very still.

"What did it look like?" asked Jack. "The block, I mean."

"I don't know."

"You must have seen it."

"Not really," Marshall admitted. "I had this fuse, see . . . and when I lit it I just ran—"

"What? You didn't even watch?" Jack shook his head. He

might have been angry, or maybe he was laughing. "All that trouble and you went and hid somewhere?"

"In the slabs," Marshall confessed. "I was scared—"

"You are such a coward. God! You really are, Marshall!"

Marshall didn't want to fight. He thought hard for a moment, his eyes focused on a point straight before his face...and his gray voice said, "I am. Yeah," while he nodded. "I'm a coward, sure." Then something bright and serene came into his face, particularly into his eyes. It was the same expression he wore whenever he solved a tough puzzle or some hairy equation—anything that had troubled him for a long while—and he started to nod and actually giggled for a moment. "I guess I am, all right."

And we *thump-thumped* into the cool darkness of the garage.

Lillith took me to Dr. Florida while the others waited. "He really wants a few minutes with you, and then we're leaving. Okay?" She looked sick. It occurred to me that Jack didn't have any clothes, only his snake sack—"We'll get some later," she promised. "In Hawaii, maybe." We were walking fast. I asked about the soldiers at the gates, and she said, "They're here to help guard us. To protect the labs and our scientists," and her tired eyes didn't seem sure of her words. As an afterthought, she told me, "They were invited. Dr. Florida invited them," and she touched my shoulder. "Let's be quiet now, Ryder. I have to think."

The hallways were as empty as the roads outside. We didn't see anyone, not even when we crossed into the research section. The heavy door to Dr. Florida's office yielded to Lillith's thumbprint. I blinked and saw a big round bed where the desk had stood. There were the same screens set in the walls, and I glanced at them before my eyes returned to the bed. Dr. Florida sat upright against a pile of pillows. He was so slight and so pale that he seemed beyond age and wear, more an apparition than a human being, and his dry, dead voice was saying, "Come here, Ryder. Good to see you. Come. Come here."

I was at the foot of the bed, unsure of myself. I glanced sideways and saw the blackness of space on one large screen, scattered stars and then a brilliant flash of light. I gasped and blinked. "Quite something," he said to me. All at once the view shifted, and I saw some enormous machine with the earth behind it, and the machine tilted a long slender barrel and squirted another dose of energy at something.

Lillith said, "We have to hurry."

He said, "We're putting up a fight," and he sighed. "Ryder? Look at me, Ryder. Please?"

I turned and said nothing.

He lifted a long arm. "Closer," he said. "Right up to here."

I approached him until he could touch my shoulder, then he told me, "You've been giving people a real headache, haven't you?"

I shrugged.

"You've made the right decision, Ryder. Coming here like this. And I'm telling you that you shouldn't feel guilty, not for anything."

"Yes, sir."

"I'm the one who is guilty, Ryder."

I watched his dry, pale face.

He wore white pajamas with black trim, and his sorry voice said, "You're going to be safe very soon. Believe me. It may not be home, this place where you're going, but with time I think you'll see its pleasures—"

"The asteroid," I whispered.

"Let me show you." He produced a control panel, changing the image on the largest screen. I saw an enormous cavern without any clear floor or roof, bright lamps scattered on wire tethers and figures drifting in the distance. I couldn't tell if the figures were robots or people, or both, but I watched them for a long moment. Then he was telling me, "I had this place constructed with the idea of some colony. Someday." He coughed into his free hand, the cough dry and tired. "The surfaces are faced with inert stone. To avoid heavy metal toxins. The soils are netted against the surfaces, and by the time you arrive—in several months, I suppose—you'll see green vegetation everywhere. And low-gee ponds netted into the low places." He paused, watching me. Then he said, "Your work is just now beginning."

I had trouble keeping my attention on the screen.

"Ryder? Look at me, son."

I blinked and turned.

"I needed to see you. To tell you good-bye and good luck."

"What's going to happen to you?" I asked.

"Nothing much important," he informed me. "I don't matter much any longer, I fear."

Lillith made a sound. A choked-off sob, I thought.

He said, "Look at me," and smiled. He made himself smile. "There are a couple of things I wanted you to understand." He breathed for strength and told me, "First, nothing is ever finished. The hounds breach our defenses and the earth perishes. Yes. But someday, sooner or later, people will quite surely return to this place. The asteroid out there, so remote? It's going to be home for a growing population of talented souls, you included; and with time and much work there will come industry and power and fresh knowledge. People will learn how to recapture the earth. With a virus, perhaps. Or a toxin. Or maybe something considerably less sophisticated . . . a series of asteroids, for instance. Your descendants might kick them from orbit—huge bodies full of momentum—and with the proper aim, and some luck, the hounds might be dashed clean off the globe. Eradicated. These old continents would be reshaped, yes, but there would be no angry tenants standing in the way of settlers. Of new life . . ."

I was tired of this talk. I could scarcely imagine tomorrow or the next day, and the remote future was beyond all of my senses. I had to ask him, "Why do you tell me these things, sir?" with my voice sharp. I surprised myself with that voice.

"Why?" he said. "Well, that's the other item I want you to understand." He forced his smile once again. "It's too simple to say that I'd like you to recall all of the things you've seen and heard. If that's what I wanted I would have used a camera and tapes," and he shook his head. "No," he said, "I know better. I do. A camera cannot tell people, 'Listen to me now! I have something to tell you!' Tapes cannot say to an entire nation, 'This isn't just what I saw! This is what I *felt!* Let me tell you what I felt—!'"

"We have to be leaving," Lillith interrupted. "Aaron?"

"In a minute." He shut his eyes and collected his thoughts, then he told me, "There will be time on the journey, in these coming months, for you to watch a number of key tapes. And for you to read certain books and private journals. What I'm asking you to do, Ryder, is look hard at my work and my life. People will come to you—your children and grandchildren will come to you—and they'll want to know about this time, and me, I should think, and you'll be the voice who can tell them, 'I knew Dr. Aaron Florida. He was this kind of man or that kind of man.' Say what you like. Say what is right. And then tell them, just please tell them, that I felt so very sorry for being so foolish. I truly did."

Nobody spoke for a moment.

Dr. Florida sobbed and seemed to straighten himself, but the effort was taxing and all at once he slumped forward.

Lillith said, "Aaron?"

He didn't seem to hear anything.

She said, "Did you know about the soldiers? When did they come?"

"Not long ago," he said. "Gracious of them, isn't it? The U.N. wishes to see our precious facilities protected. They even ignored the formality of an invitation—"

"I thought you might have asked for them. Maybe." Her voice was tense, her eyes glancing toward the sealed metal door. "Are we going to have any trouble?" she wondered.

"No, I've spoken to the field commander. A reasonable fellow." He sighed and said, "He assured me that my people can come and go as they see fit. For now—"

"I'll take the children to the airfield," she started to say.

"And go with them. To Hawaii," said Dr. Florida. "Promise me? Will you and John make sure their shuttle is launched on time?"

"I want to be here!" she exclaimed.

He blinked. "Come back," he said. "As soon as you can. I'll wait for you."

She said, "Aaron?"

His face was distant, detached and so terribly sober that I believed that nothing—not whirlwinds or explosions, or anything—could have made Dr. Florida bat an eye. He was strong in some way that required no apparent strength, turning to me and saying, "I hope you don't think too much ill about old Dr. Florida."

"No, sir," I said. After everything, I said, "I don't."

"And in the future? Will you please mention my good traits?"

"Yes, sir." He was Dr. Florida, after all, and I couldn't imagine not loving him. How could he doubt how I felt—?

Lillith said, "I'll be back soon, Aaron."

He blinked and smiled and said, "Fine," without the right voice. His mind had decided something, and when he said, "Fine," I heard what Lillith heard too.

She said, "Aaron—?"

"Go," he told us. "Go."

His smile was bright and fragile.

We went through the metal door, and it pulled shut behind us. Then Lillith froze. I watched her shiver, then she turned and said, "I forgot something," and touched the thumbprint pad. Nothing happened. We stood together in the empty hallway, and she said, "Something's wrong," and tried her other thumb. "A mechanical problem," she muttered, and then there was a sound almost too faint to detect. It came from inside the sealed office. I thought of a hammer driving a nail into living wood in the distance—a simple *pop*—and then there was nothing and Lillith pressed the side of her face against the door and cried and said, "No," once, then again. "No," she said softly. I watched her crying and saw the shine where the door was damp, and she pulled herself upright and breathed through her mouth, now turning and taking a step and stopping. She didn't look at me or in any way notice my presence. I waited. I didn't know what to do, standing next to her and feeling the silence around us. Finally I made myself touch one of her warm hands, saying, "We need to go, ma'am." I tugged on a finger. "Ma'am? We should leave, I think."

Dr. Samuelson was desperate to be driving, to be at the airfield and then airborne. Out of reach. He barely spoke to Lillith. I was scarcely down in my seat when he punched the accelerator, turning the wheel and taking us back out of the garage.

Now Cody was between Beth and me.

Nobody was talking. The darkness of the garage yielded to the almost-darkness outside, and we were driving fast for a brief way. The Dr. Samuelson saw lights, bright and graceful, just ahead of us. "Shit." He told Lillith, "I'll handle this," and braked just short of a new group of soldiers. I could see their faces in our headlights, and their guns, and they weren't the same soldiers. An officer approached the driver's side, a bright flashlight in one hand and a smooth pistol in the other. It wasn't for throwing darts, that pistol. I knew at a glance.

"Sir?" he said. "I'm sorry, sir. These roads are off limits—"

"I'm getting these kids out of here," said Dr. Samuelson. He jerked his head to one side, toward us, and added, "I'm not just anybody here, son. I'd appreciate some slack, if you can help me."

Lillith said, "John—?"

The officer walked back alongside the van. He peered at us, at each of us, seemingly hunting for someone he recognized. There was something patient and teasing about his expression. He enjoyed this extended moment, his lips now curling into the faintest of smiles.

"Aaron didn't think there'd be any problem," Lillith explained, whispering. "He had been assured—"

"Sir?" The officer returned. "Sir, I'd like you and your party to please step from the van. If you would, sir."

"Is there a problem, son?"

"Please humor me, sir."

Dr. Samuelson sat motionless for a long moment, then he said, "Fine," and the moment he opened his door I felt myself being shoved down against my seat. I felt the van accelerating without warning, the engine racing and soldiers leaping aside and one man, ahead of us and too slow, and I saw a bit of his face and then felt the van striking something. Lillith squealed, "God!" and we were past the roadblock. I turned to look behind us, and Lillith said, "They could have shot—!"

"No!" he shouted. "And risk the kids?"

There wasn't anyone behind us. Marshall asked, "Where are we going?" and nobody answered him. The van jerked to the left and went fast down the main road, and I saw headlights behind us. Where was this plane? I wondered. Where were we going? Those headlights were growing stronger. Lillith asked, "What if they're at the plane? Waiting?"

Dr. Samuelson grunted an answer. I didn't understand him.

There was a turn to the right, very sharp, and we were racing on a flat straight new road. The headlights had vanished. Dr. Samuelson killed our own lights, and I felt scared and helpless in the rushing darkness, wishing so much that everything was finished. Whatever was to happen, I wished it was past now. Done. Then headlights swung into view again, closing on us again—

"In the glove compartment," said Dr. Samuelson. "Get it!"

"What?" asked Lillith.

"Just reach inside!"

She said, "Oh goodness," and brought out some kind of gun. She said, "We'll talk to them, John. We can't outrun the U.N. in the air," and she put the gun on the floor between them.

"Give it here!" said Dr. Samuelson.

I could see the trees blurring beside us, and the van itself seemed to shudder with our speed. It seemed to say, "Don't trust me at this speed," and I saw Dr. Samuelson driving and trying to reach for the gun too, Lillith saying, "Leave it," and the engine finding a touch more power. We were going even faster, and Lillith said, "Slow—!" as we started to leave the road. I felt Cody moving beside me, and Dr. Samuelson said, "Shit," and we were diving into a ditch that I felt more than saw, down and then up again and me seeing Cody's hand reaching for me . . . and then came the awful crashing noise.

I left my seat with the impact.

I saw Lillith evaporate into the breaking glass and splitting metal. The van clipped a tree and jerked to one side, and nothing happened slowly enough for me to see it. I was out of my seat and past Cody's hand, and the world was full of motion and noise; and I fell unconscious for an age, or for an instant, and someone had me and pulled me onto a flat stretch of grassy ground. I knew that gentle strength. I breathed and said, "Cody?"

My savior said, "Who's Cody?" Then he said, "Lie still. Just lie there and keep still, son."

He was an enormous soldier. I saw him smiling. It was still night, but there were lights nearby and I could see his face now.

"Is Cody one of your pals?"

"Where is she?"

"Somewhere," he said.

"And Marshall? And Beth? And—?"

"Easy. Easy."

"Are they okay?" I wondered.

"I don't know," he admitted. "I just got here myself."

"Can you please see for me? Please?"

"I know Florida's mistress is dead. And that crazy old fart of a driver too—"

"My friends though . . . are they hurt?"

"One of them." He was watching me. "One of them is pretty badly broken up, and I don't know. It's touch and go—"

Which one? I wondered. I tried to move, to look for them; but some tiny needle pricked my arm and I started slipping into sleep. There was nothing I could do. I imagined each of my friends dead and bloody, flat beneath stained sheets, and I made a vow to myself. Whoever did die, I would remember them. I would find every moment I'd shared with them, and I'd string the moments together. I'd make them real again by remembering the look of their hair and the sound of their voice and the exact feel of their living hands—

—and then I was asleep, so deeply asleep that I didn't dream and I barely thought, the sensation pleasant and endless, not unlike floating suspended in a still pool of warm, warm black milk.

I was awake.

Doctors stood around me. The lights were brilliant, making me squint, and one doctor in white bent and said, "Hello, Ryder."

"Hello?"

"Do you know where you are?"

I said, "No, sir."

"It's been several days," he said, "and you've been tranquilized."

I felt my body wrapped snug inside white bandages. "Are we going to the asteroid now? Sir?"

"No. No, we're not."

He wasn't a doctor. I suddenly understood that few of these people were real doctors, something in their hard watchful eyes telling me.

"We're still on the earth," he told me. "Good old Earth."

"The hounds—?"

"Dead," he promised. "All dead."

A woman's voice said, "Your parents wish to see you, Ryder. But first we have to ask you questions. May we?"

"About Dr. Florida," said the man. "The late Dr. Florida."

"What happened to the hounds?" I wondered. "How did you kill them?"

"Luck and hard fighting," he said. "Plus some last-minute gear we got up into the sky." He told me parts of it, and I learned the rest later. I learned how the U.N. had watched Dr. Florida preparing his ark and certain shuttles. They hadn't been fooled; not for long, at least. And at the last possible instant the U.N. had interceded, claiming the shuttles for themselves and boosting certain freshly minted bombs into high orbits. "Enormous nukes," said the man. "Special nukes. They were designed to throw their blasts in one direction, you see. A shotgun effect." But instead of steel pellets, the ammunition was hard radiation in abundance. The scattering clouds of nest fragments and hounds and eggs were mostly killed; and the few survivors were finished just short of the atmosphere. Thankfully. While I slept in this hospital bed, unaware, the world had been saved. And now everyone was busy celebrating their good fortune, each day like an endless, breathless party—

"You mentioned an asteroid," said another man. "What do you know about the asteroid?"

"Not much," I confessed.

The first man said, "What's important is why. Do you know why you were going there?"

"I think so."

"Why don't you tell me what you know, would you please? Please?"

I tried. I concentrated and began to sort the past, working to tell the essential details. Then all at once I stopped talking. My head was spinning now. I was tired now. I said, "Sir? Could you please tell me . . . which one of them died?"

"Who do you mean?" he wondered.

My friends. I named my four best friends—

"Died?" he said.

I braced myself.

"They're all doing quite well, Ryder." He grinned and said, "Why did you think one of them had died?"

"The soldier had told me. 'It's touch and go,' he said."

"He meant you, Ryder. You're the one who was badly hurt."

I was speechless for a long moment.

He grinned and said, "Rest." All of the people were grinning.

"Yes, sir," I replied.

"For a minute," he said, "rest. Then we'll bring in your parents."

"I'd like that, sir," I told him. "I would."

FIFTEEN

I spent the rest of the summer mending—my arm and leg were broken, plus I needed an operation to patch up my insides—and when things were almost finished, me close to fit and the air tasting of fall, my folks packed everything and moved us to a different city some two thousand miles away.

It was due to business.

Real estate wasn't doing well. Not at all. Lawyers and politicians were starting to dismantle Dr. Florida's empire, and common logic said they would kill the city too. People were going to have to be paid for their pain and anguish, of course. Dr. Florida had promised to make good such debts. And there were physical damages too, particularly on the moon—farm domes smashed and industries frazzled and several cities resembling battle zones—and to raise the needed cash, without fuss, Dr. Florida's companies were being sold piecemeal. "Which means their new owners aren't going to keep them here," Dad warned me. "They'll move them closer to the action, Ryder. In a year. In five years. Eventually."

"That's why we're going?" I asked.

"We don't have a choice. Who's going to want a new home, or an old home, in a shriveling city?" He shook his head and touched the cast on my leg; he felt sorry for having to bring me the news. "I wish we could stay. I do. But we have to eat too. Son? Ryder? Are you listening?"

The TV was full of news about Dr. Florida. In death, it seemed, he garnered even more attention than he had in life.

People learned about the big shuttles full of kids and seeds and durable machinery, and they heard stories about an ark out in the asteroid belt. Sometimes reporters would call our home and inquire about me. What would have been my role in the thing? Was it true that Dr. Florida had spent his last hours with me, talking just to me? They had reports, unconfirmed but tantalizing, that I was to serve as some grand chronicler of this strange, Florida-built society. Did my folks have any comments? "No," Mom told them. "You heard it wrong and stay off this line. This is a business phone, please!" But was it true that I had a gifted memory? Ryder? Was my name Ryder? "I'm asking you to get off this line. Now!".

One final question, they promised. Certain high officers within the Florida organization, testifying to U.N. investigators, reportedly stated that Florida himself wanted the boy, your son, to learn everything possible about Aaron Florida. Even while the world was coming apart at the seams, the old man was busy finding means by which he could insure his good name—

"What's the question?" asked Mom.

Any comment on the story?

"No," she told them. Each of them. "And if you make any attempt to contact my son, or any of us again, I'll call the police." She screeched, "I mean it!" and hung up on them.

It was the harassment, in part, that made us pack and move.

Another home. A different city. My folks didn't mention it at the time, and haven't since, but I think beginning again must have had its appeal. I'm sure that was part of it.

Beth had been the least injured in the crash. She spent just one night in the hospital, then she went home.

Of course her folks welcomed her, and they exhausted themselves explaining how they had done what they had done because of fear and love. Beth heard it many times, in many moods—how they felt horrible now for having seemed so cruel, but would she please try to understand their desperate logic? They had wanted their only daughter to live. They would have done *anything* to make sure she would escape. And of course Beth took care of them as always, accepting their apologies without a word. Her mother developed an infection after having been outdoors that one time; and Beth spent several weeks at her bedside, mopping her gruesome face and singing to calm everyone's frazzled nerves.

But we noticed changes in our friend. Despite her loyalty, we couldn't help but see changes. She was darker. Sadder. Sometimes she would say things—harsh, even cynical words pointed at her folks' weaknesses. "The frail ones," Beth called them. "The old worn-outs." I felt uneasy when I heard her speaking in such ways. Even tiny doses of bitterness didn't wear well on Beth, and I tried ignoring them when they showed.

Everything was different in the world now.

Jack kept living in the treehouse. There were a string of long, loud expensive parties at the Wellses' house, and there was talk that enough people had complained to the social services office that now, at last, the Wellses themselves were under investigation for some type of child abuse. But before any action could be taken—in the dead of the night, and without warning—all of the family, excepting Jack, packed and drove away to parts unknown. Afterwards Jack said, "I watched them go. I sat up in the tree and watched and then I went back to bed. It didn't matter to me." His hard eyes didn't blink. "Not a bit," he swore, and he sighed. I think he was sad because that was the truth. He couldn't have cared less.

"So what are you going to do?" Marshall asked. "Huh?"

"I'll stay where I am. What do you mean?"

"What about the social services people? Do they know where you are?"

"Oh, sure." Jack shrugged his shoulders and smiled. "They came looking for me a couple times. They even brought cops the last time, but shit . . . they might as well have been hunting a snow dragon, as close as they got to me."

I went up into Jack's treehouse just one last time.

We were moving in a week. I wasn't entirely healed—my leg was still buried inside a massive cast with plastic and plaster and electronic therapy devices to make my muscles hold their tone—but Cody rigged block and tackle and pulled me up through a window, everyone helping me over to the long bench. My bad leg was propped up, my toe pink in the sun. It was all like old times, and it was all so different too. I halfway wanted to cry.

Everyone had gifts for me. Going-away gifts.

Marshall gave me a game to be played alone—intricate pieces and a large colorful board—and I told him, "Thanks." Beth wanted me to have a book, her personal favorite. "Thank you." Jack had found a dead pig in the woods, a little boar, and he had boiled away the rancid meat and then varnished the skull for me. "It's great. Thanks," I said. And Cody, knowing me best, slipped down into the maze wearing a smile and carrying tools. *Bwink! Bwink! Bwink!* I laid there waiting. *Bwink! Bwink! Bwink!* Then she returned, bringing me the lowest hatch on the treehouse, complete with its new lock coded to my own thumbprint.

I told all of them, "Thanks. I mean it!"

We talked and talked, darkness falling and nobody wanted to stop. There were cans of beef and beans for dinner, my folks having given me a grudging okay to eat "down there." We had our meal cold. Then Beth looked across the bottoms and said, "Remember the first time we were all up here together, Ryder?" and that launched me into a string of memories. It became night, and late, and everyone had some moment they wanted recalled—"That's what happened? Really?" —which led to other moments. And days. And seasons. "Remember when we did this, Ryder? And that? Tell us what happened again. Please?"

We slowly drifted into a conversation about Dr. Florida.

Was he a good man, or bad? There was a lot of talk defending both verdicts nowadays. In the end we decided that maybe he was both things at the same time, in equal measures, and then we paused for a long moment. It was Marshall who mentioned my old art teacher and his lover, the physical education teacher of whom lusty things had been said. Saying his name was enough to make us dip our heads in respect. He and she had been found dead after the Florida War. They had made some kind of suicide pact, it appeared. When the hounds were coming and everything looked hopeless— the earth's defenses taxed and nobody talking of victory— they had overdosed on drugs and died in bed together, in each other's arms. Curled up like spoons, we had heard. People we halfway knew—

I blinked and shook my head, then something occurred to me.

"Marshall?" I said. "Someone else died. Someone else we know."

"Who?" he asked.

"Remember those guys we saw years ago? The ones hunting snakes with pellet guns?" I could see them plainly. We were eight years old and sitting on the slabs, watching them, and then we went down on the bottoms and found the dead snake. A female, I realized. "I saw his picture on the news a few weeks ago." I told Marshall, "Faces are tough. I just realized who he was."

"Who was he?" asked Beth.

"I never knew his name," I admitted.

Cody asked, "What killed him?"

He had been one of the U.N. soldiers storming the moon's moon at the end. I remembered the poor dead snake and me thinking that someday, in some fashion, he would pay for murdering it. Now he was vapor between the planets. He was dead in some ultimate fashion, and a hero, and I was old enough to realize it had nothing to do with what I had seen. It was just one of those things. The boy was dead and sleeping beside God, I thought, and I felt rather wise and sorry at the same time. For a minute.

Then Jack asked, "How do you think we would have lived up there?" He waited a moment, then he said, "If we'd really gone, I mean."

"Up where?" asked Marshall.

"The asteroid. If things had really gone bad and we'd gotten away."

Marshall said, "It would have been strange."

Cody said, "I'm glad we're here."

"Me too," said Beth. "I like the earth just fine, thank you."

Then Jack told us what he had imagined—the five of us, plus five hundred other kids, growing up in the near-freefall with jungle around us and garter snakes in the air. And he told us, "Cody would have been in charge, see. And I would have been the top scientist. And the rest of you would have helped us run things—"

"Wait!" said Marshall. "I'd be the top scientist!"

Jack said, "No," in the dark. "You wouldn't be," he promised. There was something absolutely certain about his voice. For a moment he sounded rather like Marshall.

"You?"

"Yeah," he said. "Sure. Me."

They started to wrestle. I heard them, and I felt them through the long bench. I pulled my bad leg off its perch and sat up, looking out the windows, out toward the pasture. It was close to midnight. A pair of flashlights were bobbing in the distance, showing people walking straight for the oak. My parents, I sensed. My folks. It's almost finished now, and I sat there wishing for a few more minutes. Just a few—

Then the scream rose from the woods, harsh and roaring and unmistakable.

Marshall and Jack quit wrestling. It hadn't been a serious fight, and now they rose to their feet, Jack saying, "Quiet."

Nobody spoke, everyone waiting.

There was no second scream. My folks were nearly to the oak, and I breathed and said, "I couldn't tell. Was it the same one? Jack?"

"I don't know," he whispered. "I've heard it a bunch of times lately. But I haven't seen it." He paused, then he said, "Maybe it's one of the others. One of its clone kids. Maybe it's wandered up here."

"I bet so," said Marshall.

"I bet not," said Cody. "I bet that's ours. It crawled out of that well somehow."

"Do you think so?" asked Beth.

"I do."

Jack said, "I don't know."

"But I killed it," Marshall told us. "I know I did—!"

"Ryder?" Mom was below us.

"Ryder?" called Dad. "You there, son?"

We sat in silence for a long moment. What if I stayed? I thought. Could I hide with Jack for a little while? Maybe? Then Cody rose and bent and picked me up as if I weighed nothing, holding me flush against her broad flat chest. "We've got to get you down," she told me and everyone.

"Safe and sound," said Beth.

Which was what I wanted, I realized. Honestly. I said, "Okay," and they slipped the ropes around me, and all of them held the heavy rope as they eased me downwards in the darkness.

Which brings me to now. Almost.

A few weeks ago, by chance, I found myself in that part of the country. I drove my new skimmer off the main highway and headed through the shrunken remnants of the old city, going slow, noticing all the empty lots and the old houses collapsing to rubble and the weeds and grasses and little trees creeping out of the parklands to claim the empty ground. Marshall's old house was my first landmark. It was still standing, still occupied, and I parked in front of it and climbed out into the blazing summer heat.

Someone had painted its dark bricks a ridiculous gold color.

The yard itself was hard-packed earth sprinkled with all sorts of bikes and toys and cheap playground equipment. His folks must have moved away long ago, I realized. I waited for a minute, wondering what sorts of kids might live here now. But none showed themselves, not even at the windows, and I finally turned and strolled down the hill toward my old house.

Where was Marshall? I wondered. A few years back, I happened to run into one of his cousins—a pretty woman quick to speak her mind. "He was busy flunking out of schools for a long while," she informed me. "I'm not sure what schools and what fields, but I think he had troubles at home. With his mom. That had to be part of it." She shook her head and grinned, saying, "That old warhorse. His mom, I mean. I got the feeling he was flunking just to bug her silly. Does that make sense?"

It did. I nodded, saying, "It does. Sure."

"Anyway, the last word I heard is that he's happier now. He got away from her and all that expectation crap." She told me, "He did the big emigration," and I asked what she meant. "Up to the moon! Didn't you hear? He's some sort of accountant with a mining corporation, and I guess things are okay. The last I got word—"

"The moon?" I asked.

"The one and only." Her face brightened. "Hey, wait," she said. "I remember you. You were that one kid, right? The one with the . . . with the . . . God, which one were you?"

I deflected her. And now Marshall's on the moon, I guess.

Sometimes I'll watch the TV channels that show live scenes from the moon. I'll hunt for Marshall in the crowded places. A couple times I've seen a tall, angular figure almost graceful in the light gravity—was it him?—but I can never be certain. The right complexion and the right height, yes, but I've never quite seen the face.

A rectangular hole was all that remained of my house,

the basement walls cracked and ready to crumble. For a long minute I stood on the edge of the hole, and I let triggers trip in my head. Crystal moments flooded through me. I saw faces, parades of them, and there were robust odors and certain sounds and real objects seemed to be lying in my hands. But it wasn't this place tripping the triggers; it was me. All me. Wherever I go and whatever the circumstances, I carry that vanished house inside my aging skull.

I blinked, breathing hard and stepping away from the hole.

My hands were empty. I looked at them and shook them hard and then turned and went on my way.

The Wellses' house was gone too. But Cody's moms still lived across the street, their home and yard forever tidy. I went to the front door and wished I hadn't. The personal said nobody was home and would I like to leave a message? "Do you remember me?" I asked. The personal watched me with its single glass eye, then said, "Ryder?" I said, "Hello," and it said, "Ryder? Would you like to leave Tina and May a message?"

"No," I said. "Thanks, no."

I crossed the street and walked down the weedy graveled road, grateful for my solitude. I didn't feel in the mood to talk to anyone just now. I thought about Cody, sure. I'd seen her several times in the last ten years or so. She had played minor league ball for a couple of years, in the men's leagues; then she was hit by a pitch—a hundred-and-twenty-mile-an-hour rocket delivered by some tailored, ape-armed brute—and the doctors said, "Not again. Never again." So she quit the game, toying with some tamer games before finally settling as a coach in a little college and marrying an English professor twenty years her senior. Of all people. She has kids now, a boy and girl, and I've stayed with her a few times. She seems happy enough. The carbon plate in her head makes her content. "Go on. Touch it," she told me once. "Feel it? Do you? That's how close I came to having all my lights go out. So you bet I'm happy. And thankful. I'm just so glad to be here still."

Cody's moms would have talked about her and their sweet grandchildren, I knew. That would have been fine on most days. But I didn't want it now. I crossed the pasture alone, careful to keep alert and not to remember too much. I had too much to do. The grass was tall and ever so green, green in spite of the heat, and I lifted my eyes and found the battered old oak, one of its main limbs gone and no trace of any treehouse whatsoever.

Cody's moms would have talked about Jack too. Sure.

He was theirs for a time. They had adopted him after I moved, making some arrangement with social services. They gave him their spare bedroom when he was cold or ill, and they let him come and go as he wished. Cody had told me about it. There were tensions, sure. He wasn't an easy son. But he ended up in a very good school on pure merit. He ended up getting a string of degrees in ecology and gene tailoring too. And he became part of the huge team that's planning for the terraforming of Mars—a vast, multigenerational project sponsored by the U.N.

I'd seen him once since I'd moved from the city.

The boy is father to the man, they say. Jack was certainly that way. He had the same fierce independence and those changeless hard eyes. He told me how he was working to build predators for the new Mars—big red cats that would hunt in packs, bat-winged wolves for the thick new atmosphere, and a giant furry snake with a shrew's blazing metabolism—

"A snow dragon?" I asked.

"Better," he promised. "Faster. Larger. Smarter." He winked and said, "It's my private project. Plenty of shits don't think it'll work, but I know better. You wait. You'll see."

I passed under the old oak. Our footworn slope had grown up into vigorous weeds, and the bottoms were more grass and trees now. I strolled out into the middle, my eyes open, missing nothing. I could see new, oddly shaped treehouses in the woods beyond—lightweight, enduring things built from carbon fibers and foam metals—and sometimes I'd hear kids hollering or just laughing. I heard them and the wind in the trees too.

I considered walking toward Beth's old house for a glimpse, then I stopped myself. From this side, at this time of year, I wouldn't see anything unless I climbed the stairs and intruded in someone else's life. Later, I told myself. Later. I would pass by the place later, in my skimmer, on my way out of town.

I've been married for twelve years now.

My wife is sweet and young and a wiz at business. We inherited the family business when my folks retired, and we've had some successes selling real estate. Then five years ago, out of the blue, I learned that Beth was living not two hundred miles from me. Her folks were with her, still living, medical technologies just keeping pace with their feeble bodies; and on a whim, I drove to see her and for a little while, now and again, we tried to conduct an affair.

I don't think either of us enjoyed ourselves.

Beth would talk and talk about willing herself into some different life. She was angry for the hold her parents had on her, and for her many weaknesses; then with the next breath she would tell me how many times they had prodded her to go and get a true career. They didn't need her so much of the time, they claimed.

"So do it," I would say. "Take the offer."

"But they don't mean it," she would tell me. "That's the thing. They're just talking that way to make themselves feel better."

In the end, in a clumsy fashion, I put an end to our affair.

I used my wife as an excuse, but the truth was that what we were doing should at least bring joy. At least once in a while. And since it didn't, it couldn't continue. "Not anymore, Beth. I'm sorry."

She didn't seem to hear me.

Sitting across from me in the restaurant, she sighed and sang a slow note before asking me, "Do you know what we have to do? If we want to ever, ever be happy?"

"What?" I asked. "Tell me."

She sighed again, lifting her eyes to me.

"Betray our parents," she said. "That's the only way."

I began this account with a promise. I would pick and choose, telling only what needed to be told. I think I have done that most of the time, never pretending to know things beyond my grasp. For instance, I can't give any definitive answers about Dr. Florida's truest motives and plans. Lately some people have speculated that Aaron Florida had masterminded every awful thing with the spark-hounds. Their escape. Their growth. Even their assault on the earth. He had been an evil man, say these people. His intent had been to manipulate a small number of children and rebuild this world in his own image. Smiles and guilt were his masks, nothing more, and I shouldn't let myself be fooled now. These people weren't fooled. The man had been the biggest bastard, they claim. The vilest piece of shit ever to walk outside of Hell.

Maybe they're right, and maybe not. I don't know.

I've come to see how little I do know, telling this story.

The world is so different today. I am near my middle years, gray coming into my hair; and I feel like a traveler in time. When I walked down the bottoms I was very much out of place. The parkland I remembered was gone—the trees grown or fallen, the kids grown and gone; and even a landmark like the almost-pond was transformed. Its waters were running clear, and it was deeper and quite a bit larger. A true pond at last. I stood on its shoreline for a long moment, watching a big fish or maybe a little whale breaking the surface, and then I heard a sound. A pounding sound. I turned and started up the long west slope.

Someone had built a house on that flat stretch where once, years ago, I'd lost the snow dragon in the grass. It was a modern house, colored like wood and shaped like an Indian tipi. There wasn't a trace of that old crumbling concrete foundation, of course. There were brief slopes on three sides, all of them covered with brilliant odd flowers. A patio encircled the base of the house, and a figure stood working on that patio. I crept closer. I didn't want to intrude, no, but I felt so very curious. I saw a small hammer rising and falling. Hammers haven't changed—a clawed tool and a flat pounding tool—and the figure looked like a boy, I thought. At least the face was masculine. Sweat-soaked and determined.

At his feet was a substantial chunk of wood.

Rot and dampness had made the wood soft, and he was beating it with the hammer's clawed tool. He was eighteen, maybe nineteen, months old. He had a baby's soft golden hair and skin nearly as black as coal, and he worked with his pink tongue sticking from the corner of his mouth.

"What are you doing?" I asked him. "Kid? What are you making?"

He looked up at me. His head was oversized, and his eyes were like polished stones. With a soft, eerily clear voice, he spoke to me in some language that I didn't know. He seemed to be explaining something that was perfectly obvious to him, gesturing with the hammer and his free hand.

They do that a lot these day. Kids.

They've started to invent their own words, impatient with our own, I suppose.

Finished with his lecture, my new friend laughed. I saw little white teeth, and he took the hammer in both hands and swung again. Bits of tired damp wood flew in every direction; he paid no more attention to me. So I turned and left him, going down the slope now. I kept hearing him pounding, endlessly pounding, and then the wind rose, and all I could hear was its rustle high in the trees.

HERE IS A PREVIEW OF
DOWN THE BRIGHT WAY,
THE NEW NOVEL BY ROBERT REED

In *Black Milk*, Robert Reed explored the effects of accurate genetic engineering upon the parents and children of its first generation. In **DOWN THE BRIGHT WAY**—on sale in March from Bantam Spectra—he postulates another development strong enough to shake the very foundations of our lives.

One day, quite unannounced, thousands of Wanderers appear through a gateway from other, alternate earths. They are pilgrims, traveling down what they call the Bright, seeking the unimaginably advanced beings who created the universe-spanning road. Our earth is merely a waystop on this magnificent highway; another lies beyond.

At each new earth, a few select representatives become part of the pilgrimage. On our earth, Kyle Hastings dreams that he will be one of them.

His full name was Kyle Stevens Hastings, and he wasn't any sort of Wanderer, not even a novice.

It was a ruse on his part.

It was his elaborate strange game.

Kyle's real home was just a few hundred miles east of Lincoln. He didn't come from any odd alternate earth back down the Bright. Until the Wanderers arrived some fifteen months before, he had been a bland fellow with a sapless career and few friends and a scattered family whom he rarely saw. Kyle didn't have a happy life, but he didn't expect one either. He had security and his comfortable routines. He felt close to nobody, but any loneliness was ignorable. Wasn't it? He believed so. Besides, Kyle was smart enough to entertain himself. He existed day by day with few changes and no real aspirations. On those rare evenings when he considered what was to come, he imagined thirty-plus years of steady work and a quiet retirement and then an uncomplicated death.

Then the Wanderers arrived, no warnings given.

They pushed one of their big crystal portals up the Bright—an enormous sphere suddenly floating in the Pacific Ocean—and through the portal came their egg-shaped flying ships. Within the hour the leading wave of diplomats were scattered across the earth, ten thousand voices bringing greetings from someone named Jy. Several million more Wanderers were ready to accompany Jy. Every television set was full of the news; the diplomats were speaking to political leaders, scientists and common people. They were strange apparitions with their odd builds and odd faces, or not so odd, each one speaking perfect English or Russian or Swahili. They were fluent in whatever language was required. They told about the Bright and their grand mission, explanations brief and clear and almost simple. Then they told of the opportunities they would give everyone. *Opportunities*, not intrusions. They were to remain here for only the briefest while. And they wished this earth nothing but the best.

Kyle remembered watching the news and feeling an excitement, a runaway sense of awe. He was smart enough to learn the bare bones of everything—the Bright, the mission, the Makers—yet comprehension didn't diminish the spectacle of the thing. It was too wondrous, too strange . . . it still could make his breath come up short and his body nearly shiver.

This earth was one of many similar earths.

There might be an infinite number; nobody knew for certain.

Sitting at home, resting in his favorite chair, Kyle could practically feel the world around him changing . . . nothing able to resist this sudden whirlwind. . . .

The Bright was like a string woven through the ultimate universe. (That's how Kyle imagined it; he saw the clean geometry of a string.) The Bright itself seemed to be built from degenerate bits of matter and lumps of shadow matter, odd intricate plasmas and things entirely beyond human reach. All these elements were sewn into each earth's matrix—the core; the mantle; the crust. Nobody here had suspected the structure's existence. It was perfectly camouflaged. The Wanderers themselves thought the Bright had been constructed four and a half billion years ago, each earth utilized as a bridge might use pillars to cross a wide, wide river. A million pillars stood in a line, carrying the bridge across the fluid vagaries of time-space.

For billions of years each earth had had the same history: the same weather and the same species arising, the same individual animals and trees and twirling motes of dust. Even identical electrons, ghostly and swift, had traveled the same graceful existences on the brink of Reality.

A couple million years ago the earths had divided.

Nobody could point to a specific cause. The fossils didn't say, "This is what started things, here." The Wanderers liked to speak of tiny motions at the subatomic level and how those might lead to chaotic and profound macroscopic changes. Atoms in a single breeze might move in different directions, and those differences would mount over time. A storm would follow a variety of tracks, or perhaps not form in the first place. Weather systems would diverge. One earth might grow dry where its neighbors would flood, seeds and game herds responding in kind, and that would lead to subtle changes in natural selection and variable mutations and eventually novel adaptations.

Humans existed on most earths found to date.

They showed enormous variability in their looks and natures. A few had developed big brains and industry in the ancient past; a few had retained their primitive features, hunting game with sticks and their muscles; and the rest were in the middle somewhere, Kyle and his species included in that multitude.

One species had gotten a tremendous lead on the rest.

They were the Founders—a rigorously peaceful, truth-hungry folk—and they had discovered the Bright some million years ago. It was an accident which led to Jy defining the mission, the Makers waiting somewhere and Mankind to be united by this grand quest. Two groups of Founders had started to travel on the cosmic string, one in each direction; and after ten thousand centuries and recruits from each inhabited Earth, they were leading two enormous bodies of highly trained, highly motivated and highly diverse people.

Kyle had spent days and nights watching the strange people on his television. The Wanderers were hairy or hairless, giants or midgets, or sometimes they were indistinguishable from the average Hank and Harriet on this world. He saw them fielding questions with charm and a gentle humor, their honesty easy to see. Wanderers looked so different from one another... yet they didn't. Not in certain ways, Kyle decided. He saw their changeless gray clothes and the ways they held themselves, and he studied their wise, perceptive eyes. Immortal eyes, he realized. This was how people seemed when they had lived five thousand years. Or five hundred thousand.

Every inhabited earth was represented somewhere in their numbers.

There were the Founders from Jy's home and the Cousins who came from the most primitive earths... one or two from each, wasn't it?... and the more populated and advanced earths sent dozens, maybe hundreds of people. They were entitled because they were richer, more complicated places.

Most of the Wanderers here were high-ranking. It seemed to take time and flawless service to rise to the forefront of the mission.

All Wanderers loved talking about the Makers. Kyle felt a delicious tingle whenever he heard them, particularly when it was Jy who was talking. She would describe how all human beings would stand as one, humanity showing its best face . . . and before them would be the Makers, every mystery answered and every cost worthwhile. . . .

He used to sit and wonder how it would feel to be among the Wanderers. How would it seem to belong with them? They were so determined and passionate . . . so strange with their immortality and their apparent wisdom. Kyle found himself starting to mimic them. At first it was almost accidental. He might quote them aloud, in their own voices. Or maybe he would glance at a mirror and try a Wanderer's expression. Then he began to tape interviews, and he propped tall mirrors by the television and watched himself using the same stances and the knowing voices, polishing his act, always asking himself just who he might fool.

It was a delicious question.

Kyle hired a tailor to make the appropriate clothes, matching the fabric and even making the polished wooden buttons for the shirts and the sturdy trousers, and he managed a few cosmetic tricks with his homely face. He plucked his eyebrows and devised an odd haircut, then for several weekends he went to nearby towns and pretended to be an emissary from along the Bright. Just for fun. Just to see if he could manage it.

Kyle had had a wonderful time.

He found himself drifting into his new identity, a weekend lark becoming a modest obsession and his own life suddenly pale and dull and entirely forgettable.

How could he have lived that way? he wondered.

All the wasted years seemed like a tragedy, and he felt lucky to have realized it in the end.

People treated him differently when he was a Wanderer. Which was natural, he supposed, but nonetheless illuminating. Kyle was noticed all at once. He was a prince among happy peasants. Of course there were a few who didn't approve of Wanderers—the paranoid, the religious worriers, and so on—but they didn't matter. Groundless fears and grudges simply added spice to everything. Living on the road without a job, living on his savings . . . it was a wonderful existence. Most people perceived him as a godlike being. Kyle had the eyes and the stance and the dry smooth knowing voice. After weeks of travel, hitching rides and taking buses and meeting hundreds of innocents . . . after everything he reached a point where he felt like a Wanderer without trying. Of course it was a ruse, but it didn't feel like one anymore. Kyle got to where he was thinking as he imagined Wanderers must think, considering the Bright and the Makers and all the mysteries embodied within them. He dreamed of reaching the Bright's end and everyone holding hands, millions and millions of mismatched people standing in the presence of...

... what?

What indeed? thought the Wanderer inside him.

Indeed!

I'm often asked about immortality and how it feels and is it sweet or perhaps boring, can I describe it? Well, I like to respond first by saying that none of us are truly immortal and that we do enjoy long lives, yes, and we are protected from many forms of abuse, yes, because of our medicines and the hard-memories woven into our minds. Hard-memories augment most of our intellectual processes and they mirror what is most essentially *us*, and they can survive most tragedies. Yet the truth is that I have lost friends, countless fine friends, over these millennia. The unthinkable accident always thinks of a way to happen, in time, and not enough of the hard-memory survives to allow for revival. We might build a new body, yes, but there's nothing to put inside the body and we are far from immortals and we have precious few illusions. Please believe me.
—Jy's speeches

People in the middle of the most powerful nation-state will tend to be more reserved than their fellow countrymen. Do not expect to attract crowds while traveling through the region, particularly once they have grown accustomed to seeing us in their midst. And you should expect to have trouble measuring the moods of the most agrarian citizens. These people carry their emotions inside bottles mostly kept out of view. Shake hands only if a hand is offered. Do not make a show of returning favors; favors are granted without any overt desire for reciprocity. Compliment their land and their decency; by nature they are rather insecure people. And should all other conversation fail, try talking about the weather. . . .

—final scout report

Kyle walked south towards the campus and downtown. There was a viaduct over the railroad tracks, and the stadium stood to his left. Semis and smaller trucks were stacked up in the entranceways. Workmen scarcely noticed him. A woman wearing tight lavender slacks standing motionless beside the street held high a handmade sign, SATAN AND HER ANGELS ARE HERE!!! Kyle read. She gazed at him with fiery eyes, and he smiled weakly, stepping over the snaking cables and trying to treat the woman with the appropriate distance and reserve. He was careful to show no trace of disrespect.

He wasn't in any danger. He kept telling himself so.

True or not, people believed that each Wanderer was protected by force fields and other trickery. Everyone had heard stories about muggers and zealots left unconscious after some failed assault, no harm done to them but for the embarrassment and the helplessness. Kyle couldn't count all the unsavory fellows who had shied away from him, worried by the simple reputation.

Now he allowed himself a thin smile and a backwards glance at the woman, only she wasn't staring at him anymore. Her eyes were fixed on something else.

Kyle breathed and turned again.

Wanderers, true hard-memory Wanderers, were standing at the stadium's main entranceway, in the shade, talking to workmen.

His heart began to hammer against his ribs.

There were two of them. A man, he saw, and a woman. The woman was a glossy coal-color and brick-shaped with a mass of silver-white hair tumbling from beneath her fluorescent hardhat. The man was tall, maybe Kyle's height, brown like leather and dark-haired and narrowly built. He had a handsome, hairless face and strong forearms, the sleeves of his gray shirt rolled to his elbows. Both Wanderers seemed to belong there; they looked *right*. It was the man who happened to glance at Kyle, and Kyle felt his heart flutter and die, time in suspension. And then the Wanderer nodded at him. There was recognition in the dark eyes, a hint of a smile, and with that he returned to his work, saying something to the workmen and gesturing at one of the big semis.

Nothing happened.

It was like some test, walking past here. And Kyle continued on his way, just like that, feeling empty and feather-light and very close to joyful. He had never been so close to a real Wanderer; he had intentionally avoided all contact with them. Yet he had fooled that man. Right? Of course he had done it. Kyle had to fight the urge to throw up his hands. Was that juvenile, or what? But it was a good sign, wasn't it? Of course it was good. He started thinking how Wanderers were people, after all, and they would see what they expected to see. If he could act the role to the best of his ability... well, maybe it would work. It could be the biggest thrill of his life... fooling all of them and actually meeting Jy herself... what a thought! Just imagine it!

Summer students were everywhere: young girls with cultured tans, boyish men wearing polo shirts and cocky smiles, and foreign students, dark to varying degrees and mostly serious. Some students watched Kyle, and sometimes they nodded. Some muttered "Hello" in passing. Nothing more. Either they recognized him from the other times he had come here, or they assumed he was part of Jy's entourage. A few Wanderers were supposed to have arrived early, making ready and shaking hands and saying good wise Wanderer things to everyone, paving the way for Jy.

Kyle remembered when he first came to Lincoln. There was an all-night bus ride, and he had stepped onto the pavement with shaky legs and his overstuffed travel bag in both hands. It was midmorning, early and oddly cool for summer, and for some reason he had decided to linger. He had stowed his bag in a bus depot locker and found the campus. A tourist handout had recommended the natural history museum, and he knew Wanderers liked such diversions. So he found the big brick building and paid the flustered girl at the door, always polite, then he had roamed the long air-conditioned hallways and the towering rooms, mammoth skeletons and plesiosaur skeletons and slabs of crinoid-encrusted limestone lining the way.

He ended up in the basement, feeling alert despite the bus ride. There were a series of dioramas, large and elaborate— stuffed bison on plaster grasslands, glass-eyed deer standing behind paper oaks, a pair of battered whooping cranes rooted in a plastic marsh. A girl was sitting in front of the crane diorama, in the middle of a hard wooden bench. Kyle could remember everything. An astronomy text was beside her, closed and ignored. She was reading from a collection of Chekov stories, and Kyle walked past once while looking at her pretty face and feeling some imprecise urge that made him stop and come around again. She was pretty, he thought, and maybe prettier than her looks. Did that make sense?

"Miss?" he managed. She didn't seem to hear him, brown eyes sliding back and forth with her mouth slightly open. "Miss?" asked Kyle. "Could I join you for a moment . . . miss?"

Her face lifted, and the eyes became huge.

"If you don't mind."

"Oh, no . . . no." She looked as if she might faint, shutting her book and straightening her back and doing nothing at all for a moment. Then she set Chekov on the textbook and stroked her dress with both hands. "Let me just . . ." She bent forward and pulled a book bag from under the bench. Kyle watched. Weeks later he would remember her tropical red dress and the way its neckline dipped when she bent forward, for an instant, him gazing down at one of her little breasts with its river-mud nipple, tender and precious, and she grunted once, then again, pushing the overstuffed book bag back out of sight. "There," she announced. She sat on the bench and stared at him, chewing on her lower lip while her hands wrestled in her lap.

Kyle sat down beside the girl, not close, and told her, "Thank you."

She made a low scared sound, imprecise and endearing.

He would always remember the delicious tingle running under his skin and the way he grinned, feeling self-assured, everything easy for him. "Did you hear about the whooping cranes?" he asked, and he pointed to the diorama. "How long have they been extinct here? Thirty years? Well," he said, "we're bringing them from another earth. Did you know?"

It was true; he had read it on the bus.

The girl said, "Really?" and hugged herself. She had smooth legs with a good shape, and she was kicking them.

"As gifts," he added. "Along with some other species." He listed a few examples—sea cows and woolly mammoths and desert pupfish—then admitted, "They're not quite identical to your cranes and whatever. Not genetically, not down deep. But they look and act the same, and if you're careful with them they should do just fine—"

"It's wonderful," she blurted.

He smiled and nodded.

"What you're doing," she told him. "I think it's . . . it's all so amazing, and special. . . ."

"We want to be helpful," he stated.

"Oh, I know. I do." She nodded and hugged herself. "I'm always thinking about you—"

Kyle straightened.

"—and I'm so glad you came. To our earth," she told him.

Kyle said nothing.

The girl was obviously excited. She kept talking, thanking him for everything good done by the Wanderers and admitting she'd never been so close to one, not ever, and her legs kicked and her hands straightened her red dress, and she hoped she wasn't talking too much. It was a problem of hers. "Sometimes I get started, you see . . . when I'm nervous? And I can't stop. Oh, I can try. But the words just keep coming. . . ."

Kyle thought of a thunderous lie. "Do you know what?" he interrupted. "On my earth, way back down the Bright, do you know what? You would be one of our great beauties. That's how pretty you are."

"Me?" she gasped. She started to laugh and shake her head, startled and numbed and absolutely thrilled. "Are you sure? *Really?*"

"I'm sure you're a beauty here too," he offered.

"Fat chance!"

"No?" he teased. Then he touched her with his fingertips, stroking the soft thin fabric of her sleeve while humming. "I think you're awfully lovely. I do." He was a Wanderer and confident, and if she laughed at him she simply didn't know any better. It didn't reflect on him.

But she didn't laugh, nor did she seem to breathe for a long moment.

There was some . . . *quality* to this girl. Other people were interested in Wanderers, but she was enraptured. Kyle watched her liquid-quick expressions on that pretty dark face that might have been a little bit Chinese, or something . . . and what? Was he in love? All at once it was like a blow from a big fist. Just asking the question made him a little bit crazy. He felt a longing and a fear, and with his voice cracking at the edges he asked, "What's your name?" and she told him. Billie Zacharia. A strange name, unique and somehow perfect . . . he certainly loved her name. Then he heard her asking for his name, *sir*, and he uttered it. The phony one, convulated and intense, adding, "You can say Kyle. That's enough," and she did repeat Kyle several times, giving the single syllable an exotic taste. Then she happened to glance at her wristwatch, and he noticed. Did she have to go somewhere? Did she have class?

'No, it's nothing," she squeaked.

He remembered the textbook. "You're in astronomy?"

"It's up... well, in the planetarium." She pointed towards the ceiling. "But I don't have to... I mean, I can just... well..."

"Take me." Kyle felt alert and happy. His solution took both of them by surprise. "I'll be your guest."

"My guest?" She was dumbfounded.

"I'm here to learn," he replied. "Show me your class."

"Well... all right." She stood slowly, arms spread as if she were ready to lose her balance. Kyle kneeled and lifted her book bag, offering to carry it. All right? Then they went upstairs and into the back of the museum, arriving just as the big doors were being closed and the lights were coming down.

Nobody seemed to notice Kyle. Darkness gave him a delicious anonymity. The professor, small and bland, stood armed with a tiny blood-red laser beam he used for pointing out constellations and their slow wheeling motions. He called their home "*the Earth*" as if there was only one in all of Reality, and when people spoke among themselves he coughed ominously into a fist.

Billie watched Kyle until he glanced her way, then she focused on the lecture. Or at least she pretended to focus.

Kyle sat and listened, always aware of the girl beside him.

After a little while she leaned towards him and wondered, "Do the skies change?"

"Excuse me?"

"From earth to earth... do the stars stay in the same places? I've always wondered."

People had asked him all sorts of questions. They wanted to know about his home and traveling on the Bright, and about Jy too. But nobody had ever asked if the stars held steady.

"Yes," he whispered. "They're just as they look up there." Which was true. Kyle had read it in the science magazines when he did his early research. "Stars don't care about the earth," he informed Billie. "People can turn out any odd way, and do anything, and the stars and the galaxy just keep spinning in the same patterns."

She nodded, and he felt her body. She was close without touching, and there was a damp, sweet-scented heat. Kyle had to shift his weight, and he reported, "It's comforting. Some things never change, like the constellations, and I like that."

She cooed and nodded.

The professor heard them, and he quit talking to cough and stare into the darkness for an angry moment.

Kyle watched Billie's face in the artificial starlight. She had a sweet dreamy smile. He felt the blood in his temples and the steady rubbery hammering of his heart, and he imagined it was just them sitting close, at night, some mossy glade surrounding them. The air conditioning was the wind, moist and persistent, and the professor's steady old voice was a whooping crane muttering in its sleep, dreaming about fat frogs and cold snakes, no doubt. And then Kyle imagined pulling Billie's red dress over her head, and those small hands were touching him and he was smelling her and stroking her thick black hair, he knew exactly how that hair would feel, stiff and springy and warm beneath... and Kyle breathed and made himself look at the false sky and the changeless stars, feeling what? What? A tangible guilt... the first he had felt in a long, long while. But he resisted the urge to confess anything. Why should he? Instead he breathed again and asked Billie where she lived. On campus? Nearby perhaps? She gave him a look and bit her lip, appearing startled. "If you don't mind telling me," he added. "Please?"

The professor made an angry noise, then continued.

"Because," said Kyle, "I might stay here a few days and maybe you would show me what I should see. If you'd like. Okay?"

"Oh, yes...."

"You're sure?"

Billie sighed with her entire body and nodded yes, yes, yes... hands held close as if she didn't entirely trust them.

Watch for DOWN THE BRIGHT WAY, on sale in March 1991 wherever Bantam Spectra Books are sold.

The first book in a stunning new series from
STEPHEN R. DONALDSON
Bestselling author of *The Chronicles of Thomas Covenant*

The Gap Into Conflict:
THE REAL STORY

The Real Story is set in a detailed, dynamic future where people cross the Gap at faster-than-light speeds, where technology has blossomed with extraordinary possibilities, and where a shadowy presence lurks just beyond our view. But that's not the real story....

The rivalry between Angus Thermopyle and Nick Succorso -- two ore pirates with legendary reputations -- begins with a meeting in Mallory's Bar. With the beautiful Morn Hyland between them, the conflict was bound to escalate -- but *that's* not the real story....

With **The Real Story**, Stephen R. Donaldson takes his readers into *The Gap Into Conflict*, a five-volume cycle of novels that explore the very nature of good and evil within each of us. It is certainly the most profound story he has ever told.

What's the *real* story?
Find out for yourself.

The Real Story
is on sale now in hardcover
wherever Bantam Spectra Books are sold.

The writers that *The Washington Post Book World* called "cool dudes with a decadent New Wave vision of a plugged-in future" come together to collaborate on an amazing shared vision.

William Gibson and Bruce Sterling
THE DIFFERENCE ENGINE

"A visionary steam-powered heavy metal fantasy! Gibson and Sterling create a high Victorian virtual reality of extraordinary richness and detail." -- Ridley Scott, director of *Bladerunner* and *Alien*

What if the Information Age had begun in the Victorian era -- and Charles Babbage perfected his mechanical computing Engine before the development of electronics? With **The Difference Engine**, William Gibson and Bruce Sterling have created a very different London of 1855. Steam-powered Babbage Engines are run by an elite group of "clackers," and every man and woman has a government-issued number. When paleontologist Edward Mallory, on the verge of his greatest achievement, finds himself in possession of a box of punched Engine cards, he finds out how fleeting fame can be -- because someone wants those cards badly enough to kill for them...and place the very future of England in jeopardy.

Provocative, intensely imaginative, an irresistable reading experience, **The Difference Engine** establishes a powerful literary team.

Available now in hardcover wherever Bantam Spectra Books are sold.

Dan Simmons
HYPERION
THE FALL OF HYPERION

Hyperion, winner of the Hugo Award for Best Novel, and
The Fall of Hyperion together constitute Dan Simmons'
astonishing masterpiece, a thousand page novel that
chronicles the last days of the vibrant yet self-destructive
Human Hegemony. The story centers upon seven
pilgrims who travel to Hyperion for a confrontation with
the mysterious and deadly Shrike, and how their desti-
nies become inextricably tied to that of all mankind.

Look for *Hyperion* and *The Fall of Hyperion*
now on sale wherever Bantam Spectra Books are sold.

AN203 -- 2/91